I0649809

FALSE IDOLS

DARCY DAHLIA

Copyright © 2023 by Darcy Dahlia

All rights reserved.

No part of this book may be reproduced in any form or by any electronic or mechanical means, including information storage and retrieval systems, without written permission from the author, except for the use of brief quotations in a book review.

Edited by Luna Girl
Book Cover and Interior by Qamber Designs and Media

This book is for everyone that's ever had to become a Final Girl.
You are greater than the ones that tried to cut you down.

AUTHOR'S NOTE

Dear Reader,

False Idols is a book born of my love for 90's Slasher movies, Final Girls, and of course, Dark Romance. I got the idea for this book while watching Scream 2 and something just clicked in my brain when I went home to my college town. There are so many instances from those years that I would revisit and change, rewrite as the woman I am now, but I can't do that.

This book is my way of changing things while paying homage to the movies that have a special place in my heart.

Thank you for picking up my book and please take a moment to read the TW list below to make sure this book is for you.

Your well being and mental health matter more than I can say. If this book isn't for you, please know that I love and appreciate you.

TRIGGER WARNING LIST

False Idols includes scenes with graphic language, murder (on page and off), attempted violence, murder of a parent, mutilation, violence, attempted suicide, male genital mutilation, kidnapping, coercion, blood and gore, stalking, and sexual assault. There are sexually explicit scenes of public masturbation, public sex, breeding kink, virgin kink, and talk of forced pregnancy, edging, forced orgasm, dubcon/noncon situations between between the MMC and FMC breath play, impact play, light bondage, violent pornography(off page), primal chase scenes, praise and degradation, knife play, and blood play. Characters experience emotional manipulation, anxiety, PTSD, bullying, humiliation, grief, isolation, and depressive thoughts. There are references to parental infidelity. Child abuse to include, neglect, verbal, emotional and physical to FMC. Please note there is religious trauma and drama in this book as well, with a good portion of it taking place in the Evangelical Non Denominational Church or under the influence of its teachings in a toxic form.

FALSE IDOLS PLAYLIST

You didn't think I was going to write a book in ode to 90's slashers without absolutely curated vibes for it, right? I hope not. Here's the playlist that just set the mood for creating False Idols from the very first word to The End, bestie!

Zombie – The Cranberries

If You Could Only See – Tonic

Hysteria – Muse

Sleep Now In The Fire – Rage Against The Machine

Dead Souls – Nine Inch Nails

Iris – The Goo Goo Dolls

Who Is She? – I Monster

Breed – Nirvana

Only Happy When It Rains – Garbage

Zero – Smashing Pumpkins

CHAPTER ONE

Nevaeh

FOUR YEARS AGO...

I'M FIFTEEN YEARS old and my name is Nevaeh.

It's heaven spelled backwards, because my mother loves church. It's her favorite thing in the world. I know she would pick it over me if someone asked her. She makes sure we are front and center every Sunday morning for the first service at our church—Crown of Thorns in Bloom, Kansas. The name makes me think of the thorns on the blackberry bush outside of my grandmother's house. I always manage to stab myself on them when she sends me out to pick enough berries to satisfy her compulsive need to can and preserve on the hottest summer days. Pastor Mike said that's why he picked the name when he founded the church fifteen years ago. To remind us of the price Christ paid for our sins, which I guess makes sense. Even though it makes me sad, there must be a reason Pastor Mike wants me to be sad when I think of Christ. My mom says that Pastor Mike is always right. My mom loves church and she loves Pastor Mike, because when we go to church, folks in town have to be nice to us. Even if we live in the trailer park outside of town and she has to clean their houses.

"When we're at church, everyone's the same. That's the gift of grace."

My mom makes sure we don't just go on Sundays, like the people she calls fair-weather Christians. We're there for Wednesday Bible study, too. She even leads one of the women's life group meetings on Tuesday. At the library, because our trailer isn't nice enough. She insists I go to Youth Group on Saturday nights and I do, because she means well. I know that, even if the walls of Crown of Thorns are stifling. There is one thing that makes it all worth it.

Well, one person. And he's the most beautiful person I've ever seen.

Beau.

It's the perfect name for him, because Beau means beautiful and that's exactly what he is. His hair is dark as midnight, so black that it shines blue in the light. And while I've heard the other girls in the youth group talk about Beau's body or how tall and strong he is, I love his eyes. They're blue—the color indigo ringed with lashes so long and perfect I think they touch his cheeks when he closes his eyes. Beau comes from the Du Ponts and my mom cleans their house on Mondays and Thursdays during the week, plus every other Saturday. She made sure to only take certain days so she didn't miss any of the church meetings. Seeing as the Du Ponts are part of the church leadership, they arranged it special for her. Beau Du Pont is four years older than me and when I tag along with my mom, I get to see him. It's the only time outside of church that I get to see him. There's school, but he's a senior and I'm a freshman, so we don't really cross paths unless I manage to stay late for his football practice. There's always a group of girls on the bleachers just for Beau, so I don't do that too often. Besides, seeing him at his house is special. Almost as special as when we're in youth group together—that's when Beau talks to me.

When we're at Beau's house, he doesn't talk to me. But that's because he doesn't notice me. He's busy when he's at home. Studying, working out, watching after his younger cousins. Reading to his grandfather or driving his mom to errands. There's always something for Beau to do when he's at home. When we're at youth group though, everything changes. That's when there's nothing for Beau to do but hang out with everyone. This is the only time I understand what my mom means about grace and everyone being equal. Because even though he's four years older than me, Beau talks to me like we're the same age. When Beau talks to me, I can't help the butterflies I get or the smile on my face—he makes me so happy. Beau makes everyone happy. But I like to pretend it's only me when he sits down beside me before movie night and asks me what's playing, or when he offers me a snack from the refreshment table.

I'm always too nervous to talk much to Beau because I have a crush on him, but it's okay. I just need more time with him and he'll see how much he means to me. Sometimes he's the only nice part of my day, especially when I have to help my mom clean on Saturdays. I don't like those days, but I owe my mom. She never misses a chance to bring it up, so I guess I do. I keep hoping she'll stop saying it if I help her enough, so I never complain when she tells me to get her supplies ready for work on a Saturday morning. Today is one of those days, but I keep a smile on my face and work as fast as I can, because I know I'll see Beau. It's hard to keep smiling when I hear the scary news about the girl a town over that was found cut up in her bed.

"You better keep all the windows in the house shut and locked tonight, do you hear me?"

"Yes ma'am."

"I'm not kidding, Neveah. There's a sicko cutting up girls in their beds, and I know you sleep with that window open. Swear it now."

"I swear it, ma'am."

My mom is jumpy as a cat as she talks about the girl they found, but I try not to listen. I don't want to hear what the killer has done to her. She isn't the only girl that's been found the way she was, with a cross carved into her chest.

"Maybe it's an X," I tried to tell my mom, when she was sniffling over the thought of a cross being used that way.

"It's not an X, you idiot! It's a cross. He's a satanist. I know it! This is demonic!"

I try to ignore my mom. It isn't the easiest thing to do when she gets hysterical like this, but it doesn't help that everyone we meet in town is of the same mind. I make it through the day, but just barely, because I know I'll get to see Beau. Except when I walk into the youth group room, Beau isn't there. No one really mentions Beau not being there, so I can't bring it up, not with the way they're all going on about the murder. But I keep an eye on the door. Every time someone walks past, I think it's him, but it never is. My face must show how disappointed I am, because when my mom picks me up to go home she comments on my "ugly face."

"No one is going to want to court you if you frown like that, Nevaeh." She snaps her fingers at me. "Fix it, girl."

I force myself to smile for her. "Yes, ma'am." She won't let me rest if I don't. Doesn't matter if I don't want anyone to court me or not. There is only Beau, and he isn't around to see my face. The ride home passes like it normally does, with my mother going on about the new jobs she is hoping to get in town and what she plans to do with the money. Most of it is going to be saved to get us into a better house in the "nice part of town, where they won't look down their noses at us."

I don't have to ask who '*they*' are. It's the same people she talks about from church as talking to us like equals. I know my mom doesn't like them, so I keep quiet and nod while she goes on about what we'll have for dinner. I smile the whole time, even though it makes my cheeks hurt. It's after dinner, when my mom goes to watch her stories while I clean the kitchen and do the dishes, that my mind goes to Beau.

Where had he been? He never misses youth nights, but maybe he was upset about the murder? He's there like clock work, so what's changed? It's his senior year and I know he will be leaving soon and my chances at working up the nerve to talk to him are running out. He'll go to the college in town. Even if he stayed in Bloom, it wouldn't be the same. I bet he'll live in the dorms then and play football for the school. Beau is that good at football. There's no way I'll get to see him again, when we clean his house on Saturdays. The thought makes my chest hurt. I have to get out of the house. It's a summer night and there's no central air in the trailer we own, so it's *hot*. The rotating fan by my mom's chair really doesn't do much but circulate the already warm air. I finish cleaning the kitchen and then go to my room. It's off of the kitchen, so my mom doesn't notice, not with the way she's glued to her shows. I have to think and I can't do it here, not in the warm trailer with the tv blaring in the next room. When I'm in my room, I go straight for my flashlight and grab my notebook and Bible before I climb out of my window.

The second the night air hits my skin, I let out a sigh of relief. It's warm, but it's still so much cooler than our trailer. I flick the switch of my flashlight, giving it a smack when the light flickers, but a second later it's steady. I'm careful to keep the light away from the living room windows where I know my mom is sitting and set off on a walk through the trees to the trail that runs behind the trailer park and up the hill that overlooks town. The Mineral Belt Trail is a path that joggers and mountain bikers use. It's not paved, so I always get my shoes dirty when I use it. It makes a big twelve mile loop around town. I shouldn't be out here this late. Not with what's been going on around town lately. My mom would pitch a fit if she knew, but I know she'll be watching her shows for another two hours, so I've got time. My shoulders drop the longer I walk and the quiet sounds of the trees settle over me. I can hear the chirp of crickets and the rustle of birds settling in to roost for the night while a gentle breeze moves through the leaves. I pass by something rooting around in the leaves just out of the reach of my light. I don't bother looking for what's making the noise. It's just an animal. Even if it wasn't, I don't want to find anyone else right now. It's nice to be alone. Peaceful, even. I've walked this path so many times that my feet know exactly where to go and I can let my mind wander. I think about Beau, about school, about why my mom wants someone to court me. That's dating, but in a nice way. The way Pastor Mike says is acceptable for young ladies and men to act before marriage.

Naturally, my thoughts go to Beau. Is there anyone he wants to court? Will he wait to finish college to do that? Would he ever look at someone like me and want that? Butterflies come to life in my belly at the thought, but when I try to picture the kind of girl Beau would want to marry, I can't. I don't want to think about that too much, anyway. There's no way a girl like me would be the one for him. I live in a busted trailer with no air conditioning and help my mom clean his house on the weekends. I bite my lip and hold my Bible and journal tighter while I walk faster, as if I can outrun the thoughts.

The ground slopes under my feet. It's steeper here and I know I'm almost to the top of the hill. I have to work to keep the same pace. After another minute, I turn off my light and continue on in the dark, so I don't let anyone know that I'm coming up the path. At the top of Bloom Hill, there's a clearing high schoolers and college kids park in to drink and listen to music, but I know they smoke weed up here, too. I can smell it when I climb up to my favorite spot to write at night. It's a flat rock that's tucked to the side of the clearing, just behind some trees so I can always see who's parking at Bloom Hill. I recognize a lot of cars from church, and I make a game trying to see how many I can spot while I journal.

The most I've ever seen is seven.

Tonight there's just one, but it's the most important car I could ever think to see at the top of Bloom Hill.

It's Beau's car.

I'd always recognize the familiar profile of the jeep that I know has a Crown of Thorns Church sticker on its side window and a DARE bumper sticker on the back. If I got close enough, I'd be able to see the number twelve, for Beau's jersey number, that the high school girls stenciled onto his car when school let out a month ago. I turn and squint at the jeep from where I'm sitting in the trees and I jump in surprise when a second later I see a girl hop out of the door. She's pulling on the straps of her dress. It's short and white and it glows in the moonlight as she gets her dress on and lights up a cigarette. The cherry red butt of it dances in the air as she flicks it a couple of times and turns when the driver door opens and I see Beau get out. My throat goes tight at the sight of him rounding the jeep to stand beside her. She hands him the cigarette and Beau takes a long drag before he leans back against the jeep. She says something to him and he laughs, the sound of it is like music in the air to me, but it's all wrong.

I forget about my journal and Bible. My hands go to my flashlight and I hold onto it so tight the plastic flexes under my fingers. What is he doing here with her? She's the reason he wasn't at youth night, I know it. She's pretty, blonde and perfect looking. She can't be in high school, she's too polished and put together, even for a girl that just got out of a jeep half naked a minute before. She's elegant and grown up. This girl is in college, she has to be.

Of course, she's the kind of girl Beau would want to be with. He wasn't upset about the murder at all, he was with the college girl in his jeep. I know what that means at Bloom Hill. All thoughts of courtship, proper behavior and smiling so hard my cheeks hurt, seems stupid now. I drop the flashlight with a thud onto the rock and I look down at the journal and the Bible I placed beside it. I take in a deep breath and then another, even though my heart is pounding in my ears at what I now know, and smooth my fingers over the worn leather of my Bible. I came here to think, but I can't do it now. Beau's laugh sounds behind me and this time there's another one with it. The girl's. It's bright and happy. I want to throw up hearing them together. I grab my things and slide off the rock to head back towards the path that will take me back to my trailer park.

I pick up the pace and jog across the clearing and towards the path so no one sees me, but the second I make it past the tree line, my steps slow. Beau was with a girl at Bloom Hill. A perfect, beautiful, college girl. It doesn't matter that I couldn't see her clearly from my spot, I know she has to be beautiful if she's with Beau Du Pont. I take in a deep breath and then another. I fix my mind on being numb, on nothing but the circle of light from my flashlight bouncing on the path in front of me. I'm so focused on thinking of nothing that I don't notice the sound of rustling leaves and cracking limbs straight away. It's only when the bushes to the right of me move and shake that I freeze. There's heavy footfall and a branch snaps. There's someone there, I know it. I swing my flashlight towards the sound but can't see too much from where I'm standing, so I take a step closer to where I think I heard the noise come from. I sweep my light over the area and squint as I take another step forward.

"Hello?" Fear spikes through me like an icy blade. I want to run, but I can't. My feet carry me forward another step, because I have to see what's making the noise. I don't know why, but I do. All the while I can hear my mother's voice screaming at me to run. That there's *a sicko cutting up girls in their beds.* Why oh, why didn't I listen when my mom warned me about this sort of thing? I shuffle forward and the light shakes in my hand. My palms are sweaty now and I have to squeeze the flashlight harder to keep hold of it. I take another step forward. I'm right on the edge of the path and pebbles fall over the side of it when I move. Whatever is there, I have to be above it, because there's a drop down the hill from the path. It's the reason I started carrying my flashlight in the first place, even if it alerts people I'm up here.

The trees shake again and I jump. "H-hello? Who's there?" My voice shakes just as much as the flashlight I'm holding. Everything around me falls silent. Even the crickets stop chirping and I swear the wind stops blowing. I swallow hard and start to run through my daily prayers. I would try to say them out loud but I can't speak, I'm too scared. Why didn't I listen? Why did I come out here and not tell anyone?

What is my mom going to think when they find me cut to pieces?

"W-ho's there?" I say again, but this time it's barely a whisper. Nothing stirs and I can feel my heart hammering in my chest. It's so loud that I start to wonder if I imagined hearing anything at all. Maybe it was just my heart. My wild imagination and not-

The leaves wiggle, but there's no wind to move them. If I wasn't so close to the leaves, I might not have even noticed that they moved at all. It's all the warning I get, because I was right. I'm not alone. The tree limbs jerk and leaves explode forward when a body leaps out of the trees at me.

"Oh god!" I scream. Everything slows down when I try to move out of the way. I twist and start to fall to the side, but my light shines bright on a snorting deer that leaps away from me with an agitated flick of its tail. A deer. It was a *deer* that I heard.

Sweet relief sweeps over me, because it's not the monster cutting girls up, it's just a deer.

I'm safe.

A sob rises up in me in relief, but that's when time moves again and my sob turns to a scream as I fall head first over the path's edge and tumble down the hill.

CHAPTER TWO

Nevaeh

I DON'T FALL FOR long, maybe five feet or so, before I slam onto a dirt ledge and the air gets knocked out of my lungs. I hit my head and my ears ring from the fall. I feel like I'm deaf. I can't hear anything as I cough and try to push myself up. It's rough going, so I lay there for a bit. I don't know how long passes, but when I finally manage to move, I'm relieved that I kept my grip on my flashlight. It's right beside me when I put my hand out to roll over. I cough and try to take a breath, but it's difficult. The air has been knocked out of me and all I can do is wheeze and roll from my side to my back while my lungs ache. It feels like an eternity passes while I choke for air, but finally I'm able to breathe. That's when I hear it.

A scream.

"No!" A woman screams. "Get away from me!" She's close by and getting closer. I don't think I heard her before because of the ringing in my ears and my struggle to breathe. My coughing must have drowned it out when she was farther away. I struggle to sit up but my back aches and my head is sore from where I hit it, but I manage to get to my knees. I'm trying to stand up when a shriek rips through the air.

"No, stop! Please! *Please*!" She's begging above me. Rocks slide over the edge and hit me where I'm kneeling. I look up and see the trees move. She has to be grabbing them, trying to get away from whoever is chasing her. I should tell her to drop down where I am, or try to pull her down, but I can't. I'm too scared to move. I'm so scared that I turn my flashlight off. I can't let whoever is after her find me.

I can't. I can't. I *can't*.

"You can't do this! You don't have to do it! I won't tell anyone. I promise! *Stop*! Ple-" I know she was about to say please. That she was going to promise anything to stay safe. To stay alive. But her please stops abruptly. It turns into a howl of pain, a sob. And I know the sound that accompanies it.

Even if you've never heard it before, there's no mistaking the sound of a knife cutting into a body. It's a wet smack. It sounds like a fist making contact before it slices through muscle and fat. Before it hits bone. I clap my hands over my mouth to stop the scream that almost comes out of me and I keep my hands there to stop myself from getting sick as I hear the knife cut again and again. The girl screams and it's frantic. She's not getting away. I fall against the hillside and press myself flat. I shove my face against the dirt and shut my eyes like I can block out what's happening. I don't know what to do. I feel like a bomb is going off next to me and if I make one wrong move I'll start screaming. I'll lose it.

There's a sicko cutting up girls in their beds.

I bite down on my hands and force the puke that's burning my throat back down. It's not just their beds. He's here. The killer is *here*. If I make a sound, he's going to kill me too. Dirt falls around me and gets in my nose from how hard I'm breathing, but I don't move. I don't dare lift my head to see what's going on. What if they're done with her and they know I'm here? No, I can't look. I can hear her screaming still and somewhere in her begging, I lose the fight and puke down my shirt. It mingles with the dirt from the hillside I'm still pressed against, but I don't move. I puke silently. I don't know how I do it, but I manage to not make a sound. Vomit slides down my chin and tears blur my eyes, but it's all darkness anyways. I stay exactly where I am.

The girl goes quiet and I hear the heavy footsteps of someone big moving. They come to the edge of the path and a rock falls and hits my shoulder. I shake where I'm kneeling and still I can't lift my head to look up at them. If they see me, I won't know. Maybe it will be better that way, if he does what he did to the girl to me. I start to pray, the words stuck on my vomit coated lips, but then there's a shift and he moves away from the ledge. I know it because I can hear his footsteps. He walks heavy and he doesn't care who hears him, at least it sounds that way from where I am. Second by second, his footsteps get fainter until I can't hear them anymore, but it's not quiet when he's gone.

She's crying.

It's soft, just a moan really. The sound of someone trying to breathe but all they can do is gasp. *Oh my god. She's alive.* I lift my head then and look up. It's dark, but there's enough moonlight to see the tops of the trees. I know where the edge of the path is and can see it if I concentrate. Another rattling gasp sounds and I start to move. I have to get to her. I have to help her. I shove the flashlight into my back pocket and get to my feet as fast as I can.

There's a choking gasp, the sound hoarse and raw, I squeeze my eyes shut when she breathes again and the sound repeats. She's not going to be able to last for much longer. I have to help. I lift my hands and feel along the side of the dirt wall in front of me. When I feel a tangle of tree roots, I grab with both hands and lift myself up. I can't see much, but I keep trying. I reach up again and nearly slip when I miss the next root. I manage to hold on, but I'm not that strong and I won't be able to hold on for much longer.

I grunt and grip the roots, but I'm slipping with each second that passes. "Please God, help me," I whisper. I have to get to the top as fast as I can before I fall back down to the ledge. If that happens, she'll die. I won't have a chance at helping. Shame hits me hot and fast. I hid while someone hurt her. I'm a coward. I'm lower than low. I have to make this right.

"Give me the strength, Oh Lord." Tears slide down my cheeks and mingle with the vomit and dirt I'm caked in. I don't know what to do, but adrenaline hits me hard and fast when I hear the girl's sick rattling breath. I'm going to make this right. I'll save her. I dig my feet in to push up as hard as I can and I jump. I grunt when my chin clips the ledge, but I land high enough that I get a hand hold on solid ground. Using the roots as a base, I'm able to kick myself over the edge. I don't stop when I roll onto my side. I can't. Not when time feels like it's running out. I only make a step before I hear her move. She must be trying to crawl away.

"I'm here," I call to her and her shuffling stops. "I'm going to help you. Don't move." I tell her, but I don't know where the girl is. When I was climbing, I thought she was just above me at the edge of the path, but the killer must have dragged her away from it.

"You're safe now, I promise." I keep my voice low, I don't know how far the killer went. If he comes back, I don't know what I'll do. *You'll run. Run like the coward you are.* I flinch at the voice but I push it away and keep moving. I'm doing the right thing now. That's what counts.

I need light. I reach for the flashlight still tucked in my back pocket and flick it on. My hand shakes as I lift it to shine on the ground around me. I see the blood first. There's so much of it. I don't want to look but when I hear a footfall, my hand jerks and I see everything.

It wasn't the girl that was trying to crawl. She's not moving. She's not breathing, either. And she's not alone.

I don't have to see their face to know who it is. "Beau?" I whisper.

He's bent over her and my heart breaks when I see the blood on his hands. It's all over his chest and jeans. His head whips in my direction and I nearly drop my flashlight at the look in his eyes.

They're wild. The blue isn't the summer sky blue I know. He looks *wild*. There's a light to them that isn't right. He bares his teeth at me and all I can think of is the rabid dog that roamed the trailer park last summer. They had to put it down when it killed Ms. Samson's chickens and tried to go after her. Beau isn't the boy I think I might love, he isn't even human right now when he roars at me.

"*What are you doing here?!*"

I shake my head. I can't speak, but I know Beau isn't right. I look at the girl and that's when I see the familiar white dress that's now a shade of dark maroon. It's shredded where she's been stabbed and I almost throw up again when I see what's happened to her perfect body. She's mangled and in pieces. The only thing that looks right is her hair. It's blonde and shiny, perfectly splayed around her in a halo but the strands are starting to turn dark from the blood pooling around her in the dirt.

"She's dead," I choke out.

"And so are you!" Beau leaps at me when I speak and grabs my arms. I can feel hot sticky blood smear over my skin where he's got hold of me. I scream and jerk away from him, but I can't break his hold. It's the first time he's touched me. How can it be like this? It wasn't supposed to go like this.

"Let me go!" I scream and swing the flashlight at Beau, but I miss. He drags me forward and I don't know how to feel. I wanted to court him. I wanted to be the girl he kissed and said goodnight to while my mom looked on proudly and all the older girls at youth group stared in envy. I wanted Beau, but he's going to kill me. I know it. Beau is a killer and I'm next.

"No!" This year in gym class the coaches showed us how to do self defense moves when they needed to fill an extra two weeks at the end of the year. I took them seriously when my mom told me about what can happen when you clean for the rich. I did good enough in class that the coaches always used me for demonstrations. I use everything I learned in those two weeks as Beau drags me towards the dead girl.

His date. He killed his date and now he's going to kill me.

I slam the heel of my palm into Beau's face and wince when I feel my hand hit his nose. Beau's head snaps back and I throw myself forward, using the momentum to slam my knee into his groin. He drops just like my gym coach showed me and I don't wait. I take off running down the path, straight for home. I still have my flashlight, but I don't need it. I don't think I could stop even if I wanted to, so it doesn't matter what's in front of me. I just keep running. I don't stop, not even when I see the familiar lights of my trailer. I trip on the steps as I sprint up them and try to open the door, but it's locked. I start pounding on it immediately. I don't know if Beau is behind me or not. Even if I got the head start, he's still bigger and faster.

"Mommy! Open the door! Mommy, please! Mommy!" I scream and slam my hands on the door. I don't let go of the flash light and start hitting the door with it. "Mommy!"

I hear my mom storm up to the door and she's moving fast, stomping from the sounds of it. A second later the door flies open and hits me in the face, but I don't fall back. I shove past my mom into the trailer and only stop when I trip on the rug and land on my knees.

"Nevaeh? Nevaeh, what's wrong? Where were you?" My mom's voice is sharp and she shuts the front door with a click. "I knew you snuck out! Were you out in those damn woods? You were, weren't you?"

"Mommy, he killed her." I turn to face her and I see fear flash across her face. Her eyes widen, but it's only for a beat before she points a finger at me.

"What were you doing in those woods, young lady? You went to see a boy, didn't you?"

I shake my head. "No ma'am! I went to-"

"Where did you go?" She cuts me off with a glare and snaps her fingers at me.

"Bloom Point. I went to Bloom Point and-"

She slaps me hard. "You slut!"

I see stars from the second slap she lands on me. I hit the ground and taste blood in my mouth. It makes me think of the girl. Oh god, he killed her. I start to sob and stand even when my mom hits me again. This time it's on the side of my head and my ears ring, just like when I fell off the path.

I hunch over, my hands on the floor and hold back the vomit that's rising in my throat. "No, I didn't do anything! I'm a good girl. I promise, I promise."

"Dirty slut. You sinned in those woods, I know you did, and now you think you can come back here and lie to me? Make up some lie about what you saw to get away with it? Do I look stupid to you, girl?"

I raise my hands and try to fend her off, but it's no use. "No, mommy, please. I didn't-"

"Get to your room. You're filthy!" She jerks me to my feet by my arm and starts to pull me down the hallway towards the bathroom, but it feels too much like Beau and I scream and shove her away from me.

"*He killed her!*" I scream. "I-I saw him do it! We have to call the cops right now or he's going to kill me, too." I turn and run back to the kitchen where the house phone is. I have it off the hook and I'm trying to dial it when my mother speaks.

"Why is there blood on you?" She whispers. When I look at her, I see she's looking at her hands. There's blood on them from where she grabbed my arms.

"Beau," I whisper, and start to dial 911. But the second I say Beau's name my mother crosses the room and jerks the phone out of my hand.

"You're lying!" She slams the phone down on the cradle and shakes a finger at me. "You get Beau Du Pont's name out of your mouth, little girl. You're a liar!"

"I'm not!" I scream at her and she falls back a step. I never scream at my mother. I'm a good girl. "Beau was there. I-I saw him with his date, and she's dead. He said that I was dead too! I'm telling the truth!"

"You go and accuse that boy of anything and we're done in this town."

My blood runs cold and I feel like I'm still out on that ledge with Beau cutting his date up. *Coward.* The word bubbles up in me, but it dies on my tongue, even though I know what my mom wants me to do.

She wants me to lie

She points a finger at my face and her voice gets quiet. It always gets quiet when she's really mad at me. "You didn't see anything tonight."

She wants me to forget.

"You lied," she whispers.

I shake my head. "No m-ma'am. I saw him. H-he grabbed me and said I was dead, just like she was! I tried to help her, I promise I did!" My voice rises with every word. I make a wild grab for the phone, snatching it from my stunned mother's hands. She's not used to me yelling at her. She's always worried about the wrong things and I know she's going to be upset with me for a long time for it, but I can't help it. Beau Du Pont is a killer.

"I tried to save her." Tears blur my eyes and it's hard to hold onto the phone, but I manage to dial it this time. It rings twice before the operator picks up.

"911, what's your emergency?"

"There's a dead girl on the Mineral Belt Trail. You have to come, please hurry!"

"Where are you? Where is the girl?"

I hold the phone so hard that the plastic creaks in my hand. "I-I'm at home and she's on the trail. She's dead. Please hurry, you have to come or he's going to kill me too!"

"Stay calm. Is your home a safe location?"

I nod, but then remember she can't see me, so I answer her. "Yes, I'm safe now. But he's coming and-" I turn in time to see my mom make a run for the cord, she's going to try and yank it out of the wall. "Mommy, no! Don't!" I have to force my body between her and the cord to stop her from getting a hand on it.

"Hang up the phone, Nevaeh!" My mom screams at me. She slaps me, but I don't let go of the phone.

"Who is after you? Who else is there with you?"

"My mom is here and-and we're scared," I blurt out. I don't know how else to explain my mom beating on me while I'm on the phone with the 911 operator. Shame wells up in me just like it always does when my mom acts out. "She doesn't mean it," I say quickly.

"Who is chasing you? Are the doors locked?"

"Yes they're locked and it was Beau Du Pont."

The line falls silent, because I know they are thinking what my mom thought when I told her. It *can't* be Beau Du Pont. Someone from his family wouldn't kill. If they report this and they're wrong, there will be hell to pay, but I know what I saw.

"Are you sure of the identification?" They ask after another second.

"Please, you have to believe me. It was him. I-I saw him," my voice cracks and I start to cry again, "there was so much blood on her. She's dead."

"What is your address? We have units on the way. Stay indoors. I need you to stay on the phone with me now. What's your name?"

"Nevaeh Santiago," I whisper.

"Where do you live, Nevaeh?" They prompt again and I give them my address on autopilot. I can't stop seeing the girl or hearing the sick rattle of her breath. I squeeze my eyes shut but I can't make it stop. "Everything is going to be okay, Nevaeh," the operator tells me, but I hear sirens. I'm glad I hear the sirens. It makes me stop hearing the girl. They're getting louder and I run to the door to look out the front window.

"I can hear the cops. Are they here already?" I ask. Bloom isn't a big city, but how can they be here already? I shove my face through the curtains and look out the window in time to see the cop cars blow past us and continue on up the road. They're heading for Bloom Point, they have to be. We're too far outside of town. There's nothing past the trailer park but Bloom Point.

My mom comes to stand beside me and pulls the curtains back from the window. The road in front of the trailer park entrance is alive. Cop car after cop car flies past, sirens screaming, and red and blue lights flash and light up the night. Our neighbors come out of their trailers and stand in their driveways and on the streets that crisscross through the trailer lots. They're gathering together in groups as they watch the never ending stream of police heading up to Bloom Point. The operator is talking but I can't focus. I'm staring at the blood on my arms and the smear of dirt I left on my mom's white lace curtains. We don't have many nice things in our house, but these curtains are the nicest. She's going to give me hell for ruining them. But when I look at her she isn't busy noticing the stain on her curtains. She's pale and shaking and staring out at the scene unfolding in front of us. A cop car speeds into the trailer park and comes to a screeching halt in front of our trailer, and a second later a policeman is banging at our door.

Everyone in the trailer park is watching us now, not the cops driving past.

"Nevaeh, what did you do?" My mother whispers, while the cop keeps banging on our door for us to open up.

"I didn't do it, mommy. Beau did."

CHAPTER THREE
BEAU

PRESENT DAY

"NEVAEH SANTIAGO."

I stare up at the cement ceiling and roll my shoulders in a last ditch effort to get comfortable, but it's impossible on the state issued mattress I'm laying on. Doesn't matter though, I always try anyway. I fold my arms behind my head and clear my throat before I say her name again.

"Nevaeh Santiago."

Those two words hang in the air above my head and I hear my cellmate Ben groan at hearing them again. I don't give a shit. I've said her fucking name every day for the past four years, since I landed in this shit hole nightmare—that's 1,461 days, because of fucking leap year. Ben's been with me for the past three years and he's used to my morning routine by now, but it doesn't stop him bitching about it.

"Shut the fuck up man," he tells me, like he has every morning for the 1,095th time. "Every goddamned morning with that cunt's name."

I frown. "Watch your mouth when you talk about her or I'm going to break your jaw again, Ben."

Ben mutters something but he keeps it under his breath. Good. If I hear him talking about Nevaeh like she's trash, I'll make him pay. No one talks about her like that. I turn on my side and look at the photos that are taped up on the cement wall. Cement is everywhere here. Prison is a fucking tomb. A cold, cement, tomb. But I'm going to get out.

I'm not fucking dying here. I know that for a fact, because two days ago my lawyers came by. There's big news. Good news about what happened to me. What they say I did to Carrie. I never would have hurt her. She was sweet, more than willing to give me anything. Carrie was the girl I wanted. I never would have done anything to hurt her.

But someone did.

Someone cut her to pieces and let me take the fall. And Nevaeh helped them do it. I reach out and tap my finger on the photo I know the best. It's the one that's the oldest. I printed it off the computers in the common area a month after I got here and realized this was going to be my life.

I wanted to look at the girl that fucked my life up beyond all repair. FUBAR is what the old timers call it. *Fucked Up Beyond All Repair.* I slide my finger along the curve of Nevaeh's cheek. She's smiling big for the camera, but she's got her arms tucked close to her stomach like she's trying to hide. Her dark hair is neat and pulled back into a ponytail and she's baby faced with chubby cheeks and all that shit. She's young here. Fifteen, tops. That's how old she was when she lied and said I killed Carrie. This photo came from the Crown of Thorns website where it listed her as a top volunteer for the church. I didn't notice her then, didn't even realize we went to the same church. I don't think I ever really saw her until that night.

She was the girl that cleaned my house. I saw her sometimes with her mom and tried to be nice to her. She worked hard, so did her mom. I recognized her when she had her light on Carrie's body. Funny thing about how life works. I went my whole life not noticing Nevaeh Santiago and now her name is the first thing I say every morning and she's the last thought I have every night.

It's been that way for four fucking long years. Being locked up does a lot for a man's focus and attention. After they gave me a life sentence for Carrie's murder, I started paying attention to Nevaeh. I wanted to know everything about her. If she got an award, I knew. She wrote on a weird blog site for about a year—crappy poetry, the normal emo shit, and I knew. I had the RSS feed sent to my email. It wasn't hard to keep track of Nevaeh and her mom, Terri Santiago. My mother was all too happy to make sure she kept them as close as she could. She knew I was innocent and she wasn't going to let them get away from her. Du Ponts play the long game, and my family was nothing if not patient. Patience is the first step to power. Without patience, plans fail. Patience meant legacy, it meant deep roots. In a town with a long memory, patience created opportunity.

I could be more than patient when it came to Nevaeh Santiago. Maybe not before, when she was no one to me. But the night she pointed her finger and named me The Reaper? Oh, that's when Nevaeh became *mine*.

I might not be the sick fuck that terrorized the tristate county area, raping and murdering college coeds, but I wasn't the innocent choir boy everyone knew me as either. He died in these cement walls. Now, I'm all that's left. I don't even know what I am anymore outside of being obsessed with Nevaeh. Nevaeh is my life. The only thing that has kept me going for four years is my obsession with revenge. If my mom wasn't blinded by the fact that I'm her son, she wouldn't tell me what she does about Nevaeh. If she knew to look closer, she'd realize the son she knew is dead and gone. That I'm going to hurt Nevaeh. But even when I do, she won't believe it.

She'll take my side over Nevaeh when I'm out and so will the entire town. It won't be hard to convince them to go after her when she put an innocent man away for murder. They don't have to know that I'm not innocent anymore. That I became just as bad as the serial killer still free, in order to survive.

I yank the photo down from its spot and knock a couple of others I cut out of the newspaper with it. Nevaeh's toothy smile fills my vision. Even if I close my eyes I'd see the way one of her front teeth is slightly out of place. How her smiles are never even, but a little crooked. I've memorized every bit of her and the information my mom feeds to me helps me fill in the gaps of what I can't find online. Nevaeh uses social media just like any other nineteen year old and if I didn't know any better, I wouldn't suspect she was the girl from the woods.

The girl they call the hero of the Mineral Belt Murder. She's the girl that got away and put The Reaper behind bars. The one that saved a town and stopped a man with a trail of violence that spanned years across the state of Kansas. How no one knew The Reaper was behind over thirty rapes and murders within a 15 year span is anyone's guess, but I'm no friend to the justice system or the fucking police after what they did to me. I was nineteen when they locked me up like an animal. How the fuck was I supposed to be responsible for any of that?

The logical answer was that I wasn't. Not that it mattered. Not when the Bloom PD figured out the murders and rapes occurring across the tri state area were connected, that they were serial, they wanted it over. It's not like they cared much how it was done when they were getting heat for letting a killer walk free. The State Attorney General even issued a public warning and statement about The Reaper and called on the community to find him. He didn't directly go after the police department, but any idiot could read between the lines. The Bloom PD knew they had to end this. They looked stupid as fuck not realizing a serial killer had set up home base in their own backyard for years. When Nevaeh pointed the finger at me, she gave them their out on a silver platter and they took it.

What's more sensational than catching a serial killer? Catching a serial killer that was the town's golden boy. It was a no brainer. Roots or not, not even my family could stop it.

My hand clenches and the photo I'm holding wrinkles and folds in my grip, but I don't care. I'm not going to need the photo or any of the others I've put up to keep me focused. It's easy to get lost in here—to forget you're a human being. As much as I hate her, my little Nevaeh has been my touchstone to who I was before. A reminder of what I lost and what I'll take back from her. Not a day has gone by that I don't know what she's up to. Not even prison can keep her from me.

Her family moved from that shitty little trailer park into town, into a house near mine, and I knew. I have her address memorized and know exactly what kind of car she drives, even though she just got it two weeks back. It's a busted up blue pick up truck her mom got off some college kid. Nevaeh's socials are packed full of summer excitement. Nevaeh hasn't gone far, not even with her graduating the year before with a 4.0 GPA. She took a Gap Year, a fancy European way of saying she took a year to fuck around. I wondered if she was going to leave Bloom then, but she didn't. She didn't apply for schools or choose to go to a school where no one knew her. Somewhere she could start over.

If she was smart, she would have tried to start over, but a high GPA doesn't make you smart. That's just a number on a piece of paper. My Nevaeh isn't smart. She's staying close to home, which suits me. Her life is about to explode because of that choice. I have dreamed of nothing but hearing Nevaeh beg for mercy. If she wants to stay close and make that easier for me, then so be it. The big news I'd been given a month before is almost enough to make up for the four years I've spent locked away in a tomb because I died six months in this shithole. Every day for six months, I'd fought for my right to eat and breathe, for the right to simply exist. That changed after I made an example of the biggest fucker in my block.

That was the day I lost my grip on who I'd been. The friendly, easy going kid that couldn't hurt a fly was dead. I lost him then. And the inmate that squared up to me lost an eye. Not a bad trade. A soul for an eye feels like a one sided deal in the grand scheme of things, doesn't it? It did to me.

Not anymore, though. I've got no use for a soul, but an eye? Now that's valuable. I came out ahead with that trade, but it set the pace for the next three and a half years. I did what I had to. The only thing anyone respects in prison is focus. Focus begets strength. Strength creates brutality.

There was no room for redemption or the softness that came with life on the outside. You had to forget who you'd been before, what you'd thought your life would be, before the walls closed in around you and you simply existed. I made it for months without losing who I was before. The Beau Du Pont from Bloom, the small town idiot boy that went out of his way to be kind, giving and gracious. I was so fucking stupid playing the part of town hero that my family laid out for me. I was the star quarterback, the homecoming king. I was set for a full ride at Bloom State and even though I probably should have set my aims higher, I didn't.

Why would I, when I was a king in my hometown? Everyone knew me. Everyone loved my family and thought we walked on water. We'd been in the area for as long as the town had been in existence. That's well over 150 years in one place. With that much living and dying, our roots ran deep in

Bloom. But all of that meant nothing when Nevaeh Santiago opened her fucking mouth.

The girl that cleaned my goddamn toilet is the one that ruined my life. I'm going to destroy her the second I'm free. Because what no one else but my family and our lawyers know is that come this fall semester, I am going to be right there with Nevaeh when she starts her freshman year. Nevaeh has haunted me every day for the past four years and now it is going to be my turn to return the favor.

There won't be a safe place for her in Bloom and she's going to wish I'd died in here. She is going to wish that the fucking Reaper had killed her instead of Carrie. I'm going to make sure of it.

CHAPTER FOUR

Nevaeh

BEAU DU PONT didn't kill Carrie Salt. That was her name. *Carrie Salt.* The girl I didn't save, the one that was murdered on the Mineral Belt Trail while I puked all over myself.

Not a day has gone by that I haven't dreamed of Carrie the way she was that night. I can see her standing perfect and beautiful outside of Beau's jeep. When I remember Carrie Salt that way, her dress is spotless, so white and bright it shines in the moonlight. Sometimes in my dreams, Carrie looks at me, sometimes she talks to me, but I can never hear what she's saying. When she opens her mouth it's like a wave of static, a rushing sound that muffles every word that Carrie is saying to me. I don't need to know what she's saying to know that she wants me to follow her, though. Every time Carrie talks to me, she goes into the woods and I follow her. I'm helpless when she steps into the woods and I'm instantly the fifteen year old girl that didn't know evil was real and the devil wasn't only something I heard about at church.

No, the devil was real and he was The Reaper. He killed and cut his way through pretty girls like Carrie and I told everyone the devil was Beau. *Beau.* I loved him, or at least I thought I did. He was the only boy I've ever wanted, even after I sent him to prison—*I still wanted Beau.*

No one else compared to him. No one ever has.

It's fucked up to still want the man you put away for murder, right? It is. I know it is, because for four years I have been in love with a murderer. One that I put behind bars. Now that they're saying he's innocent I don't know which part of it is worse. The fact that I still want him, or that I always did. Even when everyone in Bloom said he was The Reaper and told me how brave I was, there was the fear—the thing that's kept me up alongside the ghost of Carrie Salt. That maybe I fucked up and got it wrong. Maybe Beau didn't do it. He was drunk when they found him, high too. The news I've read said that he was too fucked up to know what was going on when we ran into each other. That I got it wrong and he was barely keeping it together. I've replayed that night so many times in my mind over the past four years and every time it's a little different.

Now I know the truth about three things in life.

I got it wrong. I ruined Beau's fucking life. I still love him.

"Nevaeh! For the last damn time, hurry up, girl!"

I wince at my mom's shrill scream from downstairs. I'm supposed to be packing for my move to Bloom State, but I keep stopping. I can't keep packing. Every shirt that I fold or box that I tape up feels like a death sentence. A week ago, I had friends. Friends and even a boy that I flirted with sometimes, even if I didn't mean it. They were all excited to have me at Bloom State with them. I took the year off after college to work for my mother. I always knew I would go to Bloom State eventually on account of the scholarship that was waiting on me. The town started a trust the same summer Beau went away and my living nightmare started. Even with a fully paid ride, I put off going, though. I said it was because I wasn't sure what I wanted to major in, but that's not true. I didn't know what to do with myself because my life was picture perfect. The summer I survived the Mineral Belt, I went from a poor, awkward and quiet kid no one noticed to someone people went out of their way to talk to.

I didn't deserve that. Not while Beau rotted away in prison and Carrie Salt was dead and buried. I couldn't bring myself to go off to Bloom State with my friends and pretend none of it happened. That I didn't lay in bed at night and stare at the ceiling replaying that hour over and over again until I wasn't sure what I saw. Until the doubt creeped in and made me sick with the fear that I had done the unthinkable.

What if I put an innocent man away for life? I'd wondered about it since they took Beau away and I was forced into my new life where people called me a hero and gave me everything I wanted, just because of what I saw. All of that changed when Beau Du Pont's release was announced at a press conference one Tuesday morning—but it was a day I'd been waiting on.

I never thought I was going to be able to keep the dream life I landed in. I didn't deserve it. Neither did my mom, but that didn't stop her from trying to hold on to what she could. But even though I expected it, having it all crash down around me was surreal.

I didn't know how to feel standing in the middle of Rosie's—the sort of run down but tried and true diner everyone went to for greasy chili cheese fries or coffee, depending on the time of day. It was the sort of place that opened up at 3 AM which made it early enough to attract the farmers setting out for the day and late enough to catch the college crowd rolling in from the bars just down the street. I went there with my friends because even if we couldn't get into the bars, we liked to be around the college kids that could.

Minnie said they had the best weed, but I didn't know because I was too scared to try any after I did and threw up one summer at Minnie's party when I was sixteen. Now Minnie didn't even text me. I think she blocked me on socials, pretty much everyone did, but that doesn't mean they haven't kept up with me if the burner accounts calling me a lying whore or threatening me with eternal damnation are anything to go by. Somebody said they would gut me like a fish. I think I liked that better than the damnation threat, even though I don't go to church anymore.

That happened last week when they let Beau out. I had already been thinking of not going once I was in college, but Beau's release forced my hand. I couldn't walk in there with the Du Ponts waiting for me. Not with Pastor Mike, who I know would tell me not to be too hard on myself like he did when he came by after the Du Ponts' press conference.

"A lot of people are going to be angry with you, Nevaeh. But it's important to remember that they're scared. They're hurt by what they thought was the end of The Reaper. Now that Beau is out, they know the truth."

"What? That I'm a liar?" I'd been crying. Hardly able to see Pastor Mike through my tears. But I felt his hand when he put it on my shoulder.

"No, sweetie. That The Reaper is still out there. It's not over and people are going to blame you for losing that peace."

I understood what Pastor Mike was saying even if it didn't make sense. Not logically, anyhow. I thought they were mad at me for what I did to Beau. But what the hell do I know? I put the wrong man in prison.

"*Nevaeh!*" My mom screams and I hear her footsteps start pounding up the stairs. She's been after me nonstop since the news broke. She swears I've ruined her life with all the clients she's lost and is worried about the house. That's why she's scared. It's why she's always angry with me.

I tear off a strip of tape and put it on a box before I move on to the next. My door flies open and my mom only stops because she sees me with the new box in my hand.

"You hurry up and get out of my damn house, Nevaeh. The sooner you're gone, the better."

I open my mouth to tell her I'm sorry. That I didn't mean it, but she's gone. She didn't say she hates me this time, but I know she does. I can't blame her, I guess. I fucking hate me too. I deserve whatever is coming to me and I have no right to run from it. Beau couldn't run from it in prison, so why should I? I deserve it. Every bit of hate and vitriol I'm going to get from my classmates, the anger my mother hurls at me, it's nothing that I haven't earned.

I don't know what's going to happen to me at Bloom State, but I know I deserve it for what I've done to Beau Du Pont.

"Someone will be by with your boxes," my mom says when she drops me off at campus. She doesn't bother sticking around or giving me any other information than that. I'm lucky, I guess, that she at least did it in front of my dorm. Even though I have to carry my duffle bag and suitcases up the stairs to my dorm room, at least I don't have to walk across campus to do it. People stare at me and I see a few of my old friends, but they ignore me. My phone hasn't gotten a single message other than threats from people angry at what I did to Beau. At least I'm on scholarship, I guess. If I wasn't, then I'd be paying for what I did to Beau in more ways than one. But when I look at everyone around me and see the hate in their eyes, my plan to ride this out and pay for what I did wavers.

I don't think I'm strong enough to do this.

"That's her. I can't believe she came this year." I hear someone say. They aren't even bothering to lower their voice. There are others who do, though, and they whisper when I pass by. I wasn't good with attention before, but after the Mineral Belt Murder, people paid attention to me. But it wasn't like this. After the Mineral Belt, people treated me nicely and went out of their way to see if I was doing all right. They didn't look down at my mom and me anymore. I know that's what my mom misses the most right now. She's never been one to take the judgment of everyone at the church. I don't know why she keeps going, but I know she will until she takes her last breath. It's a relief to not have to go anymore. I couldn't take the stares, the sympathetic looks when someone heard that I was *that girl.*

I'm relieved Beau has been found innocent, because now I'm not that girl anymore. I'm not the survivor. The one people take care to treat like glass, even though I've doubted what I saw that night for years. It's like a weight has been lifted off of me, even though everyone hates me now. Because I don't have to be *her.*

The girl that survived the Mineral Belt.

The one that beat The Reaper.

None of it was true.

All I did was put the boy I loved away in prison and spent the next four years wishing I'd never said anything at all. Wishing that I never decided to set foot on that trail. I don't think I've wished for that more than I do right now, with everyone staring me down as I walk the halls of my new dorm. *Morris Hall.* I'd been excited to be assigned here just a couple of weeks before but did I trade one prison for another? Before, I was trapped with my thoughts—my doubt and fear about that night, but now? Now, it's made real with the students I'm supposed to be spending the next four years with watching me like they want me dead.

I don't want to see them looking at me. I duck my head and keep walking until I get to the fourth floor and find room 412.

My name is written in purple dry erase marker on the little board someone stuck to the front of the door. There's another name, O'Malley, but that's not all. Someone wrote *LYING CUNT* through my name. I freeze when I see it and I hear someone laugh. I bet it's whoever did it, but I don't give them the reaction they want. It'll just make it worse. I shoulder open the dorm room door and stick my head in to see that it's empty.

Someone else has been here, though. I see boxes in the middle of the room but they haven't made a move to set up camp on either side yet. I wonder if they're waiting for me to pick. It's a nice gesture, but I make it another step when another idea comes to me. What if they know who I am and they don't want to stay here? What if they're going to get the RA to tell them to give them another room?

I bite my lip and drop my bags. I hadn't thought of that. When we got our room assignments I'd still been a normal girl that went to choir practice and had friends. A best friend, even. My chest goes tight thinking about Minnie. She was my best friend since the summer I ran down the Mineral Belt Trail and called Beau Du Pont a killer. The weeks and months after that night are a blur to me when I try to think about what happened. There were so many people reaching out to my mom and me. Her business tripled overnight with well wishers wanting to do their part and show that "when Bloom's very own has a need, Bloom makes sure to show up for them", or at least, that's what they said when they gave my mom their business. One client led to five and that led to fifty and now she owns Blooming Heart's Cleaning Service. That rush got us out of our trailer by the end of the month and into a house in a neighborhood my mom had always driven us by and called our "someday dream home." A realtor from Crown of Thorns came through for us and made sure we were given the price the "lord put on her heart." It was sold to us at a loss, but again the community insisted on it because of what happened on the Mineral Belt. But while my mom got the house, the job, and the respect she'd always coveted—I got something out of it, too.

Friends. People that I thought wanted me around.

Minnie appeared the first day we were in our new dream home. We'd been inseparable since then. I'd never had a best friend before. She was my next door neighbor and I felt just like one of those girls in a sitcom with a perfect life, having Minnie next door. She was a year younger and a year behind me in school and when I decided to come to Bloom State this Fall, it felt perfect getting to start college with my best friend. I miss her, but her silence tells me everything I need to know.

Minnie doesn't miss me.

Maybe just because she was *my* best friend, doesn't mean that I was *hers*. Her dorm room is just a floor below mine. We'd made plans to try and get our roommates to switch with us so we could room together. All of that's over now. If my best friend doesn't want to live with me, why would a stranger want to do it? I'm sure they won't and I'll be the one to offer to move. They shouldn't be the one to do it when I'm the one everyone hates.

"Oh my gosh, *hey!*" There's a voice behind me and I jump at the sound. "Are you my roommate?"

I whirl around to see a girl in the door with her arms full of pillows. She can't see over the pile and peeks out at me from the side of her pile. There's a bright smile on her pretty face and when she marches past me to drop her pillows on her bed, I don't know what to say other than, "Y-yeah, that's me."

"I am *so* excited for this year!" She tells me and throws her pillows down. "We are going to have *so* much fun! I promise, you won't regret living with me." She's bubbly and happy, and feels like just the kind of person you would want to start college with. The girl is petite, shorter than me by a few inches, with wide green eyes and blond hair that's piled on top of her head with a clip. She has on a Bloom State tank and a pair of cheer shorts. There's no way she's going to want to room with me when she figures out who I am.

"Listen, about that," I start and try to interrupt her, but it's no use.

"I wanted to wait until you were here for us to pick sides, so let me know which one you want, okay?" She practically bounces up to me and extends her hand. "I'm Sunny. Sunny Harold."

I stare at her hand. I know I'm supposed to take it and introduce myself, but there's something about the open and sweet way Sunny is talking to me. She's genuinely excited for this year, and for me to be her roommate. I know it's not me that she's excited to see. Sunny would be…well, *this sunny* with anyone that happened to be her roommate, but it's nice to think it's because it's me that she's so happy.

"Hello?" Sunny blinks up at me and I realize I've been staring at her like a weirdo. Great. I quickly take her hand and force a smile to my face.

"I'm Nevaeh. Pleased to meet you."

I half expect Sunny to rip her hand from mine and to tell me to get the fuck out of the room, but she doesn't. She keeps smiling and shakes my hand.

"Oh my gosh, your name is *so* cool! Nevaeh," she pauses and taps her finger on her chin, "that's heaven backwards, isn't it?"

I smile weakly at her and nod. "Yeah, it is."

"*So cool.*"

"My mom is kinda, kind of a religious nut, you know?"

She gives me a knowing nod and sighs. "My mom grew up in a hippy commune down in Florida and that's why she named me Sunny. I'm lucky I didn't come out named Moon Beam, honestly. I get it."

I can't help but laugh. "Moon Beam is kinda cool."

Sunny rolls her eyes and waves a hand. "No it isn't, but you're being nice about it and I like nice."

Sunny's words hit me like a brick. I'm not nice. I put the man I love away for murder. I'm a monster.

"Hey, where's the rest of your stuff?" Sunny asks and points a finger at the duffle bag I'm still carrying. "Is that all you brought?"

"Uh, someone is coming with my stuff." I don't know who, because my mom didn't say. "And I'm sort of into minimalism, there's not a lot anyways," I lie, because for all I know no one is coming with my things.

"Minimalism? That's pretty cool." Sunny jerks a thumb at the pillows on her bed. "In case you can't tell, I'm not. I *loooooove* stuff. Love it!"

"Yeah?" I move to the side and drop my duffle onto the other bed, because one bed is just as good as the other and I don't know what else to do with myself. I put the suitcases I'm carrying down on the floor and turn to Sunny. I'm ready to try and tell her she doesn't want me as a roommate, but she's not looking at me.

She's at the door and staring at the dry erase board. "Who wrote this?" Shit. She saw the whiteboard. "You're Santiago, right? Why would someone write this nasty word here?"

"It's a long story. I did something terrible, Sunny. Th-they, I mean, I deserve it."

Sunny looks at me and narrows her eyes. "No, you don't."

"Sunny, you don't understand."

"You're my roommate and no one does shit to *my* roomie," she says and rips the dry erase board off the door before she stomps out of the room and into the hallway. I'm stunned at her response, but my mouth drops open when I hear her yell a second later.

"Who the *fuck* wrote on my board, huh?" Sunny doesn't sound bubbly anymore. I hear the sound of her smacking the dry erase board against a door and I sprint for the hall.

"Sunny, wait!" I yell when I hear her continue down the hallway. She's pissed and from the sound of it, she's not settling down until she gets an answer. I can't believe she's defending me. She doesn't even know me.

"Sunny, please, you don't understand!" I run out into the hallway and see she's a couple of doors down and arguing with a girl I've never seen before.

"What's your problem, asshole?" Sunny asks and points a finger at the dry erase board. "You think this is funny?"

"Fuck you! You don't know what she did to Beau!" There's a murmur of agreement from around us and I hear a few girls pipe up.

"She's going to hell."

"She shouldn't be in our school!"

I wince at their words. Shame burns through me hot and quick. I want to melt into the floor and vanish. When I imagined doing penance this year for what I did to Beau, I didn't imagine I would be bringing anyone else into it with me. I can't let Sunny do this.

"Sunny, it's okay. Really-" I start, but she's not listening. She's toe-to-toe with the girl that wrote on our dry erase board.

"And I don't *fucking care*! She coulda ran him over with her car and hit his mama for all I care. You don't pull this shit on *my roommate*, you got it?"

"She's a liar!" The girl screams back and then sees me approach. She points a finger at me. "You should be ashamed of yourself showing your face on campus after what you did to Beau Du Pont! No one wants you here you, fucking cunt!"

Her words hit me like a slap. There's so much hate in her eyes and I can't even make myself hold her gaze. I know what I did to Beau. I deserve everything she's saying. I hold up my hands and I see they're shaking. Oh god, why am I shaking?

"I'm sorry. I'm sorry, I didn't mean t-"

"Fuck you, you're the cunt!" Sunny explodes and slaps the girl's finger with the dry erase board. "I catch you writing shit like this again on our board and I'll beat your ass, bitch."

The girls in the hallway watching from their doors gasp at Sunny's words. I can't help but join them. It's so opposite to the happy girl I just met. It's like a switch got flipped and I'm speechless, just like the girl that yelled at me. When she opens her mouth to speak, Sunny snaps her fingers at her.

"You don't talk to my roommate. You shut your mouth or I'll do it for you."

The girl shuts up and Sunny stomps down the hallway towards me. "That goes for everyone on this floor, you hear me? I'm not playing with any of you Midwest bitches. I'm from San Antonio and I fight!"

"Come on, Nevaeh," she says and grabs my hand. I barely keep my feet as I hurry after Sunny. It's only when we're back at our room and she's fussing over getting the dry erase board snapped back into place that I say something.

"You shouldn't have done that. I deserved it."

"I don't like bullies. I don't care what the hell you did, but I will not let bullies get away with that."

"Sunny, when I was fifteen I put a man in prison for a murder he didn't commit," I blurt out, because it's better she knows who she's defending and can decide what to do with it after that. It makes sense that she isn't from around here. That's the only way she wouldn't know who I am or what I did.

Her eyes go wide and she drops the dry erase board on the floor. "Wow, what the fuck?"

"I-I'm not worth defending. I loved him and I did that to him. That's why everyone out there is so mad at me and it won't stop. I don't want you trying to defend me. It's just going to-"

"You were *fifteen*?" she whispers and comes into our room. She closes the door behind her and asks me, "What happened?"

"I was a witness to a murder. I named the wrong person."

"Holy shit, that's…that's intense."

"I know, but that's why-"

"Why that dumb bitch wrote on our dry erase board," she finishes for me. I smile at the dumb bitch and nod. "Yeah."

"You were just a kid, Nevaeh. It wasn't your fault," Sunny says. I don't expect that.

"Sunny, it is my fault."

"Two years ago, I saw a hit and run. When they asked me what kind of car it was, I couldn't remember. I was the only one that saw it."

"Sunny, I know you're trying to make me feel better but-"

"They hit a cyclist and they-they died."

I clap my hands over my mouth, because in a day of things I didn't expect this is just one more. "I'm sorry, Sunny."

"I couldn't tell them the color or if it was a car or a truck. I kept trying to remember what kind of car it was and every time I tried, it changed. They got away with it, so I kind of understand what you feel like."

"That wasn't your fault," I try, but Sunny isn't listening to me.

"I could have caught them, but I didn't. Why couldn't I remember?"

She's right, I know that, but what I did hurt someone. "You're not like me, Sunny. I'm evil. I'm a liar."

"Bullshit, Nevaeh. You were just a kid, and whether you like it or not, I'm going to be your friend and the best damn roommate you could ever have, you understand me? Don't make me kick your ass, Nev," she says the last part with a smile on her face and I smile back at her.

"Nev? Why'd you call me that?" I ask.

"Yes, Nev. It's a nickname, silly. I give my friends nicknames and that's mine for you." She holds up a finger as she goes on, "You might be tempted to try and give me a nickname too, but Sunny really doesn't lend itself to anything cool."

I've never had a nickname from anyone before, but I like that Sunny has given me one. Sunny really does want to be my friend. I don't know what to do with that.

"You don't even know me. You could just ask for a different roommate and have a better year without me around."

She rolls her eyes at me and starts to work on arranging her pillows on her bed. "My mom might not have raised me in that hippy commune in Florida, but she did teach me that everything happens for a reason. You're meant to be where you're meant to be. Who am I to tell the universe no? It put me here and seeing as I like you, I'm taking it as a sign that we're supposed to be friends."

"Oh yeah?"

"Absolutely. I'm only here because my grandma is an alumni and said this is the only school she would pay tuition for. I was shit at school, so it's not like I had a lot of choices to pick from, Nev. I'd rather give this place a go with having a friend for a roomie, than not."

"So you'd rather take your chances with me? The town pariah?"

Sunny nods and tosses a pillow to the side. "Absolutely, I would." She doesn't sound the least bit bothered at being stuck with me. That means I'll at least have one friendly face this year and the pressure bearing down on me lessens enough that I take a deep breath.

"Thank you, Sunny. I-I don't know how to thank you."

"Don't even stress. We're friends now. You can get us pizza tonight to repay me. And if you're good at math, I'm going to need a tutor."

"I'm good at math and I can get pizza. No problem. We can, ah, we can get some after unpacking, if you want?" I turn to my duffle bag and start to unpack while Sunny lets out a cheer and drags one of her boxes to her side of the room.

"Is it okay that I took this side of the room?"

"Oh yeah, I don't have a lot anyhow."

"Right, minimalism. How did you get into that anyways?" she asks and I start to try to cobble together an answer that makes sense. There's a knock at the door and I'm thankful I don't have to explain that my moM may or may not have just tossed all my things into the garbage to get rid of me.

Both of our heads whip in the direction of the door and Sunny holds a hand up to me. "I got it. If it's one of those dick faces, I'll handle it." I don't know where the fight in her is coming from, but I like it. Her spirit is so much bigger than her small frame and I wish I was as brave as her. I've never stood up to anyone like Sunny stood up to our entire dorm floor.

"Okay," I say with a nod and Sunny heads for the door with a bounce in her step, like she didn't just threaten our entire dorm floor, or like she isn't ready to do the same to whoever is on the other side of the door. I force myself to go back to unpacking but can't help and tense up when the door swings open.

"Hi, I'm Sunny. How can I help you?"

"Hello, I'm Pastor Mike. I'm here with Nevaeh's things."

I jump in surprise. That's not who I thought was going to bring my things, but it makes sense. Pastor Mike is the only person that would volunteer to bring my things to my dorm when my own mother couldn't be bothered.

"Pastor Mike?" I ask and turn to face him. I can't keep the surprise off my face, but if Pastor Mike sees it, he doesn't show it. He just gives me a warm smile and waits while Sunny sizes the man up in the doorway.

"Is he okay to let in?" Sunny asks and I smile. I know if I said no, Pastor or not, Sunny would slam the door in Pastor Mike's face.

"Yeah, he-he's okay. Thanks Sunny," I say and she gives me a bob of her head before she flashes a bright smile at Pastor Mike and extends her hand.

"Pleased to meet you, sir."

Pastor Mike is carrying two boxes but the man makes it work and manages to shake Sunny's hand before he looks my way. "Nevaeh, how are you? It's good to see you."

"I'm good, sir. H-how are you?" I rush forward to get a box out of his hands. "I'm so sorry that she asked you to do this. You shouldn't have to bring my things here."

"Now, Nevaeh, what kind of a friend would I be if I didn't make sure you got here safe and sound with all of your things? I was tasked with leading you and keeping you safe. Whether that's your soul or your books, I'll make sure it gets done."

I fall silent and nod at him. I feel bad about not going to church now. "Yes, sir. Thank you, sir. I appreciate you taking the time to do this for me."

"Oh, no worries at all. Happy to do it," Pastor Mike steps into the room and waves a hand over his shoulder. "Come on in, boys. Let's get Nevaeh set up for her first year at college. Aren't you happy to see her?" he asks and I realize he's brought other people with him.

"B-boys?" I don't know who he conned into coming with him and my stomach drops at facing the people I used to think of as friends. "You brought other people?" I ask and turn quickly away to buy myself more time. The box in my hands is heavy, I think it's books, but I don't know. I didn't think to label any of the boxes that I packed this weekend because of how much of a rush I was in. Honestly, I was just throwing things in boxes and taping them shut so that my mom didn't lose her shit at me. If she came by my room when she was home and didn't see me packing she started threatening to throw everything away so I was gone faster.

"Just bring those boxes in and set them off to the side there, Jared and Tyler." My cheeks heat because Tyler Roth was the boy that I flirted with but didn't mean it. "This is your side of the room, Nevaeh?" Pastor Mike asks and I nod quickly at him before I steal a look at Tyler.

"That's right, sir," I answer while Tyler pretends I don't exist. He's got three boxes and a backpack that I bought the summer I went hiking with Minnie up and down the prairie. We couldn't go anywhere, not really, with the way our parents were. But we pretended we weren't in Kansas, but Europe. It's silly to think about now, with how different Kansas and anything in Europe looks, but we didn't care. If we were together we had fun and nothing could touch us.

Tyler shrugs the bag off and drops it with a thud at the foot of my bed before he sets down the boxes and goes back into the hallway for more. It's then I see they brought a dolly and a handcart that's stacked 3 high with boxes. Far more than the boxes I packed for school. I'm confused for a split second and I forget all about Minnie or the fact that Tyler was sending me flirty good morning texts just over a week ago and go to the hand cart to look. My mother's neat handwriting is on top of the boxes, telling me what's inside. But it isn't stuff like toiletries I see written, it's *Keepsakes* and *Vital Paperwork*.

"Hey, I thought you were a minimalist," Sunny asks and pokes her head around the door to look at the sad little pile of boxes that contain my life.

I clear my throat. "I-I, well it's new. I don't really have the hang of it yet."

Sunny laughs and turns back to her side of the room. "Yeah, I can see that." She doesn't press the issue and I'm grateful that she picks up a box and carries it to the closet on her side of the room. It's not a big room, not with our beds and the matching desks and side tables, but it's a decent size. Or at least, it would be if there weren't so many people in it with us. Tears burn my eyes but I blink them back and grab another box. This one says sweaters. I know where that goes and go to my own closet on autopilot. Around me, Pastor Mike directs Tyler and Jared, both of which don't say a word and work with a quiet efficiency that tells me they want this over as much as I do.

My mom kicked me out. Well and truly. There's far more here than any freshman would need for a year at college, even if they were going out of state and I'm just a fifteen minute drive away. She's washed her hands of me and sent Pastor Mike as the messenger.

I always thought she would do it, but not this fast. I should have known better.

"Great, let's get those over there then. What do you say to pizza after?" Pastor Mike asks as he goes to the dolly and pulls another box off the top. *College Books* is written neatly on this one and I'm grateful I'll at least know where to start for classes.

"Pizza?" Sunny perks up and stops unpacking her things. "That would be awesome. Nevaeh and I were just talking about pizza," she says and grins at me. "Weren't we?"

All eyes come to me, even Tyler's. I'm only thankful for it because I don't have to think about my mom kicking me out and whether this means I'm homeless or not. I have the scholarship, but other than that nowhere and nothing else to my name. My mother came to Bloom to get away from her tiny town after she graduated high school because she'd gotten pregnant with me and ran away from her hometown. We've been in Bloom ever since.

She's never mentioned anything about her parents or if I have any other family to speak of.

If she's kicked me out then I am seriously on my own.

"Nevaeh?" Sunny's voice breaks me out of my mini-spiral and I give her a jerky nod.

"That's right. Pizza," I say, because I don't know what else to do. "I-I owe you pizza."

"Nonsense, it'll be my treat. It's your big day, after all," Pastor Mike tells me with a grin. "It's not everyday that it's your freshman year. There's only one first day, Nevaeh. We should celebrate it."

"I, uh, I have to get home soon and-" Tyler starts, but Pastor Mike gives him a sharp look I pretend not to notice. "I mean, pizza sounds good," Tyler finishes weakly and I remember wanting him to ask me out so badly. Why did I want that? I didn't even really like Tyler and now I'm going to have to play nice while we have pizza with Pastor Mike. It's not at all where I thought I would be a week ago, but there's no stopping it. Jared mumbles something about how good pizza will be and we keep bringing boxes in until they line my side of the room in a neat row, two high. It's awkward, but Sunny doesn't notice. She just chatters on while she puts her side of the room together. Before I realize it, we're done.

"Well done!" Pastor Mike claps his hands and gives us a bright smile. "I knew a little pizza bribe would speed things along." He sounds so happy and sure of what he's saying that I wish he was right, but I know better. It's not pizza that got us done so quickly, it's the fact that the faster we're done, the faster they get away from me.

"How about we head to The Pie?" Pastor Mike asks while he starts to fold up the handcart.

"What's The Pie?" Sunny asks.

Tyler is the one that answers, even though he's tried to stay quiet. "Only the best place in town to get pizza." He sounds normal now. The way he did when we talked on the phone at night. When I look his way, I see him smiling at Sunny the way he used to smile at me. My throat goes tight. Not because I care that Tyler is smiling at Sunny, but because I know she'll choose him.

He draws himself up to his full height and squares his shoulders. He used to do this to impress me. I didn't think it would be this lame when I wasn't the girl in front of him, but it is.

"Maybe I can show you around after we get pizza," he offers Sunny.

My new friend isn't going to pick me. Minnie didn't, so why would Sunny? I clear my throat and go to grab my jacket when Sunny steps beside me.

"I thought you had to go," she says and crosses her arms over her chest. "Didn't he say he had to go?" she asks me with a raised eyebrow. I have to hide a smile behind my hand. Sunny links her arm with mine and gives Tyler the stink eye while he turns beet red.

"Ah, Tyler is a forgetful guy," Pastor Mike covers and leads us out of my dorm. "He'd forget his head if it wasn't attached. Isn't that right, Tyler?"

"Yes, sir," Tyler mutters.

I've got a smile on my face when I lock the door behind us. The hallway isn't so scary with Sunny walking beside me. Maybe this year won't be so bad now that I have a friend.

CHAPTER FIVE
BEAU

FREEDOM IS SWEET. The sun is high in the sky above me. It's hot as shit, but damn is it good to be free. I turn my face up to the sky and inhale deeply. I can smell fresh cut grass on the wind and I know the maintenance crew has been hard at work getting the campus ready for today. I hear the telltale sound of a leaf blower and turn my head to see the crew working halfway down the block. They're at the corner, so I can only just make them out from where I'm standing, but it makes me remember the shit I had to do in prison.

Getting to work outside was a privilege then. Just to feel something alive on your skin, the wind, the heat of the sun, dirt on your hands, anything other than the cold numbness that filled my body in prison. I never got to stand around like I am now and enjoy it, so I do.

"Beau, do you have everything?" My mother asks and comes beside me. I don't look away from the clouds above me but I feel her smooth her hands over the dress shirt I'm wearing. It's pressed and perfect. Blue to match my eyes, my mother said when she insisted that I wear it. I let her fuss over me. She never gave up on getting me out of prison and that's why they didn't drop the case. That's why they found the knife that killed Carrie Salt. And the prints all over it weren't mine.

They don't know whose prints they are, but the thing that matters is that they weren't *mine*. And besides, whoever did kill Carrie made sure to have the knife delivered nice and neat to the Bloom Police Department with a note attached. I even heard they wrapped the box it was in with a red bow like it was a fucking gift. Which, you know, it was. For me.

Not for the Bloom Police Department, though. It was their worst nightmare, because the psycho fucker that killed Carrie and handed over the knife tipped off every news station in the area. They were swarming all over that damn station like maggots on roadkill. The note though, that was something else.

Fear The Reaper.

That was as dramatic as the cherry red bow. I'm not a fucking idiot. I know whoever did it is out there, but I don't care. They killed Carrie, but Nevaeh took my life away. I've got a score to settle with her before anything else. Psycho serial killer or not. I don't care who he kills next, I'm free. That's all that matters.

"Beau?" My mother asks again and I look down at her.

"Sorry, what?" I pretend I care that I wasn't listening, but I don't. I'm not the kid I was when I went in, but my mother doesn't know that. No one in Bloom knows how fucked up I am now and it's going to stay that way. I don't want anyone saving Nevaeh before I'm done with her. I'm going to make her scream.

"Your books and schedule? You have that all for tomorrow, right?" My mother is petite with brown hair that's cut to her chin. My hair is darker, much darker than hers or my father, but I do have her eyes. I look like my father in every other way, but my mother and my eyes are the identical shade of blue.

"Of course he does," my father rumbles and claps me on the back. I've got his build and stature. He played a wide receiver here and talks about it as if he's never done another successful thing in his life, even though he owns the largest construction and development group in the state. "It's a damn shame you can't play ball this year. You would have been sensational on the field back then, son. Would have loved to see you in the colors."

Back then.

He makes it sound like decades since I took the field, not four years. It may as well have been a century ago. A lifetime ago. I loved football. I dreamed about wearing the silver and royal blue my father wore, but now it's never going to happen. Another thing Nevaeh took from me.

I shrug, lifting my bag higher on my shoulder. "It'll be nice getting to a game now and then this year."

"We got you season tickets. You can go whenever you like," my mother tells me.

"Thanks, mom." I kiss her cheek but my eyes are scanning the green space around us. We're standing in The Oval, the quintessential spot on Bloom State campus that's a point of pride for how it offers the best view of the school's cathedral and the Green. It's a wide open lawn that slopes downhill to the trees that work as a living wall between the campus and Bloom's streets. The dorms are to the west of us, just behind the cathedral and the rest of campus to the East. The libraries and buildings and Unions spill out that way towards the football stadium until you reach Fraternity Row. I used to go up that way and party with Carrie and her friends before The Reaper cut her to pieces.

Why the fuck didn't we go there that night instead of Bloom Point? *So fucking stupid. Stupid fucking goddamn-*

"That little bitch is here!" My mother's whisper may as well be a scream. I see her the second my mother does. *Nevaeh.* She's walking with a girl I've never seen before. A little blonde thing that's arm and arm with her. I frown. She's supposed to be alone. Not with a friend. What the fuck is this? But then I see Pastor Mike and two dipshits I remember following me around in youth group.

"Pastor Mike is with her," I observe. I tuck my hands in the pockets of the pressed slacks I have on. I look like a fucking rich douche. Like I did before I got locked up with murderers and became one too. I found my way, though and earned my respect. If they saw me dressed like this, they would gut me and I would let them. Doesn't matter though, it's a disguise that works as good as the dark hood The Reaper hides behind. That's all I remember seeing from that night. A hooded figure, something that looked like a robe, slamming into me on my way down the path after Carrie. She was supposed to just be taking a piss but then I heard her scream and I knew something was wrong. I was drunk though, high too, and I fell more than I didn't in the dark trying to find her. The Reaper ran right into me then and knocked me on my ass, covering me in Carrie's blood.

I thought I was going to marry her and he covered me in her blood. My hands curl at my sides and anger rises up in me but then my mother steps in front of me and clucks her tongue at the sight of Pastor Mike and the bitch that put me away.

"She has some fucking nerve showing up here. I thought they took that scholarship away from her."

I nod. "I know."

My mother sighs and shakes her head. "I can't believe you're forgiving her."

I say the words I practiced a million times when there was nothing to do but pace my cell and look at Nevaeh's photos. "It's the right thing to do."

Beside us the camera crew van is pulling up. The brakes squeal when they come to a stop and I know it's showtime. My mother may be kicking up a fuss at Nevaeh being here, but we need her here. It wouldn't work without her.

"She was just a kid," I add.

My father makes a noncommittal grunt. "It's very admirable of you son. I'm proud of you."

"So am I," my mother sniffs and hugs me. "My poor baby."

I pat her shoulder and let her hug me and sniffle into my shirt, but I don't look away from Nevaeh. I can't look away, because she's smiling. I watch as she smiles, as her lush lips curve up, before I see the white flash of her teeth when she laughs. Sunlight warms her skin and bounces off her dark hair. It shines, hints of red and gold show and I want to fucking touch her. God. How many hours did I stare at my shitty printed out photos of her?

Nothing compares to the real fucking thing, even if she's a hundred feet away from me. I want to get closer, but my mother won't let go and the camera crew and news reporter are talking to my father.

"There she is!" The news reporter chirps and points at Nevaeh. I want to slap her hand away. I don't want anyone else looking at Nevaeh but me.

I waited a long fucking time for this, but I stay where I am. Still as a statue and with a dumb as fuck kid smile on my face, like everything is perfectly fine and the girl that I've thought about for four years isn't walking so close I can hear the tone of her voice.

"Are you ready?" The reporter is getting mic'd up or something, but I don't pay much attention. I just nod and say the line they expect with an easy going smile.

"Of course I am. I've been waiting for this for a very long time."

"Well, wait no longer! Come with me, young man." The reporter takes off across the green like they own the place and heads straight for Nevaeh. Adrenaline hits my body. I'm so fucking close to her. I want her to look at me. I fucking need her to. I've looked at her for so long, not having her eyes on me makes me want to break something. I want to fucking kill everyone she looks at.

"Excuse me! Miss Santiago! Miss Santiago!" The reporter has her hand up and is waving down Nevaeh's group. I don't miss the way Nevaeh's big brown eyes get bigger and she looks like she's going to faint.

I notice the second she sees me.

"Can we get a moment of your time?"

Nevaeh's eyes are on me and it's like the first hit of a drug. Like the first sip of liquor after a long fucking day. That burn is perfect. It hurts in the best possible way and I smile at her. She looks like she's going to throw up.

Good. I hope she fucking gets sick all over her fucking self. The bitch.

She falls back a step and grabs onto the girl walking with her. Nevaeh looks just the way I imagined her. Terrified and trapped. My little liar wants to run, but she's got nowhere to go. Not in broad daylight with a reporter shoving a microphone in her face and my parents standing with me. Even if we weren't here, she'd be surrounded. I see the looks from the students that recognize her. The ones that knew me. They look at me with a mix of admiration and pity. I can almost hear their whispers.

"He didn't deserve that."

"He was such a *nice* guy."

I'm not a fucking nice guy. Not anymore.

I smile at Nevaeh and ignore the reporter that's firing questions off at her like a sniper. Honestly, I don't even know what she's asking Nevaeh, because I can't look anywhere but at Nevaeh's face. She's beautiful. I didn't think that before, not before I spent hours, days…fucking *years*, staring at her pictures. I've memorized every curve and dip of her. The way her hair looks in the sun, the depth of brown of her eyes, the way she tans in the summer. I know it all.

She's mine.

But even if I hadn't, there's no denying the beauty she grew into from the gangly teenager that used to sweep my floors. She was awkward then, knobby kneed with baby fat on her face and clothes that didn't fit right.

But now?

Now she's fresh faced with curves that I want to bruise. She's fucking perfect.

"*Beau?*" She whispers and I feel that whisper hit me like a knife to the chest. It's work to keep a pleasant smile on my face. All I want to do is cross the space between us and shove the reporter and cameraman away from her. I want to drag her inside where no one is going to see us and make her pay for what she did to me, but it's then that I realize something.

For four fucking years I've spent my days and nights thinking about this moment. Staring at Nevaeh's photo until the after image of it is burned into my eyes. Even when I tried to sleep, she was there. Always, my beautiful, perfect, fucking liar was there, just out of reach. But now she's not. Now she's fucking not and something happened to me while I was locked away with the ghost of Nevaeh haunting me, because it really is true what they say.

It's a thin line between love and hate, and I've blurred that line until I can barely see it.

I don't know if I want to fuck her or kill her.

Motherfucker.

CHAPTER SIX

Nevaeh

I'VE THOUGHT OF Beau Du Pont every moment since the day I put him in prison. I didn't eat for that whole week because every time I thought of Beau, I threw up, which just made me think of that night again. I stopped eating so there was nothing to throw up and it took my mom bringing down the kids from my youth group to pray over me for me to eat anything and keep it down. I really only gave in then because I was embarrassed to see them in my room unexpectedly with pity in their eyes.

I ate then and eventually was able to think of Beau without getting sick. Right now I'm glad I haven't eaten the pizza we were about to get, because I have zero doubts that I would have thrown up all over Sunny.

"Beau?" I can't believe he's here, but there he is. Plain as day and even more beautiful than I remember him. He's so much more grown up than I remember. Before, he had boyish looks and the kind of charm that a nineteen year old boy had when you were fifteen and didn't know shit about the world. I thought the sun rose because Beau Du Pont told it to, then. But that never changed. It can't have, with the way my heart feels like it's going a million miles an hour.

"Can we ask you a few questions, Ms. Santiago?" There's a microphone in my face and I jump back in surprise from the reporter that I forgot about for the split second that my eyes met Beau's. He's smiling at me. Why is he smiling at me?

I don't deserve him to be smiling at me with the fall sun high in the sky and making him look like my dreams come true. His dark hair is slightly longer now than the way he kept it when he was in high school, but it looks good. There's product in it, just enough to keep it swept away from his face. I'd have given anything to touch his hair. His face is more angular now, jawline sharp and strong with a hit of stubble there that wasn't around before. He's bigger, too. Beau was always bigger than me, but now?

Now he feels like a mountain with broad shoulders that pull the material of his dress shirt tight and his trousers fit to a tee. Even with the changes that make him look like a man with just a hint of the boy I loved, there's one thing that hasn't changed.

His eyes.

At least…almost. Beau's eyes are a beautifully clear kind of blue that makes me think of the sea. They look the same, but the longer I stare at him, I see there's something else there that wasn't before. A hardness that's there and gone in a flash when the camera swings his way.

"We are here with Beau Du Pont and his family on Bloom State's Move In Day, but this day is so much more than that. This perfect autumn day is when Bloom's very own confronts the girl that helped put him away, in a case that rocked our small community and stole four years of his life."

That's the bucket of ice water I need to snap back to reality and I fall back a step. Sunny follows close and Pastor Mike comes up to the reporter. "Now, now, miss. I think there's been a misunderstanding-" he starts, but the reporter isn't letting up.

"Ms. Santiago, what do you have to say for the role you played in Beau Du Pont's wrongful conviction?"

"I-I-" I stammer and the words won't come. I've had a recurring nightmare where this happens. Where I'm dragged out in front of everybody and have to account for my sins, but I could never find my voice then and I can't find it now either. I look at Beau. "I'm sorry."

"You put my boy away for a murder he didn't commit and that's all you have to say for yourself?" Mrs. Du Pont is there beside the reporter and her eyes, the ones that are identical to Beau's, are angry. She looks mean as a snake and I know she'd slap me if there wasn't a camera crew filming the whole thing.

"Mrs. Du Pont-"

"Mama, I forgive her. We went over this." *Beau's voice.* My heart squeezes and stutters at the sound of Beau's voice. I've tried to remember what it sounded like, but it's not like I had any recordings. The only ones I could find when I looked were his trial and questioning. I couldn't watch either of them. Over the years, I've almost forgotten what he sounded like, but this is right. It's like a key sliding into a lock and everything just clicks.

Beau looks at me and there's an apologetic look on his handsome face. "You didn't know they'd be here, did you?" he asks and glances at the reporter. "Your mama was supposed to have told you. I'm sorry, Nevaeh. I wouldn't have let them do this if you weren't okay with the interview."

"Interview?" I ask and look around because yes, this is an interview. The reporter is there with her dumb microphone and the camera man shows no sign of letting up. There's even one of those sound guys that has the big stick with the fuzzy microphone on one end. I can see two other television vans pull up and a second later reporters and more cameramen hop out and start heading our way.

"I didn't know anything about an interview." I shake my head and back away, I bump into Tyler and he jumps away from me, but Sunny is right there and grabs my hand. "I'm sorry, I can't do this. I c-can't."

I turn to try and run before the other reporters get to us, but the one that's already there shouts after me. "And what about the school revoking your scholarship? What are your plans for college?"

That stops me.

The scholarship.

I've been kicked out of my house. The scholarship is the only thing I have. I can't lose it, I can't! If I do, I don't know how I'll afford Bloom State. I was a good enough student and did all the right things, but I didn't apply for any other financial aid because I didn't have to. I had the scholarship trust waiting on me, so it seemed unnecessary. I should have known it wasn't going to work out.

"What do you mean?" I force myself to go back. The reporter knows she has me from the smug look on her face and I hate that I have to ask her. I'm so tired of people forcing me to do what they want. First it was the questioning when things started to fall apart and I didn't know what I had seen. Why was Beau there? Why did he grab me? I hadn't seen a knife, so maybe it hadn't been him, right? That had been before the detectives. I don't remember a lot of what I said then, but it cost me Beau and my fucking conscience.

"What did you say about my scholarship?"

"Bloom State has made a motion to revoke your trust and forfeit your scholarship."

I hear Pastor Mike make an indignant sound. "On what grounds?" He sounds angry. Poor man. I don't know why he's defending me. No one should.

"On a morality clause issue, given Ms. Santiago's part in what happened to Beau. Her presence on campus could prove to be nothing but a distraction to the student body and a reminder of that horrible night."

Pastor Mike sweeps me behind him and confronts the reporter and the Du Pont's head on. "No, I don't accept that-"

Mr. Du Pont nods and holds a hand up, stopping whatever it is that Pastor Mike is going to try and convince them of. We all know what I did, so it can't be my innocence. "Now Pastor, we respect your authority at Crown of Thorns. That's what part of this is about."

"I think the school is right. She should lose her scholarship." Mrs. Du Pont's eyes on me are sharp as ever. "She can stay if she can pay her own way. It's only fair, with what she's done to our family."

Pastor Mike doesn't back down. "That's not true. She's just a girl, you have to forgive her!"

I open my mouth to tell him they're right. That it's okay and can he please help me move my shit out of my dorm, but everyone starts talking at once. A camera flash goes off and that's when I realize the other crews are here.

"Excuse me, Nevaeh, can we get a photo for the paper?" There's another flash and it's hard to focus. I can hear Mrs. Du Pont's sharp voice and when there's more camera flashes, her blue eyes are the only thing I can see. Her look tells me everything I need to know. If she could kill me, she would do it.

"I'm sorry, I have to go." I turn and try to get away, but I run right into one of the reporters. I don't know if this one is new or if it was the one that was talking to me, but her microphone hits me in the chest and I have to back off.

A voice rises up out of everyone. "Do you *really* think you're going to be forgiven for what you did?"

I go still but Sunny catches my arm and glares at the person that spoke. "Let's get out of here, Nev."

"Yeah, okay." We start to push out of the crowd and I'm thankful Pastor Mike is there. He helps clear a way, but we aren't going anywhere fast. Not with the crews and reporters shouting questions at our backs. That's when I hear Beau.

"I have," Beau blurts out, cutting everyone off.

"Are you saying that you've forgiven the girl that put you behind bars for the murder of your girlfriend?"

My gut twists. I know I shouldn't be paying more attention to the fact that Carrie was called Beau's girlfriend than their mention of what I did to him. I should not feel upset about the mention of Carrie. That's sick.

"That's right," Beau says and I look over my shoulder at him. He's standing in the circle that's formed out of everyone, his family at his back. Tyler and Jared are awkwardly to the side and the reporters, journalists, and their crews have fanned out around us, blocking us in. Students and their families have started to gather. Some close by and others further back, but everyone is watching what's happening. Everyone in Bloom is going to know about today, even if they weren't here, they'll know. I look at Beau because I'd rather look at him than anyone else. I don't know how he manages to stand at the center of it looking unaffected. I feel like I'm going to pass out.

"I've forgiven her," he says and looks around at the group of people before his eyes come to me. "And I don't want you to lose your scholarship. It wasn't your fault." The amount of camera clicks and flashes that go off when he says that are insane. A half dozen microphones swing his way and Beau keeps talking, raising his voice as he does and takes a step in my direction.

"You were just a kid," he says and gives me a warm smile. "I know you didn't mean it. We've all made mistakes and one shouldn't define the rest of your life, Nevaeh."

"And what do you think about her presence on campus?"

"I think Nevaeh should be here. It's fitting that we go on this journey together. I am personally going to visit with the school board and trustees to ensure that her scholarship remains intact. If Nevaeh goes, I go."

There's a few gasps and my mouth falls open. I can't believe he just said that. I don't move, I can't move while I watch him approach. Beau doesn't stop walking and comes right up to me.

When he extends a hand to me, I have to let go of Sunny to take it. Then it's just us.

"Nevaeh is staying right here with me at Bloom State," Beau goes on, voice still loud enough for everyone to hear. Then my dream man, the man I've loved since I was fifteen, the man that I thought of every day for the past four years and wondered *what did I do?* How could it have been me that put him away? That same man leans in close and it's like all my dreams are coming true. In those daydreams, Beau kisses me. He holds me close and tells me that he loves me, that he always has and that he's thought of nothing but me. It's a perfect fairytale after a nightmare. I hold my breath, don't dare move while Beau comes closer and the cameras flash and record around us.

No one says a word. Beau doesn't kiss me like I've dreamed. Instead, he leans in close to me, the hand I've taken pulls me right up against him and it's then, when my body touches his for the first time, that I feel his lips graze my ear as he speaks softly, for only me to hear.

"You took four years from me, you bitch. Now it's time to pay."

It's been two hours since Beau Du Pont threatened me while cameras flashed around us. Two hours since I stumbled away from him and didn't tell anyone a word about what he said. Instead, I let him stand beside me and pose for cameras like Mrs. Du Pont instructed. The reporters had questions, but Pastor Mike didn't let me say too much before he pulled the pastor card and got everyone to back off. He marched us out of The Oval and towards downtown. I sat in The Pie and ate a pepperoni and jalapeño jumbo slice because if I didn't, Sunny would probably notice and Pastor Mike ordered it special for me because he knows it's my favorite. When we left the pizzeria, things had calmed down and the sun had started to set. Pastor Mike and the guys walked us back to our dorm before they left and it was just Sunny and me. She's in the shower now down the hall and I've been sitting on my bed like I have been since we got back.

Beau threatened me. It wasn't like my daydreams at all. It wasn't even like my nightmares, either. In all the scenarios I tortured myself over, it never occurred to me that it would be Beau that hated me. That he would be the one threatening me. I was stunned. So much so that when Beau turned to the cameras and flashed them all a smile with his arm around my shoulder, I stayed put.

I figured it out, though. What was different about Beau's eyes. It was the anger. Cold, mean, dark. Anger in a way that made his mother's glares pale in comparison for all the quiet rage I now understood lived in him. I squeeze my eyes shut and drop my head into my hands. How the hell am I going to fix this? I have to think of something, especially with the entire school hating me. Beau wants me to stay and I understand why. If I'm here, he knows where I am. Of course, he's going to talk to the board and see if he-

There's a creak and a heavy footstep outside of the door and I freeze. I lift my head up and stare at the door. I can see a shadow through the space at the bottom and I watch. With my mom the way she is, I got used to watching for people like this. I never knew when she was spying on me. Waiting to catch me slipping so she could lecture me on how I'm going to hell. It was like all the bad the world dealt my mom came crashing down at me because I was the only place she could safely put it. She knew I wasn't going to fight back. Not when she'd been doing it since I could walk. I'd looked at college as the place I could escape, but now it is a prison. A place that, even though I want to run from it, is the only roof over my head now that my mom has dumped all my things off via Pastor Mike.

And my scholarship? What if I lose my scholarship? I don't know what I am going to do if that happens. Beau said he wanted to make me pay, so I know he's going to try and make good on his appeal to the board of directors. But if he is successful, then what? My heart starts to race. I have to fight from putting my head between my knees and keep my eyes trained on the shadow that moves again. The person on the other side is still there, but what are they doing? Are they writing something else on the door? What if it's Beau?

I stand up and take a deep breath. I'm dizzy. God why is it so hard to breathe? *Maybe because the man you put in prison is free now and he's going to make you pay.* I flinch at the thought but it's the truth. If I stay at Bloom State, Beau will have access to me and who is ever going to believe me about Beau? After what I did to him, no one is going to care if I tell them what he said today.

No one would give a shit if he does do something to me.

They wouldn't care. My own mother fucking had all my shit dropped off by the only man in town that wouldn't say no to doing a favor for me. My mind is racing, anxiety feels like it's bubbling in me so hard and fast that I almost miss seeing the doorknob starting to turn. Oh my god. What if it's Beau? He's coming in and I'm standing here like an idiot.

"You took four years from me, you bitch. Now it's time to pay."

I turn to look for somewhere to hide. The closet is easiest, but it's also the most predictable, so I drop to the floor and go to roll under my bed. I have to move faster. I hit my shoulder on the side as I try to get under the bed and the next second the door bangs open. I scream and spin to put my back against the bed. I'll at least be able to see him coming. But when I turn, it's only Sunny staring at me. She's wrapped in a towel with one hand on the door and her shower caddy in her free hand.

"Are you okay?" Sunny asks me and when someone walking by laughs, she shuts the door.

"I-I'm sorry," I choke out and press a hand to my chest. "I didn't mean to scream," I say instead of answering her question. I'm still sitting on the floor and when I get up, I'm shaky and have to sit down on my bed. The adrenaline that just filled my body has nowhere to go and my head throbs from the rush. I want to run, but there's nowhere to go. No one to run from. So I stay put and try to slow my breathing down. Sunny puts her shower caddy down on her desk and turns to face me.

"Why did you scream? Did someone try something while I was gone?" Her eyes go to the floor in front of me. She knows I was trying to get under the bed, but she isn't mentioning it.

I shake my head and press my hands to my knees. "N-no, no one tried anything." I don't tell her about Beau and what he said. I've already gotten so much more than I deserve by having Sunny as a roommate. She was so happy after the reporters and journalists let us go.

"I knew it was going to work out. You'll see. It has to, if he's telling them to let you stay."

She doesn't know that he just wants me at Bloom State so he can have access to me. I don't want to tell her either. Telling her will just drag her in deeper. Sunny will try to help. I don't think anyone can help me when it comes to Beau Du Pont.

"I dropped something," I lie and get to my feet shakily. "I-I'm just a little jumpy after today."

Sunny nods and starts to dry her hair. "I get that. Lots of changes. But tomorrow is the first day of classes. Are you excited?" She looks at me over her shoulder with a smile and my heart aches. Sunny is excited. She's sweet. Too good of a roommate for someone like me. I can't tell her about Beau or she'll try to do something.

"I am. It's going to be great." I grab my shower things out of the box I opened earlier and am grateful that when my mom packed my things up she kept them grouped together, enough at least that I've been able to find my things in the boxes that I've unpacked and opened. "I better shower though or I'll be rushing around tomorrow."

Sunny hums. "Good idea. It's pretty quiet right now. It'll be nuts tomorrow morning if you wait."

"See you in a bit." I head out but stop with one hand on the door. "Hey, Sunny?"

"Yeah, what's up?"

I turn to look at her and see an expectant smile on Sunny's face. Next to Pastor Mike, it's been the only friendly face I've seen today and I smile back at her. "Thanks for today. For, you know, sticking up for me."

"That's what friends do, Nev."

"Thanks for being my friend, Sunny."

"Always."

I leave the room and head for the bathrooms. Sunny was right that it's quiet. I only see a couple of girls on my way to the showers. When I enter the bathroom, it reminds me of summer camp. It's muggy and I almost trip over a forgotten shower shoe. I see a few toiletry items and towels scattered at the sinks to the right of the door. Ahead of me, I see the row of shower stalls. There's someone else here, from the sound of the shower that's running, but other than that I think it's empty.

Guess I'll be showering at night to avoid the crowd. I don't really think I'd get a lot of peace showering in a bathroom full of people that hate me. Anxiety hits me just thinking about it, but I keep walking forward with a tight grip on my shower caddy. I can do this. I deserve this. I put an innocent man behind bars and now he wants his revenge.

Maybe this is all a part of it.

I should pay for what I've done, whether or not it's Beau that does it. That means I can't leave Bloom State. I drop my shower caddy on the little bench inside of the stall, pull the outer curtain closed and start to get undressed. I'm glad this shower isn't like the ones at summer camp and actually is divided into two spaces. There's a part with a bench and a hook that will keep my stuff dry and beyond that is the actual shower. I step into the shower and frown as I turn on the taps. At home I had a bluetooth speaker I used to play music on, but I'll have to get used to the silence if I want to fly under the radar while I'm here. It takes a second for the water to heat up but finally it does and I step under the spray. I take in one deep breath and then another while I count to twenty, I hold my breath for a beat and then repeat the cycle. It helps with my anxiety—at least somewhat, and after a few minutes it slows down my heart rate enough that I can relax under the hot water beating down on me. It's then that I start to cry.

I'm homeless.

My mom definitely kicked me out. I don't even have to call her to find out.

I put Beau in prison. I stole four years of his life and now he's going to take that from me. What that means, I don't know, but I don't think I'll be able to stay at school if he doesn't let me. How am I supposed to stay here with him threatening me the way he is?

I press my hands to my forehead and fight back a wave of nausea. *I love Beau.* How could I have done this to him? He's not the kind of man that's going to hurt me. Or at least, he wasn't. He wasn't before I put him away for a murder he didn't commit.

My thoughts come faster and faster until there's nothing but worry and fear in my brain and no breath work in the whole world will slow it down, so I turn the shower off and towel off. I can hear the other shower still going and try to stay quiet. I don't want the other girls on the floor to know that I'm falling apart, not when Beau put on the show that he did today. There's a reason for it. I think I owe him enough to play the hand he has stacked against me. It's the least I can do after what I did to him, even if it hurts.

I deserve it.

There's a bang and I jump, but it must have just been the door slamming shut behind the other person that was just in here. The other shower is off now. I wrap my towel around myself and reach for the curtain but the second that I do, someone rips it out of my hand. I scream and try to back away from them but they're faster and the curtain ends up wrapped around my head.

"You're trash, you lying bitch!" The voice is a girl's, but I've never heard it before.

I swing the shower caddy out at them but I know it misses when it doesn't hit anything. There's a laugh before I'm shoved and I fall back and hit my face against the shower wall. My shower caddy hits the floor and I hear the sound of my shampoo and conditioner rolling away on the floor. I try to rip the shower curtain off of me, but I freeze when they speak again.

"No one wants you here. You should kill yourself for what you did."

I half expect my attackers to hit me again, but they don't. When I rip the shower curtain off my face there's no one there. I can hear someone running and the lights turn off before the door bangs shut again. Even though whoever just hit me knows where I am, I can't move. I'm paralyzed where I'm laying in the dark and it's a long time before I force myself to get up. I almost slip a few times on my way to the door and when I finally get the lights on, I know I'm alone.

"Fuck," I whisper and then wince, because I'm not someone that cusses. I can't think of anything else to say, though, when I see my reflection in the mirrors above the sinks closest to the doors. I have a busted lip and I can feel a bruise forming on the side of my face. I touch it gingerly and start to walk towards the sink but stop and lock the door before I do. Whoever was here is gone, but I'm not going to be an idiot and let them have another go at me while I'm still in here. I wash the blood from my lip. Thankfully it stops bleeding when I hold a wad of paper towels to it. I pick up my shower caddy and get my shampoo and body wash back from where they went.

There's already going to be questions from Sunny when I go back to the room. I don't need her to know I'm absolutely lying to her when I tell her I slipped and fell. Once I've got my things together I look myself over in the mirror again. My lip is definitely busted, but it's stopped bleeding and there's a scrape on my knee and one on my elbow, but other than that I seem okay. I don't know how big of a bruise the one I know I'll have on the side of my face will be, but I'll try and cover that with makeup as best I can so no one talks too much about it. I stop in front of the door but my hand hovers above the lock and I swallow hard.

If they're out there...what if they're waiting? What if, when I open the door, someone is going to swing on me again? My hand shakes and I don't know what to do. I can't stand here all night, but the risk of my attacker being on the other side of the door is pretty damn high.

If they're there, you fight them. The lights are on in the hallway, so you'll see them coming.

Fight them.

My hand curls in a fist. I don't know what this urge is. Where the thought that I can fight *anyone* is coming from is beyond me. I don't fight. I've never even thrown a punch in my life. But I know without a shadow of a doubt that if someone is on the other side of the door, I'll hit them.

I will fight them.

I turn the lock and jerk the door open, but there's no one in the hallway. I hurry back to my room on shaky legs and with a clenched fist that I don't know how to use. When I get back to the room, the lights are off. There's a nightlight Sunny must have plugged in by the door and its soft light is enough for me to get dressed for bed and put my things away without making too much of a racket. When I climb into bed, I don't sleep.

I cry.

CHAPTER SEVEN
BEAU

SOMEONE'S BEEN FUCKING with my shit.

Nevaeh has a split lip and a bruise on her cheek. It's not a black eye, but it's too close for my liking. Who the fuck is having fun with *my Nevaeh*?

That's for me and for me alone. I didn't do four years with nothing but my sweet liar as the prize for someone to come along and take her from me now. *I'm* the one that makes her scared. I'm the one that's going to mark her skin. I earned her.

Whoever touched her is as good as dead.

"I can't believe how forgiving you are," the girl next to me, *Carly, Megan, Ali,* something like that, sighs and leans close to me before she places a hand on my arm. "You're *really* forgiving her after everything she's done to you?"

She means Nevaeh but I shrug and play dumb like I don't know.

"Not sure what you mean." I flip open my notebook and watch the front of the class, even though I'm still tracking Nevaeh where she's awkwardly skirting the lecture hall and trying to make for the back of the room without anyone seeing her. She's failing. Everyone in the room fucking sees her. Even if they didn't, I'd see her.

I'll always see my sweet little liar. She's mine.

"Oh, um, of course. I'm sorry. You probably don't want to talk about that now that you're free, huh?" I raise an eyebrow at her and she's got the good grace to blush and look away. "I'm really fucking this up right now, aren't I?" She bites her lip and looks up at me through her lashes. She wants me to think she's innocent and sweet. Carrie used to look at me like that when she wanted something.

"Fucking what up?" I ask and take in the girl for the first time. She's similar to Carrie. She's what I would have wanted before I went away. Before Nevaeh became the first and last thought I had. I glance over at her and see her taking a seat a few rows back from me. She's just at the edge of where everyone is sitting without being against the wall. The only thing that I want now is dark hair and warm brown eyes that make me so fucking mad I don't know if it's worse to have her look at me or not.

Nevaeh freezes and our eyes lock. Her pouty lips part in a perfect fucking O of surprise before she looks away and I know the answer—not having her look at me is torture. It's hell. I want to get up and go to her. I want to drag her right out of this classroom and make her tell me what happened to her before I put my own marks on her skin.

"Making a good impression on you," the girl beside me says and I'm forced to look away from Nevaeh. I'm here to play the role everyone expects. The good All-American boy that's happy to be home. If I don't press it, if I don't show them how fucked up I am now, they can all pretend that I wasn't in prison. They'll make up a story in their head about how I was away for some reason or another and I'll become a hero again sooner than later.

I need that image to hold if I'm going to have enough time to break Nevaeh. That's why I smile at the blonde I don't give a shit about and let her go on. "I'd say you're doing just fine, Carly."

"Ali," she corrects with a smile. "I'm Ali Simpson."

I nod and hold out my hand. "Forgive my bad manners. I've been out of good company for some time, Ali Simpson. Pleased to meet you, I'm Beau Du Pont."

Ali takes my hand and gives me a sparkling smile. "I know who you are. We all do."

"I'm sorry it's that way. I hope it's not too much of a distraction."

She giggles and flips her hair over her shoulder. "You're going to be plenty of a distraction in this classroom and I think you know it."

She's flirting. Trying to show that she's interested. Good.

"Hopefully a good distraction?"

She winks. "Oh, the best. You're easy on the eyes, Du Pont, but I think you know that." I haven't been called Du Pont since I played ball. It's easy to pretend that I'm who I say I am when I've got a girl like Ali smiling and calling me Du Pont.

The professor enters and calls the room to order, but I make it a point to lean close to Ali as everyone settles down. "You'll have to let me know if I'm too distracting, Ali."

She giggles again and bumps my arm with hers. "I pinky swear."

Class starts then and I'm finally left alone to think. Someone put their hands on Nevaeh before I've had the pleasure. I don't like that. I had a meeting with the board this morning and argued for her to stay. It went my way, of course, because I had my parents' backing on the matter. Pastor Mike even showed up to lend his support. Being the pastor of the town's largest church has some pull in a place like Bloom. The board relented, even though they weren't happy about it, which is fine. I don't care if they don't like it or are calling Nevaeh's presence a disturbance to learning.

I want her. That's all that matters.

I keep a careful eye on Nevaeh and see something else other than her bruised face that I don't like. There's a fucker sitting next to her. He looks like the sensitive type. The kind of guy that reads shitty poetry and plays acoustic guitar at keggers to impress the girls. I know his type. Why the fuck is he talking to my Nevaeh? She looks nervous next to him and keeps her head down, even though he leans in to talk to her a few times. I'm going to find out who he is and put a fucking stop to that. Class lets out and everyone practically bolts for the door except for the ones trying to make a good impression that hang around to chat with the professor after and a few stragglers at the back.

Nevaeh and the sensitive dick looking at her like she's his next muse are two of the stragglers. She's got a few books and she drops them with a gasp when she sees me walking towards them. Of course fucking lover boy doesn't hesitate to scoop them up for her.

"Here you go," he tells her with a cheerful smile that I know isn't fake. Not like mine are now. He's interested in Nevaeh all right. I should slit his throat.

"Nevaeh," I say and pleasure floods my body when I watch her face go pale. She looks like a rabbit caught in a trap and I fucking love it. "Let's go." I tilt my chin to the door and when I start to pass her on the way, lover boy steps in front of me.

"I'm Dean," he says and extends his hand to me. "You a friend of Nevaeh's?" he asks.

"Sure am," I tell him and shake his hand. "I'm Beau."

"Beau Du Pont?" Dean asks and looks between Nevaeh and I. "Everything okay?" His meaning is clear. He wants to check with her if she wants to go with me. Typical good guy shit. I would have done the same thing before the pretty little bitch in front of us put me away.

"Everything's fine," I answer for her. "Isn't that right, Nevaeh?"

She answers me immediately. "Yeah, it's fine. I-I, well, it was nice to meet you, Dean."

He nods and steps aside, even though I can tell he doesn't want to. His eyes are on me and his eyes narrow. He doesn't know what I'm up to, but he's wondering now. "It was a pleasure to meet you. Remember, I'm here if you need to talk."

Nevaeh's face softens, her eyes lose the scared edge to them that I prefer and she gives him a smile. She's going to thank him. Offer to take him up on his offer to talk, but I'm not about to let her have a hero.

She doesn't deserve a hero. Good people get happy ever after. They get a hero that steps between them and the devil. But not Nevaeh. She's a fucking soulless bitch and she's mine. All fucking mine. The only thing Nevaeh's going to get is me. And I'm her villain.

I step in front of Nevaeh and level a smile at Dean. "Nevaeh doesn't need any more friends, Dean. But thanks."

His jaw stiffens and I have to give it to him, he doesn't give when I think he will. But that just shows me how stupid he is. That's the only excuse he has to be going after Nevaeh.

"I wasn't talking to you, friend."

I give him a mean smile. "It's Beau and I'm not your friend." I turn to Nevaeh and lean down to her ear, so she knows no one else is going to hear what I tell her. "Let's go, or you're not going to like what I do to him."

There's nowhere else to go but with me if she wants things to stay peaceful. I don't care about causing a scene. I can do a lot right now with the way the public sees me. The wronged hometown hero come home, so ready to forgive the girl that ruined his life. I head down the stairs and glance over my shoulder as I do. Dean looks pissed. He moves, takes a step towards us when Nevaeh falls in step with me and I smile. The easiest way to get respect is to make an example of someone and I'm about to turn Dean into a fucking lesson. The professor and their hanger-ons aren't paying attention to us. Not really. We're too far away for them to hear what we're saying and they're doing the polite Midwestern thing by not gawking.

Everyone knows Nevaeh and I have unfinished business and it looks like no one is too particular about how we settle it.

"Nevaeh," Dean starts again and I sigh. Because there's one person who *does* have a problem with it. *Dean.* Stupid goddamn dick Dean.

"Please don't hurt him." Nevaeh's hand is on my arm and I freeze. I look down at where she's touching me. Her hand looks small on my arm and her big brown eyes are wide with fear. God, the way she's looking at me like I'm the only reason her heart beats. That's my girl.

"Why shouldn't I?" I ask her.

Dean comes down another step. "Nevaeh, you don't have to go with him," he says, but we aren't looking at him. There's about five steps between us and him and I jerk my chin in his direction when he keeps coming.

"Think fast, or I'm going to break his goddamn neck." She licks her lips and when her eyes cut to Dean, I have to fight the urge to grab the dumb fuck and throw him head first down the stairs. "Speak, Nevaeh, or I'll do it."

Her eyes come back to me. "I–I'll do whatever you say. I promise. *Please.*" She's desperate. Begging me not to touch the idiot who thinks he's her knight in shining armor.

I smile at her. "I love it when you beg, angel." She sucks in a gasp. The intake of air has me wanting to make her do it again, but with my hand around her throat. I shake her hand off as I point a finger at Dean.

"Ah, ah, ah, Deanie baby. You stay right where you are, or you're going to make life *very* hard for sweet Nevaeh. You don't want to do that, do you?"

He shakes his head but he stops like I told him. Good fucking boy.

"What the hell is your problem? I know there's something wrong with you."

"You don't go where I've been and not come out fucked. Isn't that right, angel?" I ask Nevaeh and she ducks her head. Her eyes are back on the floor which is fine, because if she isn't looking at me she better not fucking be looking at Dean. When she doesn't answer, I tap a finger against her chin.

"I said, isn't *that right, angel?* You know exactly what happens to good guys where you sent me, don't you?" Nevaeh turns her head and the bruise on her cheek is big. Whoever hit her, got her good. "Look at me, Nevaeh."

Her beautiful eyes are on me again and she nods. There's tears in her eyes. Good. I want to see her cry. I've dreamed of it for years. I deserve to see it up close like this.

"I'm sorry, Beau."

"Sorry isn't going to fucking fix what you did to me. Now, tell your little friend goodbye, Nevaeh."

She obeys me instantly. "Goodbye, Dean."

I bite back a groan of pleasure. Nothing compares to Nevaeh fucking doing what I tell her. "Now walk." She moves when I tell her, doesn't look back, even when Dean calls out to her.

"Nevaeh, you don't have to go."

"Put a smile on your face, baby. We don't want anyone talking shit about this, now do we?"

She shakes her head. "No." She smiles a second later and I open the door for her like the gentleman I'm pretending to be. The hallway is busy when we leave the lecture hall and there's plenty of eyes on us as we walk out of the building and into the small plaza area in front of it. There's a few small tables here close to the stairs, but further away there's a copse of trees and a bench. That's where I want us to go. It's the perfect place for me to lay out how shit is going to go to Nevaeh. Perfectly in sight but out of ear shot, with nothing but the trees so no one is going to walk past us while we talk. I hear Nevaeh's steps slow as we approach the bench. She's realized it's a trap. Good. I like her scared.

I take a seat and drape my arms along the back of the bench in a dare to Nevaeh. She won't sit. We both know it. Instead, she stands in front of me with her books awkwardly clutched to her chest. She looks so fucking small right now. So breakable. The bright sunlight shining above us practically shows me where she's already starting to crack. I can see the fissures, the lines where she's weak and I want to force her weak parts to give. I want her to do it with my name on her lips while her body screams for me—I want her to hate it as much as I do.

I don't know how shit got so fucking twisted in my head when it comes to Nevaeh. I want her and I hate her at the same time. She's mine to torture, to smash into a million ugly pieces, but god if I don't want to take my time doing it. I want to marvel at the beauty of her shattering, because I know she's going to be a sight to see. Nothing I was able to dream up in my four years of lockup is going to compare. I know that, because this?

This moment right here is beyond everything I could have imagined. *It's exquisite.*

"What's going to happen to me?" Nevaeh whispers.

I smile up at her. "That's entirely up to how good you listen, angel."

"I said I would do anything."

"Would you suck my dick right here in front of everyone, baby? You going to drop to your knees for me?"

Her eyes go wide and she falls back a step. "W-what? No!"

I drum my fingers against the back of the bench. "I thought you said *anything*, Nevaeh," I say. "Or were you lying? You're so fucking good at lying, aren't you, angel?"

Her shoulders hunch and she shakes her head. "I didn't mean to do it. I thought it was you. I didn't-I didn't-"

"If you aren't your knees for me, choking on my dick, then shut your fucking mouth, Nevaeh." I lean forward and keep my easy going smile on my face. If anyone were to look over at us, they'd see me patiently listening to Nevaeh while she has a fucking breakdown. The girl begging for forgiveness for the fucked up shit she did. That's all the world is ever going to see where Nevaeh and I are concerned. I'm going to drive her insane. I'm going to do exactly what she did to me and make sure I'm the only thought she has, because she's that for me.

I'll never be free of her. It doesn't matter how much time passes, she's the face I'm going to see when I close my eyes. It's only fair that I do the same to her. Both of us marked and fucked up, unable to get away from each other because of how deep and dark shit is between us. Soul to soul, for better or worse. All of that starts now on this stupid little campus I don't give a fuck about, in a town I would rather see go up in flames. They all turned their backs on me the second Nevaeh gave them a reason. The Reaper could gut every last one of them and it wouldn't matter to me so long as Nevaeh was mine.

CHAPTER EIGHT

Nevaeh

BEAU JUST ASKED me if I would suck his dick in broad daylight. I've never even had a guy touch me below the belt. I'm a virgin. Why is that what I'm thinking about right now? I shouldn't be thinking that. I should be screaming and running from him, or trying to get back to see if Dean is okay. Feeling shocked over Beau requesting a blowjob is small potatoes right now, but I've heard about people fixating on mundane things when trauma is involved.

That has to be what's happening right now.

"Why were you going to hurt Dean?" I ask, because that's the question I should be asking. I feel sick. The boy that I knew wouldn't want to hurt anyone. He wouldn't, but this man? He would.

"Why not? Now get on yo-"

I know he's going to tell me I'm lying about not wanting to suck him off in front of everyone, so I cut him off.

"You're not the kind of person that hurts people, Beau." It's true. He's not. At least, he wasn't. It's also a way for me not to tell Beau I've never been with anyone. I don't want him to know that. Why that matters right now, that's anyone's damn guess. The trauma, I guess. Just like the flare of jealousy that moves through me when I remember Beau has been with other girls.

He was with Carrie the night I saw them. My jealousy is washed away, the fire that was there put right on ice, when the rational part of me makes itself known. *The night she was murdered.*

I rub my hand across my chest and try to take a deep breath. I'm not right. I've never been right. Why am I thinking these awful things?

He laughs. It's not happy. It's bitter. Stark. Sharp like a knife sliding between my ribs. "Maybe I wasn't, but I've changed, and you know what? I don't share, Nevaeh," Beau says and tilts his head to the side. The movement makes it impossible not to notice how perfect he looks. The sunlight plays over his handsome face and the easy smile he gives me looks so genuine. So sweet. If I couldn't hear him I wouldn't know any better. That's why he brought me here, I realize. He doesn't want anyone to know what he's saying.

He smiles at me. God. His smile is still so beautiful that it makes me light up just seeing it. "And I gotta be honest with you, I wasn't going to hurt him, baby."

The heavy weight in my stomach from before loosens. The only person that knows Beau isn't the forgiving hero he's shown Bloom when it comes to me is Dean, and who is going to believe him? He's a transfer student from Chicago. An art student he said, when he sat down beside me in our Psychology 101 class. It's interesting that's the class I have with Beau. I didn't think I would have any classes with him, but that was stupid. Of course I would have classes with him with the way he talked to me yesterday. Beau Du Pont has never been unprepared for a thing in his life, so why would it start now?

I hold my books tighter and force myself not to look away from him. He wants me scared, I know that. So why does a thrill shoot through me every single time I catch him looking at me? I shift from foot-to-foot uncomfortably under the weight of Beau's stare. It isn't trauma that has me excited that he's looking at me.

No, that's the fifteen year old girl that fell in love with him at first sight.

It's her that's excited by his attention, but it's also me too, because I never fell out of love with Beau. My body is so conditioned to want him that even though my brain is begging me to be smart, I can't.

It's like I don't know how to choose survival when it comes to Beau. If he's the one that's going to end it all, I'll let him do it. That's not even taking into the account the guilt that's taken root and blossomed in my bones over the years. It's in so deep that I don't know how I'd ever get it out. I can't even remember what life was like before I carried the guilt and doubt of what happened that night. Whatever is coming to me, I earned it. I squeeze my eyes shut. This is all so messed up.

"Who the fuck was that idiot?" Beau asks casually, like we're friends.

We're not even, though I always wished we would be. Now I don't know what we are. Enemies maybe, if I could find it in me to hate him for what he's promised to do to me. But I can't. I don't know how.

"He's just a guy," I say quietly.

"He wants to fuck you."

I blush hot at his words. There's no denying that I'm blushing, but I don't say anything about what Beau just said. "I don't want you to hurt him."

"Why not?"

"Because no one should be hurt over me. W-whatever is going to happen, just let it be to me."

Beau hums. "Oh, she's grown brave. My sweet little liar has a backbone now that she's all grown up."

"I'm not brave," I tell him before I can stop myself. It's hard not to talk to Beau like I would a friend. I used to wish he would talk to me and then when he was gone, I daydreamed. I pretended that we had been something when we hadn't. I can't stop myself from doing it now that he's in front of me and I know that he wants to hurt me.

I have zero self-preservation instincts when it comes to Beau Du Pont.

"Who hit you?" Beau asks and I'm caught off guard by his sudden change in conversation. I thought I covered up the bruise well enough when I was with Sunny, but that was in our dorm. It's easy to see in the brighter light of the lecture halls. I know he's got to be able to see exactly where my face hit the shower wall in the direct sunlight, so I don't bother saying he's wrong.

"I don't know. They did it fast."

"When?"

"Last night."

Beau rolls his eyes at me. "I know it was last night. You didn't have that fucking bruise the last time I saw you, now did you? Now, where were you when they did it?"

"I was in the shower," I tell him quietly. I hate how I'm blushing again from him talking down to me the way he is. Beau was always so otherworldly. So much smarter than anyone else I knew. Bigger than life. Even if I wanted him to want me the way I did him, I don't think I believed he would talk to me like we were equals. Shame fills me, because the way things are between us now feels right.

I don't deserve to be around him.

"Someone put their hands on you in the shower?" Beau asks and lowers his voice. "Before me, angel?" A cloud moves over the sun and the change in light casts his face in shadow. He looks less like the golden hero I remember now.

"What?"

"I said, someone put their hands on you before I've gotten to?" Beau *tsks* and smiles at me. "That's not the way this works. I didn't do four fucking years for you, for some fucking cunt to fast pass their way to marking you. That's for me. I'm the one that's going to tear you apart."

I feel dizzy. The look in Beau's eyes, it's possessive and dark. Greedy. There's nothing else this man wants but me. I know that.

It's everything I've ever dreamed of.

"I don't understand." I take a step back because somewhere in my lizard brain, the part that's supposed to keep me alive has woken up. "I have to go." Beau stands when I move back and purses his lips.

"Did I say it was time to go, angel? You're mine, remember?"

I open my mouth to speak but someone yelling cuts me off and I flinch. My hands come up to cover my face and I drop my books for the second time that day.

"Is that Beau Du Pont?!" The yell is closer and another joins it before there's a chorus of whoops and hollers. "There he is!"

"Jumpy as a fucking cat," Beau mutters as he bends to pick up my books, but I'm not sure what's going on, because we're not alone anymore. There's a guy next to me and behind me. When I turn, I run into another.

Beau waves them off to hand me my books. The guys make room around me, but that's not much better than when I was bumping into them, because I'm suddenly in the middle of everyone with only Beau beside me. I clutch my books tighter and look around the circle of faces and the familiar pit in my stomach I know is anxiety forms. They're not looking at Beau, they're looking at me. And from the glares aimed my way they aren't happy to see me. Some of them look familiar and I realize it's because I went to high school with them. I've seen these faces. I know them. There's Andy whose dad owns the hardware store and Mike who I went to Sunday school with and helped lead the youth group last summer.

They look so angry to see me.

"I have to go," I croak and dart forward, but Beau grabs my arm and keeps me where I am. "Beau, let go."

He doesn't let go, he just keeps me where I am. "Not so fast, angel."

One of the guys pushes forward and ignores me. His name is Jordan Davis and he was a grade ahead of me. His mom worked for my mom during the summers when we needed extra help. I don't care that he ignores me. I wish they all would.

"We've got news, buddy! The best news in the world!"

Beau's eyes leave me and he smiles at them but I see how fake it is now. I thought that was real before, when I was too young to know better, but I've seen the real Beau. The one that looks at me like I belong to him and only him. The one that promised to make me pay.

That's who Beau really is. The smiling man now surrounded by guys is a lie. It should make me sick, but all I feel is closer to him. No one knows him but me.

"What's the news, Jordan?" Beau asks. His voice is different when he talks to them. It's bright and sunny. Warm like a summer afternoon. His words don't carry the dark, hard edge they do when he speaks to me.

"You're back on the team, man!" Jordan claps Beau on the back and shoulders me out of the way. "Coach sent us to get you. You're coming with us, brother." Football players. That's who they are. Before Beau went away, he played football. I can't help but look up at Beau to gauge his reaction. I'm happy he'll be back on the team. He was so good at it and when he was on the field no one could stand against him. There were scouts that came to watch Beau his junior and senior year. I knew there was a lot of talk about where Beau was going to end up playing. Everyone in town was hoping he'd end up at Bloom State and he was more than good enough. He was supposed to be a star here before he went on to play pro. I used to think about that sometimes when I saw the football players around or when I went to a game with Minnie and her family. It used to hurt thinking about how it should be Beau out on the field.

At least my fucking mistake isn't taking away his chance to play college football.

"Are you serious? I'm on the team?" Beau moves forward with them and ignores me. I'm glad. He's the center of attention, that means there isn't any room for him to demand anything from me. At least, not yet. I know it's coming. My belly twists when I think of what he told me before.

If you aren't on your knees for me, choking on my dick, then shut your fucking mouth, Nevaeh.

I shouldn't like that. I've barely even made out with anyone before. Why do I like that?

Because it's Beau. That's why. It's always been him for me and as much as I'm scared of it, I know it's always going to be him for me, even with what's happening between us.

I shuffle to the side and start to squeeze past a few bigger guys but I can't help but hear what the group of football players are telling Beau.

"You'll be in as quarterback. Second string, but we know you've still got it. We'll get you ready in no time, man. It's going to be like you never left."

"I can't believe this. It's like a dream."

Beau sounds genuine. I wonder if he is and I can't help but look over my shoulder at him. The second I see him, I know he's lying to them. He doesn't care about football or being on the team. The smile doesn't reach his eyes and he's not ignoring me anymore. His eyes are right on me. I trip over an uneven paving stone on the path and run right into a guy who steadies me with a hand on my arm. The same place Beau grabbed me to stop me from leaving.

"You okay?" He starts and frowns at me. "Sorry about th-" he stops right in the middle of his sentence and I know why when I see his eyes. He's just realized who ran into him. He drops my arm like the touch burns him and sneers. "Well, look who it fucking is." He's loud enough that the guys celebrating Beau's return turn their attention back to me.

"It's our very own Nevaeh Santiago."

"What the fuck is she doing here?"

I know those voices. They're Andy and Mike.

"I just want to get by. Excuse me." I try to move to the side, but the big guy I ran into moves with me and blocks my way. "Please let me pass."

"Not until you apologize to Beau," he says.

"She owes him a lot more than an apology. She put him in fucking prison," someone calls out and I wince. It's one thing to think it, but when I hear it out loud it hurts all over again.

I look around the group and avoid Beau's eyes. "Look, I don't want any trouble. Just let me through, please."

Jordan throws his hands up and mimics me in a high pitched voice. "I don't want any trouble." He flips me off. "Neither did fucking Beau when you lied and said he killed his girlfriend, you bitch. What the fuck are you doing here? Going to accuse him of another murder?"

"I'm sorry, please."

"You don't belong here, you lying bitch."

I shake my head. "Just let me go. I-I don't want any trouble." I hate the way I stammer when I'm nervous. I wish I was stronger, but I'm scared. There's over a dozen guys around me and Beau's taken a step back. He could stop them if he wanted, but he isn't lifting a finger to do it. I don't know what's about to happen.

"She's fucking lying again, isn't she?" Jordan calls out to the group and they murmur in agreement. The energy is changing, shifting until I can feel it pressing down on me. It's like a pot of water that's about to boil over. I swallow hard and look around me for help. I know Mike and Andy aren't going to help me, but maybe someone else will. They have to know this is crazy.

"Grab her," Jordan says with a snap of his fingers and the guys on either side of me do. My books hit the ground and I end up stepping on them when they start to drag me forward.

"Let go of me!" I throw myself back and try to twist away, but there's no way. They're stronger, bigger, and faster than me. Even if I did get away, they would just drag me back. "Stop! Please!" No one listens and I'm forced down onto my knees with my captors holding onto my arms in front of Beau and Jordan. Beau is a step back and watching everything. It's Jordan that comes forward.

Jordan crosses his arms and comes to stand in front of me. "What do you want us to do with her?" He asks Beau.

Everyone goes quiet. They're waiting for what Beau is about to say. I don't, though. I know if he's going to break his forgiving persona he created just twenty four hours ago it's going to be for a reason. I have to get away.

I pull, try to yank my arms away and scream. "Help me! Someone!"

Jordan's face twists in anger and he starts to pull his hand back. He's going to slap me, I know it. But before he can do anything, everything goes sideways. Beau catches his hand and nearby someone screams bloody murder.

"He killed her! The Reaper is back!"

It's like time stops. The Reaper. That's the person everyone thought Beau was that killed Carrie Salt. More screams behind us erupt and students start running. It's been four years since he killed anyone, but we all know the drill.

Get home. Get safe.

The Reaper killed two girls on the same day once. The second was after they found the first one lying dead in a wheat field, but we didn't know what it was then. No one went home, so he took another and left her with a note stapled to her severed arm.

Get home. Get safe. Or I'll take another one.

Now everyone knows the rules. We all go home when The Reaper decides it's time.

"What the fuck?" Jordan asks, but he's not looking at Beau. His eyes are trained on the students running for their dorms. Beau drops Jordan's hand and jerks his chin at me. He wants me gone. The football players around me have lost their edge and I can already hear them starting to make calls to people to check if they're home. I'm grateful the guys holding me let me go, but when I go to stand, Jordan's attention is back on me.

"Leaving so you can point the finger at Beau for this one? Is that where you're running off to?"

Ice shoots through me because just like that, the attention is back on me. A serial killer is on the loose and I'm the one they want to fucking hunt.

"I need to get home. We all do, you know that!"

"Or maybe we fucking leave you out here for The Reaper to find," Mike says and I feel the blood drain from my face. Oh fuck. Oh no. "Tie your lying ass up for him to cut up. That'll stop your lying for good, won't it?"

"Get away from me!" I swing at them when someone grabs at me, but I miss.

"Grab her legs, I know where to leave her for him to find," Jordan orders and I'm picked up a second later.

"Let me go!" I scream and twist. I have to get away. I don't know where they're taking me, but I know I'm dead if they leave me outside. The Reaper will do what he did to Carrie to me. I scream and kick, but it doesn't do anything. Rage fills me. It can't end like this. Not with it being them. Boys that I went to school with. Not with Beau watching me.

"I thought you loved The Reaper, Nevaeh! Time to meet him!"

"We're all witnesses this time. Beau didn't do shit!"

I don't know who is yelling or speaking. Everything is melding and blending until it's just a roar in my ears, but I don't stop fighting. I can't let them take me off campus. I have to get free. I turn my head and see people still running. There's books and papers people have dropped on the ground. Everyone is panicking. They don't even notice what's going on with me, but I don't think they would stop it even if they did.

"Drop her."

The frenzy dies and the boys holding me stop. "Beau, come on. She deserves this."

When Beau speaks it's not summer sunshine, it's with the edge of a blade. "I said, *drop her.*"

I hit the ground so hard that I bite my tongue and blood fills my mouth. My tailbone hurts from where I landed but I'm grateful it's not worse after last night. I crawl away from the football players and, because I don't know where else to go, I end up at Beau's feet. For the second time that day he has my books in his hands.

He holds them out to me. "Get the fuck out of here, Nevaeh," he says and I expect that, but what I don't is for him to say, "Get home. Get safe."

I nod and take my books from him as I get to my feet. The guys that just dragged me away are standing nearby but they don't come any closer as I skirt around them. They would if Beau wasn't here. I know they would.

"You're going to pay, Nevaeh," Jordan calls out to me in a sing-song voice that shouldn't scare me, but does. "The Reaper is going to pay you a visit."

I ignore him and take off running in the direction of my dorm. I have to make sure Sunny is safe.

CHAPTER NINE
BEAU

THEY WOULD HAVE killed Nevaeh if I wasn't there. Not that I think Andy, Mike and that dumb fuck Jordan has it in them to actually do it themselves, but they would have left her out for The Reaper to find. I know they would. The girl he killed when he stapled that fucking note to her was a freshman when I was a sophomore. *Get Home. Get Safe.* It's probably not the smartest to use a murder's words as a mantra to stay safe, but the people in Bloom are idiots. But so am I, because I let Nevaeh go. I made sure the football team knew not to fuck with her because what was done, was done.

I shouldn't have let her go. I could have left with her then and used The Reaper as cover to play with her. No one would have come looking for her for hours. Not with a killer on the loose.

That's where I fucked up.

I look down at the practice sheet they handed off to me. It has all the times and dates for my training for the next few weeks. Jordan was lying. The spot on the team is not second string, it's third. But even that's generous for someone who hasn't played in years. I fucked around in prison when there was a pick up game, but not really. It made what I'd lost too fresh, so I stayed away from the games unless I was bored out of my mind. I'm going to be

91

riding the bench for the season and that's fine with me. With the training I'm going to be doing, my time is already more divided than I wanted it to be.

I'm here for Nevaeh, not fucking football. I don't give a shit about football. That was the old me. The one with a future and a soul. The only thing I have is revenge and my goddamn obsession with Nevaeh. I toss the practice sheet on the table in front of me and start pacing. I can see the pretty pink blush that spread over her cheeks when I told her to get on her knees. She liked it. Even though she was scared, she liked it. She didn't run either. She wanted to, but she kept giving me more time. She kept listening to me like she didn't have a choice. And when those motherfuckers came crashing down on us, I'm the one she crawled to for safety.

She knows I'm going to break her and she still came to me. This is going to be more fun than I realized. Outside a siren blares. It's close to the tornado siren that goes off when shit is getting bad and we need to shelter in place, but this siren is lower and shorter. It goes off in a series of four blasts before it sounds again.

The sirens are the signal that it's not safe. To stay the fuck inside if you want to stay alive. They started playing this my junior year when some kids threw a "Don't Fear The Reaper" party because he killed a girl on Senior Day and they refused to give up their party. The Reaper paid them a visit and they never found the hands for two of the bodies.

I go to the window and look out. It's a ghost town. The only movement is from the police car that's patrolling. It's driving the block in 10 minute intervals, which doesn't seem safe as the killer they haven't caught is notorious for stalking his victims. The police really shouldn't give him a pattern to follow if they want to actually do anything, but I know it's all a show. They aren't going to keep us safe, not really. Because he's too smart. He's so smart that he delivered the knife he used on Carrie to the police station with a fucking red bow on it and no one knew who left it. He was on their doorstep and no one saw him. Idiots.

They'll never fucking catch him.

I take out my phone and start scrolling through my socials. It's a flurry of notifications. I turned my accounts back on after I got back from prison. My mom kept them inactive after the trolls wouldn't stop commenting about how fucked up they always knew I was and how my entire family was going to hell. She couldn't take it, but she also couldn't bring herself to delete the profiles either.

I'm glad she didn't delete them, because now I can keep an eye on what's going on on campus a lot easier. The amount of friend requests I've gotten since yesterday is overwhelming. The damn apps froze up at one point and I had to turn my phone off for a while, but being home with The Reaper is as good of a time as any to start going through them. I start to tap on the profiles and approve them one by one. It's mostly girls, so many pretty college coeds who have included message like, *"I'm so sorry that happened to you"* and *"I always knew you were innocent!"* But there's also the more direct messages of nudes and offers to fuck me, no strings attached, whenever I want.

Those I pause over, because it's been four fucking years. The last girl I was with was Carrie. We got drunk and high that night and fucked like we normally did at Bloom Point. I should pick a girl that looks like her out of the friend requests I've gotten and take them up on their offers to *"suck the soul out of me,"* but I won't.

I want Nevaeh.

I take a deep breath and tamp down that feeling. No one is going to cut it but her. Pussy is pussy, but Nevaeh? Now that's going to be worth waiting four years for. Willing or not. She's going to be the first thing I put my dick in. Judging from her reaction to me, she's going to want it.

A message request hits my phone and I almost ignore it but then I see the message preview. *Nevaeh.* I tap on the message and nearly throw my phone, because the message isn't from Nevaeh, but someone talking about her.

> I saw you talking to Nevaeh today.
> Everything okay?

The message is from Ali, the girl from our Psych class. I should have known she'd be paying attention to what I was doing the second class was over.

> Everything is perfect. Just checking in with her that she's okay.

The image of Nevaeh trying to fight the football team off, twisting and kicking her legs even though they had her off the ground, dances through my mind. She had zero chance against them, but she was willing to fight. Did she fight the person who hit her the night before? The one she said got to her in the shower?

I frown and open my app to start looking for Nevaeh. There's another message that comes through from Ali, but I ignore it. She can fucking wait. I don't care what she wants. I find Nevaeh's profile a second later because, even though I didn't have this account in prison, I did have access to a burner account I made.

NotHeaveN is her username. She hasn't changed it since she got the account. There isn't any new activity on her page, but I do see she's online from the little green dot next to her name. Ali messages me again and I send a message to Nevaeh.

> Are you home?

I have to know. I told her to get home and she's a local, same as me. She knows the rules. Still, I need her to tell me where she is, which annoys me. I'm going to put a tracker on her. That roommate of hers is trusting enough she'll let me in. I'll put a camera there, too. I tuck my phone into my back pocket and go into the kitchen to look for something to eat for dinner. I'm in a loft my parents picked out for me because they didn't want me in a dorm room. My mother took one look at them and immediately hated how small they were.

"This looks like a bomb bunker. We are *not* putting you in here after where you just were."

It's a rule that freshman live on campus, but the school made an exception for me because of course, they fucking did. They're up to give me whatever I ask for while I'm a student. They don't realize the only thing I want is something they can't give me, but that's fine. I'm taking care of that myself. The fridge is stocked full and for a second I freeze. I haven't had access to a kitchen or a fridge like this on my own for years. I wouldn't even try to cook something if The Reaper hadn't shut the damn town down.

Motherfucker keeps ruining my life. First prison, now I can't even get a pizza delivered. I ought to cut his fucking head off and see how he likes it. I grab a steak and some potatoes that look like you can cook right in the container and start to work on them, but my phone buzzes. I know it's not a message from Ali.

It's Nevaeh.

I know it is.

When I open the app, Nevaeh's name is there at the top of the list and I smile. I knew she wasn't going to make me wait. I open her message and see her answer. It's direct and simple.

Yes. I'm home.

Not going to ask if I'm home and safe?

Anyone that would read this is going to think we're flirting. That's fine. I know Nevaeh won't show anyone the messages, just like I know she hasn't told her roommate about what's really going on with me. That I'm not kind and gracious or forgiving. I'm brutal, obsessed and vengeful. And this time Nevaeh is going to keep my secret.

CHAPTER TEN

Nevaeh

I DIDN'T STOP RUNNING until I got to my dorm room. I'm not the only one running for cover and I end up running into three other girls. The last time, I fell to my knees and scraped my palms on the stone path leading to my dorm.

"I'm sorry, I'm sorry!" The girl offers, but she doesn't stop running. I know she didn't mean to run into me. I understand. This isn't like when the football team went after me or the psycho that attacked me in the shower. She's not trying to hurt me. She's scared the same as me. It's in the chaos of everyone trying to get indoors that no one notices me. I'm just another scared college kid in a sea of thousands. While The Reaper is on the loose, I'm no one special.

When I throw open the door, Sunny screams and jumps. "What's going on?"

I don't say anything, at least not right away. I lock the door before I run to hug her. Everything that's happened over the past twenty four hours crashes into me and the only thing keeping me on my feet is hugging Sunny. I'm going to have to tell her about The Reaper, but I won't put more on her than I need to. That means Beau, the football team, my mom, all of that shit stays with me.

"You're okay?" I ask when we break apart.

She nods and swallows hard. "Yeah, I'm good. I was in class and they just cut us loose. Told us to get to our dorms and to lock the doors. I don't understand what's going on. Someone died?"

Sunny wouldn't understand. She's not from here. Bloom, Kansas isn't the kind of place that airs its dark secrets to outsiders. Not even locals talk about The Reaper. We don't speak of him, we just pray he doesn't see us. For four years we were safe but now there's no denying the evil.

"It's The Reaper, he's back."

"Who?"

"Remember Beau?" I start and when Sunny nods I give her a tight smile and step away from her. "The murder that I saw that night wasn't Beau. It was The Reaper. I got confused that night. I didn't know what I saw and I said it was Beau, but it wasn't him. I put Beau away while this monster is out there free and now he's back."

I wrap my arms around myself and sink down onto my bed while Sunny lets out a low whistle. "Holy shit. So the man you saw that night is the same one that's…that's…" her voice trails off and she points out the window. "He's the one out there right now?"

I look out the window along with Sunny. "Yeah, he is." The sun is still shining but it doesn't feel the same. When I woke up this morning everything felt full of promise, even if I had the majority of town and probably the whole university out to get me, the day still felt fresh and new. Of course, that was before I'd nearly been dragged off and left for dead by the school's football team or had the boy I'd loved since I knew what love was threatening to make me pay for the biggest mistake of my life.

Sunny goes to the window and puts a hand up against the glass. The sun spills over her, she's so pretty in the warm glow of the afternoon. "What's he doing out there?" she asks.

I shiver and pull my blanket up around myself before scooting back across my bed until my back is against the wall. "He's hunting," I tell her.

Sunny makes an audible swallow and turns to look at me. The sun is lower now, it slants and shadows play over her face so I can't see her eyes, but her hair is a brilliant gold. It looks like a halo.

"Hunting?"

I burrow deeper in my blankets like I used to when I was younger and The Reaper appeared yearly. The monster out there hunting kids made my childhood a nightmare. What was the point in growing up if you were going to be next? I think that's one of the reasons my mom took us to church so much. She felt safer that way.

"Yes, hunting. He does this at the start of the school year and again over winter break. He'll go quiet again until the summer time, but sometimes Spring Break is enough to bring him out."

"Oh my fucking god, you're serious. My grandma shipped me off to get murdered in the middle of Kansas. That bitch!"

I blink in confusion at Sunny who is now pacing around the room. "What?"

"My grandma said she was paying because she went here and just loved the school, but she's trying to get rid of me!"

"Why would she do that?"

"Because if I'm around then I get everything when she dies and not my stupid baby brother." Sunny strokes her chin and squints at the door. "What are the chances this psycho serial killer is going to break in through the door?" she asks.

I shake my head. "He doesn't do that. If we're inside, we're safe."

"Says who?" I open my mouth to answer her but I know how weird it's going to sound, so I hesitate. My answer isn't going to be comforting, I know this. "Answer me, Nevaeh. We're friends. I'm in this shit with you now, so you open up about your freaky little town's murder secret."

"It's not a murder secret an-and, okay, The Reaper said."

"You guys are seriously listening to rules the killer made?" She throws her hands out and gives me a 'what the fuck look' "You can't listen to *the killer*! The rules he gave you aren't real. They're just so you feel safe."

I bite my lip, because she's making sense. Shit. "He's never broken them," I point out.

"*Yet*. That's the keyword, Nevaeh. *Yet*. But he will when the prize is too good. He's going to cash in on the fact that everyone thinks they're safe at home to get the person he really wants."

"Who would he want enough to do that?" I ask and lower my voice, because it feels wrong to be talking about The Reaper like this. All my life I've done my best not to think about him, not to talk about him or the horrible, terrifying things he's done in our town, but now he's here. He could be right outside, and oh, god who did he kill today?

"That's a great question." Sunny goes to her bed and sits down cross legged. "It could be anyone, I guess. Hell, it could even be you."

Fear shoots through me and I sit up straight. "Why would you say that? Why would he want me?"

"You're the one who put the wrong guy away for a murder they did. Don't serial killers have a thing about other people taking credit for their kills?" she asks.

"I-I don't know."

"He could be pissed and now that Beau's out, he's out. Seems like weird timing, doesn't it? How long has it been since the last murder?"

"Four years," I whisper.

"And now he's back and both you and Beau are here at Bloom State." She raises an eyebrow at me. "Don't you think that's weird timing, Nevaeh?"

My heart pounds painfully in my chest. She could be right. It *is* weird timing. "I don't think it's me," I say, even though I feel like I'm trying to convince myself of it. It has to be because so many people are angry with me over Beau that I feel this way. It's not The Reaper that I'm feeling locked on to me. It's the target on my back the student body painted there. That's all it is.

"I mean, I hope it's not. I like you."

I smile and nod. "I like you too, Sunny. But why are you just rolling with this?" I ask her. She's taking it in good stride. A little too easy for someone who's in the middle of a nightmare.

"Listen, I grew up in a really crazy family. The thing I told you about with the bicyclist? That's not even the worst thing that happened to me when I was growing up."

I nod because I can relate. Families are complicated. I know that. We're both quiet. I hear someone run by our room and slam their door shut.

"Were you serious about your grandmother?"

"Serious that she wants to off me and would think a serial killer at college is the perfect way to do it?" Sunny asks and when I nod she falls back on her bed with a, "Yeah."

My mother kicked me out, but she wouldn't kill me. "Holy shit. I'm sorry."

Sunny waves a hand at me from where she's laying. "It's all right. Money makes people weird and greedy. She's old now, so I think she's acting out some kind of *The Most Dangerous Game* cosplay with me right now. If I'm gone, then she doesn't have to worry about anyone dividing the trust because my little brother has no spine and will do what she tells him to do."

I wonder how rich Sunny is if there's a trust worth getting murdered over, but that's not polite. She didn't pry about Beau or what I told her about seeing the murder, so I'm not going to ask her about the money.

"I'm sorry. That's rough. I can't imagine having a murdering grandma."

Sunny laughs and lifts her head. "It's not for the weak I'll tell ya."

I smile but then shake my head. "I don't...why does this feel really... well, *you know.*"

"Fucked up to be joking around about my homicidal grandma when there's a real killer out there?" she asks.

"Yeah, that."

"It's called dark humor. People use it to process trauma and I think this calls for it, Nevaeh."

"Good point."

We fall into a state of limbo with the horns blaring every hour. I let Sunny know they're for The Reaper and she shakes her head. "Fucking weird ass town."

There's no homework to do because of the timing. I'd only been to 3 classes and hadn't even gotten all the books for them yet. I was supposed to go with Minnie but...well, last week changed all that. Sunny and I hang out and put on a movie. There's an email in the evening announcing that a meal delivery service will drop off our dinner and to not open the door until after the food has been dropped off. It still feels weird opening the door with nightfall outside and the horns still screaming The Reaper's presence.

When we hear the knock at the door announcing our dinner drop off, we only open the door on the count of three with Sunny holding her desk chair over her head out of sight, just in case. "Thank you!" I call out to the dining staff making their way down the hallway with a trolley full of dinner before I snatch the bags with our dinner inside and we slam the door shut.

Dinner is a let down. Dry meatloaf, soggy rolls and overcooked green beans. But it's not all bad because the lemon pie that comes with it for dessert is better than good. Sunny pulls out ramen and sodas for us from the mini fridge she brought and we make dinner that way. It's when we're halfway through the second RomCom of the night that my phone beeps.

I haven't gotten any messages since I got here. Sunny has my number. Out of everyone I know, she's the only one that I would think would message me, but she's here with me. I pick up my phone and adrenaline starts to hum in my veins, because I don't know who it could be or what they might say. After Beau's release, I got the usual slew of horrible messages but I blocked them and did my best to ignore the burner accounts. I haven't posted on my socials since then. I thought about making them private, but what's the point?

It would just show them they've won. I might deserve what I'm getting, but I'm not going to let them know they broke me.

"I love it when you beg, angel."

"I didn't do four fucking years for you, for some fucking cunt to fast pass their way to marking you. That's for me. I'm the one that's going to tear you apart."

Beau. He's the one that wants to break me. Why does that feel right? I force the thought away and turn my phone over and slide the lock screen away. There's two notifications waiting for me. One is a text from Minnie, but the other is a message through my socials and I don't recognize the username.

ChiDean

I stare at the username until Sunny throws a pillow at me and yells at me to pay attention to the movie. I drop my phone and try to think who it might be or what they've sent, but it's tough. Also, a message from Minnie? What would she have to say to me now? I pick up my phone a little bit later and I hesitate, because I don't know which message to open. In the end I go with the devil I know and open Minnie's.

> Are you inside?

I miss her. She misses me. That's proof in this text, isn't it? I text her back because all I want is my best friend back, no matter how pathetic it might make me look after how she's vanished.

> Yeah, are you?

I wait for a few minutes for an answer but there's nothing so I open the other message and brace myself. It's probably a burner account and it's just someone calling me a bitch or wishing The Reaper got me today. Or at least, that's what I expect to see. So when I see a smiley face and a *Hey, it was great to meet you today!* I don't know what to think. I take a deep breath and message them.

> Who is this?

I get an answer almost immediately.

> Dean from Psych.

Holy shit. *ChiDean.* He said he was from Chicago and now I feel like an idiot for not thinking of him sooner. I didn't think he would find me, though. How did he find me so fast?

"He wants to fuck you."

Beau's ugly words from earlier come to mind, but I push them away. Dean seemed sweet and nice. There was no reason for him to come and sit beside me in class but he did it and he didn't even care that people kept staring at us. I wasn't sure if he knew who I was, but from the way he looked at Beau, I think he might have known. That makes him being nice to me all the more meaningful. There aren't many people willing to give me a shot right now. So even though I don't know what to text him, I try anyway. I can use all the friends I can get at school.

> Hey! How are you?

Not bad. Trying to wrap my head around this indoors thing. You're good, right?

"Hey, I need to go pee. Come to the bathroom with me?" Sunny asks.

"Sure, let's go." I shove my phone into my pocket and follow her to the door. She hesitates and looks around the room.

"We really need a weapon or something," she says.

She's right, but there's not a lot that we can do right now so I reach for the door. "It's okay. We're together. We'll be safe if we stay together," I lie.

My phone buzzes in my pocket while we walk down the hallway but I don't check it. I'm scanning the hallway and wondering if the bathroom will be empty when we get there. I'm relieved that it is and while Sunny heads for the toilet, I hesitate and almost go double check the showers to make sure no one is hiding back there, but I don't. We would have heard someone back there by now but there's nothing but the slap of our flip flops echoing off the tile and walls. We're alone. I go to the sinks and check on the bruise on the side of my face. It's not bad and the swelling is pretty much gone. My lip is healed up enough but it's still hard to smile without it hurting. Both are small in the big picture with what's gone on today, though.

My phone buzzes again and I pull it out expecting to see a reply from Dean, but it's not just him that's messaged me. There's another name and this one I know because I memorized it the second that I figured it out in youth group when everyone exchanged contact info.

Beau1511

The 1511 is his street address. I remember loving that I knew that. It felt special, even though everyone in town knew what the 1511 stood for. It didn't matter though, it was special to me. I should open Dean's message and delete Beau's, block him even, but I can't. I've waited to see his name on my phone since I was thirteen.

Even though he's probably threatening to hurt me, I have to open it.

I tap the message and suck in a breath when I see his message.

Are you home?

Another person that I didn't think would care is messaging me about where I am. It means more to me than it did when I saw it was Minnie. That's fucked up and I know it. Doesn't change the fact that it's true though.

Yes. I'm home.

I send back. Only a second later I see the dancing bubbles letting me know he's typing before Beau's message comes through.

Not going to ask if I'm home and safe?

I smile and lean against the counter to think of a reply, but just as I'm hitting the button, Sunny rounds the corner. "Hey, who has you smiling like that?" she asks and I almost drop my phone from her sudden appearance.

"What? No one."

She rolls her eyes and starts washing her hands. "It's definitely a boy you shouldn't be talking to if it's *no one*."

She's got me there.

I want to tell Sunny it's Beau. There's no reason I shouldn't, right? She doesn't know what he's told me so far or the way he's acted. All she's seen is the forgiving man I wronged. She wouldn't tell me I'm out of my mind for being excited that it's Beau. He's the one that's put the smile on my face. Not Dean. If I was smart, if I was sane, I'd choose to smile when Dean texted, but I'm not either of those things. It's Beau that sets my world on fire. Sunny sticks her tongue out at me in the mirror while she washes her hands and I decide it would be safe to tell her. Maybe it's the trauma of today that has me feeling this way, I don't know. What I do know is I want normalcy. I want to pretend that I'm just a normal girl in her freshman year, getting to hang out with her roommate and talk about boys while they have a movie night.

"You really want to know who it is?" I ask her.

Sunny bounces where she's standing and spins to flick water at me. "Yes! Who is it?"

I open my mouth to tell her, but that's when I hear the telltale squeak of a shower knob being turned before we hear the familiar sound of water running. My eyes go to the showers that are just around the corner. My heart starts to pound in my chest and it's hard to take a full breath.

Someone else is here.

"I thought we were alone," I whisper.

Sunny takes a step closer to me. "So did I."

A second later we hear another shower turn on and fear shoots through me. It's them. The person that hit me last night. There's no way it isn't. Why would someone be turning on more than one shower? Why would they have stayed so still and quiet when we came in chattering? The Reaper is on the loose. If it was innocent, they would have announced themselves. There's no way someone not trying to scare us would have stayed quiet for this long. I feel like I'm rooted to the floor by fear, and I don't know why. Whoever is in here already knows where I am.

God, what would I have found if I had gone to look in the showers like I almost did?

"Who's there?" Sunny calls out and takes a step towards the hall that leads to the showers, but her movement breaks me free of my fear and I rush towards her.

"No, we have to go." I grab Sunny's hand and start to pull her towards the door. "Come on!"

Sunny looks over her shoulder but she comes with me. "Who the fuck is back there, though?"

"We don't have time for this. We have to go. *Please.*" I tug her again, but she's not moving as fast as I want. "Sunny, pl-" I start but stop when another shower goes on and she shakes her head.

"Nope. Fuck this."

She finally moves it and we run out of the restroom. We sprint past a couple of girls in the hallway sitting on the floor and talking quietly, but we don't stop until we get to our room.

We wedge a chair beneath the door and I almost tell Sunny about what happened to me last night, but I don't. My phone keeps buzzing with messages but I don't check them. Neither of us sleep that night.

CHAPTER ELEVEN
BEAU

"**DID YOU SEE** the papers? They found that girl's body down by the Mill." I'm talking to Jordan or at least I am trying to. He's forced me back onto the team and now I have to fucking play along because playing football, even as a third stringer, was all I ever talked about when anyone asked me what I was going to be doing after high school.

Playing ball.

That had always been my answer. It doesn't matter that I don't give a fuck about football, or school, or this town. There is only Nevaeh. Everything else is just in the way.

"She washed up on the shore. Some volunteers picking up trash at the Mill found her yesterday."

The Mill is what people call this old water wheel some pioneers built in a river that you can't really count on because of how dry it can be on the prairie. Sometimes it's a trickle and barely a creek and other times it's a roaring torrent you have to yell to be heard over when you're walking beside it. It's a wide river and when it's calm, it's barely a foot deep. People like to park their trucks out onto the limestone that slopes down from the prairie and set up camper chairs in it to cool off in the summer.

It's not calm right now. Not with the storms that we've been having. Right now it's wild and it's flooded past the limestone onto the prairie. It's all mud down there right now from what I heard.

"What the fuck was she doing out there?" I ask.

"Bro, I don't fucking know. Heard she was a bio major, probably out there doing science shit? That or he took her there, you know?"

"Mmm, sounds about right."

I've studied The Reaper almost as closely as I've studied Nevaeh, but he doesn't interest me like she does. Funny considering everyone thought I was him for four goddamn years. Morbid curiosity about the killer everyone thought I was had me reading up on the shit he did. He picks pretty coeds as prey. He prefers to kill where he has the time to make it last from the photos I saw. He took one girl's head clean off. For all the shit he did to Carrie, at least he didn't do that to her. He isn't particular where he kills them, their home, out at a house party, somewhere remote like the Mill. It's all the same to him. The riskier the location, the better.

It's like The Reaper is a ghost. He comes and goes. He takes who he wants, when he wants and there's not a thing anyone can do to stop him.

"Too bad he didn't fucking gut Nevaeh."

I raise an eyebrow and I'm glad we aren't face to face. The way I'm looking right now would be a dead giveaway he said the wrong fucking thing. No one touches Nevaeh but me. Jordan's words have me thinking, though. He was the one who wanted to leave her out for The Reaper yesterday.

"And why is that?"

"She deserves it for what she did."

I lean forward and brace my elbows on the counter. I'm in my kitchen fucking around with breakfast. I'm supposed to be eating healthy for the workout regime I'm about to jump into for the season I'm already behind on, but I just slammed as much bacon as I could take and I fucked up the pancakes I was trying to make until the smoke alarm went off, but I didn't care. I ate it all. Food tastes great, even if you burn the shit out of it, when you're not behind bars. At least here I can choose what I want and when I want.

"That's all in the past," I lie.

Jordan scoffs. "You sound like you really did forgive her."

This little shit. Does he see what I'm playing at? "That's because I did."

"Whatever, man." He yawns and I can almost see him waving a hand at me to show me he doesn't really care what I'm saying. Jordan's the Captain of the team and he let that shit go to his head. He was a skinny little shit the last time I saw him who could barely hold onto the ball when anyone so much as looked at him. He thinks he's hot shit right now. If The Reaper catches anyone it should be this bitch.

"We'll take care of it for you since you're going to be a boy scout about her."

"Meaning?"

"Meaning she's going to make up for what she did to you. You're one of us. No one, especially not some trailer park trash cunt, is going to get away with fucking with you. Don't worry, bro. We're going to handle her."

"Listen, Jordan-"

"Hey, did you clock the workout this afternoon?" He interrupts and I have to take a deep breath. If I was acting like my real self I'd drive to Jordan's house and beat his brains in with his toilet seat, but I can't do that.

Not yet.

"Yeah, man."

"Cool, I'll be by to get you, all right?"

"Sounds good."

The line goes dead and I'm glad. Talking to Jordan puts me in a shit mood so I already know who I'm looking for when I pick my phone up. Nevaeh. I hit the app and frown. I sent her three messages throughout the night but she never replied. Not after the first couple. I don't like that she's left me on fucking read, but she isn't online either. I start to scroll through my feed for another distraction and the whole thing is filled with students losing their shit over the girl they found. There's another handful of messages in my inbox too, but I ignore those except for one that sticks out.

It's from Ali.

> Big mixer tonight! I hope you come. Everyone in my dorm is going to be there, but that means that creepy girl Nevaeh will be too. Just wanted to warn you.

That's all it takes. I know what I'm doing after practice today.

I message Ali asking what time the mixer is and she responds immediately. It'll be at nine, plenty of time to go in prepared for what's going to happen. She gives me her dorm name, Morris Hall. It's Nevaeh's dorm. She offers to meet me out front, but I don't reply.

She's not the one I'm going to be seeing.

CHAPTER TWELVE

Nevaeh

"**T**HERE'S A PARTY tonight in the dorm," Sunny tells me. We're walking back from our class, Film Studies, and everything seems normal. Or at least as normal as things can be after a girl was murdered and left in the river. All around us everyone is quiet and walking with their heads down in groups of three or more. There's safety in numbers and all that. Sunny and I are the only pair I see out.

"A party?"

"Yeah, you want to go?" she asks.

"I'd say no but it sounds like the party is sort of coming to us, right?"

She nods and looks towards our dorm. It's just up ahead of us. "Is this normal?" she asks.

"Is what normal?"

"People pretending nothing happened?"

People were shocked when I said it was Beau. Before that, it was like the town went into a weird sort of stasis after every murder. It only took a little time before they were going on like nothing happened.

I nod. "Yeah, they just…move past it."

"How the fuck can anyone move past something like this?"

"It's been happening since before I was in junior high. I think everyone is just numb to it at this point." When the cops finally realized the murders were serial, I was ten. Beau would have been fourteen then. They managed to trace back his activity to seven years before that, but who knows how long The Reaper has been killing in Bloom? Even if what I said had been true, it couldn't have been him. At least not alone. There would have had to have been two killers, but the police didn't even bother with that. They went after Beau with everything they had, even if he was too young for what the killer had been doing to those girls.

What fourteen year old boy could have pulled that off? And for that long, without being caught? They'd said it was horror movies and violent video games that pushed Beau to experiment and start killing. It hadn't ever felt right, but I couldn't tell anyone that the more time passed the less sure I was of anything.

"I don't get this town. I don't get this college. It's all so fucked up, Nev. Everyone is just at class taking notes and making study group plans and planning parties like nothing happened." Sunny walks closer to me and I can see she's getting upset.

I put an arm around her shoulders. "We can hide out from the party tonight if you want."

She leans back and shakes her head. "No fucking way."

I blink in surprise. "What?"

We stop in front of the dorm and Sunny starts to pace around. It's something I've noticed that she does when she's anxious. She did it all last night while keeping an eye on the door while the RomCom we had put on played in the background on a loop.

"We are going to that fucking party. I'm not missing it."

I rock back on my heels and ignore the girls that shoot dirty looks my way on their way past. "Didn't you just say this whole thing was fucked up though?" I ask. I'm trying to follow Sunny but it's hard. She's off one thing and on to the next faster than I realize, but it's part of what I like about her.

"Yeah, that still totally stands. This whole situation is fucked, but I can't transfer anywhere else right now and if my grandma thinks I'm going to roll over and let some dude in a robe with a knife kill me she's wrong. I'm graduating."

"Ooookay," I hedge as I watch her pace. "What's that got to do with the party?"

"If I'm staying here I need to learn to be as fucked up as the locals. If they party, I party." She stops and points a finger at me. "*We* party."

A group of girls passes and when one of them points at me, I turn away from them. "I don't think I'm exactly going to be welcome at a party here, Sunny."

"Fuck those bitches, Nev. We are going to this party and anyone that has a problem with it can catch my hands." Sunny turns and flips off the girls for good measure. They gasp and run off which makes Sunny smile. "Get out of here you assholes!"

"Sunny, *stop yelling.*"

"I'll stop yelling when they stop acting like bullies."

I smile, because in spite of how fucked up everything is. It's nice to have a friend. When we go inside I'm thankful to see my professors canceled my next two classes due to The Reaper claiming another life. Sunny and I hang out, we even do a little homework after dinner and when we come back to the dorm, I settle down for a while to rest while Sunny starts bouncing around the room getting ready for the party. I fall asleep listening to her pop music.

When I wake up, there's still music but it's coming from outside our room. It's dark out and there's only the nightlight Sunny plugged in by the door to light the room up. "Fuck," I whisper and then wince at my language. I'm not the kind of girl that cusses. I never did before now. I know it's not a big deal but it feels wrong every time I do it. Like it's someone else and not me. I don't like how easy it's getting and I just got here. I move to sit up and put my hand down on a paper that's beside me. It's a note, or at least it looks like it in the dim light. I flick on the lamp beside my bed and see I'm right. It's a note from Sunny.

You looked like you needed rest so I thought I'd let you sleep for a while.
Call me when you wake up and I'll come back to the room to get you!
Can't wait to party tonight with you!
XOXO
Sunny
PS: Don't worry about the bitches on this floor. I'll handle them.

I put the note on my bedside table and slide my legs over the edge of the bed. The clock next to my lamp says it's almost ten. When I laid down it was after dinner. I slept for five hours and I still feel out of it. I stand unsteadily and look at the door. There's people laughing and running past while music pounds so loud that I can feel it thumping through the floorboards.

I didn't think we would be allowed to have a party like this on campus, but the school must be letting us have a little freedom where we can find it after what happened. I grab a brush and run it through my hair while I text Sunny that I'm up.

> I just woke up. Should I change? I feel really out of it.

> Nah. 90% of the people here are in sweats and Carhartt, I think you're fine.

I laugh because she's right, so I pull on my shoes and head out into the party. Sunny texts me again.

> I'm in the lobby on our floor. Someone brought a keg!

Holy hell. I must be right. The school really is letting us blow off some steam. There's no way they would turn a blind eye to that normally but nothing is normal here. Nothing has been since The Reaper came to town. When I step out into the hallway, I almost go right back to my quiet dorm room. The space is packed full of people and someone turned the lights off and put on a strobe light that makes the hall look like a bad impression of a club you might see in a movie. All around me people are dancing, making out and drinking. Our dorm is a coed dorm but our floor is just girls. Until now I haven't seen a guy on our floor. I avoid looking at anyone and I don't know if it's because everyone is having too much fun or it's too dark in the hallway for anyone to know it's me, but no one bothers me.

When I get to the lobby it takes a second for me to spot Sunny. She's dancing with her hands above her head, eyes closed as she laughs and sways.

She looks every bit the carefree college coed. It's nice to see her laughing and having a good time. I can see the keg she mentioned off to the side. There's no shortage of students with red solo cups around the keg. I've only had beer once, but I didn't like it much, so I go straight for Sunny.

"Hey," I say when I get to her.

Sunny's eyes pop open and a smile spreads over her face. "Yay! You're here." She throws her arms around me and hugs me tight. "Where's your drink?" she asks.

"I'm not really one for beer."

She waves a hand at me. "Listen, after this week, we need a drink. Come on." Sunny grabs my hand and pulls me along with her towards the keg. We only take a few steps before I realize my anonymity is gone. People are noticing me and they're staring.

Fuck.

Maybe this party wasn't such a good idea after all.

"Hey, I, uh, I don't know if I'm up for a party right now." I don't want to ruin Sunny's fun and she looked so happy before I got here. There's no stopping the dark cloud that follows me on campus. If I stay, I'm going to just ruin her night.

"What? No! That's crazy. You're staying." Sunny doesn't let go of me and she ignores everyone around us on her way to grab two red solo cups from the table beside the keg.

"Sunny, I-"

Sunny grabs the spigot hanging from the keg and starts filling a cup. "You're staying and that's that," she says and shoves the cup in my hands. Sunny gives me a pout and I lose the fight with myself to not ruin the night. If she wants me here and I leave, isn't that the same thing?

"All right, fine. Fine, I'll stay."

Sunny cheers and waves her own filled cup over her head. "This is going to be the best night *ever*!"

I smile and it's a little easier to ignore the stares from everyone around us. So far no one's said anything, which is something positive. Maybe they won't at all and I'll be able to blend into the crowd. Everyone is spooked about the murder that just happened. Why would anyone be thinking about me when The Reaper is out there somewhere? I follow Sunny through the crowd and take a sip of the beer. It's bitter and cold but I take another sip because I'm nervous and it's something to do with my hands.

The music gets louder around us and Sunny spins. "I love this song!" Sunny yells over the music to me and I nod at her. I try to move along like she is but the only thing I can focus on are the people staring at me. It feels like they're closing in. More eyes are on me by the second and I take another deep drink of my beer. I can do this. I can ignore them. I'm going to have to if I want to survive the year. It's hard to breathe and the room feels like it's tilting on its side. My hands start to shake. I can't do this. Oh god, I'm going to be sick.

Someone touches my shoulder and I scream. I drop my beer and it splashes everywhere when it hits the floor. People jump back, cussing when the beer hits them, but at least it gets them away from me.

"Who the fuck are you?" Sunny darts forward and shoves the person back from me.

"Nevaeh?" I hear them say my name and relief floods my body when I realize it's Dean. I didn't think I'd see him tonight. I feel bad for not answering his texts. I didn't have it in me to go back to playing at normal after the person in the showers scared Sunny and me. God. How do I think I'm going to make any friends if this is the way I'm going to act at school?

"Dean?"

He smiles at me and tries to come forward but he can't get around Sunny. She's got her arms crossed and she's planted firmly in front of me. "You know him?" she asks.

I nod. "Yeah, we have a class together. He's okay, Sunny."

When she steps aside Dean gives her a nod of appreciation. "Nice bodyguard work," he says.

She salutes him with a smile. "Lots of bullies around here."

Dean looks around the packed room and nods. "So I've noticed."

"So, you're a friend of Nev's?"

"Nev?" He looks at me and gives an appreciative nod. "I like it. Suits you."

"I'm the only one that calls her that, but it's because I came up with it so no one else knows about it. You can call her that too though, since you're a friendly," Sunny tells him and then points at my empty cup on the floor. "I'll go get you another one. Be right back!"

"Sunny, no, it's okay!" I call after her but there's no stopping her. She's already gone and disappearing into the crowd without a backward look. I'm left standing awkwardly with Dean and I rock back on my heels. We both give each other a tight smile and I decide it's now or never if I don't want things to be awkward between us tonight. He was kind to me when no one else was. Even tried to get between Beau and me when he had no reason to.

"Hey, I'm sorry for not answering your texts."

"I didn't mean to scare you."

In the end we both speak at the same time and I laugh while Dean rubs the back of his neck awkwardly. "I hope you didn't think it was weird that I found your profile," he says and winces. "I really didn't think it through when I did that. I've been worried you thought I was a stalker or a freak since then."

I hold my hands up to stop him. "What? No. I swear I didn't. If anyone's a freak here, I think we both know it's me."

Dean frowns and comes a step closer into my space. I try to back up but there's nowhere to go really with the people dancing around us. It's not like there's a dance floor here since it's the common area of our floor. The couches have been moved from where they were flanking the room to the corner and so have the tables to create an open space, but it's still not big. He puts a hand on my shoulder and it doesn't feel right. God, why is it all red in here? Someone must have switched the bulbs in the floor lamps that I know stood at regular intervals in the common room.

"That's not true, Nev," Dean says, taking Sunny's nickname for me. I don't think I like hearing him say it, but I don't say anything. "Listen, I know that I don't know you, but I want to. I don't think you deserve everything that's happening to you, or the way people are acting on campus."

I don't know why, but it doesn't feel real. Maybe it's because of last week and the nightmare that started four years ago, those were all real. Dean's been nothing but nice to me and I don't know what to do with it. I give him a tight smile. I look around us, trying to spot Sunny, but I can't make anyone out in the dim red flashing party lights. It's like there's nothing else but the square foot that Dean and I are now standing in.

"I-I'm sorry. Everything has just been really hectic."

"I want you to know that if you ever need someone to talk to, I'm here for you." Dean's fingers flex on my arm and the dancers are still going. Someone elbows me in the back when I try to move again.

"I, ah, I mean thank you, Dean."

Dean's handsome. He's taller than me, not as tall Beau, but tall enough. He has blond hair and green eyes. When I met him I thought Dean's eyes looked kind and open and after years of people looking at me with nothing but pity and now hate, I can tell the difference. If I was a normal girl, Dean would be the perfect kind of guy to have interested in me. I should be excited that he found me online and that he came to the party tonight.

But because I'm not a normal girl, I'm not any of those things. All I want is to get away from him because, as sweet and friendly as Dean has been, I don't trust this. Or maybe it's not that I don't trust it, it's that he's not the boy that I want.

Beau Du Pont.

"Nevaeh." Beau's sharp voice cuts through the thumping bass and suddenly I can see past the space Dean and I are in. It's like someone put the air back in my lungs and I realize there's enough space around me to get away from Dean, so I do.

"Beau?" I ask stupidly, even though I can see him plain as day. He's there with a sneer on his handsome face. His eyes are dark in the red filtered light of the room. There's no trace of the blue that I know his eyes to be. They look black and as scared of him as I am, I can't bring myself to look away from him.

"In the flesh. What are you doing here alone?" he asks, sauntering up to Dean and I. The lines of his body are relaxed but I can hear the anger in his voice. It has to be from seeing me. There's no way the sight of me doesn't make him sick.

Dean steps between Beau and I. "She's not here alone. She's here with me."

I don't miss the dismissive look Beau shoots Dean's way. "That why you've got your hands all over her?" he asks.

Dean freezes. "What did you say?"

Beau flicks a finger at Dean. "You think I didn't see how you've got her cornered over here, just because you know she's too scared to tell you no."

Dean turns to look at me. "What? I would never do that to you. You know that. Right, Nev?"

"Nev? What the fuck is that? Her name is *Nevaeh*."

Dean lifts his chin and meets Beau's glare. "Maybe to you, but not to her friends." Beau's eyes are scary. He's going to do something. I can feel it. Oh god. Oh fuck. I didn't want to drag anyone else into my mess with Beau and here Dean is, putting himself right in the line of fire. I have to stop him before Beau hurts him. Dean is a big guy, but he's not like Beau. Beau was athletic before he went to prison, but now? Now there's a cruelness and sharpness to his body that none of the boys at college can compare with.

Beau looks like a killer.

"Dean, please don't," I blurt out. Even though we're standing next to each other, I don't even know if he can hear me over the music that someone just turned up, so I put my hand on his arm. Both men look at me the second I touch him. Dean looks triumphant, Beau looks murderous. I jerk my hand back but Dean is too quick. He's got a hand on top of mine and keeps my hand where it is on his arm.

"It's going to be all right. I promise, Nev."

I shake my head. "No, I mean, yes, but no." I jerk my hand out from under his and step past him so that I'm closer to Beau now. I take a deep breath and the next time I reach out, it's for Beau. "I'm fine, Dean. I promise."

He looks confused. Even in the red light and flashing rainbow that moves over the room, I can see it plain as day. He doesn't understand. "What are you doing?"

"I want to go with him, Dean."

"But, Nev-"

"I'll text you later," I tell him, but then Beau grabs my hand.

"The fuck you will. Let's go." He turns and I hate having to follow him like this, but it's the only way to keep Dean safe.

"Goodnight, Dean!" I call over my shoulder and force my way into the crowd after Beau.

"*Nev!*" Dean yells after us but I ignore it and keep walking.

I pass Sunny on her way back with two beers and her mouth drops open when she sees Beau walking in front of me. She inclines her head to him and I know what she means, so I nod. Her face breaks out into a wide smile and she raises the cups over her head in a victory cheer. She's happy I'm with Beau. I try to tell myself that it was just last night that I wanted to tell her it was him that I was texting.

Dean appears at Sunny's side and when he tries to come my way, she steps in front of him and offers him one of the cups she's holding. Thank god she's there to run interference when I know Dean would come right after us.

I take a deep breath and hurry away from them, but that's when I run right into the last person I thought I would see that night.

"Nevaeh?"

"Minnie?"

My old best friend stares at me. Her dark hair is messy and falls forward in a tangle. There's a sheen of sweat on her face and her eyes are glassy. I don't miss the red solo cup in her hand. She's been drinking and partying for sure. Minnie was always more adventurous than me. She drank and smoked pot even though I was too scared to do it. She had boyfriends when I was too scared or hung up on Beau to see anyone else. I never told Minnie about the night Carrie died. I never told her about how I wasn't sure Beau had done it. That I hadn't actually seen him do it. Maybe I should have, because now she's acting like all the rest. She hates me and blames me for what happened to Beau. But there is the fact that she texted me, wanting to check if I was okay. Maybe there's hope. Maybe I can have my best friend back with a little more time. Maybe now is the start of it?

I smile at her and take a step closer to her. "Minnie, how are you?"

Her eyes dart to the side and she looks around us like she's scanning the room for someone. "Don't fucking talk to me, freak." It's then I realize it's not someone, *it's everyone*. Minnie is worried people will see her talking to me.

I shake my head at her. "Don't do this. I want to be friends again."

She sneers. "And I don't."

"Then why did you text me?"

"Just because I don't want you dead doesn't mean that I want to be your friend, or that I want you here. No one wants you here."

I blink back tears. "That's not true."

"Yes, it is. You know it. Why are you here anyway?"

I open my mouth. The answer would be so easy to tell her but it's then that I realize I never really told Minnie the truth about me. She didn't know about how I felt after Beau got put away. She didn't know, or care about the drama going on with my mom. Not really. I hid as much of that as possible. She only ever wanted to be around me when I was fun. When I was happy. I was never any of those things. I pretended so that I could fit in. I lied to have a friend.

My eyes go over Minnie's head to Beau. He's watching me, just behind Minnie and from the look on his face he doesn't think much of her. Even though Beau's been away for years, he knows me better than Minnie.

We share the secret of what happened that night. The mark it left on both of us is the thing that binds us. He sees me.

"I have to go," I say and move past Minnie, but she swings around with me as I walk.

"What the hell? What are you doing here with him?" Minnie all but yells and I blush. More people are looking at us. "He hates you!" Minnie screams. I don't know why she's screaming like this.

"Stop it," I tell her.

Minnie shakes her head. "He hates you. You don't deserve him. You're a liar."

For me never telling Minnie what I thought all those years, she's able to say all the things that I thought when I was alone. The thoughts that played in a continuous loop and haunted me. Maybe my best friend saw more than I realized.

I try to ignore Minnie, but Beau doesn't. He comes forward and puts a hand on my shoulder. "She's my friend," he lies. His voice sounds so sincere that I know people around us are shocked. At least the ones that can hear.

Minnie's mouth drops open. "She doesn't deserve you. She's trash."

Beau shrugs. "Aren't we all?' He squeezes my shoulder and pulls me back. "Let's go."

We both turn and start walking again. I should not be following him but I don't know where else to go. It's like when the football players tried to drag me away and the only person I could crawl to for help was Beau.

He stopped them. He stopped them, but I know it's just because he has a mind to give me worse. That's it, isn't it? But is being at the mercy of the man I've loved since I knew what it was worse than being held up as a villain by everyone else?

The football players were going to leave me for The Reaper to find, my mom got rid of me, the school wanted to take my scholarship, and my ex best friend called me trash in front of everyone.

I'm safe with Beau even if he's different now, right?

I swallow hard because the truth is that I don't know. I want to be safe with him, but I'm not stupid. He wants to hurt me. He wants to make me pay for sending him away to prison. But for whatever reason, he's set on everyone thinking he's a good guy. I watch as the crowd parts for Beau and a few people even raise their glasses or high five him as he passes. Their faces darken when they see me so I don't look at them, I look at the space between Beau's shoulder blades. I focus on his back and it's because of that reason that I'm not paying attention to where he's been leading us. When he stops walking, I almost run straight into him. That's how much I've been concentrating on looking at his back that I don't even notice he's stopped.

"I'm sorry," I say and try to put distance between us, but I stop when I see Beau shoving open a door. It's a door I know.

It's my door.

"What are we doing here?" I ask. We're far enough away from the music playing in the common area that I know he can hear me, but it's still loud. Someone stumbles past with a drink in their hand and bumps into me. Cold beer hits my arm and soaks my sleeve.

Beau shoves the person away that spilled their drink on me and opens my door wider with his other arm. "We need to talk, Nevaeh."

I hesitate and shift from foot to foot. "I don't know. Can't we go outside?" I ask. I'm nervous to follow him. This feels like a trap. Why would Beau bring me to my room? How does he know it's even my room?

He raises an eyebrow at me. "With The Reaper on the loose? You want us to go outside? Is that really where you want to go right now, Nevaeh?"

He's right. It's not safe. I don't know what I was thinking. It's safer inside.

"Okay, f-fine." I tell him and step past him and into my room before I can chicken out. The room is so much quieter than the hallway and for a split second I feel disoriented. Sunny's nightlight bathes the space in a warm dim light. It feels calmer in here and I look over at my bed remembering the nap I woke up from earlier. I don't know how much time has passed, but it can't be long. Maybe half an hour has passed since I woke up? I never dreamed that I would be back in my room with Beau.

Beau follows me into the room and surprises me when he only closes the door just a little over halfway. "There, the door will stay open. How's that?"

It's a rule my mom and all the other parents at church used to use on all of us kids. The door stayed open no matter what if you had someone of the opposite sex in your room. Nothing bad can happen with the door open is what my mom used to say when I had study groups that included the boys from youth group.

I eye the door and nod at him. I'm safe if the door stays open.

What's the worst that can happen?

CHAPTER THIRTEEN
BEAU

NEVAEH IS AN idiot, but everyone else here is something worse. They're cowards. Spineless fucking little bitches I want to break over my knee and end. If they were in prison for a day, they wouldn't make it. They're too soft. Too goddamn weak. The only way they know how to live is to band together and beat up on one person. Someone they think is weak is fair game but how weak is that person if it takes everyone to bring them down? All it does is show how pathetic they all are. An entire goddamn town against one girl and they can't even do it right.

Good thing, I'm here. I'll do it.

"I won't close the door," I say and Nevaeh nods at me. She thinks it'll keep her safe, but it won't. I am fine breaking my sweet little liar with an audience. I waited for four years to do this. I knew when the day came, I'd do it no matter what. That when I was able to get my hands on my Nevaeh, it would all be worth it. She's the one that hasn't had time to understand this was always going to happen.

That it is going to happen. Door closed or open, I'm going to have my girl tonight. I knew that when I came to this mixer and ditched Ali the second I got inside. The after hours lock was in place by the time I showed, but all it took was someone inside opening the door, which Ali was all too eager to do when I texted that I was outside. She was easy enough to ditch when she caught sight of Jordan. I get the hierarchy for some girls on campus. I used to be "that guy" in town for every femme with a pulse, but that was before I was in prison. Now I'm older, I'm third string on the team and I'm definitely considered damaged goods.

Sympathetic figure, yes? The guy you want to marry for someone like Ali?

Absolutely not.

I don't give a shit about any of that either, so it suits me just fine. I need enough support to go where I want and do as I please with Nevaeh. Nothing else matters. When I see my little liar she's with that fucking try hard from earlier. He's touching her this time and I see red. No one touches Nevaeh.

She's such a good fucking girl that she took a purity pledge the year after I got sent away and I can tell she stuck to it. Not like her best friend or the other girls that go to Crown of Thorns. They're harmless enough, but they get into trouble on the regular. Nevaeh isn't the type. While her friends were updating stories showing them at parties, Nevaeh was sharing her favorite tea and cozy fucking fall read. She's lived her life doing all the right things because it's safe. She hasn't so much as stepped a toe out of line in the past four years. What she saw that night on the Mineral Belt marked her the same as me. The only difference is that I did my time in prison and she did it out here. She made her own bars, her own walls, she didn't go outside of them because she knew it wasn't safe.

Tonight I'm going to rip those walls down, brick by brick, until there's nothing left. Nowhere for her to hide. No safety to find comfort in. The only thing left is going to be me.

Nevaeh tried to get away from Dean but there was nowhere for her to go. Nowhere until I showed up. It's comical just how much Deanie Baby thought he could actually stand up to me. I'm going to find him after this night and teach him a lesson. He's going to learn to keep his hands to himself. Nevaeh is scared for him, though, I don't know why she cares what happens to the fucker, especially when she looked like she wanted to run away from him.

Doesn't matter why she wants me not to hurt him. All I know is that it pisses me off. I hate that she feels anything for a man that isn't me. I should be the only one she cares about. The only fucking thought in her head.

I'm going to fix that. She's not going to care about any of them soon. It's not like they care about her. Even with his do-gooder act, I know what he wants from her. He wants to fuck Nevaeh. Why he's picked her out of all the girls on campus is anyone's guess, but he fucked up thinking I'm going to let him have a shot at my girl and not make him pay for it.

I'm glad the party is in her dorm. It's perfect for my plans on where I want to take Nevaeh. Her room. I want her to be relaxed and pliant to what I have planned for her. She would never do that somewhere she wasn't familiar and I'm not wasting the time to take her back to her house. Nevaeh's friend—the little blonde—is nowhere to be seen, but that doesn't mean I don't see another face I know well from her social media.

Mygirl420M

Otherwise known as Minnie. Nevaeh's once best friend.

Minnie is the daughter of some of the church's biggest donors and her family has been on the board with mine for as long as anyone can remember. They're rich fucks and from what I can remember, Minnie is a spoiled little bitch that dropped my Nevaeh the second it came out that I was innocent. She made a post about *"cutting certain toxic people out of her life"* and explained just how *"refreshing it was to be with authentic people again"* the day after I got out. I knew it was about Nevaeh. So much for a fucking best friend, huh? I didn't know what they were saying and I didn't care, but I stepped in when Minnie started to scream.

God fucking dammit. Why was she making a scene? A scene meant that many more people will remember I was with Nevaeh. More eyes on where I'm going to take her, but I can work with that later.

"He hates you. You don't deserve him. You're a liar."

Minnie wasn't wrong. I do hate Nevaeh, but it isn't that black and white. I hate her and I want her. I don't think I can feel love, but the fixation I have for Nevaeh probably comes close to it.

It disgusts me.

The crowd of people watching seemed to close in as I stepped close to take Nevaeh's back. The last thing I needed is some drunk fuck trying to lay hands on her tonight. I want to play with Nevaeh tonight. I'm the only one that gets to fuck with her, and tonight I want to fuck her.

I put a hand on her shoulder and felt her go stiff. She's like a stone beneath my hand and I squeeze it. "She's my friend."

Minnie's mouth dropped open. "She doesn't deserve you. She's trash."

Trash. That was rich coming from a girl whose family got caught embezzling cash from the charity trust. They were pocketing funds earmarked for water infrastructure in Botswana, and she wanted to talk about trash? The only reason her family has anything at all is because my father caught them and gave them time to put the funds back before he went to the church elders. He's the treasurer and I know for a fact that if even a penny goes missing this little bitch's family is the first place he checks.

"Aren't we all?" I asked and pulled Nevaeh back a step with me. "Let's go."

Nevaeh came right along. Docile as a fucking lamb and ran right into me when I stopped in front of her dorm room. It's only when we stopped walking that she realized where we were.

"There, the door will stay open. How's that?" I offered. It's not going to save her, but it's easy to keep up the good guy act for a second longer. I don't expect Nevaeh to fall for it, but she does. Interesting.

"Okay, f-fine," Nevaeh stammers. She's sweet. Adorable. Fucking stammering and blushing and worried about doors being open or not. The football team almost left her for dead for a serial killer to find and cut to pieces and she's worried about shit like this?

Stupid, beautiful, fucking liar.

Nevaeh goes to the left, it's on the side of the room behind the open door and it's not visible from the hallway, even with the door partly open. Light spills out onto the opposite side of the room and onto her roommate's empty bed. Her dorm room looks like any other that I've seen. There's a bed on each side of the room, pushed right up against the wall. There's windows above the beds. Twin desks sit on either side of the door and I see the outline of closets beside the beds. There's a matching pair of nightstands as well between the beds, and a rug that covers the space. I can make out the shape of a bookcase and a few pictures on the walls. Nevaeh's room is just like any other college girl, even if she's so much more.

Nevaeh takes a seat on her bed and crosses her arms over her chest. There's a stupid little strawberry night light beside the door that illuminates the room well enough. It casts golden light and shadows over Nevaeh. She looks down at the rug at her feet and tucks her chin close to her body.

She takes a deep breath and looks up at me. "What do we need to talk about?" she looks calmer now that we're in her space.

I'm glad she feels safe. It's going to make everything so much sweeter when I show her just how fucking paper thin her sense of safety is. It's not real. Nothing is out here.

"How far have you gone with a guy, Nevaeh?"

Her eyes go wide and she sits up. "What?" she whispers.

I take a step closer. I'm still standing in the light coming in from the hallway. The party hasn't slowed down and someone put on a party light. It's rotating and spinning, shining red, blue, yellow and green light every other second.I wonder what I look like to Nevaeh in all those fucking colors. For so long my world was nothing but gray. There's no goddamn colors in prison. Blue, grey, white. Sometimes orange. That's it.

"You fucked anyone?" I ask her and drop my voice as I stalk towards her. "Tell me the truth."

"Why are you asking that?"

"Because it's my right to know."

"That doesn't-" she stops and then starts again, "what do you mean?"

I'm just a couple of steps away from her. The dorm room isn't big at all and I've closed the space between us in a second, so when I come forward and put a hand on either side of Nevaeh she's got nowhere to go. Doesn't mean she doesn't try, though.

Nevaeh jerks back from me and tries to scoot away on her bed. "Beau, what are y-"

I grab her face and my palm presses against her lips, my fingers digging into her cheeks. I squeeze and Nevaeh whimpers. "It's my right, because you're mine. And no one touches what's mine. And you," I pause as I lean towards her and jerk her forward, "have been mine the fucking second they put me away. *My beautiful liar.* For four years you have been the only thing I've thought about and tonight I'm getting the start of what you owe me, do you understand?"

Nevaeh sucks in a deep breath through her nose. I frown, not liking that she's fighting me for air. She's going to learn to trust me. To know that I understand her and her limits more than anyone. She's going to learn not to fight my control. I shift so that my hand covers her nose, blocking off her next inhale of air. Her eyes go wide, the faint glow of the nightlight shows me the fear in her eyes and I can feel her lips part against my palm when she tries to speak. I growl low in my throat and give her face another squeeze.

"I said, do you understand? Nod your head like the fucking good girl that you are."

She's struggling to breathe. Chest rising and falling with each quick gasp that doesn't bring her any closer to getting a lungful of air with my hand over her nose and mouth. Even so, Nevaeh does what I ask and nods her head. Tears start to roll down her cheeks and wet my hand before they drop from my fingers to the floor beneath her.

"You're beautiful when you cry," I tell her and stroke her cheek with my free hand. I curl a lock of her hair around my finger and tug sharply. The gesture makes Nevaeh cry out and her neck bends, awkwardly trying to follow the pull of my finger, but she doesn't quite manage it without a wince. Nevaeh has beautiful hair. Thick, dark hair that curls slightly. It's soft and shines in the sunlight. I used to look at her photos and imagine what it would be like to touch her hair. I would fall asleep to that thought. I never knew nothing would compare to the real thing.

"My beautiful liar." I roll the lock of hair around my fingers and yank her closer to me every time I wrap it around my knuckles.

Nevaeh sobs, but the sound is muffled by my hand and the noise from the hallway, making sure no one hears a thing. The door is still open where I left it. Not quite halfway and not quite closed. Nevaeh's eyes go to the door and I pull her face to look at me.

"Wanting to be somewhere else?" I ask and dig my fingers into her beautiful face. "I don't think I need to tell you that when I'm with you, your attention is mine, angel. Do you understand?"

This time I don't have to tell Nevaeh to nod.

"Good girl, you're learning so fast for me. But if you're going to be thinking about anything other than me, I should do something about that, shouldn't I?" I loosen my grip and stand so suddenly Nevaeh almost falls forward onto the floor. I catch her with a hand on her shoulder and move close to grab her around her waist when she tries to make a run for it. I hear the intake of her breath as she gears up for a scream, but I don't stop what I'm doing. I'm faster than her and by the time her scream starts to let loose, I've got her facedown and over my knee. I hit her before she can truly scream and like magic, she stops.

She freezes, that perfect curvy body of hers curled over my thighs and I know she's trying to process what just happened. She didn't expect for me to spank her. I raise my hand and spank her again. The slap of my hand on her ass is swallowed up by the music and laughter from the party in the hallway. Someone falls against the doorframe but I don't pay them any attention. I don't care if someone finds us.

Nevaeh does though.

She moves, body jerking away from the thud she heard by the door, which means she's moving towards me. "Beau, stop." She doesn't scream, she doesn't even speak those two words. She whispers them. "Please." If I wasn't right beside her I wouldn't hear her speak at all.

"Why would I do something like that?" I ask her, not worrying about whispering. "I've waited years to mark you. I'm going to have my fucking fun. I earned this."

Nevaeh starts to fight me. She tries to wiggle away and covers her ass with her hands. "Beau, no, please. Someone will see."

"Good. Let them fucking see what I'm doing to you. Do you think anyone would stop me?" I lean forward and push her hands away from her and plant my forearm across her back as I do. "You earned this," I say as I spank her. Once, twice, three times and she's trembling against me. She buries her face into my side and I don't stop when I feel her start to cry.

Her tears are a fucking drug to me. Nevaeh crying because of me is incomparable to any high in the world. I'm her everything right now. Nothing exists without me allowing it. There's nothing but the pain I'm giving her.

The way I control it. How I decide to mark her. It's even sweeter to me that she's stopped fighting me and is taking what I give her.

When I stop spanking her, she's breathing hard and holding onto my thigh so tightly I know there's going to be a bruise. I smile. I like knowing Nevaeh's marked me tonight, just like I've done for her, but I'm not finished with her yet.

"Get on your knees," I order and nudge her, raising one of my thighs to move her. She doesn't move and shakes her head. She grabs onto my thigh and shakes her head again.

"B-beau," her voice shakes and then cracks when she starts to cry again. "I'm sorry. Please don't do this. Please."

Nevaeh begging almost breaks me. I almost pull her up into my lap to take her right then, but I want this to last. I move fast, shove her right off me and onto the floor.

"On your knees, angel."

CHAPTER FOURTEEN
Nevaeh

I'M FACE DOWN on the floor and my ass is on fire. I was so stupid to let Beau into my room just because he said he would leave the door open. I turn my face and look towards the door. It's still open, the light from the party flashes every now and then when the colors change and I debate trying to make a run for it.

But the last time I tried to run, he spanked me. My face goes hot even thinking about Beau spanking me and I swallow hard. I didn't know he was going to do that, but I also didn't know I was going to like that he did it.

Why did I like it?

Every slap of his hand against my ass felt like I'd earned it. All the guilt that I'd been carrying over the past four years started to seem less and less. Like I was finally being punished for what I'd done to him. It wasn't enough, though. I need more. What Beau just did to me was barely a drop in the bucket of regret I've felt at getting to live my life while he rotted away behind bars.

I know what I have to do. What I want. It's fucked up. It's not something a girl like me should want. I'm a good girl. I took a purity pledge and didn't kiss boys like my friends. I didn't even entertain the half hearted courtship offerings from the boys at church, because I always knew it was

Beau for me. Even if he'd never gotten out, I wouldn't have wanted anyone else but him.

Even if he really was a murderer. It was always going to be Beau.

And I want him to make me pay. I want him to be rough with me and take his due out of my body, because then at least I'll have that with him and it will be enough for me. It will be so much more than any other intimacy I've had with anyone else. No one knows me. No one has ever bothered to try and see me, but Beau does. He strips me down to the scared and weak girl that I am. When he wants me, I don't feel like either of those things. I know that's wrong, but I refuse to fight it. I want it more than I want to breathe and with that thought, I know I have to push Beau to give me the punishment I crave.

I get up from the floor and launch myself towards the door, but I only make it half a step before Beau has me in his arms. He's at my back, his big body engulfing me and he yanks me back against him. The hard muscle of his chest and thighs fits perfectly against my softer curves. Beau wraps an arm around my waist and lifts me and that's when I feel it. The undeniably hard length of him. His dick.

I've never felt a man's dick before. I've never really thought about it to be honest, other than something I needed to avoid per the guidance of the church elders and the girls older than me. I knew better than to walk the line Minnie and the other girls did, because if a girl like me was found with a boy? That was something I wouldn't be able to come back from. Minnie had money and a family people respected. If she fucked up and was caught with a boy, it'd be buried and forgotten in a few months, but me?

No such luck. I knew what happened to girls without a family and with hardly any money. Girls that survived off the charity of others and weren't really embraced by those around them. I'd seen it with my own mother. She'd had to leave and start over because she made a mistake with the wrong boy, so I'd avoided physical contact and anything beyond holding hands because it wasn't worth the trouble. Or so I told myself.

The truth was, I avoided it because none of them were Beau.

I kick my legs and try to wiggle free, but all it does is force my behind right up against Beau's dick and he moans. One of his hands comes to my hip and he moves me the way he wants.

"Such a good girl, aren't you?"

I shake my head. "No."

"Don't lie to me."

"I'm not," I whisper and blink away the tears. Shame rolls through me and wars with the lust heating my blood. I sink back to meet the next roll of Beau's hips and it's me that moans this time. I reach back and grip his thigh, my fingers digging into his hard muscle. "I'm not a good girl."

Beau scoffs and leans close to my ear. "You're *my* good girl," he whispers and then turns me around to face him. He looks me over for a second and my knees go weak. He's so beautiful it hurts me to look at him. He's also terrible and horrifying. I don't know what he's going to do to me and I shouldn't like that, but I do. He forces me down to my knees with a hand on my shoulder and this time I don't fight him.

"Undo my belt." Beau isn't trying to be quiet like I am. He's speaking like he doesn't care who sees him and that makes me nervous. I do what he says but when I look towards the door, he slaps my cheek. "What did I say about looking at anything but me? When you're with me, I am everything to you."

"I'm sorry."

"When I am with you, I am your god."

I gasp before I can stop myself. I don't know why I do. I don't think I believe in God anymore. I don't think I've believed in him since the night Carrie Salt died and I probably should have too. If there was a God, why would he put Beau and I together like this?

He chuckles and rubs a thumb over my bottom lip. "Oh, angel, you're going to have to get used to a lot more from me than that. Now, suck my dick." I should be scared, but I'm not. At least not truly. I'm curious. I've never touched a man like this. I've never done anything like this before and now I get to do it with Beau.

My hands shake as I unbuckle his belt and work down his zipper but I manage it. I don't know what to do and I freeze with my hands just above the top of his boxers. The warm glow of Sunny's night light washes Beau in a gentle light. The sharp lines and the glare on his face is softened in the warm light. If I concentrate, I can pretend Beau doesn't hate me. That he isn't angry with me or that he isn't doing this to punish me. I can pretend that he actually wants me for me. That what we're doing is something we both want.

I can pretend that he loves me.

Beau puts a hand to the back of my head and he strokes his fingers through my hair. The gentle touch is light and I almost give into the make believe world where Beau loves me the way I want him to. God, why do I still want that? I shouldn't. Beau's light touch turns sharp and he grabs a fistful of my hair and jerks my head back to look up at him. I can see him better at this angle and there's nothing soft about him.

His eyes are black and he bares his teeth at me in a snarl.

"Faster, Nevaeh or you won't like what I do to you," he says and shoves my head away from him. The party is still going on, the light of it pours into the room through the half open door and none of this feels real. How can it be? A week ago Beau Du Pont was locked away and I spent every night in bed thinking about him and hating myself for what I saw that night. Now he's free, The Reaper is on the hunt again and I'm caught in this twisted thing with Beau.

"I'm sorry," I whisper. I don't know where to look so I drop my eyes to the floor. I don't know what I'm apologizing for. Not going fast enough to satisfy Beau's demand or for getting it wrong all those years ago. Either way. "I'm sorry," I say again and pull his pants and boxers down. Beau is big. Bigger than anything I could have imagined, even though I've never seen a dick before. Beau's dick lays thick and heavy against his thigh. The width of it makes me nervous. I don't know how I'm going to get my mouth around it. There's a slight curve to it and the mushroom head of it has a drip of precum already beading at the tip. His balls are big too, they're darker than his dick and anxiety shoots through me, because I don't know what to do.

If I mess this up is Beau going to get angrier? What will he do then?

Beau grabs me by the throat and squeezes. "Goddammit, Nevaeh."

I grab Beau's hand and try to scream but there's no air getting to my lungs. The scream is cut off before it makes a sound by the hand on my neck and all I end up doing is choking. I thrash in Beau's hold but he doesn't let me go. He holds me tighter, squeezes harder and strokes a hand down my throat while I claw at his hand. I swing a hand at his dick but he catches that with a laugh.

"Oh, angel. I don't think so."

I keep fighting Beau, but it's not long before my vision starts to darken and I feel my arms getting heavier. I sag forward and almost pass out but Beau's grip on my neck loosens. My body reacts on instinct and my lips part as I gasp and choke. Air fills my lungs, but a second later, Beau grips the side of my face and forces my mouth wider. I can't take in enough air to stop the burning of my lungs, but I try to manage it anyway. I sob and take another ragged breath as tears slide down my cheeks. I can't see past my tears and reach out, grabbing onto Beau's thighs to steady myself, but he slaps my hands away and I almost fall over again. He steadies me with the hand gripping my face that still keeps my mouth from closing. I try to speak, but I can't form words, not with the way he's holding me. He digs his fingers into my cheeks and I cry out from the pain of it. It feels like he's prying my jaw apart, but no matter how hard I try, there's no getting away from him.

Beau gives my face a shake. "I said you weren't going to like it, now didn't I?" He growls as he shoves his dick into my mouth and down my throat. Fresh tears fill my eyes when he hits the back of my throat, but I'm powerless with the hold Beau has on me. I'm still weak from the lack of air and all I can do is brace my hands on his thighs while he starts to thrust. I'm grateful he's at least letting me hold myself up now. He rolls his hips and the fat length of him moves over my tongue. I can taste him. Salty and musky. It's a taste I've never had before, but I've heard the girls in youth group talk about it.

They made it sound terrible. Like the taste of cum is worse than death, but it's not like that with Beau. But what do I know? Maybe the worst is yet to come, but I don't know if that's true with the way Beau's hand on my face has started to relax. He isn't digging his fingers into my face like he wants to rip my jaw in half. He's touching me softer now and his hand moves lower until it's cupping my jaw. He slides his thumb along my bottom lip before he moves into my mouth. He slides it in and out of my mouth in a mimic of his dick. He shifts closer and moves a hand to the back of my head before he gives a hard thrust and feeds me the full length of his dick. I choke and try to pull away from him when he holds himself there. He's so deep in my throat and I can't breathe. I push at his hips but he's too big to move and he feels like solid stone beneath my hands. I'm not moving him. I'm not getting away from the hard length shoved down my throat and cutting off my air. Panic fills me and I try to jerk back, but then I hear Beau speak.

"Nevaeh." Beau's voice is low and deep. Beau says my name like a whispered prayer and the sound of it surprises me. It's almost tender. "Filthy, beautiful, Nevaeh."

My body feels warm because, even though he isn't saying the sweet things I always imagined from him, the way he's saying these dirty words to me is just how I thought they would sound. The tone. The timbre. The longing. I can hear it all there and I want more.

"That's it. You're going to be my dirty fucking slut now, aren't you?"

I stop fighting him but I don't know what to say. I've never had anyone talk to me like this. I try to pull myself off of his dick, it's still filling my mouth and throat. Spit pools in my mouth and drips down my chin and onto the floor.

He groans and grabs one of my hands and brings them to his balls. He cups my hand around them and gives my hand a light squeeze. "Gentle, or I'll slit your fucking throat. You can be gentle for me, can't you, angel?" Again the praise mixed with his cruel and filthy words sets my body on fire and I feel myself start to get wet. I press my thighs together and try to breathe through my nose, but Beau's free hand is back around my neck and no matter how hard I try, I can't get enough air. My throat tightens and I can still feel his hand on my neck, cutting off my air. I thought Beau wouldn't hurt me. Not really. But I don't know anymore. Even so, I can't deny the rush of adrenaline that floods my body, or the way my clit aches when he touches me.

He grunts and starts to thrust, the wet sound of his dick moving in and out of my mouth mingles with my stuttered gasps for air and I blush. It's stupid, I know it is. Why am I blushing like the bashful virgin I was trying to muster up the courage to talk to my crush and not like the woman Beau's forced to her knees like a supplicant to an angry god.

"You're perfect."

Those two words make me dizzy. When I look up at Beau, I see he's watching me. His eyes are on my face and it's like nothing else exists in the world to him. Every move I make, he sees. Every breath I choke on, he drinks up. I know he likes it when I choke, because he thrusts deeper then, the hard length of him sliding past my lips and down my throat with a satisfied groan. I should hate it and want to get away from him, but I don't. Because that's also when he praises me the most.

"You're mine."

"That's it, angel."

"You take me so good. I knew you would."

It's all like a drug to me and I'm addicted. I don't know how long I'm on my knees or how I've managed to stay conscious with so little air but one second bleeds into the next and all there is in my world is Beau. I stroke him the way he likes best from the moans he gives me, cradling him in my palm and sliding my fingers over him while I take him down my throat and swirl my tongue over the tip of his cock when he slides past my lips. I bring my free hand up and start to slide it along the length of his dick, squeezing it hard at the base when I hear his breath hitch.

"That's it, angel. Faster. That's my fucking whore."

I work him faster, bobbing my head along the length of him until he's no longer forcing me with the hand at the back of my head.

"Fuck, Nevaeh." Beau grunts and rocks his hips, bringing them forward to meet my mouth as I slide down the length of him. "I've wanted you for years."

My clit throbs. Years? I almost bring my hand to my clit to touch myself but I don't, because I don't want to make Beau angry. I want him to be happy with me, so I keep touching him, but I almost cum from hearing those words come from him. The man that's been my greatest fantasy, the one that's ruined me for everyone else, has wanted *me*. He wanted me after I put him in prison. Are we both as fucked up as the other one? We have to be for any of this to make sense. I moan and start to work Beau faster. I want him to cum, I need him to, because then maybe I will too. Maybe he'll touch me then. No one's ever touched me before. The only time I've ever felt like this is when I did it. When I was alone at night and the only thing I could think of was Beau and what I would do with him if he was free.

What I had always wished I'd done when I had the chance. But that was with the Beau I knew before. The kind boy, the one that all the girls wanted to date, the ones every family wanted to see turn up on their door asking for permission to court their girls. He was everything I'd been told to want by the church and it had been so easy to fall in love with him as an awkward teenager. Beau had been the standard that I measured every other boy I met. Even with that horrific night, Beau continued to be everything I wanted. Somehow, he'd gotten into my bones, into the marrow and blood that kept me upright and I wasn't stupid.

I knew Beau hadn't noticed me. Not with the girls fighting for his attention. They had been just as perfect as him. That's why he'd been with Carrie that night, but now...she was gone and he was with me. I didn't care that he only wanted to hurt me now, because no one else had ever had this version of him. The old Beau belonged to everyone, but this one? The dark and angry man that put me on my knees?

This man belongs to me and me alone.

"Get your tits out." The order is harsh and I can barely understand him, but I try to do what he says. I pull down the front of the top I'm wearing. It's a sweetheart cut blouse which makes it easy enough, but before I can get my bra down, Beau's big hands are there. He steps back, his hard dick slides out of my wet mouth when he does. Beau grabs the front of my bra and pulls it forward. I hear the faint snick of a blade opening before he brings the knife to my bra and cuts clean through it with a rough jerk of his hand. I feel a slight sting from the blade sliding over my skin and I know he cut me. I press a hand to my chest and feel the sticky heat of my blood against my palm.

"You cut me," I whisper. I should scream. I should run. I don't. I stay exactly where I am while Beau's knife glints in front of me. He moves it slowly, brings it close and drags the blade along my jaw.

He turns it and presses the flat side of the blade to my lips. "I did, angel."

"Beau-" I start, but he isn't done speaking. He turns the knife and flicks the tip of it below my jaw. I freeze, because I can feel the change in energy. The man that whispered my name like a prayer is gone.

"If I cut you, what do you think I'm going to do to that fuck boy out there that thinks he's going to pop your cherry?" He presses the tip into my skin and I feel the sharp sting of the blade breaking the skin. He cut me again, I know he did. There's no way he didn't with the pain in my neck and I swallow hard as a stream of blood comes forward and heats my skin on its way down my neck. Blood drips onto the floor beneath me with a soft tap and my heart starts to pound.

Just because Beau isn't The Reaper doesn't mean he won't hurt me. He's done it already. The cut on my chest burns more with each second and I can hear my blood dripping onto the floor. Just because he wasn't the person that killed Carrie Salt doesn't mean he won't kill me.

"I don't know," I whisper.

"I'll kill him," Beau says and digs the blade into me for a second more before he pulls it away and I let out the breath I didn't realize I was holding with a whimper. "If he touches you again I'll cut his heart out and tonight, angel, I'm claiming what's always been mine." I hear the telltale snick as Beau closes the knife up. A second later he's grabbing me. His hands are rough on my body and he hooks his hands under my armpits to hoist me up from my knees. I turn and struggle, because I know that's what I'm supposed to do.

I'm a good girl. I don't do this kind of thing. I'm not supposed to have this happen to me. I struggle, but I don't mean it and I think Beau knows that. He picks me up and carries me forward before he throws me down on my bed. I cry out when I land on my bed face first and hit my bed with a hard bounce. I push myself up and there's blood on my hands and the sheets in front of me. I can see the dark color of it in the warm light of the nightlight still cheerily lighting the room.

"B-Beau, what are you doing?"

For a split second I don't know where he is and when I hear the floorboards creak near the door, I think he's left. It's then I realize the door is still halfway open and the party that I was terrified someone would hear us from is still raging on outside. Oh god. How did I forget that the party was still going?

I hadn't cared how loud I was or who heard when Beau had me choking on his dick. I grab at my sheets and try to draw them to my chest when Beau slams the door shut. He locks it, the snap of the lock sliding home is deafening in my now quiet room.

"Beau?" I whisper and slide back on my bed until my back is against the wall. "W-what are you doing?" My voice is shaky and weak. I hate it, but I don't know how else to be. God what is happening right now? Why do I want it to keep going? Even if Beau hurts me, I want more.

I deserve more from him for what I did. Maybe this is my penance. Maybe this is what was always meant to happen to right the scales for what I did to him.

"I'm making sure no one fucking sees what's mine," Beau snaps. He's angry. I can hear the venom in his voice but I stay where I am as he comes to me.

"I don't understand." I'm lying. I know exactly what Beau's going to take from me tonight.

"Sweet angel, I think you do understand." My cheeks heat because he knows. He knows me just like I know him. "Isn't that right?" he asks.

"Yes," I whisper. I hear the sound of Beau's belt sliding free and my pulse picks up. What is he going to do with that belt?

"That's my filthy little liar. You know what you owe me, angel. You are going to give me everything tonight. Isn't that right?"

Again I whisper my answer. "Yes."

"You will never let another man touch you. Never let another one fucking feel just how good that mouth of yours is." Beau's in front of me now. He plants a knee on the bed and grabs my foot with one hand. He yanks me to him and I cry out when my back hits my bed.

"I'm going to be the first one to feel that perfect fucking virgin cunt," he says and I squirm in his hold. He drags me forward, right to the edge of the bed and pulls my jeans off with an angry jerk of his hands.

"Beau, please."

"Please, what?" he asks and tosses my jeans to the side. He leans over me and presses a palm to my still bleeding chest. "Are you going to beg me not to do this, angel?"

I bite my lip. I should say yes. I know that's the right answer, but the words are stuck in my throat. I lick my lips and I can still taste him on my tongue. I want this. We both do, but still. I do what I'm supposed to do because I'm a good girl.

"Stop, don't!" I raise my hands and try to kick out at him but Beau catches my legs with ease and forces them apart. His hands are rough on me and he grasps my thighs and jerks me towards him with a satisfied groan. "Beau, no!" I yell at him, even though I don't mean it. I want this. I want him to take from me. The guilt I've carried for four years is heavy and Beau's unforgiving hands on my body are the way I can finally let my burden go. This is my penance to pay with the man I love. The one I've always wanted but never thought myself worthy of. I want it to happen this way. It's the only way that makes sense to me.

Beau leans over me and captures my mouth in a cruel kiss. "I hoped you'd fight me. I wanted it like this," he whispers against my mouth. He moves his hand between my thighs and I cry out when he strokes two fingers into me. It's the only thing I've ever had inside of me and he curls his fingers and starts to thrust them in and out. The stretch of his fingers, drag of his fingertips against my walls, is unlike anything I've felt before. When he presses his fingers to a spot I didn't know existed in me, my back bows off the bed and I scream his name.

"Beau!"

He laughs. The sound of it is harsh and cruel and I know he's mocking me, but none of that matters because he continues to tease me, fingers stroking me faster and faster while his thumb slides over my clit.

I whimper from the pleasure of it all and wrap my legs around him. I want him deeper inside of me. I need more than the two fingers filling me. "Beau, please. Please." I'm begging again, but this time it isn't for him to stop. "Please give me more."

He leans over me, his big body on top of mine pins me to the bed and it's bliss. He might hate me, but this is everything I've always wanted. "I'm not going to be gentle with you, my sweet liar," he says while he speeds up. The fingers in me move quicker with each second and I can't catch my breath. I'm dizzy when he presses his thumb down hard on my clit and rubs a circle quick and rough against my sensitized flesh. I'm wet. So fucking wet. The sound of Beau's fingers moving in and out of me is obscene, but there's no denying it. My body wants him as much as my heart does.

"Do you hear that?" Beau asks and bites my ear. "You're wet for me. Soaking. Your slutty little virgin cunt knows exactly what it wants and it's getting you ready to take me inside. Isn't that right?"

It's all that I need to lose myself to the orgasm Beau's built in my body. My eyes roll in the back of my head and I scream myself hoarse as I cum. "Beau!"

I turn my head to the side, because I can't look up at him with the way he's over me. He has a shoulder pressed against my chin and one hand curled around my head. The blood from my chest smears between us and I can feel his shirt sticking to me. He's fully clothed, even though I'm almost naked. My shirt is barely hanging on to me and shredded from the knife he cut my bra away with and I don't know where my pants are, but I don't care. I let my legs fall open around Beau when he settles himself between my legs. The rough scratch of denim chafes my skin when he hikes one of my legs higher on his hip.

"Nevaeh," Beau whispers my name. His lips graze my cheek and then my mouth when he speaks. "You have always been mine, angel." The blunt head of his dick slides against me and I gasp when he slides the tip inside of me. He's big. Bigger than his fingers were and the stretch makes me wince.

"I'll kill anyone that tries to stop me. You're mine."

His words wash over me. They're dark and needy. Possessive and I want more. I know Beau isn't lying to me. He cut me earlier. My blood is on both of us.

"I know."

Beau moans, the sound low and humming in my ear and he thrusts into me with a sharp jerk of his hips. I cry out in pain from the stretch of him. It feels like he's splitting me open, but I want more. I put my hands on Beau's shoulders to keep him still but it doesn't do anything. Neither does my grabbing his waist to hold him in place. He moves even as I plead for him to slow down.

"Beau, wait. Please, I can't. I can't."

"You can and you will, you fucking liar."

He grabs my hands, and wraps his belt around them and ties the leather tight around my wrists before he pins them down with his full weight onto the bed above my head and uses the leverage to ride me as he pleases. "That's it, angel. Take me."

I'm trapped. I tug at the leather binding my wrists but it holds fast. There's nowhere to go with the hold Beau has on me. He doesn't stop. He's relentless in how he consumes my body. In the way he fucks me until the edge of pain that makes my breath come short starts to blend into something that feels good.

"You were always going to be mine, Nevaeh. You're always going to be mine."

"Beau, yes," I sob when the thin line between pain and pleasure blurs and vanishes, until there's nothing but bliss. It's good. It feels so good. Beau shifts his angle and I see stars. It's like everything I'm feeling is turned up to a hundred and I shatter again in his hands.

"Beau!" I scream while he takes me apart piece by piece. Beau fucks me through my orgasm. He wrings out every bit of pleasure crashing over my body until I'm weak and shaking beneath him. He moves faster, his hips slamming against mine and he keeps my hands pinned to the bed. I can't stop him and I don't want to, but he doesn't know that. For all he knows, he's forcing me. There's nothing left for me to do but enjoy what he's doing to me. God, it feels so good to let him do this to me. I'm dimly aware that he's about to come. I can feel it in how tense his body is. Hear it in the way he's gasping my name with every thrust.

"Nevaeh."

He has to pull out. He has to. But even as I think it, I don't say anything. I want him inside of me. I want him to fill me up and make me his in every way, but in the end Beau doesn't give me what I want. Not like when I told him no.

He pulls back and slides out of me with a strangled moan and warm cum splashes over my thighs and on my aching pussy. When Beau stops cumming, we're both silent. Our ragged breath is the only sound either of us makes. Outside the party is still going strong. It's loud and someone falls against the door before they hit the floor with a thud but neither of us moves.

Beau reaches out and rubs his thumb across my stomach and then my thigh, before he finally touches my pussy. He rubs his cum into my flesh. I stay quiet while he touches me, because I don't care what he's doing so long as his hands are on me. When he's done, he speaks.

"I see that fucker touching you again, Nevaeh and I'll cut his dick off and choke him with it."

I wince at his words. "Please don't. I-I, Beau, he's my friend." I shouldn't say that. I know it. I don't even like Dean, not really. He made me nervous earlier, which makes no sense. How can I be nervous around Dean when he's a nice guy and I'm here with Beau, calm as can be? He cut me, he forced me to suck his dick with the door open before he took my virginity.

I'm not safe with Beau, so why is there no other place I'd rather be than exactly where I am?

Beau unfastens the belt from my wrists and pulls it free before he moves off my bed. The leather slides so fast across my skin that it burns. My wrists ache, but I still don't move to rub them. I watch Beau instead and wish he would stay.

"You don't get friends, Nevaeh. You don't get anyone *but me*." He spits those last two words at me like a curse. I hear the lock to my door click free and he leaves my room a second later, slamming the door behind him.

I lay in the dark for another minute before I cry.

CHAPTER FIFTEEN
BEAU

HAVING NEVAEH WAS even better than I imagined it would be, and that's saying something. Not a day went by that I didn't think about what I would do when I got her alone. In the beginning, I only wanted revenge. I thought about making her cry and beg for forgiveness. When I was depressed and lost, I even thought about what it would be like to choke the life out of her beautiful body. But some time in my four years behind bars, things changed.

I didn't think about what it would be like to have Nevaeh's lifeless body in my hands anymore, but I did think about what it would be like to have her under me. What hearing her sweet moans would be like while she rode my dick. I thought about her wet pussy, how fucking good it was going to be to sink into her—even in my imagination, I knew I was going to be the first one to do it.

Nevaeh was a good girl. She didn't fuck around. In another world she would go to college and break her purity vow to some idiot she met at a campus ministry group. She'd be in love with him and they'd have fucking boring sex before they went on to have a boring fucking marriage and life. That was how Nevaeh was supposed to pop her cherry. To someone she loved. Instead, she got me.

I don't love her. I'm obsessed with her.

She is fucking mine. Now, she always will be. Nevaeh isn't going to tell anyone what happened tonight, just like she didn't tell anyone about what I told her the first day I saw her or what happened with the football team. She could have gone to someone with that limp dick Dean, but she didn't.

Four years ago she ran her mouth and ruined my life, but this time it is going to be different. *She is going to keep this secret.* This time, Nevaeh isn't going to run her mouth. I know she won't, just like I know Nevaeh won't turn in the man that took her virginity. I read a lot of fucking books and had a lot of time to think and take the classes the prison offered. I know the standard shit as well as anyone, that virginity is a social construct. It has as much meaning as you let society convince you it has. Power and control are the reasons virginity is even an issue and even then, it's only for girls.

Girls like Nevaeh.

Girls that might get too big an idea of what they might want in life or who they might want to do it with. Shit like that is dangerous. It's just like the guards that watched us in lock up. They knew we were better controlled when they kept us apart. When they helped the stupid little sects and schisms grow until the prison population would rather turn on each other than the one turning the key in the lock to their cell. But even knowing all that, I wanted to be Nevaeh's first. I wanted it to be me and, from the way she reacted, so did she. My good girl is tied to me now. She won't give me up easily and that's the way I want it.

"Oh my *gawddddddd*, Beau!" The screech is undeniable. It's Ali. Fuck. I thought I ditched this bitch already.

I turn my head and see her stumbling down the hallway towards me with a smile on her face. Her eyes are glassy and she's spilling beer out of her cup and onto the dorm floor as she walks. She's definitely wasted.

I'm still in the hallway. Only a few feet from Nevaeh's door. I left her room ten minutes ago, but I haven't been able to leave. Something is keeping me here just a few steps to the left of her door. I'm curious to see if she leaves her room after what I just did to her, but I'm not stupid. She's got a target on her back and there's too many drunk fuckers in her dorm tonight. I know Jordan is here and I saw a few of the guys from the football team here tonight.

I know what could happen.

Someone falls against the wall and stumbles toward Nevaeh's door, but I shove them away. "Keep fucking walking." They trip and fall, get up and glare at me, before they do like I said.

The energy in the dorm has shifted. Before, it was light and free. Just a bunch of kids having fun. I remembered that feeling from the boy I was before, but now it's different. There's a heaviness to it. A frenetic sway and pull that feels the way my block felt before all hell broke loose and we all ended up in lock down because someone got gutted in the showers. Nevaeh's dorm is like a powder keg with a lit candle on the edge of it. Just one wrong move could send it up. Bloom was always like this after The Reaper made an appearance. Everyone was scared, but what is fear but the other side of anger? Nevaeh is the easiest target for that kind of rage.

All it would take is one dumb ass with just enough jungle juice in his system to feel brave enough to teach Nevaeh a lesson. I'd rather die than let someone fucking touch Nevaeh.

I'm the one that bruises her skin. I'm the one that makes her cry. I'm the one she fears.

That's for me.

My filthy liar belongs to me in every way possible. Tonight I took her virginity, but what I really want is her life. I want her heart, her mind, her soul. Every last bit of what makes Nevaeh human is going to be laid out in front of me to take apart at will. And when I do, she's going to thank me for it. That means I protect her from drunk hicks, which suits me fine. It'll play right into the "good guy" bullshit I've got going for me.

But Ali showing up now?

That's a problem. From the looks of her blitzed ass, she's horny and up to no good. I glance down the hall trying to spot Jordan, but he's nowhere to be seen. He must have ditched her and now she's trying to rally for a plan B. I grit my teeth and lean back against the wall beside Nevaeh's door. I look casual, but just barely. If anyone was sober enough they'd probably realize they shouldn't bother me, but there isn't anyone on this floor that hasn't had more than a few.

"Hey, how's it going, Ali?" I greet her.

She stumbles up against me and throws her arms around me with a giggle. "Oh my *gawddd*, what a night. Where have you been all night?"

I turn to the side, angle myself away and clear my throat. "Around."

Ali pouts and shoves her tits up against my chest. "I haven't seen you for hours. I thought you went home."

I cross my arms and use them to put space between us. Having Ali on me, having her touch me, smelling her sickly sweet perfume that's turning sour from sweat, after I fucked Nevaeh, makes me sick. I've eaten a lot of figurative and probably literal fucking shit while I was in prison and kept my cool, but Ali makes me want to puke all over the goddamn floor. I roll my shoulders and glance towards Nevaeh's door.

What is she doing in there? Is she thinking about me?

Those are the thoughts making me crazy while Ali giggles up at me and the party shows no sign of letting up. It has to be past midnight, but the party won't be over until the sun comes up. No one is safe while The Reaper hunts, but seeing morning break usually calms everyone down after a night like this. Tomorrow, everything will go right back to normal. Everyone will go right back to pretending there's nothing wrong in Bloom, but I'll know. Nevaeh will, too. It's what makes us perfect for one another.

She sees what I see. She knows what I know. We aren't cowards like the rest of Bloom. They pretend, but Nevaeh and me? We don't know how to pretend. I've known that truth from the second the cops threw me in a cell and left me there. There was no going home or waking up from the nightmare. No do overs or chances for mercy.

Tonight showed her that, too.

"So when are you taking me out?" Ali trips over her words as she closes the space between us and as much as I want to knock her on her ass, I can't. The hallway is still packed full of students. Down the hall someone is doing a keg stand and there's kids smoking a joint a few feet away. I throw Ali off me and it's going to draw attention, so I stay where I am.

"What?" I ask, pretending I don't hear her slurred words.

"A date," she says and spit hits my cheek with how loud she's yelling. The stoners nearby lift their heads to look our way, just like I knew they would. Except I didn't think it was going to be from Ali causing a scene.

"You want to go on a date with me?"

"Um, obviously. You're, like, so hot and smart!" Ali throws her hands out for emphasis and then gives me a slow shit eating smile, "And besides, how long has it been since you touched a woman? Did they let you have conjugal visits?"

I think of Nevaeh beneath me. Her cries in my ear while I fucked her into the fucking mattress so hard her bed frame squeaked and bounced.

"No, they didn't."

Ali trails a finger up my arm and makes a show of pressing her tits up against me. "Why not? I could treat you right. I bet you were real lonely in there, weren't you?"

I scan the hall again. It's just the stoners around now. They won't bother Nevaeh if I leave to deal with Ali. "Not allowed for what I was booked for."

"But you were innocent!" Ali yells and stumbles back from me with a glare. "That bitch did that to you."

"Her name is Nevaeh," I correct with a sharp look. I'm not going to let Ali talk about Nevaeh. Ali is shit on my shoe. She has no right to Nevaeh.

Instantly the drunk girl act in front of me sobers and she straightens up. "Right, right. Sorry about that." Ali tucks a lock of hair behind her ear and gives me eyes that I know are supposed to be innocent, but all I see is bullshit and greed, "I know you're big on forgiveness, which is just another reason why I want to get to know you better."

She means fuck. Jordan turned her down for whatever reason and now she thinks she can fuck her way into being my girlfriend. I might not be the top choice anymore, but I come from a rich family with a lot of connections in the area. I can't fault Ali's change in tactics. It's smart, especially if she thinks I'm hard up. She doesn't know I have Nevaeh's cum still wet on my dick or the knife with Nevaeh's blood on it in my pocket, though.

"I'd like that," I lie and shoot her a smile. I can use Ali when it comes to hurting Nevaeh. I plan on making her miserable. The easiest way to do that without touching her is for her to see a girl like Ali on my arm. Ali reminds me of Carrie. They have the same look, the same way of speaking and moving on campus, but Carrie had a soul. There's nothing of substance in Ali, which is a shame, but not for me. It'll make this whole thing easier, because Ali will see exactly what I want her to see.

"Let's get another drink and chat!" Ali smiles at me and bounces forward again. She grabs my hand and tugs me away from Nevaeh's door and towards the main lobby where the music is louder. "I just think we have so much in common!" She's screaming at me over her shoulder, a lot louder than she needs to be with the level of music playing, but she's doing it for attention.

Ali wants everyone to know she's with me right now, so I play dumb and let her take me with her, because I'm already thinking about my next move when it comes to breaking my beautiful liar. She's so fucking pretty when she cries. Especially when she cries for me.

I can't fucking wait to watch her do it again.

CHAPTER SIXTEEN

Nevaeh

AFTER BEAU LEFT, I was scared to leave my room. The party was still going and I was too nervous to make a go for the bathrooms alone after the attack, but I had to do it. There was too much blood. God. The blood. The cut on my chest was shallow, more of a deep scratch than anything from what I could see in the mirror Sunny and I had in our room. It was the wound on the side of my neck that was deeper. That's where the blood had come from. Beau's hand around my neck had kept the wound open while we'd had sex. I tried to clean the blood off of myself, but it was useless. It was in my hair and on the side of my face, under my fingernails. I don't know what Beau looked like, but I was a wreck.

"Fuck, Nevaeh," I whisper and shift from foot-to-foot in front of the mirror. If I didn't do something, Sunny was going to come back and find me like this. There would be no denying what had happened then. I'd already changed the sheets on my bed and tried to remake it as best I could. I look to the side and swallow hard. My bed looks so normal. So completely normal. How is that where Beau took my virginity? There had been blood on the floor, but I'd cleaned that up with my ruined shirt that I shoved to the bottom of the dirty clothes hamper I kept in my closet. I'd throw it away later when there wasn't a damn party going on in the dorm.

Someone laughs outside the door and I hear the telltale creak of a footstep in front of the door. I hold my breath and wait, but thankfully they move on. Every second that I don't do something, I'm risking Sunny coming in here and catching me with blood on myself and a wound on my neck. I shove on a hoodie to hide the damage to my neck and chest before snagging my towel, a fresh change of clothes and my soap. I don't need everything. There's a first aid kit in the bathroom and I just need to get the wound clean enough to patch up. I run my finger over it gingerly and wince. It's throbbing, but I'm lucky it isn't bleeding again. I'm lucky Beau didn't cut me any deeper than he did. I don't know how he didn't, with what we were doing. I hesitate in front of the door but after another second, I force myself to move. I unlock my door and slip out into the hallway.

The first thing I notice is the smell of weed. It's heavy in the air and I wince. It stinks, but Minnie said that meant it was good. I try to hide my cough when I see a circle of stoners passing a joint around. One of them laughs when they see my cough but the rest of them don't look my way. Good. I don't want anyone to   stop me in the hallway, so I keep my head down and hurry towards the bathroom at the end of the hallway. It's close to the lobby where most of the students are right now. The music is still as loud as it was before I went to my room with Beau, and the lights are just as frenetic, which is good. It means I shouldn't worry about anyone seeing me and following me, but even as I think it…I feel eyes on me.

It's like a prickling sensation on the back of my neck. My skin goes hot and I know someone is watching me. It's the same feeling I used to get in youth group when the older boys would linger a little too long to talk with me and Minnie. My mom always showed up before anything happened, but I know what this feels like.

Someone's watching me.

I don't let myself look until I'm right outside the bathroom door. If anyone is going to come after me, I want to see them coming. That's when I see who is looking at me. It isn't the person that attacked me in the showers. That voice was a woman's and the person watching me is a man.

It's Beau.

He's lounging against the wall at the mouth of the hallway with a drink in one hand and a girl wrapped around his other arm. She's pretty. Blonde and perky. She looks familiar and I wonder where I've seen her. Knowing my luck, she's in my dorm. My gut turns sour while I watch them together. Beau looks right at home with this kind of girl all over him and when she leans up on her tiptoes to press a messy kiss to his mouth, I want to scream.

He's mine.

I just had him inside of me. He took the thing I thought I was going to save for the man I married. My virginity was supposed to be for someone I loved. Someone that loved me. Only one of those things is true tonight and it's all my fault. If I hadn't run down that trail four years ago and called the cops, Beau wouldn't hate me like he does now. But if I hadn't told, I wouldn't have had Beau in my room whispering my name like a prayer, either. He would have never noticed me.

The blonde drops down from her kiss and gives Beau's chest a smack before she goes on to lean against him as she talks. I don't pay attention to her. I look at Beau. He looks perfect. Where I looked like I was murdered by the amount of blood on my face and neck, there's only a slight red smudge on the side of the shirt he's wearing. Other than that, he's spotless.

How is that possible?

When we were together, it was like he was everywhere at once. The way he was holding me down, how he was inside of me and whispering in my ear, his breath warm on my neck and chest, his mouth on mine. I touch my mouth. I can't help it, not when I remember how he kissed me.

I used to dream about Beau kissing me. Nothing prepared me for how good it would be, even when I was terrified of what he was going to do to me. That's not normal. I know it's not. You shouldn't want to be with a man no matter the price. And Beau's price? It's my life. That might be why I'm so angry seeing the girl with him. I *earned* my place with Beau. I earned his wrath and his passion.

What the fuck has she ever done for him?

Nothing. She is perfect and unmarked. She is free to live her life and have Beau out in the open while what we do only happens behind closed doors or where no one else can see. Anger clouds my vision and for a wild second I think about going over to confront them. I want to slap him and scream at him, but it's the girl I want to hurt the most. I want to rip every hair out of her head and claw her eyes out. I want her to know that Beau is mine. I want her to know what he did to me tonight and how she'll never have him that way. It'll never be her that wears Beau's scars. I touch my neck and Beau smiles in my direction. Just like that, with the knife wound stinging like hell beneath my fingers and Beau grinning at me, I realize how crazy I'm being.

I'm not going over there, that's insane. I can't do that. What the hell is wrong with me? Beau purses his lips and blows a kiss my way while the girl nuzzles his neck and wraps her arms around his waist. I watch as he tips his cup back and takes a swallow. Never once does he look away from me and that does something to me.

Watching Beau goes straight to my clit and I wince. Oh no. I can't want him. Why is my body like this? I whirl around and slam the bathroom door open with my palms and sprint to the showers. I can't want Beau. I have to get clean and into bed. The sooner I'm clean and in my bed, the easier it will be to pretend that nothing happened to me tonight.

I shower as fast as I can and use the hottest water my body can stand. The water swirling around the drain turns red and then pink before it finally runs clear. This time no one comes for me in the shower. I'm also not alone in the bathroom, which helps settle my nerves. I can hear girls coming in and out while I shower and dress. There's someone throwing up in a stall and another girl sobbing while her friend consoles her.

All in all, it's what I would expect for a college party. Everyone is in their own world and I dress the wound with the first aid kit I find fixed to the wall beside the sinks. There's a lot of bandages in the box, but I settle on one that looks close enough to flesh colored and is flexible enough to curve to my neck where Beau cut me. It's not too noticeable if you don't look at me closely, or at least that's what I tell myself. I'm sure Sunny will spot it right away, but seeing as she's my only friend on campus, I'll be okay.

When I leave the bathroom, I'm glad Beau isn't there with the girl anymore. I get into bed and turn the lights off while I try not to think about what they're probably doing together now that they aren't in the hallway anymore.

Anger flares in my belly at Beau for the first time ever. It's sudden, sharp and bitter. I almost choke on it with how strong I feel it, but I breathe through it and let it roll over me until I'm left exhausted and finally, I fall asleep.

"Welcome to Death and Dying."

Professor Mrose smiles at us as he walks the length of the lecture hall and claps his hands over his stomach. "I am extremely pleased to have you all joining me this semester for what I know will be a truly memorable educational opportunity for all of you. As you know The History of Death and Dying is only taught in the Fall every two years. It is the university's most sought after history course for undergraduate and graduate students alike." He pauses and scans the room. "For some of you, it has been a long hard road to gaining entry into this lecture hall and I commend you for your tenacity." Professor Mrose lifts his hands to the room and raises his voice. "A round of applause for our tenacious seniors who never thought they would cross the threshold to this illustrious room!"

I laugh as someone lets out a whoop and the room claps and hollers along, while the professor encourages it with a cupped hand to his ear. A minute of cheering goes by before he throws his hands up and waves us off.

"All right, all right. Order! Let's bring order to our meeting of the minds! However, I would like to make it known that we do have a handful of freshmen in attendance." There's a handful of booing and shouts but Professor Mrose shakes his head and wags a finger.

"Now, now! Is that anyway to receive the luckiest among us? "Blessed is he who has learned to admire but not envy.' Who are we to begrudge those with Midas touch?"

My cheeks heat, because he's talking about me. I wish I didn't know who else was a freshman in the lecture hall, but there is one that I can spot without thinking.

Beau.

He's here with me. I saw him the second I hit the door, but he isn't alone. The girl from last night is there with him too. I hate that she's smiling at him. I hate it even more that he's looking at her and not me. I've seen Beau in two other classes this week—Psychology and Biology.

That's three so far. I'm praying there isn't a fourth, because I don't know if I can handle it.

"Now as you know, this history class will be unlike any other that you have encountered. There will be field work with each of you assigned fifty headstones to collect headstone rubbings of. We will supply the materials for this, courtesy of the lab fee each of you paid, and you will be responsible for cataloging and identifying noteworthy features of each headstone and grave. We will then pair this with a comprehensive overview of our wide and beautiful Kansas at the time of immigration and settling within the early part of the 19th century to create a vibrant narrative designed to illuminate just how integral early Kansans were the development of the United States as we know it today," Professor Mrose pauses and looks us over with a raised eyebrow. "This is, of course, going to be a demanding and exacting course, but you would not be here if you were not capable. Now, who is ready to venture into the underworld with me?"

A rousing cheer sounds and even though I'm upset that Beau is here with another girl wrapped around him, I join in. I might have thought to drop a class with Beau in it, but it won't be this one with how engaging Professor Mrose is. The class is everything I wanted when I dreamed of finally going to college. Even with Beau being in the same lecture hall, no one gives me a second look. I'm no one special when we are in Death and Dying and the feeling is a heady thing. I can be just like everyone else when I'm in class and that only solidifies my decision not to drop the class. Even with the craziness of the last couple of weeks, it's impossible not to be in a good mood when I leave the classroom. I smile the whole way back to my dorm. I can't wait to tell Sunny about my class. She's going to love it. I know it.

It's weird how normal things go after the night with Beau. I'm right that Sunny loves my news about being in Professor Mrose's class, and while she does give my neck a few lingering looks, she doesn't press about the bandage I'm wearing. I'm grateful, because even if the cut between my breasts isn't deep, it hurts. I made a mistake in not wrapping it and I make sure I do once I'm alone in my shower stall. Thankfully, Sunny is with me, so I don't have to worry about anyone hurting me. We watch another Romcom and skip dinner to order stuffed crust pizza. It's such a good night and when I fall asleep it's with a smile on my face.

After that, things slow down. People stop talking about The Reaper and life goes on. I don't hear from my mom, but Pastor Mike texts to check in. I feel bad and think I should probably go to church this Sunday as thanks. A week goes by and it isn't just in my Death and Dying class that people leave me be. It almost feels safe on campus. I've even started to venture out alone. I think the novelty of people hating me is slowly wearing off with PSL season about to hit. That or the excitement for our first football game next week outweighs someone beating my ass in the shower. Things have been quiet enough in our dorm since then, but I don't trust it. Not even Beau has messed with me. I see him in the classes we share, but he hasn't made a move to mess with me. I watch him just as closely as he watches me and even though he doesn't corner me, I know he's waiting for the right time.

He has to be. Nothing that's happened would make sense if he wasn't and I don't think it's a good omen that we both end up in Death and Dying together. The upside is that Professor Mrose does a lot of great upkeep of the cemeteries in town and I'm enjoying it so far. When I volunteered with Crown of Thorns, it was with a goal to volunteer and give back as much as I could to Bloom. The sad thing was that once I did start volunteering Pastor Mike and the rest of leadership made it clear. We weren't there for the sake of the work, but for souls. Winning souls was always our goal in the mission of saving and converting the people we were meant to serve, but here with Professor Mrose?

The work is selfless to the core.

The names and families we preserve and serve are already gone. Their souls forgotten to another time. All the work we do is for the joy of it. For a job well done and the preservation of Bloom's history. That feeds me on a level I never knew existed. But even with loving Professor Mrose and the class as much as I do, I've still thought about dropping the class but I can't bring myself to do it. I don't want to let Beau win. So I don't drop any of my classes, which is stupid. So very fucking stupid. I don't know if I'll have the same bravado in three months as I do right now, but I'm hopeful. It seems possible. At least, it is when I don't think about Beau using his belt to tie my hands while he fucked me and came all over me.

"So you really just went to bed with that party going on?" Sunny asks me. We're in the quad and she's eating fries while I try to get some homework done. The party she's talking about is the only night that I think about anymore. It's been two weeks since then and I look up from my homework to look at her. I don't know why she's bringing that party up now. Sunny throws a fry at me and I clear my throat.

"Yeah, I did. Why?"

"You didn't even talk to that cute boy?" she asks and flicks another fry at me.

I bat her fry away and raise an eyebrow. "Where is this going, Sunny?"

"Look, Nev. I just think a nice guy like that is a good move for you this year."

"Playing matchmaker?" I ask with a smile. It's nice that Sunny wants to try and give me something normal this year, but Dean isn't for me. The only normal thing I want from Sunny is her friendship. That's worth everything to me.

"A little," she sighs and slumps forward on the table and picks up her phone. "But also he found me this week and was asking about you."

"Why would he do that?" I ask and look back down at my paper and start to write again. I'm working on a headstone engraving that I did a rub of yesterday. Bloom is unique in its history. So many homesteaders and pioneers came through here when it was a trading post, and they either settled or kept moving on towards California or Utah. The ones that settled made the foundation for what Bloom is now, but so many pioneers were never given the chance to make Bloom their home. At least not while they were alive.

Our town has six cemeteries. All but two were founded with the settling of the town in 1803. That being said, there's a lot of graves no one has paid attention to and our class was given a map with over five hundred headstones that haven't been cataloged yet. We are supposed to do fifty of them this semester. We will catalog the names and dates along with any details that stand out and input them into a shared database. It's interesting, even if it's depressing when I really stop and look at the dates for birth and death.

I frown and run a finger over the rice paper I used. *Maxwell*. That's the only name for the one I have right now. I don't know if it's their first name or their last. It's for an infant, just a few months old. The headstone was so small when I did the rubbing. There wasn't much else to it and I didn't see any headstones marked mother or father near it, which makes it all the more heartbreaking. I don't like to think of the baby being all alone. Where did their family go? Did they stay in Bloom or did they move on?

"Ummm, *helloooo*. Because he likes you!" Sunny exclaims and breaks through my brooding session over Baby Maxwell.

"I don't think that's true," I lie and tuck Maxwell's paper into my binder before I close it. A gust of wind blows hard and kicks leaves up around us. I shove my hair out of my face while Sunny scowls at me.

"He is *so* into you and you know it. He said that you have a class together."

I nod. "We do."

"Okay, so why haven't I heard anything about him?"

I shrug and lean back to stretch my arms over my head and turn my face up to the sky. It's a nice day. The sun is out and the weather is perfect. It's easy to feel normal sitting here with Sunny talking about boys, but there's a feeling I can't shake that comes with Dean.

Talking about Dean unnerves me.

"There's not much to tell. Dean is my friend. He's a nice guy." Again, I lie. Dean seems like he's a nice guy. He hasn't done anything weird or made any moves, but it feels like he's waiting for something. He watches me almost as much as Beau does, too.

"You don't think it's weird that he found you on socials?" I ask her. Dean found me and I didn't give it much thought. Not until he showed up at the party. He's been nice in class too. Sticking by my side in Psych while Beau pretends I don't exist, while the blonde girl I've seen with him giggles and leans into his side. My fingers clench. I hate that girl.

"Nah, he said I had Algebra with him, but I guess I didn't notice. That class is really, really, huge, though," she tells me and I pause. Sunny doesn't sound worried. She's a lot more normal than me and she didn't let the guy she put in prison cut her and take her virginity, but then again...I don't think many people can relate to what I've done with Beau, so being more normal than me is pretty easy. In any case, she's not worried about Dean, so maybe I'm just overreacting.

"Dean is just a friend and I'd like him to stay that way," I tell her.

Sunny looks like she might throw another fry at me but when she takes in the look on my face she stops and straightens up. "Oh, wow, you're serious, huh?" She shoves the fry in her mouth and chews with a nod. "Okay, I'll stop playing matchmaker, even if I think you two would be cute."

I let out a sigh of relief. Sunny is actually going to listen to me. I'm not used to anyone listening to me. Not my mom, not the cops when I wasn't sure about that night, not Beau when I tried to say I was sorry.

I smile at Sunny. It's nice to be listened to. "Thank you for listening to me."

She gives me a salute with one of her fries. "Of course. That's what friends do. Speaking of friends…how is everyone else? People leaving you alone?"

"They are. I think they're too excited for the football game to care about me right now." I tell her and close my binder and put it in my backpack.

"Yeah, I kind of don't get that."

"What do you mean?"

"I mean, after what happened to that girl they found in the river. Everyone just…went back to normal. It's like someone pressed the reset button around here. It's so weird." She looks around the quad and shakes her head. "This place is kind of messed up, Nev."

"Yeah, I know."

"We're going to that football game though."

I snort. "What happened to 'this place is messed up?'"

"I mean, it is messed up, but we have to carve out as much of a college experience as we can. That means we are going to the first football game. If you aren't going to let me be a matchmaker, then come to the game with me. What's the worst that can happen?"

The last time I did as Sunny asked for the sake of a college experience I ended up alone and bleeding with Beau. I won't tell her that, though.

"I don't know…"

"Come on, Nevvvv. Please? It's going to be so fun! It's all anyone is talking about on campus. We have to go. Say we will," she raises a finger in the air and leans back to look at me, "and before you try and get out of it, you need to come to this game. You're going to graveyards and spending way too much time studying."

"It's for the Death and Dying database!"

"I said what I said, Nev."

"Ugh. Fine."

CHAPTER SEVENTEEN
BEAU

I'M GIVING NEVAEH distance. Space or whatever the fuck it is. I didn't want Nevaeh thinking about what we'd done and running home right after I finally got my first taste of her, so I let off the gas. I fucking hate it, but I'm doing it. Seems like the student body is taking its cue from me and are giving her breathing room too. I'm still keeping an eye on her, though. It wouldn't suit me for someone else to sink their teeth into my girl while I'm taking a step back.

So far no one has made a move. I haven't seen her go home once or her mother visit, which seems odd. From what I know, Nevaeh never spent any time away from home other than the church summer camps she helped at or the youth conferences Pastor Mike organized every year. My mother made sure to keep tabs on Nevaeh and her mother while I was locked up. She kept a close eye and did everything she could to keep them close and well connected in the church for fear they might move away from Bloom, but they never even made a move to spend time away, not even for vacations.

She's not used to being away from her mother, so why is she now? Something doesn't feel right there.

No one from Crown of Thorns talks to Nevaeh. There's only her roommate that sticks by her and that fucker I want to gut when I see him sit next to her in class. If I'm reading things right, Nevaeh doesn't like him much, but for some reason she doesn't tell him to fuck off.

"The game is tonight. You ready, man?" Jordan claps me on the back so hard that if I wasn't bigger than him it might make me stumble forward a step, but I just smile.

I plaster a fake as hell smile on my face. "Ready as I'll ever be. Grateful for the opportunity."

"Don't worry about a thing, brother. I'm going to take care of you out there. You'll make that bench look good, but we're going to bring you in for some action, okay? It's not a conference game so no worries on how it goes. We all know you're not going to be solid right out the gate, but all you have to do is watch me." He takes a deep breath and puffs his chest out as he walks. The sight is comical, because Jordan isn't a big guy. You can't be if you're going to be a QB. You have to be fast, smart, and lean. Not big. So he looks like a fucking chicken with the way he's strutting, but I keep my mouth shut while he talks. "I know you used to be top dog, but times are different. You're doing good in practice and with the footage, though. I've been getting the run down on your progress and it's good for what you're working with. I guess they don't really push cardio in the clink, right?" He laughs and it sounds like nails on a chalkboard. Like a fucking donkey braying with how loud and abrupt it is. He reaches back and claps me on the back again. My skin stings and there's no denying that he's trying to send a message with that hit. "You'll learn everything you need. If you're lucky, we'll let you get some touches in a low stakes conference game. How does that sound?" Jordan sounds like a condescending fuck. It's not what he's saying but the shit eating grin on his face and his tone.

He thinks he's better than me. He wants me to understand that tonight. Interesting. Why is he so threatened by ex-felon? I don't give a fuck about the game, even if I've been going to practices twice a day faithfully and attending the team meetings and running footage with the rest of the team and coaches. I'm under no illusions that I'm not a charity case, being on the team as a third string QB as a twenty three year old freshman, but no one on staff or any of my teammates lets on they see me that way. Even if football isn't something I care about anymore, it is nice to sink into a little bit of normalcy. I'm surprised I even recognize normal anymore, considering that I'm fucked up as they come.

In love or not, cutting Nevaeh shouldn't have made fucking her all the sweeter. It did though. The control I had over her with the knife in my hand when we were together. Ecstasy. I played my role perfectly. I was exactly who she told the cops I was, told the entire town even, but she liked it. I could hear it in her cries. The way she moved under me. Nevaeh wanted to be with me, even when I spanked the shit out of her.

"It'll be good to just get out on the field," I tell him while memories of Nevaeh's ass jiggling beneath my hand play on repeat in my head. In prison I got good at retreating into memories. Into those perfect slices of life that you swear you won't forget but we all do, because they happen so fast. In prison, I learned to slow down my life enough that the seconds and minutes I took for granted were easier to grab hold of and stay a while. It helped me keep most of my sanity, most of the time. I suspect I'll be doing it again here while I try to play it cool with Jordan and the others. Ali is already on my last fucking nerve. I let her kiss me at the party but that's it. She's arm candy for campus and for pissing off Nevaeh, but nothing more. My phone buzzes in my pocket. It's probably Ali bringing up the football game, too.

Exhausting. I'll have to cut her loose soon, even if her presence is a nice fuck you to Nevaeh. That only entertains me when it's not inconvenient to me, and Ali is starting to become a burden with her uncanny ability to materialize wherever I am. I don't like that she's watching me that close. I glance over at Jordan. He's talking again, another guy from the football team is with us now so at least I don't have to pay attention to what they're saying.

We're walking across campus. Towards the quad for food. We had a pretty low key workout today more meant to keep us warm rather than push us to our limit. That's going to come tonight. Right now we need fuel. With Jordan calling me brother and falling into step beside me, I'm going to fucking get stuck eating with this asshole, I know it.

I hate that I'm right and end up at a table with Jordan and half the team. Everyone is hyped for the game though, so it's easy enough to blend in and watch Nevaeh. She's just outside the doors. I can see her through the windows that line the dining area. She's with Sunny and working on something. She's bent close to it and even at a distance, I can spot the distinct dark smudges of the gravestone rubbing.

I don't know why the fuck Nevaeh wanted to end up in a class called Death and Dying but she did, so I made my advisor make it happen. The class seems interesting enough, even with the time we're going to be alone in graveyards. A dumb fucking choice given the fact that The Reaper hunts at random, but whatever. Bloom doesn't seem to care much about the killer in the everyday scheme of things. The class is good though. I have Nevaeh close and I plan to make use of our alone time for the database project soon.

"Hey, Beau!" Ali's voice makes me wince but I force it down and lift my head to see her approaching the table with a smile on her face. Somehow, Ali is in the class with Nevaeh and I even though it's hard for underclassmen to get in.

"Hi, Ali. What's up?" I ask. I catch Jordan straightening up across the table from me. I thought he cut her loose, but from the look on his face he doesn't want anyone else talking to her. I decide to have a little fun since it's a sore spot with the fucker.

"Haven't seen you in a while, beautiful. You mad at me?"

Ali blushes and giggles while the guys at the table settle down. They were all busy laughing and eating but Ali is a pretty girl, so they'll pay attention if she's here. "Oh, I'm not mad at you. I tried texting you earlier but you didn't answer me, so don't push it." She wags a finger at me in a flirty move but the only thing I want to do is slap her hand away from me.

I lean back in my seat and shrug. "Busy with the game and school, but I knew you'd catch me." I'm not lying. I knew she would find me, which is why I have to get rid of her. Maybe having fun isn't the play I want to make right now. I glance over at Jordan and shoot him a smile. "You know my friend Jordan though, right?" I ask.

Jordan perks up when I mention him but Ali crosses her arms and shrugs. Maybe he didn't cut her off. "Yeah, sure. We've talked before."

"Nice to see you again, Ali," Jordan offers and a few guys snicker and elbow one another. I shoot them a sharp look and the laughter dies down. Even if I'm third string, they want me to like them. Fuck if I know why. "Uh, h-how are you these days?"

He's nervous. The fucker that wanted to establish pecking order to a too old third string QB, is nervous around a girl like Ali. She was definitely the one to cut it off. I wonder what a golden goose like Jordan did. He's the man to be on campus. Looks like I read her all wrong at the party. Ali was using me for sure, but not in the way I thought. Ali can't be talking to me for any other reason than to make him jealous, I decide.

"I thought I saw you two talking at the party last week. We're supposed to have another one tonight. You invite her yet, man?" I ask Jordan.

His eyes go wide and his cheeks go pink. "W-what?" he stammers.

"The party," I say, feeding him the answer. "Weren't you going to invite her?"

Jordan is a dumb fuck so he stares at me for a hot second before he bobs his head. "O-oh yeah, yeah, I was. Uh, thanks for reminding me."

"No problem, *brother*." I want to puke after saying that but 'When in Rome' and all that shit.

I look at Ali and she's got her hands on her hips. She raises an eyebrow at him. "Well, are you going to ask me or was that it?" she snaps with a tap of her foot. She's wearing heels so there's a definitive click to punctuate her question. I have to hide my laughter, but the guys at the table don't bother. They burst into hysterics and start fucking with Jordan, who ducks his head and mumbles a, "Do you want to go to the party with me, Ali?"

"No," she snaps.

Yeah, Jordan fucked right up somewhere. Maybe he didn't pick up dinner, I don't know. Seems like the type of thing Ali would lose her shit about. Instead, she looks at me.

"How about *you* take me to the party, handsome?" It's a question, but it sounds like a statement. I don't want to do it, but at least if I do, I'm fucking with Jordan.

"Yeah, all right. I'd like that."

"Awesome! I'll meet you after the game tonight, okay?" Ali bounces on her toes and winks at me before she gives me a little wave. "I have to go, but call me okay?"

"Sure thing."

"We are going to have so much fun," she tells me while she makes a point not to look at Jordan. She flips her hair over her shoulder and struts off. The whole table falls silent to watch her leave. Ali might not be my kind of girl, but there's no denying she's got an ass on her.

No one says anything for a beat before someone clears their throat and tosses a wadded up napkin at Jordan. "What the fuck did you do, man? Cheat?"

"No, I didn't fucking cheat, asshole. I didn't text or whatever when she wanted and she's been like that since the goddamn dorm rager."

"Thought I saw you making out with that one girl. The redhead," someone else says. And Jordan ducks his head.

"Look, I was really drunk that night."

I clear my throat and shrug. "It happens," I lie. I'm a lot of things and I've been a lot of things, I've killed and stolen, lied and broken laws to get what I needed, but I've never cheated. I'm a one woman kind of man. Always have been and always would be. Lucky, fucking Nevaeh. She's never going to be free of me.

Jordan glares at me. "Don't fucking start with me. You're taking her to the party."

"I couldn't tell her no. It would have embarrassed her," I say and gesture around the table. "You think she was gonna talk to you again if she got embarrassed in front of the entire starting line?" I ask.

Jordan stops, his mouth opens like he's going to speak but then he closes it and nods. "Yeah, okay, that makes sense."

I lean forward, brace my elbows on the table and pitch my voice like I give a fuck about him, or Ali, or anyone at the table. "Listen, it's easy. I take her to the party as a way to get her there and you swoop in like prince charming and ask her to talk. I'm not going to stand in the way and you can fix whatever the fuck happened, okay?"

"That's a pretty good plan," Billy chimes in. The rest of the guys murmur in agreement and Jordan stops pulling his bitch ass face.

He smiles at me and nods. "All right, brother. Sorry, I read that shit wrong. Shoulda known you got my back."

"Always man. You know it. Besides, I'm into another girl, all right?" It feels safe to tell them there's someone else. They'll have to see Nevaeh and

I together soon enough. I'm breaking my liar, my beautiful fucking angel, shattering her into a million little pieces that I can put together in the way I like best. But when I'm done, I don't plan on being shy about showing the world she's mine.

"Ohhh, so there's a lucky lady for you then? Nice to see you didn't waste any time from being locked up." Jordan is a loud fuck and as much as he swears that he's my friend, he sure does bring up me being in prison an awful fucking lot. I'll have to watch his ass for more than the jealous boyfriend and insecure athlete bullshit.

I nod and brush past his mention of my time behind bars. "There is. Four years was a long time to go without a good woman. Don't plan on wasting time now that I'm free."

Billy grins and raises his soda can to me. "That's fucking beautiful, man. Good luck with her." The rest of the idiots raise their cups to me and give me their blessing like it means anything to me.

I lift my cup and take a quick sip. "Appreciate it. I'll need all the luck to make a woman like her mine."

I did four years for her, after all. She's mine and they're all going to know it. But there is the problem with tonight that I now suddenly have. How do I get Nevaeh to come to the party? There's no way she'll put herself in the line of fire if she doesn't have to. The dorm party was easy enough because there was no getting away from it when it was happening right outside her door. Tonight is going to take some planning.

I pull out my phone and think as I scroll. I pull up Nevaeh's profile and stare at the light. It's green. When I lean back to look out the windows where I saw her earlier, I see she's on her phone while her friend chatters away. She looks so carefree and happy. I type out a message and hit send and just like magic, I watch her change. Her shoulder tense and she drops her phone on the table while her friend looks at her in surprise. God, seeing her panic goes straight to my dick and I can't look away from her. There's no one else but Nevaeh. Just my beautiful fucking liar panicking while the world falls away. I can't read her friend's lips, but I know she's asking Nevaeh what's wrong.

Nevaeh looks around the quad. She's trying to find me. When she doesn't see me, she stands quickly and starts to gather her books while she gestures for her friend to follow her. The girls leave a minute later with Nevaeh looking over her shoulder the entire time. I love seeing her panic, her fear is like an aphrodisiac to me and I want more.

I'll always fucking want more.

My phone buzzes with a message and I smile when I see Nevaeh's name. I knew she was going to respond. Just like the good girl she is, she tells me exactly what I want to hear.

"Okay, I'll be there. I promise."

CHAPTER EIGHTEEN

Nevaeh

> Come to the party after the game tonight. 1570 Mathias Ave. Promise me you will, or else, Angel. I'll come find you and we both know you don't want that.

I **DON'T KNOW WHAT** to do. It's from Beau. I freeze and drop my phone on the table with a gasp though and look like an idiot.

"You okay?" Sunny asks. She's concerned and I have to give her my fakest, brightest smile for her to let it go.

"Yeah, I'm fine. I just remembered I have a report due that I forgot about tomorrow. I have to go work on it now if I'm going to go, ah, to that party later."

Sunny perks up. "Party? What party? I thought I just talked you into going to the football game. There's a party we're going to now?"

I nod quickly and stand fast as I grab my books and start shoving them into my bag. I have to get out of here. Beau's close, I can feel it. I don't know how or why, but I can. I look around the quad and don't see him anywhere. I can still feel eyes on me though. I need to get out of the open.

"Um, yeah, it's like, an after party or whatever, I guess? I forgot about it."

"Since when do you go to parties?" Sunny asks as she skips ahead of me. "I'm not mad about it but like, I had to talk you into the game so...." She twirls and gives me a raised eyebrow. She's curious. That's what I love about her, but I have to throw her off the scent of why I want to go to the party, because I didn't think *The guy I'm in love with who definitely took my virginity and threatened to slit my throat, also threatened to come find me if I didn't* wasn't going to go over well with Sunny.

"Maybe the ghosts told me to do it," I tell her, opting for a light approach. "All that time in the graveyards really has them concerned about me lately, you know?"

Sunny laughs and I know it worked. "Yeah, I bet they're a real scream."

"You don't even know the half of it," I joke and then shrug as I offer her a more genuine smile. "I just, well, maybe you're right that I'm missing out on the college experience because of what's happening. I heard about the party in a class and decided what the hell?"

"You promise not to ditch to sleep at this party?" she asks with a wag of her finger.

Sleep. That's what she thinks I was doing. I think about Beau and what it felt like to have his body on mine. His hard dick inside of me while he whispered my name. There was no denying the orgasm that he forced out of me. I've never felt anything like it before. He forced bliss and ecstasy on me, all the messy and beautiful parts of my body that the church made me think were dirty. Beau took those parts and turned them into something new and overwhelming, he made it feel like my life was ending and beginning in those seconds and minutes that he touched me the way I was never brave enough to explore fully.

Guilt and shame always stopped me from reaching orgasm, but when I did touch myself it was to him. It was always to Beau. I wasn't dumb enough to think that there would ever be anyone else for me but Beau. There couldn't be. As fucked up and twisted as it was, there was no one else for me. It makes sense that it was him that woke that part of me up and forced it into being.

The sad truth of it is that Beau didn't have to threaten me to get me to go to the party. He didn't have to tell me he would come find me. The *Or Else* wasn't needed, because I would go anywhere and do anything he asked me, even if I put up a fight at first.

"This is going to be even better than the dorm party!" Sunny whoops and runs up the steps to our dorm. There's people outside but they ignore me. I'm glad for it. I don't know how long it's going to last. This fragile peace that's marked the past two weeks of my life on campus can't go on forever, and with Beau contacting me, I feel like it's over and something big is on the way. I felt this way before the trial and after for weeks on end. My therapist said it was anxiety and Survivor's Guilt, this feels the same now. I rub my palms on my thighs as I follow Sunny up the stairs and into the dorm. There's only a few hours before the game tonight. It's an evening game with a late afternoon kickoff, so I don't have much time left before I see Beau. Because against my better judgment, I'm going to do something stupid and reckless. Almost as stupid as agreeing to see Beau tonight, but stupid and reckless is all I've ever been when it comes to him.

Tonight, I'm not waiting for the party to see Beau. I'm going to take it straight to him at the game and force him to tell me what he wants from me. Let's see how much he likes getting surprised on his home turf this time.

"What the fuck is going on down there, really?" Sunny yells as we move with the crowd. There's a cheer moving through the student section. Every other student moves forward where they stand, while the one next to them leans back with the drum beats from the band. I have zero clue what's happening on the field, but I know this cheer— the Bloom Beat. It's the same one that we did in high school to our school fight song and they do the same thing here at Bloom State.

"I don't know!" I yell back as we move. I have to put my hand on Sunny's shoulder and force her to move opposite of me because she keeps syncing up with my movements. We both laugh hysterically and Sunny throws her arms out.

"I can't help it! I have no rhythm!"

"It's okay, I got you!" I keep my hand steady on her shoulder and help her along. Even with the party looming over me and the decision I made to see Beau after the game weighing on me, I feel light. Maybe I'm getting desensitized, what with everything going on lately. Which, considering the town I grew up in, is saying a lot. Sunny is right, though. What's happening isn't normal, but I don't think I would know what to do with normal. That's probably why I'm not scared off from Beau. He's everything I want, but it's warped and twisted into a dangerous package no sane person *should* want. Sunny shrieks and throws her arms out in frustration when she slams into me, but I force her back into the right rhythm again and laugh with her. A cheer goes up on the field and I see someone score a touchdown.

"Nice!" I yell and jump with everyone else. Someone I don't know high fives me while the student section loses its collective shit. We're having fun. It's a perfect fall evening before the bitter chill of winter sets in, one of those perfect nights that you think of when someone says football season. And it's all mine. The smile vanishes from my face when I see hard eyes staring up at me.

Minnie.

She's about six rows down and dead center in front of me, but while everyone else is jumping, clapping and screaming, she's not moving. She's staring straight at me with her arms crossed over her chest. Hate. That's the only way I can describe how she's looking at me. I've never really seen Minnie hate anything, except for when the truth about Beau and what I saw that night came out. She hated me then and she hates me now. God, why is she staring at me?

A chill passes through me and I go still under her hateful gaze. I don't know what to do or where to go, but then Sunny throws her arms around my waist and lifts me.

"This is so *fun!*" she screams.

When she puts me back down on my feet, Minnie isn't there anymore. I scan the audience trying to find her, but there's nothing. Everyone is a stranger and there's nothing but smiling faces, no hard eyes or glares. Minnie vanished in that split second. I don't know why, but that scares me worse than when she was looking at me. The light energy I felt during the game is gone and I spend the rest of the game tense and watching for Minnie. She never pops back up, which is a good thing. But I can't get the way she was looking at me out of my head. I'm so focused on trying to find her that I don't even really realize that the game is over until Sunny is nudging me in the ribs.

"Do you want to get some food before the party? What time was it again?" she asks, pulling her phone out. I see 8:30 flash on the screen. I have zero clue when the party is starting. The only thing I have is an address and a threat from Beau, but I know exactly what I need to do to find out.

"I have a friend I can go ask," I tell her, stepping towards the aisle. "Stay here and I'll go ask them."

"Awesome! I'll stay put!" Sunny gives me a thumbs up and I don't miss that she's already got some guy talking to her.

"I'll hurry. Text me if you need me to come back," I tell her and look at the guy meaningfully.

Sunny rolls her eyes and makes a shooing motion at me. "Don't worry, I can handle him. Go talk to your *friend*." From the singsong tone in her voice, I know Sunny's guessed I'm sneaking off to talk to someone I like. She was so excited to get me to talk to Dean, that I bet she hopes it's him. I really don't know how I'm going to tell her it's Beau. Maybe when I see him tonight he's going to tell me that he's done with me. That he wanted to scare me and he did it and things are over.

Maybe when I confront him, he'll tell me everything was one huge mistake.

I know that's not going to happen, but I can't help but think it. It's a last ditch effort to make sense of everything. That all of this is a bad prank and now it's over. I wrap my arms around myself when the wind picks up. Kansas is a windy place, sometimes the wind blows so hard and so often that it feels like you're at the beach. I'm happy right now isn't one of those times, but the breeze blowing through the night is chilly. All around me everyone is happy and laughing, running down the stairs and sprinting towards the football field. I don't really know why since it's a small game, but I'm not going to begrudge anyone their happiness. The band is still playing in the stands while fans cheer and dance along, but it doesn't feel real. For some reason, not a lot of things have felt real in my life since the night Carrie died. But there is one night that makes me believe things can change.

The night of the party. The night Beau took what he wanted from me and made me see stars. That's the night everything feels like it's hinged on. One wrong move in either direction can send the fragile deck of cards holding up my life to the floor. I don't know what's going to happen to me when the semester lets out and the school forces everyone out of the dorms. It's radio silence from my mom, which means I'm not welcome home. Maybe I'll stay here. Maybe I'll leave. Transfer somewhere new and try to start over. The thought of leaving Sunny makes my heart hurt.

She's a real friend. I haven't had a real friend in a long time. Maybe ever.

I duck my head and keep walking down the cement steps and head into the stadium. I know where the locker room is because I made sure to find the signs earlier. It's a few minutes walk away from the field and I find it without trouble. When I get there, players are filing out and joining their waiting families and friends. They have wet hair and towels around their necks, duffle bags on their shoulders and smiles on their faces. I lean against the wall and clasp my hands in front of me because I don't know what else to do. I know people are noticing me.

I get why, even after a week of peace, they're stopping to look my way on their walk down the hall from the locker rooms. It would be weird for the football team to ignore me when they tried to leave me out for The Reaper like a sacrifice and all that. But I'm proud of myself, because I do something I haven't done before. Not really.

I ignore them.

I outright ignore the stares and let it roll off me like water off a duck's back. I don't care, I tell myself, as I force myself not to. Maybe everyone I see that seems like they don't care really does, but they're pretending. Maybe pretending you don't care is how you actually get there. I do my best until a familiar figure walks out of the locker room and stops a second later. I should have known it wouldn't take long for Beau to see me. I push away from the wall and stand taller while he looks me over. His eyes move from my feet to my head and back again, before they come to my neck. I'm wearing a Bloom State shirt with a V-neck. It's a cute shirt with a cougar on the front, the school's mascot. It's one of my favorites that I've had for a few years. It was an easy choice for the game, even if I know what Beau is looking at.

His eyes are my neck. The bandage on my neck. The wound he gave me wasn't deep and it's scabbing over nicely, but it still looks angry around the edges. I'd rather get a look because I'm wearing a bandage than have people see the cut he gave me.

Beau walks up to me and stops a foot away. "You're covering my mark, Nevaeh. Can't say that I'm a fan."

I cross my arms and shrug. "Can't say that I'm a fan of your mark, Beau."

His blue eyes light up and he grins at me. "You're sassy tonight. Good. I like it when you fight me."

That surprises me. I fall back a step but I hold his gaze, even when he comes a step closer. I feel like prey trapped in front of a snake. He's tracking my movements. Any wrong move and he's going to strike. God, why did I think this was a good idea? I feel out of my depth now that I'm standing in front of Beau.

"I don't know what you mean."

"I mean, I like it when you struggle. I like it when you convince yourself you don't want what I'm doing to you. I want you to run, angel. Are you going to run for me tonight?"

My breath hitches at his words. Why is what he's saying making my body go hot? My clit throbs and I have to force myself not to rub my thighs together for the friction of it.

"Stop it, Beau," I snap at him. "I'm here because I'm not doing this anymore."

"Oh, is that right?"

"Yes. We need to talk. I mean it."

"Talk about what?" he asks and I want to scream at him and the lazy look he sends my way. It's not fair that he's perfect. Even after all these years, even after he played a game of football, he looks calm and collected. Perfect and beautiful. His dark hair falls over his eyes. It's wet from a shower, so there's a natural curl to it. His blue eyes draw me in like normal, though they're darker today. I like it because they only look that way when Beau's eyes are on me. He's dressed well, in a pair of slacks, a linen shirt and a jacket slung over one arm while he carries his duffle bag over one shoulder.

I swallow hard. It's getting harder to talk to him the longer I'm standing here, so I may as well just get it over with. "Us," I blurt out.

Beau's grin turns into a smile and then he throws his head back and laughs. He genuinely laughs. People stop to stare at us while the sweet sound of his laughter echoes around us. Anger fills my veins. Beau laughing at me like I'm crazy while he's dressed perfectly and looking utterly untouchable is how I always thought this would go when I was fourteen. Back then, he was the fixation of my every obsessive daydream. As much as I tried to focus on what it would be like to tell him that I had feelings for him and have him take me seriously, I could never make the daydream work.

There was always some flaw that got in the way and ruined the fantasy for me. Beau laughing at me was the number one thing that I was fearful of. Having it happen to me now after years, after what we did together and what he took from me, I'm angry. He knows what sex means to me. What having him as my first would mean to me and he did it anyway, because he wanted to hurt me again. I hate that he's hurting me right now with his laughter. That's probably why I say what I say.

"Shut the fuck up you asshole."

Instantly Beau's laughter stops and he stills. If I wasn't standing as close as I am to him, I wouldn't even be sure he was breathing with how quiet and calm he gets. Those marble statues roped off at museums have more life to them than Beau does right now.

"What the fuck did you say to me?" His voice is a growl. Low and rough. It feels like the jagged edge of a blade slicing across my skin and I instantly put my hands up, blocking where he cut my chest when he had me on my knees.

"I'm sorry."

"No you're not." Beau shakes his head, tilts his head to the side and looks at me like he's seeing me for the first time. "Kitten has claws after all," he murmurs.

I shake my head. "I was angry. I didn't mean it, I-"

Beau grabs my wrist and jerks me forward with him when he starts down the hallway. "Oh but you did mean it, angel. You did. Lucky for you, I liked it."

"You did?" I ask. I don't believe him. He has to be trying to make me feel safe, but for what?

We round the hallway and I stumble, but Beau's grip on me keeps me upright. A second later he puts an arm around my waist and keeps me pressed close. To anyone looking at us, they would see friends, lovers, people that are close.

We aren't close, though. Beau is my tormentor, an angry god out for vengeance. I'm the idiot that just pissed him off.

"I did. I like my women with a little fight in them. Last time you let me down, angel." He unlocks a door and shoves me in before I can answer him. "This time, why don't you try getting away." There's nothing but darkness in front of me. I stumble forward and hit my hands on something and my foot catches on the edge of it as I try to steady myself. I cry out and almost trip but then Beau flips on the light and I see that I ran into an old sponsorship sign for one of the local car dealers in town.

"What are you going to do to me?" I back up from Beau and almost trip again. He sighs as he watches and crosses his arms over his chest. The dress shirt he's wearing stretches tight in all the right places and he tosses the jacket he was carrying over an old table that's turned on its side, stacked against the wall beside the door.

"Where are we?"

"Somewhere no one is going to look for you, angel. Your ass is mine. You think running your mouth to me is going to get you off, just because I want you to fight me?" he asks and snaps the door lock in place.

Oh fuck. What was I thinking? Why did I curse at him? I called him an asshole. This isn't going to end well for me, I know that. I have to get away from him, but where? There's nowhere to go now that he's locked the door. I look around the room, desperate for an escape. It looks like an old supply room and it's surprisingly big. There are folding tables everywhere. Some are stored in stacks while others are up, like someone decided not to bother breaking them down when they stored them. I see signage from old games, sponsors and concessions in here, along with metal gate barricades that are haphazardly stored. There's a line of windows that run the length of the room, but they're tinted so hardly any light from the field comes in. I see what looks like volleyball netting strung along a wall, but other than that, there's nothing. No doors or hallways from the room. It's just me, alone and trapped in this room with Beau.

Oh god. Oh no.

"What? How-I don't understand." I point at the door and try to sound braver than I feel. "Beau, let me out or else."

"Or else? That's my line, Nevaeh. You know I'm going to have to punish you even more for that, don't you? You don't threaten me, angel." Beau stalks towards me, dropping his duffle bag on the ground as he approaches and points a finger at me. *"Ever."*

Or Else. Oh fuck. I can't believe I just said that.

"I'm sorry," I whisper. It's quiet in the storage room. Even though it feels big, it's like the walls are shrinking around us, moving in closer until I can't turn without running into something. Everywhere I look there's something blocking my path. I take a quick step back and slam my hip into a table.

"I'm sorry," I try again. I hear the band in the distance. The drums are still going and if I listen hard enough, I can hear cheers from the remaining students who are still having fun and partying on the field and in the stands. The windows. What if I get to the windows? I scan the wall of windows and see handles at the top of them. I bet they're the kind that you can pull towards you. The ones that don't open all the way, but would open enough if I was trying to squeeze out of one. As crazy as it feels, I know it's my only hope. The windows. I have to get to the windows.

"Beau, listen, I-I-" I stammer and stop before I try again. "I wanted to talk to you. I shouldn't have talked to you like that."

Beau clicks his tongue and walks towards me. He rolls his sleeves up as he does and looks completely at ease. He looks like we're just having a pleasant chat and not like I'm considering the best way to shimmy out of a window to get away from him.

"Oh Nevaeh. You really shouldn't have, but I'm glad you did."

I take a step back, it's a miracle I don't hit anything, because I'm not looking. My eyes are on Beau. My only thought is to get as far back as I can and then make a break for the windows.

"What? But you're mad."

"Doesn't mean my dick isn't hard."

I gasp at his words and I can't help the blush that makes my face hot. "Beau..."

"What? Don't use that language?" He laughs. The sound of it is bitter and sharp. It cuts me just like his words do. "I already fucked you raw. What's the point in pretending you're a lady, Nevaeh? You're not a lady, angel. You're just my dirty whore now."

Tears sting my eyes and I have to bite my cheek from telling him to go to hell. "No, that's not true." My voice shakes. I don't even sound like I believe it.

What if he's right?

"Nevaeh, that pussy has been mine since you put me away."

What if I want him to be right?

"Every day I did behind bars was another day I earned in breeding you so fucking full of my cum that I'm going to have you pregnant and shamed like the slut everyone knows you are."

"*No!*" I point a finger at him.

"Everyone is going to see it when your belly gets round with my baby. They're going to know you let someone fuck you. I'm not going to claim you or the bastard you're going to push out." He takes another step towards me and gives me a mean smile. "You're going to give me that baby and another and another, angel. What you did to me is going to be your very own fucking *Scarlet Letter*. What do you think your dear mommy and the church elders are going to think of that? I don't see you getting to stay here, trying to take care of a baby on your own. Do you?"

I should be sick to my stomach with what he's saying but, like usual, all logic leaves my body when it's Beau saying these terrible things to me. When I take another two hurried steps back from him, I can feel my panties starting to get damp.

"I-I'll leave!" I shout at him. I don't think anyone is going to hear me, no matter how hard I yell, but I want to do it. I'm angry with him. I'm so fucking mad.

"Where are you gonna go, Nevaeh? I'm not going to let you take my baby from me."

"You're not doing that to me!" I scream at him, even though my body is screaming for him to do exactly what he's threatening me with. I can't be doing this. I have to get away from him. I wanted to talk to Beau to find out what he meant to do with me and I've done that.

He just told me his plans for me. He's going to make me a single mother. Someone that's scorned and shunned. A girl that has to drop out of college with nowhere to go. He knows that's what would happen and he loves it.

Beau shrugs and tucks his hands into his pants. He doesn't come forward but he watches me bang into another sign as I make a blind turn and try to run for the wall of windows. I only make it a few steps when he speaks and I almost trip and go flying into a table. The volleyball net that's leaning against the wall wobbles and falls forward, crashing onto the table with a bang. The windows aren't that far away from me, but I don't go for them. I can't. Not when the words Beau says are ringing in my ears.

"How do you know I haven't already done it?"

Jesus. No.

I spin to face him. "What are you talking about?"

Beau examines his sleeves and makes a show of smoothing them just so, holding them at his forearms as he speaks. "Biology 101, Nevaeh. Even a girl that took a purity pledge should know what happens when you get fucked like you did. I didn't use protection. I know you're not on the pill. Good girls don't need it, right?"

I bite my tongue. I wanted to be on the pill, but my mother didn't let me. She swore that I was going to start having sex if I had protection, so she kept me off of it.

"Try that shit without the pill. You'll get exactly what's coming to you acting like a whore."

Odd that she talked to me like that when her own pregnancy brought her to Bloom. She was accusing me of the very thing she did. Blaming me for future wrongs when I hadn't so much as kissed a boy before Beau took my virginity. And now he's threatening to make me into my mother. But when he does it to me it'll be so much worse. There won't be any escape or starting over. I won't even be able to carve out a little place for myself to hide in and grow bitter like my mother did. He intends to keep me right here in Bloom, with my shame and powerlessness on full display to everyone in town.

If I let him, he'll make me into my mother's daughter.

Beau laughs and something snaps in me. All I've done is try to keep the peace. I want to make it through my days without feeling like I'm a prisoner in my own home. My own body. I want to be happy and free. I want to love myself. Why does it always seem so far away?

"Get away from me!" I scream and reach out blindly to the table I ended up falling into. There's a collection of old helmets there. They look vintage or antique or whatever it is that a football helmet is when it's old. I grab one by the face mask and throw it at Beau as hard as I can. It hits his shoulder. He laughs again and I grab another helmet and throw it at him.

"Fuck you! Go fuck yourself, you asshole!" I launch another helmet at him, but this one goes wide. It crashes into a sign and sends a whole precarious tower of signage to the floor. I grab another helmet and swing it, but I don't get the chance to throw it at Beau because he's closed the distance between us. He crowds me back against the table. Strong arms wrap around my waist and his hard chest leaves me nowhere to go. He rips the helmet from my hands and tosses it to the side while I start to swing on him. My fists go wide and nothing really connects. I don't know what I'm doing but it doesn't stop me from trying. I scream and scratch at him and when that doesn't work, I try to bite him. I manage to get my teeth on his forearm when he shoves me down on the table. He grunts in pain as I bite down as hard as I can. I hope I draw blood. Right now, I want to rip his flesh off his bone and spit it at him. Beau forces his arm into my mouth with his weight and I can't keep my bite strong enough. It feels like my jaw is going to shatter from the force he's using and I have to let go.

"I hate you!" I scream. Spit flies out of my mouth and I snap my teeth at him, even though he has me pinned and I have no chance of biting him again. I don't feel human right now. I feel like a wild animal, desperate for freedom from Beau's cruel hands.

"Oh angel, we know that's not true. *You love me.*"

Love.

"If you didn't, you wouldn't have let me do what I did to you. You enjoyed that, angel."

He's right. I hate that he's right.

"Been thinking you've loved me for a long while now, Nevaeh. Isn't that right?"

I feel raw and exposed. Like my whole body has been cracked open and every sensitive part of me is on display for Beau. His smile, that smile I've coveted, adored, and feared over the course of my life, turns mean. It's always mean when it's on me now. And as weak as I am, I can't help but want even his meanness for myself. I'm greedy for every part of Beau that he gives me. Sharp edges, thorns and all.

Why do I still want his smiles?

"No!" I try to kick at him but he's too strong. I push back, trying to get away from him by rolling off of the table, but I'm yanked back and held down. Beau leans over me and grabs something before he's on top of me and my arms are pinned. I can't move them more than a few inches and when I look down I see that he's grabbed the volleyball net that fell and is using it to tie me down.

"No! Don't!" I shriek and try to wiggle free, but it's no use. He grunts as he rips through the netting and twists it into a rope that he loops around my neck and face. The netting burns and it's so much heavier than I would have thought. Beau winds it around my neck and uses it to force my head back over the edge of the table I'm on top of. "Beau, no!" I'm frantic and my throat feels raw from how loud I'm screaming, but Beau isn't phased.

He laughs.

His laugh tells me everything. He loves that I'm scared. The more that I struggle, the better this is for him. Oh god. He's going to kill me. And, because I don't know how else to be when it comes to Beau, I give him exactly what he wants and I fight him.

CHAPTER NINETEEN
BEAU

NEVAEH ACTING LIKE a bitch is a turn on. Who knew that was going to be my thing? I fucking didn't. Not when I spent every day dreaming of having her on her knees and begging for mercy. Never once did I dream of Nevaeh fighting me, of her talking shit or putting her hands on me. There's a scratch on my neck, but it's nothing compared to the wound she's got covered by the bandage on her neck tonight. I've watched her over the past two weeks wearing the bandage and it's made me hard knowing she was covering a mark I gave her. I've also watched her relax.

Nevaeh let her guard down, especially in our Death and Dying class. We have those other classes together, but it's different in Death and Dying. She relaxes enough to smile. I don't like seeing her so carefree and happy. She's not allowed to look that way without me. Rage is all I've felt since seeing it. I want her happiness to be mine. I want to bend and break her until she remembers there is no happiness without me.

She's not allowed it.

"Beau, no!" Nevaeh shrieks and I pull the netting I've got wrapped around her tighter and towards me. I pull it back until I'm able to loop it around the table leg closest to me and hear her cry out when I tie it off with a jerk.

Joy and smiles only exist when Nevaeh is with me. She screams again and it's sweet to me. No one is going to hear her here, so I let her.

"Don't have any more fucking smart ass things to tell me, angel?"

I take a beat and look down at her. She's beautiful, even if she's got a net wrapped around her neck and head. Nevaeh stares up at me with wide eyes through the netting. The nylon from the net digs into her and marks her skin with a diamond pattern across her face and neck every time she struggles to get free.

"Fuck you," she spits out at me and I smile down at her.

"That's my good girl. You always do what you're told, don't you?" I ask her, while I run a hand down her side. She's gorgeous in front of me, splayed out like my own personal feast on the table. She's wearing the school's colors in a pretty blue shirt that I recognize from her socials. She's had the shirt for years. I'm glad she's wearing it now. I've wanted to touch her with this shirt on for so fucking long.

I move my hands down to her thighs and grip them. I want to take my time with her, but this isn't the right time. It never is with us, but I'll make it good for my beautiful fucking liar. I'm going to give her a reward for being so good for me.

"Yes," Nevaeh whispers. She's gone still beneath me and when I look at her face, I see that she doesn't look scared. She looks defiant. There's an edge to her that wasn't there before. I like seeing it in her eyes. This is the real Nevaeh.

"You're going to scream for me, aren't you?"

"Yes! I swear I will!"

Hearing her scream that one word is life giving. The only other moment that comes close to hearing Nevaeh scream yes was when I took my first step out of prison, but even then it pales in comparison to what freedom is for me—what freedom means for me.

Freedom is fucking worthless to me if I can't have Nevaeh telling me yes. I want her to want this. I want her to show me. I want to hear her say it. The night I fucked her, she told me yes. She told me yes even while she hated it. It confused her, but my sweet fucking girl wanted it as much as I did.

Hearing her say yes makes me want it even more than she does.

I grab the waistband of Nevaeh's jeans and use it to pull her towards me before I pop the button and yank her zipper down. "Tell me you want this. I want to fucking hear you beg to cum. You want to cum, don't you?" I move a hand down to cup her pussy and palm her through her underwear. There's a wet spot when I move my fingers lower and start to stroke her. She's going to be soaked in a minute.

"Yes, please let me cum. Please, Beau."

I drop to my knees in front of her and yank her jeans off of her. "Say it again," I tell her as I force her thighs apart. I want my girl's pussy on my tongue. I need her screaming my name and creaming on my face. Nevaeh's cunt is warm and open to my fingers and mouth. They talked about putting me on death row. They never managed it, but it made me think. It made me think about what I wanted for my last meal. What would suffice when you knew it was the last thing you would ever taste? No matter what I picked, nothing was right. That's because I didn't want food.

I wanted Nevaeh.

I'm going to fucking eat her pussy like it's my last meal.

"Again," I order and slap her pussy harder before I rip off her panties like I did last time. I grip her thighs and yank her towards me. Nevaeh's pussy is goddamn beautiful. I've never seen anything I've wanted more than her dripping cunt.

"Please let me cum."

"Louder."

"Please let me cum, Beau! Please!" Nevaeh thrashes in my hands and I hook her legs over my shoulders. I circle her clit and Nevaeh kicks out hard before she digs her heels into my back. "Please, I need you. Oh god, Beau."

I thrust two fingers into her with a growl and jerk back to look up at her. "I am your god, Nevaeh. You know that." I grab the netting still keeping her tied down and yank it hard.

She chokes and sputters, her big beautiful eyes fill with tears but she nods at me. "I-I'm sorry, Beau," she manages to get out while I keep working her. I press down on her clit and lick into her cunt. Her body trembles and her back bows off the table while she struggles to breathe. She's so wet now, there's a mess on her thighs and my face. I fucking love it. I pull harder on the netting and Nevaeh whimpers.

"I can't breathe, Beau. I can't. Help!" I can hear Nevaeh trying to suck in air, but it's hard. Her breath comes in quick gasps and when she digs her heels into my back, I don't know if it's from panic or pleasure. If I wanted her to breathe, I would let her, but I don't tell her that. She's going to learn to trust me. I might bring her right to the brink, but I'm not going to kill her.

If I did that, I wouldn't have her to torment anymore, now would I? I would haven't Nevaeh to love if she was dead. I'll never do that to her. No matter the scars and tears, the blood and the near calls, my fucking beautiful liar is mine and I'm going to make sure that she stays alive for every last bit of what I have in store for her.

I let the netting go and Nevaeh sobs as air fills her lungs. "That's it. I know it hurts, angel. You're doing so good for me," I croon to her as I pepper her thighs with kisses and move back to suck her clit. I pump my fingers into her faster and bring a hand to her hip to urge her forward. I want her on my face. If I didn't have her tied down with netting like I do, I would have her ride my face until she fell apart into a million pieces. It doesn't take much to get Nevaeh's hips moving the way I want and she starts to rock against me with desperate little moans.

"Beau," Nevaeh keens and rolls her hips. "Beau, oh, please. Please, Beau! I need you."

I lift my head long enough to look at her and Nevaeh cries out in frustration. She must have been close. I smile and press a kiss to her thigh. "What do you need, angel?" I ask, dragging my tongue across her flesh and back to her pussy. When I bury my face between her thighs and fuck Nevaeh with my tongue, she moans happily.

"Oh, yes! Yes, Beau!" I pinch her clit and she screams. My meaning is clear. I want her to tell me what she wants. "I need you inside of me. I need you to f-fuck me."

Music to my fucking ears. Hearing Nevaeh telling me to go fuck myself is second only to hearing her ask me to fuck her. I rise from my knees and undo my belt without a second thought. The only thing I want is to give Nevaeh what she's asking for. There's no way I can deny her. I want to break her, but she's mine to protect. Mine to violate and dirty. I pull my dick free and moan when I drag my dick over her pussy. Nevaeh whimpers and reaches for me but she's held in place by the netting. Good. I don't want her touching me. Nevaeh is mine to defile. I'm her destruction and now she's begging me to ruin her. She's going to know that loving me comes at a cost. That she's never going to have happy ever after with me. But she's not going to want it, either.

I grab her hips and bring her legs up to circle my waist. "Wrap your legs around me," I snap at her. I give Nevaeh half a second to process my words before I slam forward and bury myself to the hilt in her wet pussy.

"Fuck," I groan, and put a hand down on the table to keep myself steady while I start to fuck my girl. Nevaeh wraps her legs around me and pulls me deeper when I thrust forward. "That's it, angel."

"Beau!"

"Good girl, pull me in. Just like that," I encourage her and grab her hips to hold her down when she tries to lift her hips to fuck me back. I don't want her taking more than I'm ready to give. "I fuck you," I tell her and press her hips down onto the table. "You get what I give. Do you understand me?"

"Y-yes, Beau."

I fuck Nevaeh harder. The table shakes beneath us and it feels like it might break but I don't give a shit. Nevaeh feels perfect. She feels like ecstasy. The table could break to fucking pieces and I wouldn't stop fucking her.

"B-beau, I'm going to cum. Please, let me."

I smile down at her. She's learning. "Good girl. I'm proud of you for asking me," I praise her and the transformation I see on Nevaeh's face is instant. She looks blissed out, like she was just given her Holy Grail and my balls tighten when I realize it's because I praised her.

"You're doing so good for me, angel. You deserve a reward, don't you?" I ask and Nevaeh's walls flutter. I can feel them tightening around me. Oh, she's fucking close. She's about to lose her mind for me.

"Yes, please. Beau, please. Please, let me cum."

I want to see her come unraveled for me. In her room it was too dark to see her the way I wanted. The storage room is dim but the lighting is better.

Next time I have her on my dick, I'm going to do it in my home. I'm going to do it when I can take my time taking apart Nevaeh.

"Cum for me, Nevaeh. Cum for me now. Give it to me, angel. You earned this."

Nevaeh's eyes hit mine and I watch her eyes darken for a split second before her eyes roll into the back of her head and she screams my name.

"Beau!"

"Fuck!" I yell, watching Nevaeh. I can feel her as her body rides the orgasm I just let her have. "You're so fucking beautiful. I-" I grimace when that comes out of my mouth and stop myself from saying anything else. I won't think about what I was going to say, or the fact that I'm not ready to be saying shit like that to her, but I can't take the words back now that I've said them.

"Beau," Nevaeh whispers and I grab the netting I used on her and pull it tight to cut off her words. I focus on her body, refuse to think about the fact that I've called her beautiful, or that I was about to say so much more when I stopped myself. As much as I want to stay right where I fucking am, I can't risk it. I speed up, fucking into Nevaeh harder and faster, until I'm cumming on her thighs with a strangled moan.

"Nevaeh." It's the only thing I let myself say when I cum, because I don't trust myself with saying more.

Hating Nevaeh is too much like loving her and the more I touch her, the more I fuck her, and have her screaming for me, the harder it is for me to tell the difference between the two. Love. That's not what she's supposed to get from me. I'm a dumb fucking asshole thinking I was going to manage my revenge without ending up in deep shit, because I almost said those fucking three words to her— *I love you.*

CHAPTER TWENTY

Nevaeh

I JUST HAD SEX with Beau again. I don't know how it happened, but it did. I was so angry with him that I wasn't thinking straight. I touch my neck. The area where he had the netting wrapped around me is tender. After we finished, Beau surprised me because he didn't just leave right away. He helped me take the netting off and got me cleaned up again.

It was different this time.

I watched Beau as he went to the door and hesitated. We were both just standing there. I didn't know if I should go out first or not, but I was also in a daze from what just happened.

"I'll go out first. Wait here."

I didn't answer, just nodded. But that's when Beau grabbed my face and forced me to look up at him. "I want to see you at the party tonight. Don't do anything stupid, Nevaeh."

I shoved his hand off me and glared up at him. "Don't be an asshole, Beau."

Beau laughed and moved into my space so fast that I jumped back out of instinct. My back hit the wall and he put a hand beside my head. "Angel, just because I like you mouthing off to me doesn't mean you have free reign."

He trailed a finger through my hair and gave the lock in his fingers a quick tug. "Watch that tongue or I'll cut it out. Do you understand?"

"Yes," I spit out at him and crossed my arms over my chest. "Can you please leave?"

Beau chuckled and stepped away from me. He smoothed his hands over his dress shirt and gave me a once over. He looked fine. He looked perfectly at ease and not like he just fucked me senseless in a storage room. I bet I looked like a mess.

"Trying to kick me out of bed, already. Ouch, Nevaeh. I'm hurt."

"This isn't exactly a bed, Beau," I snapped and pointed around the room.

He looked around the room as if it were the first time he'd noticed and nodded. "No, it's not. Next time."

"Next time?"

He nodded and hefted his duffle bag higher on his shoulder. "Yes, next time," he said and reached for the door. "You think I'm giving that fucking pussy up now that I broke it in?" he asked and laughed. "I don't think so, angel. It's too fucking good, Nevaeh. You're mine."

Exhilaration went through me. I shouldn't like this. Why do I like this? *Because it's Beau. I only like this because it's Beau.*

Beau left before I could say anything. That was fifteen minutes ago and my phone has buzzed twice in my pocket. I know one of them is Sunny, but I'm too guilty to look. I'll look once I'm on the way back to her. I reach for the door and slip out of the room and hurry back to the bleachers. I hope she's still there. I pass the locker room, it's empty and quiet now. There are no friends and families waiting for the players that are filing out anymore. I reach for my phone when it starts to ring, because I'm sure it's Sunny. That's when a hand grabs my shoulder and slams me against the wall.

The air gets knocked out of me with how hard I hit the wall behind me. "Beau-" I start with a wheeze, but that's when I hear an unfamiliar voice.

"Shut the fuck up, bitch."

Fear shoots through me. It's not Beau.

"Jordan?" I whisper. I try to back up from him but there's nowhere to go, not with him blocking me in and the hard wall behind me. I look frantically up and down the hallway but it's empty. "What do you want?"

Jordan smiles at me. It's a bad smile. It's not a smile that's like Beau's. Beau knows how to turn his on and off, but I don't think Jordan can do that. The only smile that Jordan knows how to give is a mean one.

"What do I want? What I want," he says and shoves my shoulder as he talks, "is for you to fucking disappear. That's what I want, Nevaeh."

"Leave me alone, Jordan." I straighten up and try to shoulder past him, but I don't get anywhere because Jordan punches me in the stomach. My knees give out and vomit rises high in my throat but I manage to keep it down while Jordan holds me up.

"Hey, hey, keep it together, Nevaeh. We've all gotten hit hard every now and then by life and you deserve it more than most." He shoves me against the wall and I'm gasping like a fish out of water. "Now, what the fuck do you think you're doing around here lately, hmm? Because it looks a whole fucking lot like you think you're going to get to have a normal time at college and that's just not fucking happening, you dumb bitch." He takes a step back from me and gives me a once over. I can see his mind working. He wants to teach me a lesson. He's going to hurt me, I just don't know how yet.

"And if The Reaper isn't going to be the one to fucking teach you a lesson, then I will."

He's just going to have a damned soliloquy about it before he does it. I never liked Jordan, not in youth group or in school. He always had to have the last word, but at least that's buying the time I need to get away from him.

"You know they should have never let you into this school with the rest of us. Not with what you did, you fucking freak." Jordan turns his back on me and that's when I grab my still ringing phone.

"Nevaeh, where are you? Is everything-"

I hit the video call button for the call and point it at Jordan while he's still talking. "You're trash, Nevaeh. I'm going to make sure you regret ever setting foot on this campus. They're going to think The Reaper did it. I'm going to kill you and nobody's gonna stop me."

"Hey, fuck you!" Sunny screams and I almost smile. I can't talk, not with the way I've just got enough air in my lungs to not be leaning against the wall. I'm glad I don't throw up while Sunny starts to scream at him.

"Where the fuck are you, Nevaeh?" Sunny yells.

"What the fuck?" Jordan looks surprised but it only lasts for a second before his face twists into anger. "Give me that phone you stupid cunt."

"Nevaeh, get out of there!" Sunny screams and I do what she says. I bolt down the hallway and my side aches with every step I take. My lungs burn and my throat is on fire from where Beau used the netting on me. I don't know how my day has gone so wrong. Today it all seemed so normal, but I knew this was coming.

I knew I wasn't going to be able to keep normal. I don't deserve to keep normal. Jordan is right. They shouldn't have let me in here with what I did, but they did. They did and I have nowhere to go, so I'm staying. I run hard, pump my arms as fast as they can go. I can hear Jordan screaming at me while Sunny begs me to tell her where I am but I can't stop long enough to get the words out. I just keep running. I nearly sob with relief when I see the opening to the student section up ahead. I sprint up the slope that leads to the level I was just on and I'm going so fast that I can't really stop and end up slamming into the railing at the top.

"Nevaeh!" Sunny yells and then she's right there beside me. "Are you okay?" She wraps her arms around me and I burst into tears. I hold on to her and let her pull me away from the entryway that I expect Jordan to come barreling out of any second, but he never does. Another few seconds tick by and then a minute before I realize he's not coming. He didn't follow me.

"Who was that guy?" Sunny whispers to me when we break apart.

My hand is shaking and I lift my phone to see that I still have it on. I hit the end call button and shake my head. "He's one of Beau's friends."

"What was he going to do to you? Was he the friend you were going to talk to?"

I shake my head. My legs feel like they're about to give out, so I sit on the first bleacher seat I see. "No, I-that was someone else."

"I thought he was going to kill you. What the fuck was that villain speech?"

"Are you okay?" I look up to see a girl I've never seen before looking at me with concern.

"I'm fine," I tell her quickly and duck my head.

"Yeah, but-" A girl grabs her arm and pulls her back from Sunny and I. "Don't talk to her. That's Nevaeh."

"What the fuck is that supposed to mean, huh?" Sunny whirls around to face the girls but I stand quickly and take her hand.

"Let's go," I tell her.

"Yeah, but you heard that guy. He was going to hurt her!" The other girl argues with her friend, but I'm not sticking around to hear what her friend will tell her to explain why I'm not worth being worried over.

"People here are psychos," Sunny tells me while we walk. We're taking the long way out of the stadium. Anything not to go back down into the hallways that lead out to the parking lot. "Everyone heard what he was saying. They know you weren't safe and no one was going to do anything to help you."

"They're just angry with me. For what I did."

"You were just a kid, Nevaeh."

"So was Beau."

Sunny falls silent and I know she isn't going to push it. I'm glad for it, but I don't want to go to the party alone, so I force a smile onto my face. "Hey, you know where you want to eat?"

"We don't have to go to the party," she tells me with a worried look.

"Sure we do. I promised we would." It's true. I did promise, but Sunny thinks it's to her and her alone.

She sucks in a deep breath and shakes her head again. "Let's stay in the dorm. You can put on a scary movie or something."

I wrinkle my nose at her suggestion. "A scary movie? Really?"

"Sure, one of those slashers where the dumb kids don't just run out of the house and keep running up the stairs."

"Those are the movies with the rules, right?" I laugh and look up at the sky. It's dark now that we're in the parking lot. We didn't drive because we're so close to the stadium in our dorms, so we walk past it and keep heading towards our dorms. There's people here, they're laughing and running by on their way to parties. The energy is back again. I can feel the excitement over the win bubbling up and it feels nice after my run in with Jordan. I rub my stomach where he punched me and bite my lip. How is that when I think of tonight, Jordan is what makes it bad for me?

Not Beau. When I think of being with Beau again, I don't know what I'm feeling. But I want it to happen again.

"Duh. There's always rules to survive a horror movie. Everyone knows this." Sunny looks around us and tugs me closer to her. "Sometimes I feel like we're in a scary movie, Nev."

"What are you talking about?" I ask, because I know I should. I know what she means. The Reaper is back. I'm being terrorized at school. I just ran from Jordan because I was sure he was about to hurt me and Beau… every dark and twisted encounter with Beau leaves me feeling more confused about who I am. And on top of that, I'm taking eighteen credit hours.

Sunny's right. Life does feel like a scary movie right now.

"I mean, all of this." Sunny sweeps a hand out to the street and people around us. She gets a funny look from someone walking past but ignores them as we walk. "There's a literal killer on the loose and a girl was murdered on the first day of classes. Don't you think that's pretty fucking scary movie-ish?"

I tuck my hands in my jeans and shrug. "A little…" I hedge. I don't want to think too hard on the reasons she's right. The girls in those movies are brave and smart. They aren't girls like me that mess up over and over again. I'm not the kind of girl that makes it to the end. Or at least, I wasn't until Beau came back.

"A little? It's literally the script for a horror movie because of how everyone is being with you, too. You know, maybe it isn't a bad idea if we stay in and watch some scary movies. Get some tips on how to survive all this shit, you know?"

I smile. Sunny would think a slasher movie marathon would be the answer to keeping us safe. "I thought the rules were just like, don't say you'll be right back and stay out of the basement. Seems pretty straight forward."

"You forgot no sex or drugs and definitely no splitting up."

I've had sex twice and I wouldn't have ended up with Jordan chasing me down if I hadn't been on my own. I clear my throat.

"Totally doable," I lie.

Sunny hums in agreement. "I think we can do this if we stick to the rules. We can make it to the end of the year." She sounds earnest, like she really believes it. People deal with trauma in different ways and all I've known Sunny to be is strong and brave. She doesn't care what anyone thinks and that's why she's my only friend. That doesn't mean she isn't scared by what's happening either.

"Sunny, this isn't a movie," I say quietly, because I don't want to take the only hope she might have to make sense of what's happening all around us.

She looks at me and I see her eyes shine with tears before she inhales deeply and nods. "Yeah, I know but…it would be nice to think it was, right?"

"It would," I agree.

"If there were rules, i-if there were rules then we could stay safe. If there were rules it would make sense why this is happening."

"We haven't heard from The Reaper for a while."

"It's been two weeks. That's nothing."

"He was gone for four years, maybe that's it for another four years," I point out before Sunny can go on. She looks like she's ready to tell me I'm wrong but I don't like seeing the tears shining in her eyes. The tears she hasn't let go, so I clear my throat and point ahead of us.

"There's a Chinese place up the road that's really good. Let's go there before the party."

"Nev, I don't-"

"Listen, life isn't a movie and there aren't any rules right now. I know that's really scary but you were right before. We have to live and we have to enjoy school. I don't care if it's The Reaper or if it's bullies. No one is going to take this from us. That means we're going to go eat potstickers and then we're going to make terrible decisions at a party."

If I didn't know better, I'd think I meant what I was saying. But I'm terrified. I'm only putting on a brave face because I hate seeing Sunny look scared. She's not supposed to look like that.

I refuse to let her look like that, so I pretend everything is going to be okay.

CHAPTER TWENTY ONE
BEAU

I SMELL LIKE NEVAEH and it's bliss. I've got her scent in my nose and her taste on my tongue. I barely bothered to clean myself up after we were done. I wanted the reminder of what I'd done to her. As good as memories are, it's the physical reminder of being marked by Nevaeh that's helping me keep my shit together while I'm walking to the party I don't want to be at.

Ali texted that she was running late, which suits my plans. The less time I have with her the better. I stopped by my place and thought about calling the whole thing off. I thought about bringing Nevaeh to my apartment.

The night is cool and calm. I can hear the music from the party and laughter from the other students walking up the block with me to the party. It's within walking distance of my apartment, up on the hill where all the Frats and Sorority houses are. The houses are an odd mix here with a lot of new development, like the frat houses the community allowed to come in to cover up the fact that the houses might be older here, but they aren't nicer. Most of the houses are in good repair, but there's still the odd house that's more derelict than charming in this part of town so close to the university. Mostly college kids live here and there's a mostly blocked drainage ditch that runs behind these houses and the hill they're built on. I remember it being a huge fuss and someone made a 'Clean Up Bloom' initiative, because of the underbrush that filled in the drainage ditch when it stopped being used in the 80's. The town said it was an eyesore, that it was a prime hiding spot for The Reaper. He never put anybody there, so the town let go of their initiative. Besides, it's not like there was anything to really clean up in Bloom. This was just a shitty college neighborhood so the houses mostly looked like that, but the party tonight won't be in one of the older houses.

It'll be at Jordan's house and that means it'll be nice, because the big dumb fuck is in a frat.

Omega Beta something, I don't know and I don't fucking care. All I know is the address sent to the team. Even without it I'd be able to find the party by the amount of people spilling out of the house and into the front yard. There's a table set up for beer pong and a circle of guys passing around a massive mug, chanting 'Macho Mug!' as they drink. Yup, this is the fucking place.

It's a big plantation style home, which is weird in it's fucking self. This is the Midwest, not the South, but that doesn't stop the faux rich from faking prestige or whatever high it is people with money get from pretending they got here with the Mayflower. I'm acutely aware my family, my mother, is cut from the same cloth as the founders of this shitty frat. I might have been too once-upon-a-time, but that changed in prison. Prison has a way of breaking you down into so many little jagged pieces that you stop being worried about who is related to who, or who donated the most to the collection plate on Sunday. You don't care about any of that. What you care about is survival. To survive you need true power.

Power doesn't come from pedigree. Power comes from brutality. Power comes when you give up your soul.

I haven't had a soul for a very long fucking time.

I roll my shoulders and force myself back into the All-American mold everyone thinks still fits me, but I barely get more than a few steps before the smile on my face cracks.

"Did you hear what Jordan did today to that crazy chick?" A girl asks. She's standing in front of me, tottering in her heels on the wet lawn. "Fuck, my goddamn heels are going to be trashed from this mud." She bends down and yanks at her foot, grabbing her friend's arm to hold herself steady.

"Yeah, I mean, she lied, but…" the girl standing beside her starts, but she loses her voice when her friend stops tugging at her heel and looks up at her.

"She did more than lie. She fucked Beau's life up. She's a fucking monster and she deserves what Jordan did. I wish he'd caught her."

I've never seen the girl that's talking like she knows me. She doesn't give a fuck about me. She cares about the idea of me. Of who I was. She's eager to prove just how much she matters by tearing Nevaeh down. My hands curl into fists. I'm the only one allowed to tear Nevaeh apart.

What the fuck did Jordan do?

"That doesn't mean he should be as bad as her. I-I was there at the game and she looked so scared from him chasing her. I heard what he was saying. H-he said he was going to kill her."

The other girl snorts. "That's not what he said."

"Yes he did! He said he would or The Reaper would, Denise. It's the same fucking shit. He said he was going to get away with it. That's insane. I can't believe we're at his party. He's fucking crazy."

"Whatever. Bitch deserves it." Denise waves a hand at her friend. "And besides, he's already trashed, okay? He texted me earlier. He's around the back of the house near the fire from his last story he posted, so let's just stay inside and drink, okay?"

Outside. Jordan's outside by a fire. That I can use. I take a step back and look behind me. The group I'd been walking with have surged forward and joined the chaos of the party. No one's seen me yet.

I know what I have to do.

"Now let's get off this fucking lawn before my shoes are…" I block out their voices. Everything narrows and mutes. There's nothing but the thudding of my heart and the adrenaline now moving through my body. I used to feel this way in lock up when there was word out someone was coming for me. The anticipation, the gear up to the fight, the knowledge that it was either them or me.

I chose me every time. This time I'm choosing Nevaeh.

I don't go inside the party like I was about it. Instead, I circle the house and head to the back. I'm not ready for anyone to see me yet. There's only one person I want to see, but he's not going to see me coming. At least, if he's lucky he won't see me coming. Because no one is going to stop me from ending him.

Jordan.

Goddamn, motherfucking Jordan. That limpdick motherfucker thinks he can chase my girl. That he can threaten to kill her. *Jordan. Jordan. Jordan. Jordan.*

His name is the only thing I can think as I walk forward in the shadows surrounding the big house. I see a fire just like the girl talked about. It's burning bright, maybe a hundred feet from the house. I stick to the shadows of the trees and hedges growing around the perimeter of the frat house and survey the backyard. It's a big yard with a sprawling lawn and a few small storage sheds that sit along the far end of the lawn. The trees look bigger there and I see the telltale outline of chopped wood beside the storage sheds. I stop and look over the hedge to my right and see nothing but darkness. The drainage ditch is there. There's nothing to step on past the hedge, so I can't creep up the other side like I want. It's all right though, everyone is too drunk to notice me on my way to the sheds.

My feet take me there, it's closer to the fire and I'll be able to get eyes on Jordan easier. I can decide what to do from there. I make it to the stacked wood and pause when I hear voices nearby.

"You shouldn't have done that. If coach hears about it, you're going to be riding the pine pony. We fucking need you, man."

"Coach isn't going to hear about shit and if he does, who the fuck is anyone going to believe? Her or me?"

It's the same words I said to Nevaeh, but hearing them from Jordan makes me want to step right out of the shadows and kill him in full sight of whoever the hell he's talking to. I take a deep breath and steady myself before I do what I'm fantasizing about. I can see Jordan's blood on my hands and on the knife I've got in my pocket. It's the knife I bought the second I got to Bloom. The cashier recognized me, but they also knew I was innocent. They hadn't said a word about me buying the weapon. It's a tactical knife, something that's small enough to be in my pocket or tucked into my boot without notice, but big enough to do exactly what I need it to do.

A lot of people get caught up on the size of the weapon. What they don't think about is if you *really* want to kill someone, anything is a fucking weapon. The knife is plenty big for what I'm about to use it for.

I crouch low and move closer while the two talk. "Listen, all I'm saying is that it was fun or whatever to fuck with her, but that's too far, man. You're not The Reaper."

"Maybe I fucking should be."

Silence falls and I know Jordan surprised whoever he's talking to. "That's not cool, man. You don't say shit like that."

"Whatever. Get the fuck out of here."

There's a grunt of a reply and then I hear footsteps retreat. I wait a beat and then another before I hear the sound of moaning. It's a woman. She isn't just moaning, she's letting out almost high pitched yelps now. A woman screams and I hear the sound of someone being hit. There's the distinct sound of a fist connecting with flesh. Once you've fought your way out of enough corners, you recognize it. I hear a crash and a scream, but it's not the standard scream associated with porno. She's in pain. It sounds like a fucking horror movie. I half expect to hear a chainsaw with the way this shit sounds.

"Fuck yeah," Jordan groans.

What the fuck?

I know he doesn't have someone there with him. If I listen close enough, I can hear someone else. There's the telltale slap of skin-on-skin and another man groaning along with the woman's sobbing. When I get close enough to the end of the woodpile I'm able to get a clear shot of Jordan. He's standing with his back pressed up along the shed, his dick in one hand and his phone in the other.

The woman screams on the screen and Jordan beats his dick faster. "Fucking bitch. You like that, huh?"

From the look of Jordan, I have maybe another minute before he blows his load all over the hedges. Good. I don't want to look at the piece of shit while he gets off for much longer. If I slit his throat from this angle, he might see me, but no one from the party will. There's no getting behind him with how he's leaning on the shed, so if I want to circle the shed and approach from the other side, I'll have to move fast.

"Suck that dick, Nevaeh." My planning freezes. Red hazes over everything when I hear him moan her name. Jordan's breath picks up. "Nevaeh, you fucking dirty slut."

This piece of shit thinks he's going to get off thinking about what belongs to me and live. Cute. Fuck going around the side of the shed. I want him to know it was me that cut his dick off. I rise from my crouch and cross the space between us in three strides. Turns out I was right about Jordan, because it's when I'm bringing my knife up to his neck that he cums with a groan. I cut his throat while he's still got his hand on his dick. When he opens his eyes in shock and sees me, I grab him by his stupid fucking letterman jacket and bring my knife down again on his still cumming dick he's holding. And just like I knew it would, my knife gets the job done in two slices of my hand. I wipe my blade on his jacket and close it with a flick of my wrist.

Jordan tries to scream, but hardly any sound comes out. There's only the gurgle and choking wet gasp that comes from his cut throat. I cut his vocal cords with how hard I brought the blade into him.

I can see the question in his eyes. *Why?* He doesn't get it. Dumb fuck. He reaches out a bloody hand to me but I step away and kick him. He stumbles back towards the hedges and lands on his knees. The bonfire light catches on his face and there's still that question. I've never had anyone look at me like that. Everyone I've ever hurt knows why. They know what they've done and that only retribution brought me against them, but this is different. Jordan doesn't know and that just won't do.

"Nevaeh," I say her name, reverent as a prayer and I see the realization hit Jordan's eyes. It's beautiful seeing that knowing settle into the dickless fuck.

"You thought you could have Nevaeh," I tell him with a *tsk*. "Nevaeh is mine."

Jordan gurgles and tries to stand, but he can't manage it. I just took his dick off, after all. He's done. He knows it. Still, he manages to get to an almost standing position. It's almost impressive and just in time for me to kick him in the chest and send him through the hedges and into the drainage ditch below us. Jordan falls with hardly a sound. There's only a rustle of the underbrush and a few branches breaking on his way through. The only thing left of him is what's left of his dick.

The Reaper might not have put a body there, but for Nevaeh I have. For Nevaeh I'll bury this whole fucking town in bodies and blood. Jordan was just the beginning. I take another minute staring at the spot Jordan was just standing in before I pull out my phone to answer Ali's text and head in to the party.

CHAPTER TWENTY TWO

Nevaeh

THE CHINESE FOOD mostly worked, which I knew it would. The dumplings there are my favorite and they turn out to be Sunny's too. It was good to get her out of her head for a little while before we headed to the party. Beau's text wasn't just a text. It was a command. Like it or not, I had to go to the party and even if Sunny didn't know what was going on, it was nice to have someone to walk with me. I felt less afraid with her there and I was free to do what I did best.

Pretend.

I pretended the entire walk to the party that everything was fine. It's not that long of a walk to the party from the restaurant, which is nice. It'll be easy getting home after. The house we're going to sits on a hill just above campus, but the dorms are just at the bottom of the hill before you hit campus. Even if Sunny gets drunk it'll at least be a downhill walk for us after the party. I pretend and think about that. I pretend and smile at Sunny like my week of peace hadn't been shattered by Beau and I having sex again or that he'd told me to fight him. That I hadn't gotten a rush of power that had made me want to make *him pay.* I pretended that Jordan hadn't threatened to kill me or chased me through the stadium halls while Sunny screamed at him through my phone.

I glance over at her and worry. She seems like she's settled mostly, but I know it was seeing what Jordan did, or hearing what he threatened to do to me that rattled her. It's what made her want to pretend this was all just a scary movie that would end with the villain getting a taste of their own medicine, while we lived happily-ever-after. I worry that Sunny won't stay and that I'll be left alone. But because I'm pretending right now, I don't let myself think about it.

When we get to the party it's in full swing. The telltale buzz of my phone has me moving to see the message before I realize and Sunny whistles at me.

"So, when are you going to share who the mystery man is?" she asks when I open my phone to see that it's not Beau. It's Dean that's messaged me.

"It's just Dean. No mystery man here," I tell her with a little shrug and show her Dean's message.

Hey! Are you at the big rager tonight?

Sunny sucks on her bottom lip and wiggles it but doesn't say anything, even though I can tell she wants to say something. "What is it?"

She holds her hands up as we walk across the lawn where there's beer pong set up and a group of guys passing around a giant mug and singing what sounds like show tunes. "Nothing, nothing."

"Sunny…"

"Look, I'm not allowed to play matchmaker, but if I *was*, we both know what I think about it."

"You're right, you're not allowed and Dean is just a friend, so let's get a drink and I'll tell him we're here, okay?"

Texting Dean back is dumb, but it feels like a way to prove to myself that things are normal. Dean has been nothing but kind and considerate to me. He's been just as steady as Sunny in the class that we share. He's always offering to walk me places or to study. He's even tried to take on Beau for me, even if it's dumb. He doesn't stand a chance where Beau is concerned. Then there's the fact that I don't want him getting between us. I want Beau in all of his fucked up glory, which doesn't make me any better. I'm just as wrong and depraved as Beau. I keep letting what's happening between us happen.

> Yeah, we just got here! Getting drinks now. Where are you?

We walk into the house and it's nicer than a lot of the other houses around here, but that makes sense because it's a fraternity. All of the Greek houses are nicer than the almost kind of ramshackle houses the students rent. This part of town used to be nice back in the day, but it went downhill when people wanted newer homes and moved. I've never been in a fraternity though, so I can't help but feel a little starstruck as I take in the chandelier over our heads and the winding staircase that makes me think of an old fashioned movie.

"This place is nicer than I thought it would be," Sunny says and walks through the foyer to the kitchen like she's seen these kinds of places hundreds of times. The closest I've come to this kind of luxury is when I helped my mom clean some of the nicer homes in town. Even then, they weren't this big. There's no way this house wasn't created for parties. Everywhere I look there are people. There's a massive den area to the left of the staircase that people are playing drinking games in and to the right, there's a darkened living room where couples dance. Huge glass doors are thrown open at the far end of the foyer we're in and lead out to what looks like a bonfire.

Sunny taps me and jerks a finger over her shoulder. "Kitchen is this way! That's where *alllll* the drinks will be. Come on."

I follow Sunny through the living room and it's hard not to feel like there are eyes on me. Mostly because someone points at me and I hear them say, "She came to Jordan's house!"

What the fuck did they mean this was Jordan's house? Fear runs through me and I look around for Jordan. I don't see him anywhere but that doesn't mean he isn't coming for me like he promised.

"Sunny," I say, fully prepared to tell her what I just heard. That we have to get the hell out of here and fast, but then I see her face. She's smiling and moving with the same carefree energy she had before I ran for my life from Jordan. I can't tell her that we need to go. If I tell her we need to leave, she's going to freak out. She's going to go right back into panic mode and I can't risk losing her.

"You want shots?" Sunny asks, holding up a bottle of red liquid and a couple of little neon colored plastic shot glasses.

"Oh, I think I'm good," I tell her and hold up my hands. I angle my body so that I'm against the wall with the doors leading out of the kitchen in front of me. There's what looks like a backdoor in here, but I'll hopefully hear that open even with the loud music going.

"You have to have a drink, Nev. It's a party."

I've never drunk more than the one beer from the last party but I don't tell Sunny that. I don't want her to think I am any weirder than she might already. I nod and grab a plastic shot glass while she uncaps the liquid and pours it for us. Maybe a drink would be okay with how scared I am about Jordan. I heard it's supposed to calm your nerves. I could use a little calmness right now.

"Oh-okay," I tell Sunny with a quick nod. I lift my glass tentatively as she cheers.

"To an amazing night with my roomie! I love you, Nev!" Sunny yells and holds up her little shot glass in a toast.

"I love you too," I tell her and clink my cup to hers. We throw back the shots and I wince at how sugary sweet it is. It burns going down my throat and when Sunny brandishes the bottle at me again, my eyes water at the smell of it.

"What the hell is that?" I ask her while I try not to choke.

She shrugs. "I don't know. It's good though, right?"

I wipe my mouth with the back of my hand and wince. "I wouldn't exactly call that good."

Sunny sticks her tongue out at me and gets to pouring two more shots for us. "Listen, we have like three more of these and you'll think it's good. I promise."

My eyes widen. "*Three?*"

"At least," Sunny says without looking up from where she's pouring shots.

"Sunny, I don't think I-" I start, because even though it's one shot, my throat still feels warm and I'm paranoid I won't make it past the next shot. God, if I'm going to keep an eye out for Jordan, I can't be getting drunk. There's no way I'm going to get away from him with three shots in me.

"Hey, you two!" A pair of arms wrap around me and someone lifts me up. "Nev! I missed you."

"H-hi, Dean," I stammer and try to wiggle out of his hold, but he's too big and strong. Plus, anytime I shift away, he just holds me tighter. "How are you?" I ask when I finally manage to get my feet back on the floor. I take a quick step away from him and give him a tight smile. The plus side of Dean being here is that it's one more person and that might make Jordan back off long enough for Beau to be appeased that I made an appearance. A group is useful right now with trying to stay alive, so I don't let on that I don't want Dean touching me when he slings an arm around my shoulder and pulls me back against him.

Dean beams at us. "I'm great now that my favorite ladies are here."

Sunny shoves a refill of my mystery shot in my hand and smiles at Dean. "Aw, that's sweet. You want a shot?"

"I'm not a shot kinda guy. I've got this," he says, raising a beer to us. "You two take the shots though."

"Done and done!" Sunny salutes him and turns to face me. "Come on, bottoms up, Nev!" I don't want to, but I take the shot. I don't want to disappoint Sunny. "That's so good! Isn't it so good?" she asks and I nod because honestly, maybe she's right. The second shot didn't seem so bad compared to the first one I had. My throat definitely burned a little less that time.

"You think they got any mixers around here? I want a cocktail." Sunny looks around the crowded kitchen and starts to grab bottles out of the large plastic bowls that are filled with ice sitting on the counter in front of us. "You want a Cosmo or something?" She asks me.

"No, I'm good." I tell her. Thankfully, she doesn't press and starts making her own drink. It's a blessing and a curse that she doesn't ask me to have a cocktail, because I don't know how to say no. But it also means that now I'm kind of alone with Dean.

"How are you?" I ask him, because I can't think of anything else to say while I'm craning my neck, making sure that Jordan isn't going to come around the corner and grab me. God, I wish Beau was here. Where is he? If he was here then I would feel safe and-I bite my tongue and cut the thought off. Beau isn't afraid to hurt me. The only difference between him and Jordan is that he likes it when I fight back. That doesn't mean that he won't hurt me to get what he wants from me. I just wish he would tell me what he wanted. If he did, I would give it to him. We both know I would.

"Hey, uh, hello?" Dean snaps a finger in front of me and I blink in surprise. "You okay or did those drinks go straight to your head?"

Annoyance wells up in my chest at Dean. I don't miss the accusing tone in his voice. After a lifetime of church, I know exactly what reproach and disapproval sounds like.

"We're at a party," I snap and point at Dean's drink, "and that's a beer if I'm not mistaken, so maybe knock it off."

Dean's eyes go wide and he takes a step back like I slapped him. Even though it felt good to tell him what I thought, regret fills me instantly.

"It was just a joke," he says quickly while I rush to apologize.

"I'm sorry, I don't know what got into me. I didn't mean-I mean, I know it was a joke." I give him a weak smile and because I'm an idiot, I do the thing I shouldn't and ask him to dance. "You want to dance? I'm really sorry I said that. I'm just stressed, you know?"

Dean brightens when I ask him to dance and I know he's over it when he grabs my hand and starts to take me to the living room. "Wait, I have to tell Sunny where I'm going," I tell him and turn back to the counter. The second I do, I see Sunny grinning at me and giving me a thumbs up.

"Get it, girl! I love it, I love it, I love it!"

I flush hot from her cheers and swat at her. "Knock it off. People are looking."

"Good, maybe then they can see you're a fucking normal girl at a party and not some fucking villain."

"It would be nice," I agree but sigh. "It's going to take time, Sunny. You know that."

"Here," she pauses, grabs the bottle of red liquor we were drinking earlier and pours it into a cup, "drink this. You look so nervous about going out there to dance. No one is gonna mess with you, okay?"

She thinks I'm nervous about someone starting shit and that's true enough. I am. I'm more nervous about Dean, though. Jordan I would know how to handle. I'd run or I don't know, scream. I'd fight him. Dean isn't that black and white. He's my friend and he's a nice guy. He hasn't done anything to make me nervous at all. So why do I want to scream every time he touches me? Probably because I'm fucked up and think the only thing I deserve is brutality and pain. Probably because I don't think I'm worthy of the kind of guy that wants a white picket fence, perfect house and a couple of nice kids. A quiet life.

I want that. No, I *wanted* that. I wanted that before The Reaper marked me and made me whatever the fucking kind of girl is that wants what Beau has been doing to me. I don't want perfect. I don't want a white picket fence. All I want is Beau.

I take the shot from Sunny and down it in one swig. It doesn't burn going down this time, but it does warm my belly and I feel my limbs start to loosen. My shoulders drop and I let out the breath I'd been holding so tight my abs hurt.

"Thanks, I-I needed that," I tell her and take in a deep breath before I let it out. "I'm good now. Promise. I'm going to go dance but I'll be right back." Sunny waves me off with a thumbs up and when I head back into the living room where Dean is she's already offering to make everyone else in the kitchen a drink.

The living room is dim with purple LED lights along the top of the walls. Someone shoved the furniture off to one side, but there's still enough seating with all of the couches and chairs facing the dance floor. I'm grateful that whatever playlist is coming in through the speakers around the room is fast. All around me people are dancing and swaying, some of them have their eyes closed and others have drinks above their heads while they shout out lyrics and jump with their friends. Everyone is having so much fun. Maybe it's the alcohol warming my belly, but I want to have fun too. I want to be just a normal college kid and I'm so tired of pretending that everything is fine when it's not. My thoughts start to come faster and faster and it's not the party or the dancers around me that I'm seeing.

It's my thoughts. It's the ghosts and memory of that night so long ago. It's Carrie's screams and the way she would look at me in my dreams. It's her murderer on the loose. It's the boy I loved not being quite right. He's wrong, dark, and twisted. He's a monster. But even with knowing that, I still love him. I still want him.

Someone bumps into my shoulder and I jump. The thoughts scatter and vanish around me like morning mist on the prairie and I blink. Nothing changed. Everyone is still happy and laughing, dancing and carefree. The music rolls over me when the song switches and it changes into something I would hear in one of those clubs in an action movie. That fast pace means I'll be able to get out of a lot of contact with Dean, but I'm also a little less worried about dancing with him with the alcohol warming my belly and making my head feel light. Maybe dancing with Dean won't be so bad. He's fun, right? I think he's fun. I don't really know, but I'm all smiles when I walk up to him.

"Hey!" I yell and wave at him, but when I get close I see Dean isn't smiling so much anymore. He's looking around with a frown on his face. "What is it?" I ask him and look around the room too. I'm not sure what he's looking for but I immediately start to look for Jordan. Maybe someone tried to start something while I was in the kitchen with Sunny.

Dean leans in close with a hand coming to the small of my back when I try to take a step away from him and shouts in my ear. "The music is too fast. What is this?"

"The music is fine!" I insist with a smile up at him while I shimmy out of his hold and start to sway with the rest of the crowd. Dean doesn't move to dance, so I grab his arms and move them side-to-side. "Come on! You wanted to dance. Dance with me!" Dean looks like he's going to tell me no, but then a second later the music switches.

Deal smiles the second we hear the fast paced bass beats change to a slow and sultry song. "All right, let's dance," he says, now seemingly okay with the song choice. I'm glad that I'm tipsy or buzzed or whatever it is that happens when you have three shots in fifteen minutes, because if I wasn't feeling as pleasant as I am I'd probably find a way out of this. Dean comes close and wraps a loose arm around my waist while the other comes to rest on my hip. Despite the alcohol, I feel awkward. I never learned to dance like this. The only dancing that I ever did with anyone came with steps to follow and the annoying little chirp of the youth leader saying "leave room for the Holy Spirit!" any time anyone got a little too close to their partner.

That's the only dancing that I know how to do. I don't know how to do this kind of dancing, but I try. I don't think Dean would buy me calling a rain check after I just begged him to dance with me. He'd know something was up. Even if I was willing to fight with Beau earlier, I'm not one for confrontation. Making Beau angry is fine with me, because it's Beau. Any attention I get from him feels good. It's what I crave. It's not like that with Dean, so I keep my mouth shut and sway as best as I can with him. I turn my face to the side because it feels safer than looking directly up at Dean. If I do that, I'm worried he's going to take it as an invitation for more. But when I look to the side I almost scream at who I see staring back at me.

Beau.

Beau and the blonde girl that's always hanging all over him. Anger flares through my body at the sight of them together. They're on one of the couches facing the dance floor, but it's set further back than the rest. No one is looking at them because they are in the shadows. I wonder how long they've been there together. Maybe the whole time I was taking shots with Sunny in the kitchen. Did Beau see me come into the house?

I bet he did.

Shadows fall over them and the purple LED lights cast them in an ethereal glow. It makes the girl's hair shine platinum while Beau's seems to get darker. I swallow hard and look her over. She's wearing a short little white dress that flares out and I'm struck by deja vu. The dress looks so much like Carrie's dress. The light makes it hard for me not to think of Carrie Salt's hair. All of that beautiful hair stained red with blood. I bite my lip and the pain chases away the thought of Carrie. This girl isn't Carrie. But just like Carrie, she's someone Beau wants even though I'm here. The girl is sitting turned to the side, with her legs over Beau's lap as she plays with his hair and smiles up at him. I see her mouth move. She's talking but Beau doesn't say anything, he just inclines his head so I know he's listening to her while he stares at me.

Why is he watching me if she's here with him?

I think of the night he took my virginity and how I saw them kissing right after. That had felt like a knife through my chest. I'd hated every second of it and here they are, after Beau and I had sex again. Is she his girlfriend? Is he cheating on her with me? Bile rises in my throat and I suddenly realize I've had too much alcohol in too little time. I clap a hand over my mouth to keep it down.

Oh god, what if I puke right here in front of everyone? Just one more thing for me to try and live down at Bloom State. I swallow hard and force my stomach to keep it together while Beau watches me. He looks lazy. Bored. At least, if I didn't know him. His eyes have the same cruel and sharp edge to them they had in the storage room today. It's a look that's only for me. Even in a crowded room, no one else sees this side of Beau but me. I don't turn my face away when I feel Dean's hand move lower. His fingers are dangerously close to my ass. When I see Beau's eyes track the movement, the sharp look goes dark.

His jaw tightens and he leans forward just an inch. He's pissed Dean is touching me. Good. I'm glad he's angry, because he's here with another girl. Right on cue, the blonde girl throws her head back and laughs. The sound of it cuts right through the soft music that's playing and a few people glance their way, but Dean doesn't notice. His attention is all mine.

He lowers his head and murmurs against my ear while I watch Beau. "You're a great friend, Nevaeh."

"You are too."

"The best. I'm so glad that we're getting to spend some alone time, you know? I want to get to know you better."

"Mm-hmm."

Dean's hand on my hip starts to move but I beat him to it and turn away from him, so that my back is to his front. Giving him my back is bad, at least from what I remember from some of those self-defense seminars they make all the girls go to every year to be ready when The Reaper comes for us. I don't really care about giving Dean my back though, because none of the girls The Reaper came for escaped, and wherever Dean was about to touch me is stopped. Plus, I can keep eyes on Beau this way. It seems like the best move I can make in the situation.

"I think you're really smart," Dean says while I watch Beau and the girl. Beau's pissed all right and he's moving the girl closer. Her legs aren't in his lap anymore. She's sitting in front of him with his legs splayed on either side of her with her back to his front, facing me. When he forces her legs wider, I can see everything. My face goes hot while I watch Beau's hand. He's got one on her hip, but the other is moving. It slides up her leg and under the hem of the dress she's wearing until his hand is hidden beneath the fabric.

I might have been a virgin until last week but I know exactly what's going on. The girl's eyes flutter closed and she leans her head back against Beau. When her lips part, I can practically hear the moan that comes from her mouth. I know what she would sound like, even if I can't hear her. The music is too loud and there's too much space between us. They're across the room—there's no way I can hear her. It doesn't stop my memories from filling in the blanks.

I know what she sounds like because Beau's made me moan for him.

"Nevaeh, I have to tell you. I like you. I like you a lot."

Dean's arm comes around my waist and I grab it. I dig my fingernails into his arm when I see Beau's arm move faster. The girl grabs his thigh and opens her eyes to look up at him. I watch the needy and hungry look on her face until it's the only thing I can see. I should look away, but I don't want to. I want to watch her come apart, because that's something I know too. Her forehead furrows and her eyes go wide. She doesn't dare look away from Beau, but he's not watching her. I don't have to look at him to know where he's looking.

His eyes are on me while he's touching her.

"I know you like me too."

I don't respond. I just keep my eyes on *her*. I have to see what Beau's going to do to her, because I can't be the only one he tears apart so carelessly. I have to see him do it to her too. Her cheeks have gone pink, probably as pink as mine from watching them, and her hair falls forward across her face. I see the smile start to form on her full lips before they form a perfect *O* of surprise before Beau's big hand is there, covering her mouth and stealing the sound of her cry.

"Nevaeh, look at me."

My eyes go to Beau and just like I knew he would, he's looking back at me. The girl in his lap is writhing, but other than the hand over her mouth keeping her quiet, he doesn't notice what she's doing. Beau's lips curve up and the smile he sends my way is arrogant, cocky, self-assured. He knows how affected I am by what I just saw and he loves it. He licks his bottom lip and I almost moan watching his tongue move. I want to be the girl in his arms. If I was, he would care.

I know he would.

"Nevaeh."

I jump because it isn't Beau that is telling me to look at him. It's Dean. Oh my fucking god. *Dean*. I whirl around to look at Dean and see he's looking at me with a dreamy smile on his face. He looks content to be here with me. Why? There's nothing special about me. Why would he be looking at me like that?

"Dean, I-"

He grabs my hands and brings them to his chest. "Nevaeh, go out with me."

"What?" I whisper and stare up at him.

"I don't care what everyone says about you. They're wrong."

What everyone says.

I'm never going to outrun what I've done to Beau and I don't deserve to either.

"I-I have to go, Dean. I'm sorry."

Confusion clouds his face and he grabs my wrist when I try to push past him and back to the kitchen. "Nevaeh, what did I do wrong?"

"Nothing. Nothing, I just have to go. I need some air. That's all," I lie and Dean immediately tries to follow me again.

"I'll come with you. It's not safe."

"No!" I blurt out and take a deep breath. "I just, I need to be alone," I tell him and pull my wrist free. Because I don't know what else to do when Dean shoots me a hurt look, I add, "I'm sorry." I take off before Dean can reply. When I go towards the kitchen Beau is there blocking my way. He's leaning in the doorway with his arms crossed over his chest and watching me with another one of his lazy fucking smiles.

"I'm not talking to you," I say, even though I'm sure he can't hear me over the music that's changed again. It sounds like death metal and when I storm off in the opposite direction I have to push past a group of drunk frat guys who are doing their best to headbang to the music as they scream lyrics I can't understand. It's music I was never allowed to listen to, but it sounds angry. Right now I'm angry. I'm angry and confused and hurt, but I'm not a bad friend. I pull my phone out and call Sunny.

"Hello!" She screams when she answers the phone. "You good?"

"I-yeah, I just, I need to go home now."

There's muffled talking and then Sunny says, "Do you want to get a rideshare or do you want me to come back to walk you?"

There's something in her voice that makes me hesitant. Normally, Sunny would jump to come with me, but someone else is there if she's trying to stick around. "I can get a rideshare," I say quickly as I walk blindly through the party. There's so many bodies around me and the lights aren't bright. I think I'm going towards the front door, but I don't know.

"Oh my gosh, thank you. There's a cute guy here, Nev. I really like him," Sunny tells me in a whisper scream.

"I knew it!" I scream and clap. I don't think I'm drunk, but maybe I am. I feel good, even if I just watched Beau do what he did to his date. God. Why did I watch him do that? Maybe I *am* drunk.

"Sorry!"

"Don't be sorry, text me when you're on your way back."

"Totally. Text when you're home."

I squeeze past a few girls when I see a door ahead. That's got to be the front door. "You got it. Have fun tonight," I tease her and Sunny's cackle sounds before the phone goes dead. I'm smiling down at my phone when a hand grabs my arm and drags me back. Fear cuts through my happiness and sobers me right up. I suck in air to scream, but the sound never makes it past my lips. A hand clamps down on my mouth and muffles my scream, it forces the sound back and makes me swallow it as I struggle to get free. I kick my feet but I'm lifted up off the ground and I feel my body moving back, away from the busy party. I'm in a hallway and then a door slams.

Oh my god. It has to be Jordan.

My heart hammers in my chest so hard that it's hard to breathe. I struggle harder, kicking and trying to claw the hand at my mouth free. Moonlight pours in through a window behind the man that has me and hides his face.

"You're safe. *It's me.*"

I almost fall to my knees from the relief that sinks into my bones at those words. It's Beau. He shifts forward to look at me and the pale moonlight shines on his face. We stare at each other for a beat. It's hard for me to catch my breath, especially with his hand on my mouth. I reach up to pull it away but that's when I realize what hand he's using to keep me quiet.

It's the hand he used to get the other girl off.

I can smell her on his hand. The musky scent of her cum is there. *Oh my god.* I know he didn't have time to wash his hands. I scream at him and swing as hard as I can and end up connecting a slap to his face. The crack of my hand on his cheek scares me. I've never tried to hit anyone other than Beau. I've thought about it, like when I was attacked in the shower, but I've never done it until Beau. My palm stings from where I hit him and he laughs. His grip loosens, so I shove his hand off my face and wipe my mouth with the back of my hand.

"I can't believe you did that."

"Did what?"

"You know what!"

"There's a few things to pick from, angel. Are you talking about dragging you back here?" he asks and holds up a finger as he begins to tick off the possibilities of what he's done to piss me off. "Or are you talking about finger banging that bitch while you watched?" He snaps his fingers at me. "That can't be it, because you fucking loved watching. Which, I gotta say, I never pegged you as a voyeur. But you know what they say about the 'good girls' being the freakiest ones of all."

My cheeks burn, because I did watch him and the girl. It was hot. So hot. I couldn't have looked away if I'd wanted to. I'd been dancing with Dean the entire time and barely realized he was telling me his feelings for me until it was over.

"That's not-"

"Not it?" Beau interrupts and clucks his tongue as he throws his hands out and makes a show of pacing the space we're in. I watch Beau as he walks, the swagger in his steps makes me spitting angry. But as I'm watching him I realize we're not inside anymore. We aren't in a room, we're in a screened in porch. The cool night air feels good on my skin after being in the frat house packed with other people. I can see a bonfire shining bright not that far away from us. There's people walking around the porch and hanging out near the bonfire, but no one looks our way at all.

What the fuck? How does no one notice anything when it comes to Beau? Or is it that they're determined to turn a blind eye to whatever it is that he's doing because of what I've done to him? It's probably the latter. If he hurts me out here, they won't care. But even as I watch Beau turn to face me, I know he's not going to hurt me.

"Could it be that you're pissed that I just put the hand I was using on Ali on your face? You smell her, angel? Taste her?"

"Fuck you."

"I love it when you talk dirty to me."

"What do you want, Beau? I need to go home."

Beau tilts his head to the side and looks me over. The moonlight paints him in black and white. He looks more like a nightmare than human, but he's still the most beautiful thing that I've ever seen. Monster. Man. It doesn't matter.

"Sure, sure. I don't want to keep you, Nevaeh. I do have one very important thing to tell you before you head home for the night." When I don't say anything, Beau sighs and crosses the porch to come stand in front of me. I don't even bother trying to scramble away from him. It doesn't matter. Not when Beau reaches right for me and shoves me back against the wall. He leans into me and settles his hands on my neck as he stares down at me.

"You've become such a beauty, Nevaeh." That surprises me. His words feel almost tender. He reaches out a finger and brushes a lock of hair off my face with a sigh. "Absolutely breathtaking. Like a work of art," he continues on, voice gentle and soft while he toys with my hair. Then his hands tighten on my neck and I cough at losing my air.

"So why the *fuck* are you letting that piece of shit touch you, hmm? Didn't I already fucking warn you what would happen if I caught him touching you again? Do you remember what I told you, angel?"

"I'll kill him. If he touches you again, I'll cut his heart out and tonight, angel, I'm claiming what's always been mine."

My eyes go wide and I start to shake my head at Beau, but he cuts me off and presses a kiss to my mouth. "Shhh, shhhh, don't cry, Nevaeh. You know what I'm going to do to him. It's all going to be just fine."

I shake my head back and forth and try to tell him no, but Beau isn't listening to me. His hands tighten and his hold on my neck gets worse. I can't breathe and the only thing holding me up is the wall at my back.

"Shhh, don't fight me, Nevaeh."

Everything around me starts to flicker and the ground under my feet feels like it's slipping away. I start to sink into the black, but that's when Beau lets go of my neck and air comes rushing into my lungs so hard that it's painful. I gasp and choke, limbs thrashing as I fully regain consciousness.

"Get off of me, you psycho!"

"I'm *your* psycho."

"I don't want you. I don't want this," I lie.

Beau chuckles and kisses my cheek. His hands are around my waist and he rubs his hands over where Dean touched me earlier. "Angel, you're a terrible liar. You want this. You want every fucked up minute I'm giving you. Do you know how I know that?"

I don't want to ask, but I have to. There's no world where I don't ask how Beau knows that I want this from him.

"How?"

"You would have told everyone what I said at the television conference on day one. There's no way you wouldn't have told someone. Anyone. That roommate of yours, for instance, makes a lot of fucking noise. If you had told her, someone would have known."

"You stay away from her," I order before I think about it. Things don't go well for me when I have a mind to tell Beau what to do or fight him. I'll risk it for Sunny, though. No questions asked. I'll always risk it to keep my friend safe.

Beau smiles down at me and leans down to kiss my nose. "Don't worry, angel. She's off limits."

"W-what?"

"Your roommate. What's her name? Moonbeam, Rainbow or some shit. She's off limits."

"Why though?" I don't correct him. I don't want Beau knowing Sunny's name, but he's close with his guesses, which surprises me even more than him saying she's off limits.

"Because if anything happened to her you would be upset," Beau tells me matter-of-factly.

"Why does that matter? You love to make me upset."

Beau snorts. "No, I like to fuck with you. I *love* to fuck you, but I don't want you upset."

My mouth drops open. "Then why have you been torturing me? That's fucking with me. You've been-I-you're *hunting* me! I'm a pariah at school! How is that just fucking with me?"

Beau raises an eyebrow and crosses his arms. "I don't know if I like it when you cuss," he says.

"Beau, what are you-"

He snaps his fingers, silencing me. "I mean, I like it when you cuss at me, but not when you cuss. You don't cuss. Stop fucking doing it."

"You don't tell me what to do."

"I do. You're mine. That's how this works. That brings me back to the fucking douchebag you let put his hands all over you while I watched. You're lucky I didn't gut him right there in front of you."

"You were getting another girl off, Beau. I think what I did was fine."

"It wasn't fine, Nevaeh. You don't let anyone touch what's mine or there's going to be a price to pay, because I'm not going to let them live."

I lift my chin and stare at Beau. "No you won't. You're not a killer."

"And why do you think that?"

I hesitate. I don't know if I want to tell him why I know, but I do anyway, because Beau wants the answer from me. I always do what Beau wants.

"I'm not scared of you."

Beau snorts and shakes his head. "That's not saying much, angel. Maybe it's not that you feel safe with me. Maybe it's that you just have no sense of self preservation. You ever thought of that?"

"That's not true."

"Isn't it?" Beau asks and looks up at the moon shining down on us. He's so achingly beautiful. His inky dark hair is darker now, the sharp line of his jaw and at odds with his lush mouth. He's breathtaking. How is this man in my life? How are we tangled up the way we are? "You came to school this year when any sane person would have left town, but you didn't."

He's right, but he's also not.

"I don't have anywhere else to go," I confess and Beau looks away from the moon to me.

"What do you mean?"

I clear my throat and wrap my arms around my chest. I want to get out of here. Away. The weight of what my life is feels too heavy right now. There's a door at the far end of the screen porch and I take a step in that direction as I speak.

"My mom kicked me out. On the first day of classes she sent Pastor Mike with all my stuff and I haven't heard from her since. If I didn't come to school here, I'd be homeless."

"You could go stay with other family," Beau counters. "Bloom is nothing but some shit town. You could go anywhere."

I give him a sad smile and keep going towards the door that leads to the backyard. "There is no other family. I have no one. That isn't the only reason I stayed here, though. I knew what was going to happen if I came to school here but-" I stop, swallow past the lump in my throat and then continue on, "I came here because I owed you. I did you wrong and this is my penance. Every terrible thing you or anyone does to me because of what I did to you, I've earned. I'll give you the four years you want, Beau. It's the only thing I want to do with my life. Whatever you want to do to me? I want that too. I want you to punish me. I want to earn your forgiveness, even if it ends with me in hell. Because you'll have put me there." My voice shakes and it's difficult to speak, but I'm not done.

"I love you, Beau. I always have."

Beau's eyes widen slightly when I say that. We stare at each other in silence for a second and then another, before I unlatch the door, push it open, and slip out into the night without looking back.

CHAPTER TWENTY THREE
BEAU

"**H**URRY UP IN there!" There's a bang against the door. Someone is drunk and screaming in the hallway, but I ignore them. I'm washing my hands. Meticulously scrubbing them under scalding hot water. I have to get every trace of Ali off of my skin. My hands are calloused and rough from the years I fought to stay alive, but my skin is red from the burning hot water. I turn them again and add more soap while I wash them one more time.

I don't want a fucking centimeter of my flesh to be tainted by Ali's body. I'm not touching Nevaeh with another woman on my hands again.

"Hey, come on!" There's another bang at the door and it rattles in its frame. Interesting. I cut the water but don't bother grabbing a towel. The bathroom has been run through at this point, so it's just as dirty as Ali was. I wipe my palms on my thighs and unlock the door. It swings open and there's a big guy there. The type that lifts heavy and tells everyone about it. A crossfitter or something. He looks pissed, but the second he sees me he stops.

"Oh, shit. Sorry, brother."

What the fuck is it with everyone calling me brother?

I nod at him. "No problem, man." I walk out of the bathroom and into the hallway. The party is still in full swing, but there's no reason for me to stay here. Nevaeh's gone. I'm done. I stride through the room and out into the cool evening air. It's been a fucking hell of a night and it's barely even past midnight. My father used to have a saying that nothing good happens after midnight and it's true, so I start walking home.

The evening air is cool and calm. There's no students running past me or people screaming and laughing this time when I walk towards campus. It's nice. The street is quiet and winds down towards campus at a gentle slope that will end near the dorms. I have to go past there to get to my apartment, but I'll make sure to swing past Nevaeh's dorm on my way. I haven't had much time to myself since I got out of prison. My only thought since I've been back in Bloom has been Nevaeh. I haven't taken the time to settle. I do it now and unpack the last couple of hours of the night.

Nevaeh said she loved me and I got Ali off in a room full of strangers. Interesting way to end a Thursday evening that started when I killed someone an hour ago. Or maybe it was longer, I don't know. Haven't been paying attention to much other than the door to watch for Nevaeh.

I didn't have to wait long after I'd taken a seat in the best spot in the house—the couch sitting the furthest back in the living room. I'd been sitting for maybe a minute or two before Nevaeh wandered in with her roommate in tow. Funny to think Jordan's body was still warm and Nevaeh was getting drunk off some sugary shit in the kitchen. Ali came by a few minutes later and like I knew she would be, she was all over me. Even though I knew it was for Jordan, it was believable. It made teaching Nevaeh a lesson easier. I'm not into girls that fight me. I only like it when Nevaeh fights me, but she's not like the others.

She's my fucking girl. My filthy liar. Gorgeous, terrible fucking liar that's bringing me to my knees.

"I love you, Beau. I always have."

Nevaeh said that. It's different when I've taunted her with her feelings for me because, deep down, I never believed them. How could she love me? She doesn't even know me. And after all this time?

"I came here because I owed you. I did you wrong and this is my penance. Every terrible thing you, or anyone does to me because of what I did to you, I've earned."

Penance. Nevaeh came to Bloom State to do penance. It makes hurting her feel cheap. The hunger I have for her isn't the same anymore. It was manageable before, but after what she said? It's unbearable now.

I'll never be satisfied without Nevaeh.

She's the only thing that will ever give me peace. I turn the corner and the campus comes into view. It's all lit up like a fucking pretty picture. No one would ever guess there's a sadistic monster roaming it, looking for girls to take apart, piece by fucking piece.

The Reaper.

It's too quiet. I know he's still out there. As much as I studied Nevaeh while I was in prison, I made sure to take the time to do the same with The Reaper. I wanted to understand him. The other inmates thought I was just up my own ass. Whatever. I learned a lot about how and when The Reaper kills. It's always more than once and it's never in the summer. It's always during the school year and always around the holidays, but this is different.

He killed someone on the first day of school. He's off his pattern and it has to be because of Nevaeh and me. We're both here and whatever makes him tick is going fucking nuts. Why else would he have sent that knife to the cops? Carrie's murder weapon all wrapped up pretty with a bow. He didn't like that I was getting the credit for his kill, so he waited until he was ready.

He waited until we would be exactly where he wanted us. Where he wanted Nevaeh. She's the only one that's ever gotten away. Doesn't matter if he didn't try to kill her first. She was there. That puts a target on her back and my gut is telling me we don't have much longer before he goes for her.

And when he does, I'll be ready for him.

That motherfucker isn't killing the girl I love again.

CHAPTER TWENTY FOUR

Nevaeh

WHEN I LEAVE the party I walk for a while. At first I was walking towards campus, but at some point I started wandering. I don't know when I did it, but eventually I realize I'm not on the way to campus, I'm in a few neighborhoods behind all the Greek houses. All around me the houses are nicer than the ones in Jordan's neighborhood. These are family homes with nicer lawns and perfectly trimmed hedges. I hear a sprinkler go on nearby and frown. It's late. I need to get back to the dorms.

"Shit," I whisper and spin in a circle, taking in my surroundings. It's not a neighborhood I normally spend time in, but I know exactly where I am. Perks of living in a small town and all that. I take in a deep breath and then another and start walking back towards campus. I'm not that far off where I need to be. Maybe ten minutes and I'll be back on the hill and on my way to campus. I rub my arms as I walk. It's chillier now than it was earlier and the shirt I'm wearing is thin. I need to speed walk if I'm going to get warm, so I pick up the pace. That's when I realize my shoe is untied. I huff under my breath before I stop and bend down to tie them. I don't like being so still in the dark. The air is too quiet until I hear a pebble skip and skitter across the road. A prickle goes down my back when another pebble joins the first and

249

the two of them end up bouncing in front of me. My hands freeze. It's hard to breathe as I watch the pebbles bounce off into the darkness.

The road here is level. It's not like the continuous slope the frat houses were on. Those rocks shouldn't be rolling like they are. Someone kicked them. Someone behind me. Fear makes it hard to move. I remember this feeling. I've felt like this one other time in my life.

The night Carrie Salt died.

The night I thought The Reaper was going to kill me.

It's him. I know it is even before I look. I can feel him. He's darker than the night. The evil and hate that comes off of him could kill me alone if I let it. It chokes the air right out of my lungs and I can barely manage to turn my head to look. Why I look, I don't fucking know. I should be running, not looking at the devil that I know is there. But I do, because I have to. It's like my head turns all on its own and the second I see him standing there in the road it's like I'm fourteen all over again.

The Reaper is big. He's tall and the robe and hood he's wearing reminds me of the pictures we saw monks wearing in our history books or in the illustrations Pastor Mike showed us during service when he talked about the history and the foundation Crown of Thorns was built on. But those monks had on brown or tan robes, sometimes white ones.

The Reaper wears black.

I can't see his face. It's hidden from the shadow the hood throws over his face. I stare into the black void where his eyes should be. How many girls looked at his face before he died? Did they see him or was it only shadows that stared at them while they gasped their last breath? I'm frozen in place, too scared to move. I'm so scared that I can barely breathe as I stare at death incarnate. There isn't a person alive in Bloom that's laid eyes on The Reaper and made it out. I escaped him, but I didn't see him the night he killed Carrie. I was too scared to look. And then when I thought it was Beau, I ran. Until now, I didn't know what he wore. No one did. If I don't get away, no one might ever know. My eyes drop to his hands. Gloves. He has black leather gloves on. That's why no matter how gory the scene, there's never been any fingerprints.

One second goes by and then another. Or maybe it's a minute. Every tense moment that passes feels like an eternity. Finally The Reaper moves and I'm glad. I was too scared to do it first, but seeing him move unlocks my body. I leap to my feet, but I don't move yet. I can't, not when I see what he's holding. The Reaper jerks one hand to the side and the unmistakable flash of steel shines beneath the streetlights. The knife he has in his hand is big. It looks like a hunting knife, the edge of it cruel and sharp, serrated at its wicked tip. It's perfect for cutting and tearing, ripping flesh. He's killed countless girls with that knife and now he wants me.

I'm not ready. I refuse to let him end me like this, on a street I barely recognize, in the town I grew up in. Not on the night I told Beau my secret regrets. Not when I confessed my love for him. No matter what happens tonight, I'm getting back to Beau.

"*Fuck The Reaper*," I spit out into the night and he growls. The sound is low and sharp, like steel on stone. I don't know if he answers me aside from that, because I'm gone. I run as fast as I can, blindly sprinting down the street. The sound of my ragged breathing is the only thing I can hear over the heavy soles of The Reaper's boots pounding on the pavement behind me. I have to get off the street or he's going to catch me. I know that. He's fast, faster than me. I can hear him gaining on me while I run. I cut left and head across someone's lawn. There's a fence in front of me, but I throw myself over it and somehow manage to land on my feet. I sprint to the back of the person's lawn and round their house. Up ahead I see an above ground pool and a playhouse. There's nothing else in the yard, so my choices are limited. I hesitate and then decide on the playhouse. I throw myself at it, crawling on my hands and knees until I'm able to get inside. I have to be silent. I have to be quiet. I clamp a hand over my mouth and squeeze my eyes shut while I force myself to breathe evenly. All the while I listen for sounds of The Reaper.

For a minute there's nothing and I start to wonder if I really saw him. Was he standing there? Am I finally going crazy? It would explain why I told Beau what I did. Is any of this real? How can it be real? Why would he come for me now? If he wanted to kill me, he had all the time in the world while Beau was in prison.

Why now?

Another minute creeps by and then another, but then I hear the footfall. It's soft. Barely there. I only hear it because I'm listening as hard as I am. There's a rustle of a robe nearby. He's close. I'm not crazy. Not about this. The Reaper is here and this is really happening. It's not one of my nightmares. Not this time.

I shuffle forward, just an inch so that I can look between the two pink plastic shutters of the playhouse and I see him. He's in front of me and he's lifting the cover of the pool looking for me. Oh god. There's nowhere else to go but the playhouse once he realizes that I'm not in the pool. I have to move now, or he'll find me. I back up slowly. The wet grass beneath me sticks to my knees and palms as I move out of the playhouse. Once I'm out of the playhouse, I rise to my knees and look over the playhouse's plastic roof to see The Reaper is still by the pool. He's moved to the opposite side of the pool and looks like he's considering the black water beneath the pool cover. He'll realize that I'm not there in a second or two. I know it. I back up, rising to my feet and head off in a crouch towards the front of the house. It's only when I get past the corner of the house that I stand and start to run at full speed.

Oh my god. The Reaper is here and he's after me. I pump my arms and run faster down the street. I take a left and then a right. I'll pass Jordan's frat house and be going down the hill in a few minutes if he doesn't catch me. Oh my god, he's going to catch me. He catches everyone. Knowing that I'm done, that realistically The Reaper will win and that I've been dead since he decided on me, doesn't stop me from trying.

I have to make it out of this alive. I have to get back to Beau. I *will* get back to Beau.

Beau is the only thought on my mind as I run until my side hurts and I feel like I'm going to throw up. He's what keeps me going when I hear the steady *thud thud* of someone running behind me. Beau is what keeps me calm even as those footsteps get closer and closer. Up ahead, I see the frat house I was at with Beau and Sunny, even Dean. It's bright and happy. Music spills out and there's people in the front yard, but I don't stop there. I veer to the right and go down the hill. Maybe it's the scared fourteen year old in me that sees The Reaper as so much more than a man. He's a monster, a living demon. I'm sure that if I went for the party, The Reaper wouldn't just kill me.

He'd kill the people at the party. It wouldn't be all of them, but it would be some. I can't do that. I ruined Beau's life when I sent him to prison. I refuse to ruin one more. Whatever is happening is between me and the psycho fucking killer demon chasing me down. So I run on and when I hit the hill I get faster. I think my choice surprises The Reaper because he slows, almost as if he was sure of what I was going to do and now I've forced him to change direction and lose momentum.

The lights overhead are bright and pass in a blur. I don't see anything but the pavement as I sprint. My muscles burn and my lungs scream for air, but I don't slow down. I get faster and when I hit the bottom of the hill, I'm moving so fast that I nearly fall. I keep my feet and stumble on towards the sidewalk that leads to my dorm, but I only get a step down the way when I'm tackled from behind.

I scream and go flying face first into the pavement with The Reaper's heavy weight on top of me. I turn and pull them towards me and manage to flip us so that when we hit the ground it's with The Reaper hitting the ground first. I'm lucky he takes the full impact of the ground but I still slam my jaw against the pavement and blood fills my mouth. I'm disoriented and everything spins around me while I struggle to sit up. I roll onto my back and see a flash of steel.

"No!" I scream and kick. My foot connects with The Reaper's stomach and I hear them grunt, but that doesn't stop them from swinging the knife down at me. I roll to the side and the blade grazes my forearm before it slams into the ground with a screech. I kick again, but miss this time and roll onto my side. My arm is bleeding and it's hot, almost like a sunburn where The Reaper's blade cut me. I don't know if it's deep, but there's no time to look now. Not if I want to make it out of this alive. My decision not to stop at the frat party suddenly feels dumb.

What the hell was I thinking?

I'm going to die trying to save people that don't care about me. People that would bully me and hurt me before they so much as asked me if I was okay. I should have stopped at the party and brought The Reaper down on them.

I try to get to my feet but The Reaper grabs my ankle with one gloved hand and jerks me back with yank. I scream as I hit the ground with a thud and land on my wounded arm. I can feel blood smearing over my skin and sticking to my shirt. Oh my god. There's so much blood. Just like Carrie. The world flickers and the memory of that night rushes over me. I can see her laying there, butchered and taken apart, barely clinging to life.

He wants to do that to me too. He wants to hurt me like he did Carrie.

"Fuck you, you murdering psycho!" I scream and brace my hands on the ground and kick back as hard as I can. My foot connects with the hand still wrapped around my ankle. I kick him again and barely manage to avoid a swing of The Reaper's knife. Adrenaline and anger rush through me in equal parts and I know I have to get his knife away from him. If I do then I have a chance. Not much, but I'll take a chance over nothing. I can't just let him win. He brings the knife up and when I kick this time, I aim straight for the hand wielding the knife and a miracle happens. I hit his hand just right and send the knife flying. It lands a foot away from us, but I don't stop to see The Reaper go for it. I leap to my feet and run. I'm hurt, but I have to be faster than I was before. If I'm not, he'll catch me. There's not going to be a second chance.

If he catches me again, I'm dead.

"Help me!" I scream, finally finding my voice. Earlier I was so scared, I couldn't make a sound, not even when I ran past the party. It was like I was underwater and everything was happening just above the surface. My brain wouldn't even process screaming for help.

"Help me! The Reaper is here! Help me, *please*!" I scream again and my voice bounces off the sidewalk and buildings around me. Up ahead is my dorm. It's maybe three hundred feet away. That's nothing when you think about the grand scheme of things. How can three hundred feet be the decider between life and death? But if you think about it, lives have been decided by so much less.

"Help me! He's going to kill me! Someone!"

I can't hear the heavy steps of The Reaper, but that doesn't mean he isn't there. I heard how quiet he can be when he searched earlier. I didn't even notice him on the street until he kicked the rocks at me. If he hadn't warned me then, he could have killed me easily. He wants to stretch this out though and play with me. He wants to enjoy the kill and it's hard not to feel like he's going to slam his knife into my back any second as I run. Even as I run up the steps of my dorm and slam into the wall beside the keypad that lets me in. I can see the brightly lit lobby of the building with the student worker on duty at their computer.

"Help me!" I scream and slam my fists against the glass door, but they don't look up. They have headphones in and whatever they're watching on their laptop has their full attention. They aren't going to see me in time. I have to get in on my own. I tense, wait for the sharp bite of The Reaper's knife, but it doesn't come.

My hands shake as I punch in the code. Blood smears over the keys and I sob when the code flashes red, telling me it's wrong. "*Nonono!*" I scream and punch it in again, but I must miss a number because it flashes red another time. "Come on, come on!" I punch in the code again and look over my shoulder. I hear the telltale ping letting me know I put the right code in but I don't move, because there's no one there. Behind me the night is calm and quiet, just like it was when I was walking earlier.

The lock to the door clicks open and I grab the door without looking and yank it open to step inside. It's only when I'm crossing the threshold that I see him. He must have been off to the side, just beyond the steps, but now he's rushing up at me with his knife in his hand. I scream and pull the door shut a second before The Reaper slams their fist against the glass of the door. Behind me, I hear the student worker scream and their computer crashes to the ground.

"Oh my god!" They scream when The Reaper hits the door again, this time with the butt of the knife handle. The knife bounces off and I turn to run to the worker who is staring at me like they're about to faint.

"Is that going to hold?" I ask them.

"Oh my god, he's real! He's REAL!" She screams and I reach out and grab her, giving her a shake. Her eyes come to me and her mouth drops open. "Oh my god. He got you. H-he got you!"

"And he's going to fucking get you too if we don't call the cops! Is that fucking door going to hold?" I bark at her and pull my cell phone out to call the cops. I look around the lobby for something to use while the phone rings and spot the Fireman's Axe behind the glass emblazoned with Break In Case Of Emergency.

"Yes, it's bulletproof. They upgraded it last year after that guy shot up the capitol," The student worker whispers while she watches The Reaper continue to beat at the door.

"911, what's your emergency?"

I slam my elbow into the glass and yank the axe out of the box while I answer the dispatcher. "I'm at Morris Hall on Bloom State Campus and-"

"That is out of our jurisdiction, ma'am. You'll have to call campus police. I'm very sorry."

"I'm not going to fucking call campus police, because The Reaper is here!" I scream the last two words and turn to face him with the axe in hand. I put them on speaker and hold the phone out towards the glass windows and doors where The Reaper kicks the door. "Do you hear that? That's him! He's trying to get in to Morris Hall, and if you don't figure out your goddamn jurisdiction he's going to fucking kill all of us!"

BANG!

The Reaper throws their shoulder against the door and the student worker screams. "Please help us! He's here, she's not lying. He's going to kill us. Oh god, I don't want to die!"

The dispatcher is silent before they start to talk. "We need a description. What does he look like? We have units in route."

"He's dressed in black, all black. Black robe and hood, I can't see his face. He has gloves. He's big."

"Big?" she asks and I throw the phone to the student worker.

"I don't have time for this. You deal."

"Oh-okay," she stammers while I stare at The Reaper and heft my axe. He stops when he sees the weapon in my hand and tilts his head to the side. The hood still hides his face, but I can read his body language. He's interested.

"Fuck you," I bite out and take a step forward. "Fuck you, you coward. You kill girls and think you're a big fucking man?! You can't even kill me! I'm nobody, you sick piece of shit and you can't even kill me!"

The Reaper hears me. I know he does when he raises a hand and drums his fingers on the glass. A second later he steps back and points at the handle. He wants me to come outside. I watch as he raises the knife and wipes it clean of my blood with his robes. It shines dully in the lights from the lobby when he's done and he beckons me forward with it.

He's taunting me. Trying to draw me out with that display. What he doesn't know about me is that I've eaten people's shit for years. A little fucking taunting from a serial killer isn't going to get me to go outside.

"Please hurry! I think she's going crazy. Hurry!"

The student worker is crying, but she's wrong. I'm not going crazy. I'm finally seeing things straight. I grip the wood of the axe handle and the weight in my hands comforts me. I like having something to hurt him with, but I don't need to beat The Reaper. The only thing I need is to outlive him. So I don't go outside. I do walk right up the doors though and stare into the place where his face should be. There's only shadows there and the curve of a chin and lip that I see raised in a snarl to me. He's pissed.

"Not used to someone talking shit, huh?" I ask him and smile. All my life I've tried to be *the good girl*. The one that does the right thing and never breaks any rules. The girl that doesn't draw too much attention to herself and is sweet to a fault. I never drank, smoked, kissed boys or stayed out late. I listened to my mom no matter how crazy her rules were and she abandoned me here. I tried to be a good friend to Minnie and she dropped me the second I wasn't perfect. I tried to tell the truth about what I saw that night but no one listened.

None of it helped. None of it worked. I still ended up with The Reaper's knife marking me. I ended up right where I should have been all those years ago. But this time it's different. I'm older now and the veneer of fear that kept me trapped and docile, forced me to make myself small within the walls of the church, is gone. Fury floods my body, steady and strong in its hatred. Church. How I twisted myself to fit in the only safe place in my mom's world. Her faith in church demanded so much from me. If I stepped even a toe out of line, I was not worthy—I was not valuable. She made sure to beat that into me and that lesson breaks now. I feel it slipping off of me with each second I stare down The Reaper.

He's death. Evil incarnate and *he could not kill me.* I fought and clawed my way until he couldn't stop me from living. Not even the devil himself could end me. For the first time in my life, I feel powerful. It's the same feeling I brushed against earlier when I fought Beau. That's only a fraction of what I feel now. As banged up as I am right now, I'm electric. Pure energy and rage. An army couldn't take me down, let alone one fucking serial killer.

I bare my teeth at him and consider unlocking the door for the sheer fact that nothing would keep me from him then.

I want to fight. I want to scream. If I could, I'd swing the axe and take The Reaper's head clean off. I want him to suffer and die. I want to see his fucking blood and guts spilling out onto the sidewalk for everyone to see. People said I was the girl who survived The Mineral Belt Murder, but I don't want to survive anymore.

I want to live.

I'll kill The Reaper if that's how I'm going to get the life I should have had. I'm done letting the past control me.

"I hate you!" The words rip out of me. They bounce off the walls and floors of the lobby and out to The Reaper. I watch as they lean forward. They hear that too, but this time they don't taunt me. They slide the knife away into their robes and head down the stairs. I watch them, craning my neck to try and see which way they go. But, like magic, The Reaper vanishes into the night the second he's past the stairs.

"Where did he go?" I ask and walk the length of the windows. I look out into the bushes for him but I don't see him. "Where is he?" I scream and slam my hand against the window.

"The police are on their way."

I turn to see the student worker staring at me with wide eyes. She holds my phone out to me and her hand shakes. "I-I just thought you should know."

I take a step forward and she takes one back. She's scared of me. I don't care.

"Thanks," I say and take the phone from her before I shove it into my pocket. I readjust my grip on my axe and head back to the windows. "Is there another way in here?" I ask her.

"W-what?" She sounds dazed. I look at her over my shoulder and a pang of sympathy hits me.

"Hey, look, we're going to be okay because the cops are coming, right?" When she nods, I point at the door with my axe, "And we know that he can't come through there. But is there anywhere else that he can?"

She thinks for a minute but then she points behind her. "There's the door where we take the garbage out and get supplies through. It's around the back."

Around the back. That's where I saw The Reaper heading before I lost sight of him. "Fuck. That's where he's going. Where is it?"

"It's through those doors at the end of the hall," she says and I take off at a jog to the door. I'm surprised when she follows me down the hallway, but it's nice to have someone else there. I feel inhuman right now. My jaw is throbbing from where I landed earlier and I know I busted my lip back open again from a week ago. My arm feels like it's on fire and every time I move, blood drips from my arm onto the floor. I have to wipe my hand on my jeans to keep my grip on the axe I'm holding. "You really think he's going back there?"

"Yeah, I do."

"Why?"

"Because he's a fucking psycho rapist killer and he's angry that I got away. He's going to find a way in." We're standing in the middle of the hallway, the door she's talking about is just a few feet away. There's a thud on the other side of it and I raise my axe. Motherfucker is out there all right.

"I knew it."

She starts to cry. "Oh my god. I have to get out of here. I have to go hide."

I nod, my eyes on the door. "Do what you have to, but tell everyone else so they know what's happening."

"What? You're not hiding?" She asks and grabs my shirt. "You're already so bloody. He's going to kill you. You know that, right?"

I grip my axe tighter and keep watching the door, whose handle is starting to jiggle. "He can try, but I'm going to kill him first."

"You can't kill The Reaper. No one can!"

"I will."

"You're crazy!"

"Definitely," I agree, but she doesn't hear it. She's running down the hallway and on her way to the upper floors. I hope whatever happens happens before anyone comes down. I don't want them to see this. Seeing something like this marks you. It changes you, even if you're a college kid and not a scared fourteen year old. Violence, anger and trauma don't care how old you are. They take their fill, hollow and empty out everyone no matter when they come to you.

Even if the people in this dorm hate me and one of them even attacked me, I don't want them marked like me. I take a step towards the door. When it opens, I'm going to rush him. I'm going to slam the handle of the axe into their face and go from there. It's not a great plan, but it's a plan. So I hold steady and I wait. I watch the door handle that stops jiggling until finally, it turns.

The door clicks as it releases and when it swings open, I'm ready. I see the outline of the man in front of me and I leap forward and swing the butt of the axe up as hard as I can. It makes contact and The Reaper goes down.

"Fuck you, you psycho!" I scream and turn the axe in my hands so that I can bring it down on them. But when I heave it over my head, a light shines in my eyes.

"Freeze! Bloom PD! Drop your weapon!"

I freeze. I drop my weapon and hold my hands up as red and blue lights fill the night sky.

"Fuck," I whisper. It's just the cops.

CHAPTER TWENTY FIVE
BEAU

I'M ON MY way to campus when my mother calls. "Good morning, mother."

"Don't you good morning me," she snaps. I look around at the day. It's a beautiful, crisp, late September morning in Kansas and the leaves on the trees lining the street to campus are changing colors. A bird chirps nearby and when a breeze ruffles my hair, I clear my throat.

"Listen, it's a good morning where I am, so you're going to have to be more specific in your brooding."

"Jesus, Mary and Joseph, Beau. Did you not hear the news?" she asks.

"No, what news?"

"The Reaper killed Jordan Davis last night! At that party you went to, Beau. Are you all right? Did you see anything?"

"How did you know I went to a party?" I ask. I don't like her keeping tabs on me the way she is. I get it, because for four years I was locked up and she had no trouble knowing where I was then.

"I'm your mother. Of course I knew you were there," she says and I have to take a deep breath to keep calm. Old habits die hard now that I'm free, but if she keeps poking around she's going to find something out she shouldn't.

I can't risk that.

"Mother, stalking me is the quickest way for me to vanish."

"Beau, I-you wouldn't do that, would you?"

"I'm partial to my freedom, seeing as I didn't have it for four years. So yes, I would if you insist on keeping eyes on me."

She sniffs and sighs on the phone before she speaks, "I wasn't following you. Marcy's boy is on the team, too. She said there was a party all of you were going to at Jordan's fraternity. That's how I knew. I wouldn't violate your privacy like that, honey."

I nod. "Good. I wouldn't disappear either," I lie. I would. I think she knows it, even if she's playing along with my innocent act. After all, it's easier to believe that I'm exactly who I was before I went to prison. If my mother does that then there's a great many things she can overlook to keep her fake and happy world alive.

"I know, Beau. I know you wouldn't leave. And I'm sorry I called in a state, but I just heard the news about Jordan and I'm very emotional."

I raise an eyebrow and keep walking. So far she hasn't said one thing that makes this not a good morning. Knowing they found Jordan and are blaming The Reaper makes it a fucking fantastic day as far as I'm concerned. Let's see how that fucker likes it. I hope he knows it was me. It would make drawing him out into the open a lot easier.

"What's wrong, mother?"

"They found him in that drainage ditch behind the hill. You know, the one the town wanted to clean up?"

"Yeah, I know it."

"And well, he was, he was mutilated, Beau! That awful—that deranged demon *mutilated* Jordan. Slit his throat and," she lowers her voice to a whisper, "he cut his penis off, Beau. Oh my god, I'm sick to my stomach thinking about it. How could anyone do such a thing?! He's an animal." My mother starts to weep but I know the sound of it. It's fake. She's forcing the tears, but she *is* disgusted. That much is true.

"I'm sorry, I know it's hard to know something like that happened," I tell her while I wave at one of the guys from the football team. I've just hit campus and I'm walking up the long drive to the Oval. My mind goes to Nevaeh. I have class with her today—Death and Dying. I'm glad tracking her down won't be a pain today. I should install a program on her phone, something that shows me where she is 24/7. It would be a lot more convenient than tracking her down on campus. After what she told me last night, at least I know she won't be anywhere else but on campus.

"And then, I can't believe he went to campus! How did no one see him until they called the cops and, oh, it was *that girl*. I know I shouldn't say it, but I wish he'd caught her. She's the one that deserves it. Not Jordan!"

My mother has my attention now. She had it from the second she said *that girl*. "What girl?" I ask. "What do you mean he was on campus? The Reaper?"

"Yes, The Reaper, who else would I be talking about? He was on campus last night and the police were called to Morris Hall, and-"

"That's Nevaeh's dorm," I say and I change direction. I was going to the Union, but not now. I have to get to Nevaeh. Where the fuck is she and what happened last night? She left before me. How did something like this happen and I not see it? Wouldn't I have walked up on it on my way home? I run through my memory and try to think if anything was off, but I can't think of a thing. Everything was calm and quiet on my walk home. After I'd had my feeling about The Reaper, I even stopped by Nevaeh's dorm for a while to make sure everything was settled.

I sat on the steps for half an hour and the only interesting thing I saw was a possum walking across the green space in front of Nevaeh's dorm. I left before I'd been there an hour. It must have happened after I'd gone home. If it had been before, her dorm would have been crawling with cops when I showed up.

My mother barks out a bitter laugh. "I know it is. That's why I said that girl should have been the one to-"

"Been the one to *what*?" I snap, cutting her off.

"You know what, Beau," she says and I clench my jaw, because I do know. But if she's going to be wishing Nevaeh dead, I'm going to make her say it. Women like my mother always get away on polite society and how everyone else is just too fucking nice to call her out on what she means. She's passive aggressive to a fault when it comes to getting her way.

I'm going to fucking make her say it.

"No, I fucking don't know what," my mother gasps at my cussing at her but I ignore it. I'm done playing her dutiful son with the shit she's saying about Nevaeh. "So why don't you just say it. Come on, I know you want to, mother. I bet you've been thinking about what would happen to her if you had your way the entire time I was gone."

"She put you in prison," my mother snarls at me through the phone. "That bitch ruined *our* lives. Nothing has been the same since you went to prison."

"We weren't the best family before I went away. You know that."

It's true. My family might be pillars in the community, but we've never been close. Or healthy. My parents barely spend time with one another and the only time they really paid attention to me was when I was playing sports. Whatever my mother is talking about happening when I got put in prison is probably because she finally had to talk to my father.

"Our problems don't exist because of Nevaeh."

"I don't care! I *hate* her!" My mother explodes and I hear her throw something onto the floor, it's glass, whatever it is. I hear it shatter. "She should have been the one to die last night, not a good boy like Jordan. It should have been *her*! She should have died, not Carrie! It should have been her!" My mother's scream ends ragged and raw and I sigh.

"Are you going to tell me what happened at Morris Hall?" I ask, even though I could just as easily search it. If I do that, then I'll have to call her back. It's better to stay on the line with her for now. Besides, my mother is well connected enough in Bloom that I know she knows something that won't be in any search engine. The police chief came to our Fourth of July cookouts and my parents went to school with half the force.

If there's anything important to know, she'll know it.

My mother takes in a deep breath and lets it out slowly before she begins to speak. "The Reaper chased that girl to Morris Hall. He tried to get in, but she fought him off. The cops arrived in time. Everyone is talking about that. What they don't know is that for the first time ever we know what The Reaper looks like."

There. That was the insider knowledge my mother was going to deliver on. Holy fucking shit.

"They got him on security camera, didn't they?"

"Yes, the dorm's security system was able to film about five minutes of footage. That and Nevaeh's a true eyewitness now. From what I heard, she was at the station all night helping them compile a sketch."

I stop walking. "Where is she now?"

"How should I know, I'm not her keeper, Beau."

"You know if she's been released. Did they let her go?" I press.

"I don't know why you're so concerned with her. She left you to rot in prison while pretending she was perfect for four years."

"I'm not concerned, I'm obsessed. Learn the difference. Because Nevaeh isn't going anywhere, mother. Not when she's going to be your daughter-in-law."

"What are you talking about?"

My mother is a fucking dead end. If she knows where Nevaeh is she isn't going to tell me, but that's all right. I've got another connection that will tell me exactly what I want to know. I start walking again. I need to get to my answers.

"I have somewhere to be," I say and end the call. She'll call back and it'll blow up into something I have to smooth over later, but maybe I won't. I'm tired of pretending to be the perfect son my parents remember. That version of me is gone and it's taking far more out of me to keep him alive than I care to do right now.

What's the point anyways? I've got what I want. Nevaeh.

"I love you, Beau. I always have."

The second she said those words, she sealed her fate. The intensity of what I've felt for her, the obsession, the bone deep need to own her, to force her into something stronger than she is. All of that bloomed into love when Nevaeh said the words I couldn't. I'll say them now though, because I'm not going to torture Nevaeh. I'm going to marry her. I'm going to spend my fucking life with her at my side. We're fucked up, I know. But other couples have had worse starts. I'm sure of it, even if it doesn't seem likely.

In front of me I see the telltale signs of police at Nevaeh's dorm. There's yellow tape and police standing guard at the entrance, but I see students coming and going from the side door. On either side of the door, there's a couple of cops and a woman checking student IDs and writing down the names of every student that enters and exits on a clipboard. Not great for hiding the fact that I was here today, but it's doable if I'm pushed to explain.

I approach the woman at the door and plaster a smile on my face. I already have my ID in hand and hand it over to her when she reaches for it. One of the cops nudges the other and I know they've recognized me with how they're leaning together and talking.

"Good morning," I tell her and she smiles at me.

"Morning, son. You visiting or live here?" she asks as she starts to flip through the papers on her clipboard.

"Visiting a friend," I say.

"We're real glad you're out, Beau. You settling in all right?" The cop to the left asks me. He doesn't look familiar but I bet we've had him over at a cookout.

I nod at him. "Yes, sir. Everyone's been nice and accommodating. Feels like I was never gone."

"You're Beau Du Pont," the woman says, staring at my ID with wide eyes. She looks up at me and swallows hard. "I'm sorry, I didn't realize."

"Nothing to apologize for. Glad someone didn't recognize me for once in Bloom. It can be a lot," I tell her and take the ID back with an easy smile.

She nods at me apologetically. "We're keeping all visits to a thirty minute limit today, Beau. I hope that's all right. We're sorry if it's an inconvenience."

The cop that spoke, puts his hand on his belt and makes a show of adjusting it. "I'm sure we can bend the rules for Beau, just this once, Brenda."

"Of course, I understand after what happened here," I tell them and make a show of looking around the area like I'm worried The Reaper might come back. "Have you heard anything about him?" I ask.

The woman with the clipboard holds up one hand and shakes her head. "We cannot officially release any information on last night's events or what might have happened here."

The cop that talked to me snorts. "Official statements, fuck that. He's got a right to know, with what he went through because of those psychos."

Psychos. He means Nevaeh and The Reaper but I play stupid. For now, I'm fine letting them think I've got nothing to do with Nevaeh.

"What happened?" I ask him before the woman can stop me.

He jerks his chin at me and waves me over. "The fucking Reaper was here, Beau. In the flesh and that little bitch that did you wrong took him on."

My stomach drops. Nevaeh can't fucking fight. "What do you mean *took him on*? How is she?"

"She's fine. Couple bumps and bruises. A cut here and there, but nothing she can't walk off. Kinda surprised on that one. She's not that big, you know?"

I nod and the other cop laughs. "Big enough to lay out Jason. Man, that door opened and *BAM*!" He hits his hand against the other with another laugh. "She knocked that fucker out stone cold."

"Gotta hand it to her, she's got a lot of power in that body of hers," he says and gives the other cop a knowing look while the woman clutches the clipboard to her chest and looks uncomfortable. I hear what they're not saying about Nevaeh's body. These men could be her father, easily, but it doesn't matter to them.

"Nevaeh knocked out a cop?" I interrupt. I don't want these fuckfaces talking about Nevaeh. If they do, I'll end up doing what I did to Jordan to them. I really don't have the time for that shit today.

The cop chuckles and nods. "Yeah with an axe. She was going to split him in two if we hadn't been there to stop her. Isn't that right?" he asks the other cop.

"Shoulda seen her. She was crazed. I thought she was completely out of it for a second till she dropped the axe. That bitch-"

The woman clears her throat. "She went through something very traumatic. It's normal."

They both fall silent at that. Whatever is going on here on campus isn't entirely police run. I bet the woman is a campus advocate. Whoever she is, her words bring the cops back into line and they stand a little straighter when they say, "Of course. Anyone would have done the same."

"I appreciate the info, but I won't take up anymore of your time today," I tell them and nod at the door. "I've just got to ask my friend about the homework. Won't take but a minute."

The woman nods at me and raises her pen to write. "We're keeping track of that today too. Please know that any of the information we take today won't be shared with anyone else."

"Unless there's a murder and you're a suspect," the first cop says with a laugh. I give him a tight smile while the woman glares at him.

"Hey, you won't catch me a second time," I deadpan, because I mean that. I was innocent the first time they brought me in and now that I'm an actual killer, I have zero plans to let the Bloom PD bring me in.

The cops burst into laughter while the woman stays silent. "Good one, man." I get clapped on the back and shoved towards the door. "You're a riot, Beau. Tell your old man, Glen said hey."

"You got it, Officer."

"Glen," he corrects, like I know who he is.

"Glen," I repeat back so he lets me the fuck go. I make it one step inside the door before the woman calls out to me.

"Wait! What friend are you seeing today?" she asks, pen ready to write my answer down. I could lie, but I don't. There's no need.

"Sunny. Her name is Sunny."

CHAPTER TWENTY SIX

Nevaeh

IF ANYONE WERE to make a list of places you should probably avoid after a run in with a serial killing rapist it would probably have a graveyard on it. I look around and take in the bright sunshine and crisp morning air. A cardinal swoops by and lands on a headstone nearby with a flutter of wings. It's idyllic here. Quiet. The graveyard is the oldest in Bloom. It was founded in 1803 with its first soul interred the day of Bloom's founding when they died from being stabbed to death by another settler.

It's fitting that Bloom's first murder victim is buried here where so many of The Reapers victims have been put to rest. Five of them, to be exact, are in the newer parts of the cemetery. It's not something I would want to tell anyone about, but it's a factoid every conspiracy theorist in town likes to trot out for visitors. I shield my eyes and look off to my left. That grave doesn't have a headstone, but it does have a plaque the town put there when I was in elementary school. It always felt like a morbid thing to memorialize, but it's not like my town is known for shit other than murder and death. Makes sense that a soul as twisted as The Reaper would choose it as its hunting ground.

Murder and pain is ingrained into Bloom, right down to its founding. Blood soaked the ground from day one here. What else were we expecting to come to us with that in our DNA?

I look back down at the rice paper I'm using for my rubbing and adjust the pressure of the charcoal stick I'm using to pick up the almost vanished name at the top of the headstone. I shouldn't be alone right now, but I had to be after last night. The graveyard feels like a haven after the chaos of the police station.

It was loud there. The excitement in the air was palpable. The Reaper was the only thing anyone wanted to talk about and that's not even with the questioning I had to go through. All night sitting in that hard metal chair under the harsh fluorescents of the interrogation room like I was the one that had done something wrong.

I guess it didn't matter if I was the victim or not this time, the Bloom PD wasn't going to let me forget what I'd done before. Never mind I'd tried to tell them almost immediately that I didn't know if Beau did it. No one wanted to listen to me. I was scared, they said, and I should stick to what I told my mother.

I wasn't the one that was scared. They were. They were terrified of The Reaper and they'd wanted the attacks to stop. My IDing Beau was the easiest way to do that. If they locked him up then they didn't have to face the fact that there was a monster in their town, someone that walked right along with them and probably smiled right in their face before they went and cut up girls in little fucking pieces for them to find.

If it was Beau then they had a name and a face. They could rest easy at night knowing they'd done their jobs, so they forced me to stick to what I'd said had happened, even if I wasn't sure anymore. The same bullying tactics had come out last night, too. But I was stronger now. Older, wiser. I also didn't fucking care if they got the answers they wanted now.

I'd fought The Reaper and I'd won.

The Bloom PD suddenly didn't seem all that scary anymore.

I rub my charcoal stick on the rice paper in short strokes and make sure to add another piece of tape to the corner when it starts to curl up. Doing this at least helps me in one of my classes, so it's something. There's no way I was going to be able to go to class. Everyone would know. I got dropped off by the police just after the sun came up and when I set foot in my dorm I was struck with deja vu. My mom says deja vu is witchcraft and to not say a word about it, but she hasn't contacted me since I got to school and she lives fifteen minutes away, so I don't really give a fuck what my mom thinks. I walked into the dorm and the lobby was full of students keeping watch. They were everywhere. Sitting on the floor, at the student workers desk, standing by the windows, some had even brought their own camping furniture down to sit and sleep in. Everyone fell silent when they saw me and I froze. It's hard to move when you have a roomful of eyes on you.

What the fuck they were keeping watch for I didn't know. Did they think The Reaper was going to come back? Was that why they were all down there? I didn't know and I didn't want to find out. When one of the students said my name, I started moving. I kept my head down, made for the stairs and didn't stop until I got to my room.

When I got to the room Sunny was there sitting on her bed and waiting for me. I didn't have to explain much about what happened. From what I'd just seen the entire dorm knew what happened. All of Bloom had to know what happened with the way the cops had been on the phones all night.

"I heard you tried to take his head off with an axe. Pretty hardcore if you ask me."

"I hit a cop in the face on accident. That's not hardcore."

"That's the definition of hardcore, Nev."

I left a few minutes later after a quick hug. Sunny was the only one who knew where I was going and I promised to let her know if anything happened. I'd been in the cemetery all morning, working away. It'd been nice. Sunny texted me saying the dorm was locked down with everyone being carded and logged when they came and left. Visits were limited to thirty minutes.

Feels like prison.

She texted and my gut had turned sour.

It wasn't prison. If she knew what prison was really like, she wouldn't say that. Beau knew what that was like. I look down at the paper in my hands. It's a nice rubbing so far and the fourth one I've managed to get. That, plus the ten I already have, puts me in a good spot for the fifty I'm supposed to collect. If I keep this up. I'll be done in no time. I press harder on the paper and it rips.

"Fuck," I whisper and stare at the ripped paper in dismay. Tears prick my eyes and I press the heels of my hands against my eyes to stop the tears from coming. I want to cry. I almost do, but I hold the tears in. I have to be exhausted if this has me wanting to sob. I didn't cry even when The Reaper tried to kill me. I'd gotten mad then. Fury, not tears, had fueled me.

I slowly undo the tape holding the rice paper in place and ball it up. It's ruined now. A rip right through the middle means I can't use it for the database. I'll have to start over if I want a rubbing of this headstone. I shove the ruined rice paper in my bag and start to measure out a new length to try again. That's when I see a shadow move. It's off to the left where Bloom's first victim is buried.

Just like last night, I go still, but I'm not scared. I'm waiting. I want to see where the shadow went. It could just be another bird, or maybe it's the wind shifting the tree limbs that reach overhead. It could be anything. It doesn't have to be The Reaper. I wait patiently for the shadow to move and it does, but it's closer now. Whatever it is is making its way towards me through the headstones and statues. It's making an effort not to be seen. The list of what it might be is now considerably smaller, but I don't panic. I put my things away and start to go through my bag. I have pepper spray in here, or at least I normally do. After a few seconds of going through my bag I can't feel the pepper spray but I do feel the handle of the soft bristled brush I've used to clean lichen off of the older headstones.

Fuck. Someone is in this graveyard with me and the only thing I have is a fucking brush to defend myself. I drop it in my bag and grab my keys. I'm getting back to my car. I'll make a run for it and hopefully put enough distance between me and whoever is here that I can get eyes on them safely.

Not who, my brain corrects—The Reaper.

"Fuck it," I whisper. I'm scared, but I'm not going to go down without a fight even if all I have is that brush in my bag. I grab it back in my hand and shove the strap of my messenger bag over my shoulder as I rise from my crouch. I stare in the direction I saw the shadow drop and for a second it's all calm. I know not to trust it and keep a watchful eye as I take one step and then another, walking backwards in the direction of the gate. The headstones Professor Mrose wants us to catalog for the database are at the back, in the oldest parts of the cemetery. Which means I'll be walking backwards for a while if I don't make a run for it soon.

Running. I don't want to run. Just thinking it makes me angry. I'm tired of running and hoping no one notices how much space I'm taking up. That I'll get by if I'm quiet enough. Obedient enough.

Why do I have to run?

The shadow moves, the darkness of the coat the person is wearing stands out in the sunlight and despite my anger at it, I run. I sprint off towards the largest thing around me. A mausoleum decorated with gargoyles and stone roses. I drop and slide when I get to the mausoleum and press myself to the ground while I catch my breath. I'm quiet as I listen, but there's only the sound of the wind and birds chirping to hear. I get up and look around the edge. Right as I do, I see someone. They're there and then they aren't. A stone angel covers them, but they're moving fast and they're coming my way.

It's not The Reaper, but that doesn't mean I know who it is either. Someone that sneaks up on a girl in a graveyard isn't the kind of person I want to get caught by either, so I keep moving. I push off from where I'm hiding and sprint to the next thing. A big cross with a Christmas wreath hanging from it. This one looks newer. It's dated 1956. Good, I'm getting closer to the front of the graveyard. I'll be at my car soon. I just have to keep moving and stay out of sight.

"Nevaeh. You can come out. It's me!"

I freeze when I hear that voice. What is he doing here? How did he know where to look?

"Dean?" I call out from where I'm hiding.

"Nevaeh, where are you?" he yells and I sigh as I rise from my crouch and hold out a hand to him. Dean is turned around, his back to me with his hands on his head while he searches the graveyard for me.

"I'm here!"

He jumps and turns to face me. "Nevaeh. Oh my god. You're okay." Dean rushes towards me. There is concern on his face but there's something off about it. I push the thought away. I'm tired and jumpy, that's all.

"I was so worried," Dean tells me and sweeps me up into a hug when he's in front of me.

"I, ah, I'm okay," I tell him and awkwardly pat his back.

"When I heard the news I went looking for you, but I couldn't get into your dorm," Dean said with a frown. "There were cops at every door and I forgot my ID. They wouldn't listen that I was just trying to see my girlfriend."

I freeze. "Girlfriend?" I ask. "What would you say that?"

Dean gives me a duh look and reaches out to ruffle my hair. "You're cute, but you're not that cute, Nev. You know why."

I shake my head. "No, I don't, Dean. Why would you say that to them?"

"Because you're my girlfriend."

"No, I'm not. I-I'm not your girlfriend."

Dean crosses his arms and narrows his eyes at me. "Then what have we been doing, Nevaeh?"

"W-what?" I don't know what he's talking about. I've been nice to Dean. He's made me nervous, but until now there hasn't been anything that he's done that I can point to definitely as not okay.

But this?

This is definitely not okay.

"We're friends, Dean. I don't understand what's going on."

"You've been leading me on, is that what you're saying?"

"No! Of course not. I haven't led you on, Dean. What are you talking about?" Aside from classes and the texting, I've never spent much time with Dean alone. Last night was as much as I've ever done. The dancing. Oh god, the dancing and what he said.

"Nevaeh, I have to tell you. I like you. I like you a lot."

"I told you how I felt. I know you feel the same way about me, Nevaeh. Why are you pretending that you don't feel it?"

"I know you like me too."

I hadn't been paying attention to what Dean has been saying because I've been too wrapped up in Beau. Too dickmatized to really pay attention to what it was that he was saying to me and then I'd run off. I'd run off and told Beau I loved him. Serial killer attack notwithstanding, I wasn't thinking about anything Dean had told me last night.

But it looks like I should have.

Dean steps towards me and I see the look that passes over his handsome face. He's always been friendly. Open faced and smiling when it comes to me. It's gone now, though. His eyes are hard and angry. His hands clench into fists and I feel the same dark energy The Reaper carried coming from Dean.

I'm not safe. Dean wants to hurt me.

"You think it's okay to play with people's feelings? *That's not how you behave when you're in a relationship, Nevaeh!*" He shouts the last sentence at me and I flinch. I've never been good when people yell at me. Men especially. Normally, I'd be too scared to do much, but not now.

I'm the girl The Reaper couldn't kill and this asshole isn't going to yell at me.

"We are not and have never been in a relationship, Dean!" I scream at him.

"You're only saying that now because you want him."

Him. How does he know about Beau? There's no one else he could be talking about other than Beau.

"I watched you last night, Nevaeh. I followed you. I saw you with Beau. When did you start cheating on me with him?" Dean takes a step forward and I take one back to match it.

I look around the graveyard. I need something else other than the hairbrush in my hand, but there's nothing around. I don't even see the candles people sometimes leave at graves to use as a weapon.

"What did you see, Dean?"

"I heard what you told him. You love him? *Him?!* He hurts you, Nevaeh!" Dean throws his arms out at me as he continues to approach. "Why would you pick him? He doesn't love you! He doesn't know how. I would treat you so good. You're making the wrong choice, Nevaeh, because you don't know what's good for you, but that's fine. *That's fine.* I know what's good for you."

I hold out a hand to stop him. "Stay away from me. Stay right there," I order when he doesn't listen and keeps stalking towards me. "I mean it, Dean! Stay back!"

"You're not going to get in the way of us anymore, Nev. You aren't." He laughs and pulls something out of his coat. It's a length of rope and Dean wraps it around his hands as he walks towards me. "I've been good to you. Do you know what the other students say about you? Have you heard the foul things the boys say? And I still want you! You're lucky I still want you! Because I've seen you. I've seen what you do with that fucking asshole!"

My eyes are on the rope. What is he planning on doing with the rope? I'm still too far from my car to make it without trouble. I'll have to fight Dean and the bandages they've used on my arm won't hold if I do.

"Dean, listen we need to calm down and-"

"I saw you at the party! I know you fucked him that night!" Dean's face twists in rage and he lifts the rope in his hand with a sneer. "You would let him do that to you? After everything he's put you through?"

"Beau hasn't done anything to me," I lie.

"He hurts you!"

"You don't know what you're talking about." I dart to the side and put a few smaller headstones between us. I want to keep eyes on him or I'd run, but giving my back to Dean right now is a dumb thing to do. I go to the side but so does Dean. He has the rope between his hands and he pulls it tight when he sees me watching his hands.

"I do! I've been watching you and I see what's happening. I know exactly what's happening. He hurts you and you like it, so you let him. And you know what I think, Nevaeh?" Dean tilts his head to the side and smiles at me. It's such a cold smile. Even in the mean smiles Beau gave me it was never like this. Beau was pushing my limits. Finding how far I'd let him go. Dean isn't doing that. The wild light in his eyes tells me everything I need to know. It's manic. Intense and obsessive.

He's making a decision to hurt me.

"Dean, please, don't do this." My voice shakes but I can't help it. I'm panicking, because facing The Reaper makes sense. He's evil. A killer. A monster. But Dean? What is Dean doing? He's a normal guy that I thought was nice to me. This isn't who I'm supposed to be fighting. Nothing about this is normal.

"I think if I hurt you, then you'll like me too, Nev. So I'm going to hurt you now."

After last night I'm not strong enough to win in a fight against Dean, so I don't wait for Dean to move. I shove my keys in my front pocket and throw my bag at his face with a scream before I take off through the graveyard towards the parking lot.

"Get back here, you bitch!" Dean's voice echoes and bounces off the gravestones and statues of the graveyard. I loved it before for how empty it was. How safe and calm it felt for me after the chaos.

Now that quiet has turned deadly. Dean is going to hurt me out here and no one is going to know it. Everyone is on the hunt for The Reaper. They won't be looking for Dean. If anything happens to me they won't expect it. I was so fucking stupid coming here on my own. Why did I do that? No one even knows where I am but Sunny.

I should have told someone else, I know that. As I run, I realize something. There was no one else to tell. Up until this morning when I ran into that lobby full of students, no one has really looked at me. Yes, they've stared and hated me. Yes, they've made it a point to leave spaces where I am.

But looked at me? Seen me? No. That only happened today.

Sunny and Dean were the only people that were kind to me. My gut turns sours. How the fuck is it that out of the two people I thought liked me, one of them is now chasing me through a graveyard.

What is it about me that makes people hate me?

My toe catches on a headstone marker and I scream when I go flying. I land on my injured arm and I know the bandage isn't doing its job when I feel my wound open up again. Fuck. Of course I would land on my arm. The air has been knocked out of my lungs and I roll onto my back, coughing. I barely have time to open my eyes and suck in a lungful of air when Dean is on me.

"You're done running from me," he growls and grabs my arm. I scream in pain when his fingers dig into the gash The Reaper gave me. "Is this what you like?" He asks me and twists my arm. I sob and almost throw up from the pain that hits me. It's too much.

Dean gives me a shake and loops the rope around my neck. "Why are you so fucked up that you want me to do this to you? Why would you *make me* do this to you?!" he asks and ties off the rope. The knot he's made digs into my neck, putting pressure on my windpipe and I can't swallow because of how tight it is.

What is he talking about? Why is it always someone blaming me? I didn't force him to do anything to me. Men like Dean are all the same. He would hurt me any chance he got, I know this. He's just taking the first opportunity given to him because he's a sick fuck that loves hurting someone weaker than him.

"Stop, Dean! No!"

Dean stands and gives the rope a yank as he drags me behind him. "I would have treated you good. You ruined everything."

I claw at the rope and try to dig my feet in but I can't get a foothold on any of the headstones before Dean drags me away.

"You did this. This is your fault. How can you like this?"

I look up at Dean while he rants. He glances over his shoulder at me and I see disgust there. He really believes what he's saying. That I've done this. That somehow this is my fault and that I deserve it.

It's the same lie all abusers tell themselves when they don't have the fucking spine to face what they've done. They aren't a bad person. They were forced. How dare their victims push them over the line. They aren't monsters when the world is against them. When they've been left with no other choice but to hurt those weaker than them

I bet The Reaper tells himself he's a good person too.

It's all fucking bullshit. The Reaper and Dean are cowards. They prey on the weak and that's the only way they have power. What kind of a life does someone have to lead to do that kind of thing? They're pathetic, chasing power this desperately. They think I'm the weak one?

Fuck that.

Dean and The Reaper aren't just cowards. They're men that underestimated me and I'm going to make them pay for it. Dean jerks the rope. It burns as it slides across my skin and I bite down a scream. I don't want to give him the satisfaction of hearing me. He won't get another sound out of me. I grab the rope and wrap the slack of it around my uninjured arm and grab the rest of it with my free hand. I watch Dean. He's been pulling me along with him, giving the slack a yank every few seconds, but other than that he's focused ahead of us. I have zero clue where he's taking me, but I'm not going to let him. If he gets me there he's going to do god knows what to me, so the next time I see slack in the rope I sit up and force my heels into the ground. By some miracle there's a tree root for me to brace myself on.

Before Dean can notice what I've done I throw myself back, throwing all of my weight into it and manage to rip the rope out of Dean's hand.

Dean lets out a surprised sound and turns to face me. "What the fuck?" He's holding his hand to his body like it's hurt. Good. I fucking hope I gave him rope burn when I did that. Let's see how he likes it.

I grab the rope and gather it up in my arms so I don't trip and stand. "I'm not letting you do this to me. I never fucking liked you, you sick fuck."

"Give me the rope, Nevaeh." He holds out his hand and I sneer at the sight of that hand. It's soft. A red mark blooms across his palm. I did hurt him with the rope. I squeeze the rope tight and wish for the axe I had before. If I had that axe, I'd split Dean's head in two.

"You don't have what it takes to kill me," I spit at him.

Dean falls back a step and shakes his head. "I don't want to kill you. I want you to like me." A shadow moves. I barely see it out of the corner of my eye but when I focus, I know someone is there. I know exactly who is there, steadily making their way towards us while Dean gets more delusional with every second. I just have to keep him talking.

"You were supposed to like me, Nevaeh. I'm the good guy. Not him!"

There's a stone angel with a sword in their hand standing on a raised marble platform. The angel's wings are spread open as if it's about to take flight with its blade raised above its head. Dean stands with his back to the angel. The figure is just behind him. It moves slow and sure, circling the avenging angel and my heart rises in my chest. I'd know that silhouette anywhere. They've left their mark on me in a way that no one else could ever hope to come close to, least of all some random stalker that's fixated on me.

"Good guy? You think you're a good guy?" I laugh hysterically, because I can't help it. "What, you show up here and I'm supposed to just like you because that's what you want? What the actual fuck, Dean? This isn't junior high, you just wrapped a rope around my neck!" I scream at him. "You're crazy! This isn't what good guys do!"

Dean looks like I slapped him but he recovers a second later. "At least I don't fuck killers," he spits at me and moves to come towards me but he stops a second later, because the shadow I've been watching clears their throat.

"I would say I was found innocent, but that's just the one you know about. I've killed plenty, fucker."

Dean freezes and his eyes go wide when he realizes we aren't alone. I smile at the look of fear that flashes in his stupid fucking eyes and look at Beau over his shoulder. The statue's stone wings frame his body and he looks every bit an avenging angel.

"How did you find me?" I ask him.

Beau rolls his neck and leans back against the avenging angel statue with a sigh. "Rainbow told me."

I pull at the rope around my neck and glare at him. "Her name is Sunny."

He shrugs. "Whatever you say, angel."

"What the fuck is going on here?" Dean interrupts. He moves back so that he's facing the both of us. He bumps into a headstone when he tries to take a step back and stops to scan the area. He looks like he's finally realizing where he is for the first time. The light in his eyes is gone. He looks so normal, so like the normal Dean that I'm used to seeing, that I almost feel bad for what's about to happen.

Beau doesn't look away from me when he answers Dean. "Oh Deanie baby, you really fucked up. You know that, right?"

"This is between Nevaeh and me. W-what are you doing here?" Dean's trying to sound tough and in control. As if he thinks he can convince Beau to leave me here with him. Delusional fucking monster.

Beau's eyes go to Dean now and he chuckles. "It's pretty fucking simple, Dean. I'm here to kill you."

Dean splutters. "You're insane." He looks at me and points a finger. "You both are insane!"

"You think we're insane?" Beau asks with a shrug as he pushes off from the statue to stalk towards Dean. "That's valid for me honestly, considering my history. But you know what?" He reaches behind him to pull a knife from his belt and points it at Dean, who looks like he's about to pass out at the sight of Beau's blade.

"I'm not the one that was just dragging a girl through the fucking graveyard by a rope!"

Dean raises his hands in front of himself. "I'm sorry! I don't know what I was thinking. She made me fucking crazy. I'm sorry, okay? *I'm sorry!*"

"You're sorry?" Beau keeps advancing and when Dean tries to run, he grabs him by the back of his shirt and drags him back. "Sorry? Sorry, isn't going to fucking cut it, you limpdick." Beau kicks Dean's legs out from under him and slams him against a headstone. The scream that rips free from Dean when his head cracks against the headstone makes me smile.

"Please!" He raises his hands over his head trying to protect himself when Beau brings the knife down and slashes at Dean. His blade cuts into Dean's forearm and shreds the sleeve of his jacket. Dean howls with pain and clutches at his arm to try and stop the blood that's now running down his arm. "I'm sorry, oh my god! OH MY GOD! You cut me! Oh my god, stop. I wasn't going to hurt her!"

His pleas land on deaf ears. Beau grabs Dean's head and slams it back against the headstone behind him, once, twice, and a third time that ends up smearing crimson across the weathered stone.

"You did hurt her, motherfucker. And now, I'm hurting you. How do you like being hurt, huh?"

Dean stops pleading and starts screaming. It's not words anymore, it's just sounds. Pure terror while Beau drags him by his hair to a raised crypt and throws him on top of it.

"You think you could touch what was mine and live? That I wasn't going to fucking end you? That I wouldn't find out?"

"I was just trying to scare her, man. I'm sorry," Dean sobs and tries to roll away from Beau, but there's nowhere to go.

"Scare her? Nevaeh is mine to torture. *Mine.* I did time for her fucking soul. I earned her tears, you little fucker. She belongs to me and me alone."

"I didn't know." Dean sounds weak. He's crying, snot and tears are all over his face and the blood from his busted head and arm are making a mess on the crypt. He doesn't look at all like the man that was threatening to hurt me. "I didn't know she was yours."

The stalker that I hadn't even realized I'd had is being cut down before my eyes and it's beautiful. I didn't know that I had a streak for revenge in me, but watching Beau act as my vengeful hands is addicting. I want him to hurt

Dean. I want him to make him scream. To turn him inside out for me. Beau crowds the other man and grabs his jaw and jerks his head to the side so that he's looking at me.

"Look at her, " he orders and gives Dean's face a shake. "Look at her!" Beau waits until Dean's eyes come to mine and then he continues on in a calm voice, like he wasn't just bashing Dean's head against a headstone, "Now, tell Nevaeh you're sorry."

"I-I'm sorry," Dean whimpers. "I'm sorry, Nevaeh."

I'm sorry. Those two fucking words. They were all that I wanted to hear from everyone after what happened, but they were the words I wanted to say the most. They were the ones that I woke up everyday wishing I could give to Beau.

Those two words mean nothing coming from Dean.

"It's not enough," I whisper. I look at Beau and shake my head. "It's not enough."

"Didn't think it would be, angel," Beau says with a sniff. "But don't worry, that's what this is for."

Dean freezes and looks up at Beau. "No, nonono, don't, n-" His voice is cut off when Beau cuts his throat. Dean struggles and reaches up to try and push Beau off, but he's too weak and there's too much blood. Dean kicks his feet and there's the sound of wet gurgling when he tries to breathe. I close my eyes and turn away. I can't watch anymore. I might not be the girl I was and Dean might have been about to torture me, but I can't fucking watch this. My thirst for revenge is short-lived. I can't stomach it anymore, but Beau has no problem.

"Fucking dick," Beau snarls and slams the knife into Dean's chest. He rips it free and the sound makes me sick. I press my hands to my eyes and take in a measured breath to keep from getting sick.

"B-beau?" I call out when I start to feel dizzy. Adrenaline and shock hit me so hard that they nearly knock me off my feet. I sway and almost faint but press a hand to a statue near me to stay on my feet.

"Angel." Beau's arms wrap around me and he holds me to his side. He kisses my cheek and then my neck before my lips. When I open my eyes, he's staring at me. "I thought I almost lost you."

I give him a weak smile. "It's going to take a lot more than a random stalker to take me down. I much prefer to go down to the ones I know," I tell him and lean against him.

Beau raises an eyebrow. "Getting cocky after taking on The Reaper, I see."

"Just trying to own my trauma."

"How progressive of you."

I wince when the rope rubs against my skin. "I want this fucking thing off of me," I tell him and tug at the rope.

"As you wish." Beau cuts through the rope and loops it around his arm. He shoots a glare towards Dean's body as he coils the rope up. "We need to go. Someone might come this way and I really don't feel like going back to prison for his dumb fuck ass."

"You could tell them you were defending me. It's the truth," I point out, but he's right. We do need to get out of here.

"Truth or not, they're going to wonder why I stabbed him through his fucking heart and slit his throat. I was a little overzealous, but can you blame me? He deserved it," Beau says and grabs my arm. "Let's get your bag. Does anyone else know you're here?"

"No, just Sunny. I didn't want anyone else to know where I was." I shake my head and look over at Dean's lifeless body. Blood spills over the edge of the crypt and stains the grass black.

"How did he know you were here then?" Beau asks. He scans the graveyard as he leads me forward and I realize we're holding hands. I don't think Beau has ever touched me gently before. Funny that it's happening now because of my dead stalker.

"He was watching me. Stalking me," I tell him. "He knew about us."

Beau growls but doesn't stop walking. "Do you think he told anyone?"

"I don't know. Maybe. But who would have listened to him?" I ask and clear my throat. "And even if they did, what would it matter? We weren't doing anything wrong together."

"Not entirely, no," he says and stoops to pick up my bag. He shrugs it on his shoulder and grabs my hand. "Let's go. I'm taking you back to my apartment."

"I have to tell Sunny where I'm going first. We have to go back to the dorm." As much as I hate the thought of going back to the dorm, I have to. I can't let her wonder what happened to me and there's no way I'll be able to explain what's happening over text.

"She's not there," Beau says and I stare at him in surprise. "Good timing really. They won't be able to ask her where you are. By the time anyone realizes you were here, it won't matter."

"What? How do you know that? Where is she?"

"She's on the way back to Texas right now." We're in the parking lot now. My car is just a few feet away and Beau holds his hand out to me when we're in front of it. "Keys. Where are they?"

"How do you know she's on her way back to Texas? W-when did you talk to her?" I reach in my pocket and hand them to Beau.

"Went by your dorm to find out where the fuck you were, because I knew you weren't there. You don't like attention. Figured you would have made a run for it but I didn't think you were going to be this fucking reckless," he says and sweeps a hand out over the graveyard behind us.

"I wanted to be alone!" I argue.

"You were a sitting fucking duck for any half assed psycho that had half a brain cell out here, Nevaeh!" Beau explodes back and grabs my throat. He slams me back against my car door. "The Reaper is out there hunting for you. He wants you and you came here to be *alone*? This is the stupidest fucking thing you could have done!"

Tears fill my eyes and I sag in his hold. "I'm sorry. I'm so sorry, I didn't think."

"No, you didn't and now we have that dead fucker out there. If I hadn't come looking for you, he would have killed and raped you."

"I know," I whisper and grab onto Beau's hand. He's squeezed my neck and it's hard to breathe, but I know he's right, so I don't fight. I relax in his hold and take what Beau's giving me. "You're right. I know. I'm sorry, Beau."

Beau's hand tenses and my air is cut completely. Just as my panic rises, he lets go. "Goddammit, Nevaeh. Don't you ever do that to me again. I'm not losing you now and definitely not to some wannabe killer like that jackass." He wraps his arms around me and pulls me to his chest in a bear hug.

He kisses the top of my head. "You should have let me kill him when I wanted to the first time and none of this would have happened."

I smile because Beau *would* say that, but in his fucked up way I know he cares. "You're sweet."

"No, I'm not. I hate everyone but you. I'm not fucking sweet, but I love you." He leans back to look at me and brushes my hair back from my face. "I love you, angel."

My breath catches and I forget about the rope burns on my neck, The Reaper's attack on me, and Dean's dead body in the graveyard. Nothing else matters anymore. I don't care about any of it. The only thing that matters are those four little words, Beau just said to me.

"Say it again," I whisper.

He leans close, presses his forehead to mine and does as I ask. "I love you, angel," he says softly. "Now, get your ass in the fucking car before the cops show up and we both go to jail."

CHAPTER TWENTY SEVEN
BEAU

THE FACT THAT I've almost lost Nevaeh twice in twelve hours doesn't sit fucking well with me. In fact, it pisses me the fuck off. I glance over at her to see how she's doing and she seems fine. She's looking out the window, eyes on the sign for the Burger Shack we all went to in high school. Even though it's the afternoon, the neon red light shines bright in the window and reflects on her face. It's hard to tell with her though. Nevaeh is good at keeping her feelings close to her. We're in her car because I didn't drive. The cemetery Nevaeh went to was close enough to her dorm that, after I saw Sunny, I walked. At the time it seemed smarter to head over on foot than doubling back to my apartment to drive, but so much could have gone wrong today because I took my time.

I fucking walked.

I should have ran, but I didn't know what would be waiting for me in the graveyard. If I had shown up any later that motherfucker would have killed her. I can't believe I fucking walked. I squeeze the wheel tightly and take in a deep breath before I let it out. I have to calm down. It's not like I can kill him again, but if I could? Done deal. I'd do it again and again. As many times as Nevaeh wanted me to do it. I'm her weapon, the only thing she has to do is point me in the right direction and pull the trigger. Whoever gets in my fucking way to give her what she wants is dead.

"You okay?" Nevaeh asks. She's not looking out the window anymore when I look at her. She's watching me. She's probably been watching me for a while.

"Fine," I tell her.

She frowns and reaches over to put her hand on mine. "Everything is fine. I'm not hurt."

I nod at the angry red rope burn around her throat. "Then what the fuck is that?" I ask.

Nevaeh ducks her head and tries to pull her blouse up to hide it, but it doesn't do the job. "It's nothing. It'll heal. Yours did," she says. She means when I cut her. She's not wearing the bandage for that, but the mark is visible. It's not the same though, when I look at where I used my knife on her.

That mark shows she's mine. I don't want her covering it up. "Don't hide that," I tell her and brush her hand away when she keeps trying to pull her blouse higher.

"But you're looking at my neck!"

I press my fingers to the healing wound. "Looking at where I marked you. That, you show. I want everyone to see what I did to you."

Nevaeh sucks in a sharp breath and she drops her hand away from the collar of her blouse. "Okay," she whispers and looks out the window, but I don't miss the blush coloring her cheeks pink or the way she presses her thighs together. She's turned on. Good. I'm going to fuck her brains out the second we get to my apartment. I think about that and it calms me down some. The image that I can't get out of my head is Nevaeh being dragged through the cemetery and begging for him to stop. That sonofabitch did that to her. Made her weak and wrapped a rope around her. He was dragging her behind him like a fucking dog when I showed up at the cemetery. For a second I thought I was hallucinating. There was no way this was happening in broad daylight, not after what she survived last night, but it was. Of course it fucking was. It was Nevaeh. She attracted evil like a fucking magnet. I saw her fight back though. She surprised the fuck out of him when she ripped the rope away from him. I have no doubt she would have used it on him if I hadn't been there. The thought makes me proud.

My girl is vicious. Warms my fucking heart knowing she's just as much a menace to the world as it is to her. Nevaeh fiddles with her phone and I see her texting someone. It only takes one glance her way for her to tell me what she's up to.

"Sunny," she says and holds up her phone. "I-I wanted to make sure she was okay."

I nod. "Good. She was in a hurry about everything. Said her grandma was calling her back because of what happened at the dorm, but that she was going to try and get out of it."

"Her grandma?" Nevaeh sounds surprised but before I can ask her why, her phone trills.

"Hello?" She answers and the sound of a video call connecting sounds.

"Oh my god! I'm so sorry I had to leave!" Sunny cries, bypassing hello. I can hear the sound of a loudspeaker going off as well as the dinging sound of an elevator and people talking. "I'm sorry, it's really loud at the airport, but are you okay? Did Beau find you?"

"He did, yeah. Thanks for telling him where I was, but where are you going?"

"Back home to Texas. The ol' ball and chain doesn't think it's safe for me to be here with you know, what happened to you last night." Sunny sighs. "I didn't want to go. She just started using my brother as leverage and I had to, Nev. I'm sorry."

"Hey, it's okay. I get it."

Whatever Sunny's grandma has on her, it's big. When I got to their dorm room that morning, she was packing as fast as she could without bothering to look at what she was actually shoving in her bag.

"That old bitch needs to die," Sunny says and Nevaeh gasps.

"Sunny!"

"What?! You remember what I told you about my grandmother! I'm surprised she's bringing me back when a serial killer could finish the job for her and *oh my god*, I'm so fucking insensitive after what happened to you. I'm sorry, Nev. I'm such a dick."

She's right, she is being a dick, but it's fine. Who isn't a dick these days? I pull into my parking lot and cut the engine. My apartment is nicer than most in town. Definitely the nicest a college kid could hope to be in. From what I've seen, the other inhabitants in my building are professionals. I think there's a doctor across the hall from the scrubs I've seen him wearing when he comes home. There aren't going to be any parties or keggers thrown here this year or any year for that matter, which is good. I'm glad it's quiet. I'm not used to the noise of college. I don't think I ever will be, if I'm honest. The apartments are really lofts set in a historical red brick building that comes with every luxury bell and whistle imaginable. It also comes with a state of the art security system and a door man. I'm glad for both considering Nevaeh has been attacked twice in the last twelve hours. At this rate, I'm going to have to sleep with one eye open if I want to keep her alive.

"Sunny, it's okay, I promise. It's weird right now. I'm glad you're at the airport and not here. You don't need to be dealing with the whole dorm situation."

I open my door and that's when I hear Sunny say, "Wait, you aren't driving. Oh my god! Are you with Beau?!" I shut the door while Nevaeh splutters a response to her friend and round the car to open her door. When I open the door, Nevaeh is still trying to come up with a response to Sunny's badgering, so I lean into the frame of the call and wave at her.

"Hey, Moonbeam."

"What up, Mister Du Pont! I'm so glad you found *our girl*." She winks at me and I nod while Nevaeh blushes. I like how she can go shy even after I watched her ready to throw down with that dumbass in the cemetery. Nevaeh. My perfect fucking match.

I reach out and run my hand through her long, dark hair and kiss the top of her head. "She's hard to get a hold of, but we're good now. I'm moving her in here till shit calms down."

"That's a great idea! She's got this really cute pink bag that would be good for a weekender bag."

"Good to know."

"It's under her bed and she keeps her toiletries on her desk next to where we put the mail," Sunny offers.

Nevaeh covers her eyes. "Sunny, stop!" she pleads, but when I offer my hand to her, she takes it and lets me lead her out of the car and towards the apartment building.

"I'd throw a fit wanting to know when this happened," Sunny says and looks over her shoulder when there's the telltale sound of an announcement going off, "but that was them saying my flight is boarding. I'll call when I'm in San Antonio, okay?"

"Thank god, honestly. But yes, let me know when you're in San Antonio. I wish I could have been there to tell you goodbye. I'm sorry I wasn't."

"Hey, you needed to lay low. I get it," she says and then calls out, "Thank you for taking care of my roomie, Beau!"

"No problem," I say and swipe my key fob on the door. It pings when it opens and we walk inside as Sunny lets loose a whistle.

"Wow, so he's like *loaded* loaded. I love that for you, bestie."

Nevaeh laughs and I love that sound so fucking much. I thought I knew which sounds I liked the best from Nevaeh, but this—her laughter is the one I like the best. Not her crying or begging, or moaning sweet for me. It's her laughter that I love the most. *God, I'm so fucked if she knows that.* I squeeze her hand and lead her into the elevator while she talks to Sunny. I'm busy opening the door and scanning the hallway when Nevaeh starts to say goodbye to Sunny, but her friend stops her.

"Dean was trying to get a hold of you," she says and Nevaeh freezes.

"What for?" she asks. Her voice is normal and even. Good girl.

"I don't know, but he was acting fucking weird," Sunny replies. "I saw him outside. He was trying to get past the cops but he must have weirded them out and they didn't let him. He kept walking back and forth in front of the dorm and then he messaged me wanting to know where you were."

"Really? That's so weird. What did you say?" Nevaeh plays her part perfectly. I glance over at her and see she looks fine. I'm going to have to watch her ass when it comes to lying. She's too good at it.

I open the door and usher her inside while Sunny talks, "He wanted to know where you were. Started saying some wild shit about you two dating and it just...it felt off. I know how you feel about him, so I ignored the whole dating thing. Didn't tell him where you were either. Figured having him around wasn't going to be the vibe you wanted for today."

"But you told Beau," Nevaeh laughs.

"Well, yeah, Beau makes sense. Plus you two have the whole past connecting you. He didn't freak me out, so I told him. Should I not have? Oh no! Did I fuck up?"

"You didn't fuck up, it's okay. I'm here with him, aren't I?" Nevaeh says and pans the camera around my apartment. It's got exposed red brick and windows all along one wall that let in plenty of light. The appliances are all state of the art and the furniture is expensive shit that I'm sure my mother had a designer pick out. It's a place, nowhere special to me, though. After being locked up for four years, everywhere with four walls just feels like a place.

"Damn! That is a nice ass apartment! We are totally having a party there when I get back."

"No you're not," I say while I walk ahead toward the bedroom.

"Yes, we are," Sunny whispers and Nevaeh giggles.

I tune them out when I hear something coming from my room. What the fuck? It's like the rustle of sheets that I can only hear because the door is open. I pause outside of my room and look around the apartment. Everything looks in place. If someone is here, they didn't touch anything. What the fuck are they doing in my room with my sheets? I reach for the knife at my back and move close to the wall while I try to get a look inside of the room, but it's too dark and I can't get a decent view from where I'm standing. I'm going to have to go in. I take a step closer to the door and reach out a hand to push it open but then Nevaeh is right there at my elbow. I nearly swing on her.

I take in a deep breath and when Nevaeh opens her mouth, I hold up a finger to my lips and gesture with my knife at the bedroom door. Her eyes go wide and she nods. She knows what I'm saying.

Someone is here.

There's a thump and Nevaeh backs away from the door. She runs into the kitchen and grabs a knife of her own from the butcher block on the counter and I give her a nod of approval. If this fucker gets past me, they aren't going to take her down easy.

I start to edge forward but I'm not about to let the person camping in my room get the drop on me. I kick the door open and bum rush the room, ready for a fight to the death. But it's not The Reaper that I see.

It's fucking Ali.

"That's not quite the hello I expected, but I can work with it," she purrs and drops the sheet she has wrapped around her to the floor. "Now, why don't you come over here and get comfy, baby."

I almost laugh. This is better than The Reaper. Or at least, I think it is until Nevaeh comes storming into the room with her knife in hand.

She points the knife in Ali's direction. "You better get out of that bed before I drag you out."

CHAPTER TWENTY EIGHT

Nevaeh

THE FUCKING PERFECT girl that I hate is in Beau's bed. I thought she might be his girlfriend at the party, but I haven't really given her much thought since I decided to tell Beau I loved him. I don't care who she is. She's not supposed to be here and the rage that fills my chest is so close to what I felt when The Reaper came for me that I have to take a deep breath to not do something I might regret. I don't hurt innocent people. I'm not like The Reaper. Still, the thought is tempting and the knife in my hand probably isn't the best thing for me to point at her when I feel like this. It's such an easy move to using it on her and the thought shocks me.

Oh no. Fuck. *What's happened to me?*

"What is she doing here?" The girl shrieks and grabs a sheet off the floor to cover herself with.

"I feel like I'm supposed to be asking you that," I snap and Beau steps in between us.

"What the fuck are you doing here, Ali?" he snaps.

Ali.

Her name is *Ali*. I fucking hate that name.

She sits up and pushes back until she's against the headboard and the sight enrages me even more. She looks so comfortable in his bed, like she's done it a hundred times before. I want to rip her hair out of her head.

"Coming to finish off what we started at the party last night."

"Nothing happened between us last night."

"Oh really? Didn't seem that way when I came all over your fucking hand!"

Beau sighs and puts his knife away. "Get out of my fucking apartment. Give me that knife, Nevaeh." He snaps his fingers at me when I don't immediately surrender the weapon to him. I don't want to give it to him, but I know it's easier if I do.

"Fine," I slap the knife into his hand and storm off into the living room. I don't want to know what they're going to talk about. I want her gone, but that's between Beau and her. I perch on a stool at the kitchen counter and wait. I can hear them talking through the open door and when I turn in my seat to listen, I see Beau close the door. My gut turns sour when I see him close the door and it's hard not to run out of the apartment. A minute goes by and then another and another. What are they doing in there? If she's getting out of his apartment should it take this long? Are they doing more than talking? Is she convincing him to pick her over me?

He said he loved me. That has to count for more than whatever she can offer him, right? I bite my lip so hard that I taste blood, because I'm not sure. I don't know where I stand when it comes to Beau's life. Not when I'm put up against a girl that reminds me so much of Carrie Salt. The papers and gossip said they were an item and that Beau was serious about her before The Reaper took her. Is he serious with this girl too?

What if the twisted thing between us isn't enough to keep him and I lose him after everything? My hands shake and I have to sit on them to stop the tremors. I might have told Beau I loved him in a moment of bravery but I don't feel brave right now. Not after facing down The Reaper and Dean. There's so little left in me right now. I take in a deep breath and then another to calm myself down. Everything feels too sharp and bright right now. I sag forward and cover my eyes with my hands while Beau and Ali stay in his room. I hear a thump and jump in surprise when the door swings open and slams against the wall. I sit up taller when Beau drags Ali out of his room by her arm and throws her out so hard that she nearly falls onto the floor. I'm glad she's dressed now. She staggers and manages to keep her feet and whirls to face us while she clutches a tote bag to her chest.

"What is she doing here? Are you insane? After what she did to you, why would you have her here and not me?!"

Beau scrubs a hand over his face. "That's the second time someone has accused me of being insane today and to be honest, it's kind of getting on my nerves," he says. "And Nevaeh is here because I want her here. End of story. Get the fuck out."

Ali's eyes cut to mine and she lifts her chin. "Ruining four years of his life wasn't enough for you? You really want the rest of it? You're poison!"

She's looking at me like she hates me, but there's confusion there too. I can hear it in her voice. She doesn't understand why Beau wants me and not her. That's why she's angry. She doesn't care about him or if I'm good for him or not. She's angry because she thinks she's better than me and I'm the one Beau wants.

I don't answer her, she doesn't deserve it.

"Out. Now." Beau points a finger at the door and Ali tosses her hair over her shoulder. She stomps to the front door and opens it but pauses in the doorway and looks at Beau.

"You're going to regret this, Beau. You really fucking are."

"I don't take kindly to threats, Ali. Ask Jordan."

That makes her freeze and her eyes widen slightly when Beau approaches her. "But Jordan is-"

"Dead," Beau finishes and grabs the door from her hand. "He's fucking dead. Be smarter than Jordan, Ali. You were never fucking here." Beau forces her out with one hand and slams the door shut with the other on her face.

"That wasn't smart," I tell him quietly.

"She broke into my apartment. Let her go to the cops, she'll incriminate herself first and besides," Beau turns to face me with a smile and presses a hand to his chest, "I have a witness to what just happened. I never said that."

I lean forward on the counter again and watch him. "Did you really do something to Jordan?" I'd heard the news at the police station. They'd found Jordan when they'd canvassed the area for The Reaper. His body was in the old drainage ditch that ran the length of Greek Row. It surprised no one to find his body there after what they'd captured on the security cameras outside of Morris Hall.

"I didn't do *something* to him. I killed him."

But it hadn't been The Reaper at all. It was Beau that had done it.

I flinch because it's still fresh to think that Beau has killed and that he's done it for me. "Why?" Dean made sense. That was in the moment and forced, but Jordan? Why had he done that? I thought they were friends.

Beau approaches me and stands behind me. He puts a hand on either side of me on the counter and leans close so that his lips brush when he answers me. "He threatened you. I heard all about him chasing you. Nobody makes you scared and gets away with it, Nevaeh."

I lean back into his arms and close my eyes. "Nobody but you, you mean."

Beau turns his face and I feel his lips curve into a smile against my cheek. "Now you're getting it. I did years for you. Hard fucking time. I'm the only one that gets your fear."

"You might want to tell that to The Reaper," I whisper and close my eyes. It feels good to be in Beau's arms. This is what I've wanted for as long as I can remember. What I dreamed of. Relaxing into his touch feels surreal in the very best way.

This is heaven.

Beau growls low in his throat and wraps his arms around me. "He's next."

I open my eyes and my heart starts to pound. Beau can't go after The Reaper. It's too dangerous. Fear tastes bitter in my mouth just thinking what might happen if I lost Beau to The Reaper. My life and my rage are one thing, but Beau? I refuse to lose him.

I turn my head to look at him. "I don't want you near him. He's dangerous, Beau and I-"

Beau moves back from me and the change in position surprises me into silence. "You think you're the only one that can face that fucker down and live?" Beau picks me up and turns me. I cry out and grab at him when he lifts me up onto the counter. "Do you forget where I spent the last four years of my life, angel? Because it wasn't sitting here in Bloom getting soft. They had me in there with killers, because that's what they thought I was. All it did was make me exactly what they thought."

A killer.

He doesn't have to say it, I know what he means. Beau's killed for me. I've seen him do it and then there's Jordan on top of that. "Beau, I'm scared." I grab his shoulders and lean into him. "Everything feels like it's getting worse."

"Because it is," he says simply. "The fucking world is on fire, but you have me now. I'm going to keep you safe."

I believe him when he says it. No one has ever worked to keep me safe before. Not really. There's always been a condition. A caveat. I had to be obedient to keep the protection of the church. Crown of Thorns' love was not so easily bestowed and I don't think Pastor Mike would be as kind to me if he knew what I'd done with Beau or the thoughts I've had about hurting other people. My own mom hasn't even reached out to me since she made her decision to kick me out. Respectability and obedience were the ways to earn her approval.

It was never love. I don't think my mom knows how to love. The only thing she ever loved was power and position, of which we had precious little until the summer of the Mineral Belt Murder. I wrap my arms around Beau.

"I know," I whisper and hold him tight. "I know you will." Beau's hands are gentle, they trace my thighs and hips and my breath catches when he slides his hand to the front of my jeans and begins to undo them. "Beau," I whisper and lean back to look at him.

"I'm not taking you to my bed after that bitch was in it. This is going to have to do," he tells me and kisses me. His mouth isn't gentle on me like his hands are. He's demanding and brutal. He bites my bottom lip and bruises my mouth with his greedy kiss while he unbuttons my jeans and pulls them down with my underwear. His hands stroke my skin gently. They move over my thighs and down my legs as he pulls my jeans down. Beau kneels in front of me to pull them completely off, along with my shoes. When he stands again, it's to push me down onto the counter. The marble is cold on my ass and the backs of my thighs, but Beau's warm between my thighs. He leans over me and presses his mouth to my aching cunt.

"Beau!" I bring my thighs together on either side of his head and pull him close.

"Nevaeh," Beau moans and grips my hips. He grabs one of my hands and settles it onto the back of his head. "I would kill a hundred more men to stay right fucking here. This," he licks into my cunt, "is mine. You're mine. Say it," he orders and pumps two fingers into me. I'm wet, so fucking wet for him.

"I'm yours," I choke out while Beau starts to thrust faster into me. My body lights up when I remember last night. This is how he touched that other girl, but *I* get his mouth. She didn't. "Beau, I'm yours. Oh yes, it's so good. P-please don't stop." I pull on his hair, twist the strands and move him where I want. The other times we were together were good, but this feels different. I feel in charge now. I feel powerful with Beau's face between my thighs and his tongue inside of me.

"Nevaeh!"

Beau spits on his fingers and sucks my clit into his mouth. "B-beau!" My voice cracks and I shatter in Beau's hands. My back arches off the counter while I scream myself hoarse. I sob and try to move away from Beau, but he doesn't let me go. He holds me where I am and keeps sucking my clit until he forces a second orgasm out of me. I can't hold onto him anymore, I'm delirious. Nothing has ever felt this way. My hands fall to my sides as I struggle to breathe.

Beau presses a wet kiss to my inner thigh and grips my hips in his hands. "I know, I know, angel." His voice is low, the bass of it vibrates against my flesh and I squirm in his hold. I don't know if my body wants more or if I'm trying to get away. I tremble while Beau continues to eat my pussy. The sounds he makes are greedy. Desperate. Like he can't get enough of me.

"Angel," he croons against my aching slit. "You were perfect for me."

When Beau is done with me, he pulls me up into his arms and lifts me from the counter. Exhaustion crashes over me. My bones feel like they're made of lead and I can barely lift my head. It's easy to close my eyes and settle into Beau's arms while he brushes my hair away from my face and kisses me. I can taste myself on his lips. The musky taste of my own spend on his tongue marks him as much mine as he's marked me. He carries me to the couch and sits down with me in his arms and that's where I fall asleep.

CHAPTER TWENTY NINE
BEAU

I HAVE TO GET Nevaeh out of town. Definitely out of my apartment. It's not safe if Ali waltzed in here and planted her ass in my bed. While Nevaeh was out, I made a call to security and found out Ali passed herself off as my sister. Creepy that she picked the role of my imaginary sister and not my girlfriend, but whatever. She's gone now.

I look at Nevaeh. She's asleep on the couch with a spare blanket tucked around her. I frown and look her over. She looks so small like this on the couch. I want her in my bed, but I'm not taking her there after Ali dirtied the sheets. Nevaeh isn't going to sleep on something another woman had her ass on. As annoying as coming home to Ali was, I'm glad for it, because she exposed one huge flaw in my plan to hole up in my apartment with Nevaeh.

If Ali can get in, then so can The Reaper.

It's not safe here. But I do know where we can go that will be safe. My family has a lake house outside of town. We'll go there. It's secluded enough that we'll know if someone else is there, and it's not somewhere that many people necessarily think about when it comes to my family. My dad bought it on a whim two months before I got sent away to prison. Without me around, it's not like my parents had much of a reason to be around each other. And going out to your luxury lakefront home doesn't really scream remorse to a town when your son was just locked up for murder.

My parents should have sold it, but they didn't. So the lake house went unused and now it's more or less forgotten except for the staff that maintains it and keeps it stocked and ready in case my father gets a wild hair to go fishing on the weekend. It's the perfect place to go with Nevaeh. No one will bother us there. No one will even think to look for us. Even without The Reaper on the hunt again, people will notice Dean's gone soon. The further away from that scene Nevaeh and I are, the better.

I reach down and nudge her shoulder. "Time to wake up."

"What?" Nevaeh raises her head and blinks a few times. She's cute when she's like this. The thought is concerning, because I don't think anything is cute. But Nevaeh is. She wipes at her face and frowns. "Where are my pants?"

I nod at where I folded them on the couch beside her and Nevaeh groans and reaches for them. "What time is it?"

"Just after five."

"What?" The sleepy look on her face vanishes and she sits straight up. "That means I slept for hours."

I shrug. "You needed it," I say and play for nonchalant. Of course she needed the sleep. She fought off two psychopaths in twelve hours. Nevaeh was running on fumes, if that. "Drink this," I tell her and bring a glass of water to her. "We're leaving."

"Where are we going?" Nevaeh asks, but she takes the glass from me and drinks obediently. Satisfaction settles in to me watching her finish the glass. My good fucking girl always listens. I love it when she listens to me, even if she's a pain in my ass most of the time.

"Somewhere safe. My apartment is fucked if Ali got in here. We're going to my parent's lake house."

Nevaeh nods and follows me but I watch her face darken when I mention Ali. I catch her hand and lead her out of the apartment and into the elevator. "Nothing to be jealous of, angel." The doors slide shut and Nevaeh tries to move away from me but I keep a firm hand on her. I don't care if we're in the elevator and there's nowhere to really go. I want her with me.

She scowls at me and pulls on her hand but I hold fast. "I'm not jealous. I just…I don't like her."

I jerk Nevaeh right up against me and wrap an arm around her waist. "Neither do I," I say and watch the elevator lights flash before it stops on the ground floor. Nevaeh doesn't say anything, but I know she liked what I said. When we step out of the elevator, she's leaning into me like the good fucking girl she is.

"We're going to your dorm. We need to grab a bag first."

"What about you?"

"I've got plenty out there. Doesn't matter," I say, but I'm not looking at her, I'm scanning the lobby of the building. Things are tense. There's cops in here and I see three cruisers and an ambulance out front along with a fire truck. Nevaeh grabs onto my side and we both stop in the middle of the lobby.

"What's going on? Is someone hurt?" Nevaeh asks. Her eyes are on the cops. She's twitchy around them, which I get after she spent the whole fucking night with them.

"Mister Du Pont," the door man steps and waves me down. "There's a few officers here that would like to speak to you."

"About what?" I ask, but it's not the door man that answers me, it's the plain clothes cop I clock as a detective that speaks.

"Beau Du Pont, we're here to question you on the murder of Ali Simpson."

CHAPTER THIRTY

Nevaeh

A S MUCH AS I didn't like the girl I'd seen with Beau, I didn't want her to die. I rub my temples and lean back in the armchair I'm sitting in. It's leather and plush, much nicer than the metal chair I had to sit in during my questioning with the cops earlier today. But that's because we aren't down at the station like the officers who arrived wanted. We're still in Beau's apartment building and he's refusing to let them take us.

I glance towards the doors and see Mr. and Mrs. Du Pont power walking up to the front doors. The door man must have called them, or maybe their network of cronies did, because I haven't seen Beau reach for his phone once and yet, here they are. Right on time. Mr. Du Pont shoves open the door and Beau's mother wastes no time laying in to the officers present.

"What *exactly* in God's name do you think you're doing questioning my son?! After everything you've put him through!" Her voice echoes through the lobby, loud and strong. I guess it's good that Claire Du Pont has never thought herself below anyone in this town, because she's ready to go toe-to-toe with the police department and I know this time she'll win.

Mr. Du Pont puts an arm around her and shakes the officer's hand that just sauntered up. He's local, dressed in a uniform, not like the detectives that had us pinned from the second we stepped out of the elevator. The detectives must be from Kansas City with the way they're handling this. I can tell they don't give a shit who Claire Du Pont is, which is a mistake all in itself.

I look outside at the rapidly darkening sky. It's going to be well and truly dark soon. The sun set half an hour ago, but it's still painting the sky in orange and pink. It's hard not to feel nervous with the dark falling. Dark is when The Reaper strikes. The curfew is going back into effect, I know it is.

Get Home. Get Safe.

The Reaper's warning is hanging over all of us. It's just a matter of time before I hear that first siren. My hands shake and I tuck them under my thighs. There's a flash of a camera going off outside. Beau's building is all floor length glass windows on the bottom floor, so I can see just about everything happening outside.

I really wish I couldn't. If I couldn't, then I wouldn't know that Ali's body is just around the corner. I can see the corner of the yellow marker they're using to mark the crime scene. The photographer takes another photo and the flash lights up the area again. I look away and try not to replay the past few hours in my head. If we had let her stay, or Beau had walked her out, would she still be alive?

Why did The Reaper kill her? How did he do it in broad daylight?

When is this ever going to end?

Never.

The word comes to me so quick and fast it leaves me breathless and scared. It's never going to stop, not until The Reaper is behind bars. Or I'm dead.

"You really think this is his fault? That killer was after her, not him!" Beau's mother's voice carries again. I know what she means by her. She means me. She isn't wrong, and I hate that, because it means that I have to leave Beau. I can't keep bringing danger into his life. I put him in prison because of The Reaper. It's on me to face him, not Beau.

I stand and awkwardly make my way over to Beau and his parents. They're arguing with the detective, but whatever is happening looks like it's about to be over. Even if it's not, I'll finish it. If they want to question anyone, I'll go with them. It's not like I have anyone waiting on me. Sunny is on her way to Texas and my mom still hasn't contacted me.

"She's with me and we're fucking leaving. End of story." Beau turns and when he sees me, holds out his hand. I don't know what else to do, so I put my hand in his and he brings me close. "We're not staying here any longer. There are witnesses to show we had nothing to do with what happened to Ali."

"Then why was her murder called in saying you did?" One of the detective drawls. He's got a mustache and a tired look in his eyes that tells me he wants to be anywhere else but here when Mrs. Du Pont starts in on him.

"Are you dense? The person who called the murder in was obviously trying to incriminate my son and you all fell for it. *Again!*"

The other detective raises their hands. It's a woman and she looks more interested in what's going on. She's younger than her partner, so maybe that's why. "Even so ma'am, we're going to have to take them down to the station for questioning. We're doing our due diligence with this homicide. There's been quite enough blood spilled in your community and they've called us in," the detective shoots back. When everyone starts to yell again, I hold up a hand and interrupt.

"I'll go," I say. I see glass doors the Du Ponts just stormed in open as I'm talking and I recognize Pastor Mike hurrying in with a worried look on his face. "You can take me if you want someone for questioning."

"See," Mrs. Du Pont says and waves a hand at me. "She'll go. You don't need Beau."

"You aren't going anywhere without me, Nevaeh," Beau snaps and steps in front of me when I move toward the officers.

"Beau, this is the easiest way," I try, but I can tell from the stubborn look in his eyes that he's not going to go for it. "Please, let me do this."

"What's going on here?" Pastor Mike asks as he joins our group.

"Pastor Mike, what are you doing here?" Mr. Du Pont asks and Pastor Mike gives him a quick smile before he shoots me a look of concern.

"I'm here on Nevaeh's behalf. You all right?" He asks me and puts a hand on my shoulder. "I came as soon as I was notified."

"I'm fine, sir. Thank you. I was just offering to go with them for questioning. They want someone to ask about," my voice catches, because it feels weird saying her name when I thought about how much I hated it hours before, "about Ali," I finish quietly.

"It's just Mike, Nevaeh. You know that," he tells me with an easy smile, but I still can't do it. I just mumble a quick *Mike* to satisfy him. He turns to face the detectives and the local cop with a frown. "From my understanding, Nevaeh has already had one run in with you, isn't that right? I'd say she's had her fill of this for the day."

"I'm Detective Dans and this is my partner Detective Lucien," the woman introduces herself and holds a hand out to Pastor Mike. "And you are?" she asks.

Pastor Mike shakes her hand. "I'm the local pastor of these good people and I'm seeing that Nevaeh has someone in her corner. Her mother is tied up at the moment. Asked me to come down on her behalf."

Tied up. That's a delicate way of saying what's happening between us and I'm grateful he's not telling them the full story.

Detective Dans nods at him and looks at me. "Very lucky to have such an involved pastor."

"We all are," I say quickly, because The Du Ponts are far more important than I am at Crown of Thorns. I'm surprised to see Pastor Mike, but he was the one to help move me in, after all. I bet my mother has told him everything and he's too good to leave me out to dry.

"Now what seems to be the reason you want to take Nevaeh?"

"They think Beau and Nevaeh," Mrs. Du Pont says and I'm surprised she only sort of chokes on my name, "had something to do with the girl that was killed. I've told them they have nothing to do with it just because someone called it in on them."

"How are we not sure The Reaper didn't call in the murder?" Pastor Mike asks and we all fall silent. "Clearly he's after Nevaeh."

Mrs. Du Pont snaps her fingers and points at Pastor Mike. "Thank you! Now *that* makes sense. Who else would know about the murder but the killer? We have a witness," she points back to the door man being questioned, "that neither of them left their apartment, plus there's security footage of what happened. It wasn't them!"

"Oh, really? The Reaper made another appearance on camera?" Pastor Mike rubs a hand over his face. "All of this feels like a nightmare. All of this pain and anger isn't right."

"The Reaper was not identified on the footage, but we do have a side angle from one of the cameras of what happened. You can clearly see the victim in distress before she collapses and someone runs away on foot after a time."

"What do you mean *after a time*? What was he doing?" I ask and everyone looks my way. Detective Dans looks like she's going to tell me it's none of my business but Detective Lucien doesn't care much to keep quiet about it.

"He cut her heart out. Found it a block away with the K-9 unit."

"Oh my god." I grab onto Beau when I hear that. "H-he took her heart with him? For a block?" I whisper.

Pastor Mike doubles over and has to brace his hands on his knees. "The evil in this world grows."

"He did, left it sitting on top of a dumpster," Detective Lucien says and his partner glares at him while Mrs. Du Pont and I cover our mouths in horror.

"Lucien, zip it."

He shrugs. "She was going to find out anyway, if she comes to the station."

Beau grips my hand tighter. "Which, she's fucking not. We're going out of town."

Beau's mother drops her hands and glares at us. "You are not taking that girl to our lake house."

"I am," Beau returns, "and unless you're going to charge me with something, we're leaving. I know my rights, remember? Doing time does that."

Everyone falls silent. I know Beau bringing up his imprisonment is the right button to push with how quickly the fight goes out of the detectives. The glare from his mother tells me she isn't going to let my part in all of it go anytime soon, but I can swallow that pill when the detectives relent and agree to let us leave. But not without giving us a police detail. Pastor Mike showing up when he did was a blessing really, with his insistence that my safety be looked after.

"He's not going to stop coming for you, Nevaeh. We have to keep you safe."

The detectives agree and after a hasty goodbye and a hug from Pastor Mike, they usher us towards Beau's car with the promise that two officers will accompany us out to the Du Pont lake house.

"They'll stay nearby and monitor your safety. We'll make sure they report in regularly. If you see anything suspicious, you let them know and they'll make contact with us."

"Sure thing. We're going by her dorm first. She needs clothes," Beau tells them, but Mr. Du Pont speaks up, stopping us.

"She can use what's there. Go on to the lake house, son."

"Those are my clothes!" Mrs. Du Pont snaps, but her husband waves her off.

"For Christ's sake, Claire! It's only clothes. They need to get indoors now! If Beau wants her, then he's going to have her. End of story."

Mrs. Du Pont snaps her mouth shut but the murder in her eyes has me thinking she is on par with The Reaper. If she could kill me, find some way that I didn't exist, she'd take it.

"Your mom hates me," I whisper to Beau while he puts himself between me and everyone else and opens my door for me.

"Oh yeah, she fucking hates you."

CHAPTER THIRTY ONE

Nevaeh

THE RIDE TO the lake house is longer than I thought it would be. It's about a half hour outside of Bloom and tucked away on a road that I've never even noticed. But that's easy all the way out here. Besides, I never had any business coming out to the lake. This was a place where only Bloom's rich went. It was reserved for them and them alone. I don't even think my mom had any client's out here. If she did, she never brought me along with her.

"How painful do you think her death was?" I have to ask it, even if I shouldn't. I can't stop thinking about what the detective said. I look in the rearview mirror to see the headlights from the cop car bouncing along behind us. Beau's car is newer and he's driving fast, so the car is always just coming around a corner when we're moving on to the next. The headlights vanish from sight when Beau sighs and speeds up. The roads here are winding and rise up on hills. When I look out, I can see Bloom glittering below us. I always thought Bloom Point was the highest you could go, but I should have known there was more to see.

"I-I didn't know her but I wish-that shouldn't have happened to her," I whisper.

"Fuck that guy for saying that in front of you. Don't think about it."

Beau doesn't want me to think about it, but I can't help but ask him the question that's been on my mind since I stood up on that deserted street and there was no one there but The Reaper looking back at me. "Do you think he's going to do-"

"No," Beau spits out. "No, Nevaeh."

I fall silent. We drive for a few minutes longer before he turns onto an access road and drives up to a gate with a keypad. "The code is 4289," he tells me while he punches the code in and the gates part. The cop car rolls in behind us and then parks at the bottom of the hill I see stretching in front of us before we go on.

There are lights that go up the length of the driveway and the lake house rises up in front of us, all lit up. It's a two story house with so many windows it almost feels like the house is made of glass.

"Everything is on an app," he says. "They made sure to turn on the lights so it felt safer."

I nod. The gesture is nice, though I know The Reaper would come for us even with a fully lit house. It isn't like when we were kids and thought every bad thing was just under the bed or in the darkness of our bedrooms and would vanish with the flick of a switch. There isn't enough light in the world to keep him away. He killed a girl in broad daylight today. He did that and no one saw him carry her heart for a block.

I follow Beau out of the car and up the steps of the house. Beau unlocks the door and it's only when I hear the lock click in place that I relax slightly. Even so, I look towards the windows.

"Can we close the curtains?" I ask him. There are curtains hanging nice and thick, even if not a single one of them is being used.

"Sure, I'll get them." Beau starts to work on closing the curtains by the door while I move into the living room. There aren't as many windows in here, just ones facing where I know the lake is. Maybe I'll spend more time here.

I pull them closed and look over my shoulder while Beau continues to close curtains behind me. "Thank you, it's just-I mean, I feel like a sitting duck with all these windows."

"I don't think I noticed it before, but I was only out here a few times before."

He doesn't say before what. I know what he means. I'm glad he doesn't bring it up. It hurts when he does. I finish closing the curtains and look around the living room. It's a big room that opens up to the second floor above it. There's a big comfy looking sectional in front of a massive stone fireplace. The floors are dark wood and the walls are white with the kind of rafters above it that looks like rough hewn wood. It adds a warmth and down to earth touch to the room, even if the lake house is easily the nicest house I've ever been in. There's a wall of built-in bookshelves beside the fireplace. When I go look at the shelves, the only books I see are photo books and what I think of as coffee table books, of National Parks and Cooking. The knick knacks on the shelves look like someone else picked them out. There's a dish full of glass orbs and a set of scented pine cones. Plain wax candles sit on the mantle, but there are no photos. Interesting. When I turn and look at the walls, I see there are no photos anywhere. At least, none of the Du Ponts. Everything is artsy or looks like it was picked out specifically to match the decor.

I'm staring at one photo that I know. It's of the Konza prairie at sunset and a storm is rolling in. It's beautiful, with a line of dark clouds and the last burst of sunshine breaking through the gray storm clouds that darken into night. It looks surreal, but it's not. Storms roll in unfettered and wild on the prairie and create a beauty so surreal it makes everything fall away.

Life here has a beauty to it. A beauty that people wouldn't think existed in a flyover state like Kansas. I wonder if it would have been more beautiful if The Reaper hadn't been bloodying it over the years. What would it have been like to take everything Bloom has to offer without a madman terrorizing us? Would it have made any difference at all? I don't know.

"They won that at some auction," Beau says when he walks into the room and sees me staring at the picture. I'm not really looking at it anymore. My thoughts are a jumbled mess, so I've just been staring in the direction of it for god knows how long.

"There's no pictures of you or your family," I say.

"They didn't spend much time out here," Beau replies and looks around the house. "It was decorated this way when we bought it."

"Really?" I look around the house with new eyes. To think Beau's parents left the house empty and frozen in time for four years is eerie, but it makes me feel like I understand the house. I was frozen in time without Beau too. Reliving that night over and over, dreaming of Carrie, guilt-ridden and praying for Beau's release.

I never left that night, not until Beau came back and freed me.

He nods. "Yeah, they never came up here after that. I think my dad does sometimes when he wants to tie one on or have a poker night, maybe do a little fishing, but my mother?" He snorts and shakes his head. "Absolutely not. No reason for her to leave town."

"It's pretty out here," I say and Beau snorts.

"Sure it is, just look at those views," he says, sweeping a hand out to the now covered windows.

"It could be worse," I point out. I don't know how much worse it could be given the past twenty four hours, but we're still alive and at this point that's a win.

Beau doesn't say anything, he just grabs both of my hands and pulls me to him. He cradles my face when my body is flush to his and strokes my cheek. "I'm going to keep you safe."

"I know," I whisper.

A knock at the door makes me jump but Beau doesn't react. He turns towards the door, calm as you please, and motions for me to move behind him. "It's just the cops, but stay behind me. There's a gun safe upstairs. First bedroom on the left, you'll find it in the closet. The code is the same as the gate. Repeat it."

"I, uh," I stammer and panic because it's hard for me to remember, but I manage it, "it's 4289."

"That's it. I want you to run for that gun and blow that fucker's brains out," he tells me while we walk towards the door.

"I don't know how to shoot a gun."

"You'll figure it out. I know you."

Beau opens the door and I hang back a step. Sure enough, it's the local cops that followed us from Bloom. "Evening, you two. We just finished doing a perimeter check. Everything looks good. We're going to go head on back down by the gate for the night but we'll be up to do a check every other hour. Anything about the property that we should know?"

"You've got the codes?" Beau asks.

"Your parents had them sent over."

"That's all there is to know then."

"Sounds good," The cops says and looks at me over Beau's shoulder as he hands him a couple of cards, "that's going to be the direct line to me and this one is to my partner." The cop doesn't look at me like I've done anything wrong. He looks at me like he feels sorry this is happening to me. I hope nothing bad happens to him while he's out there keeping watch for The Reaper.

"Thank you, sir. Have a good night out there."

The cop nods at us. "Good luck you two. Don't open this door if it isn't one of us," he says and then turns to walk back to his car.

Beau watches him for a second before he shuts the door and bolts it. He opens a security panel next to it and taps a few buttons. "Is that a security system?" I ask, even though my question sounds dumb because what else would it be?

"Yeah, if any doors or windows open, it'll go off. The station in town will get the signal too."

He doesn't say what I'm thinking.

"That's good," I say and don't say it either. We both know we're too far from Bloom for anyone to make it out here in time if The Reaper comes knocking. Alarm or no alarm, we're on our own.

Beau and I get ready for bed and everything feels oddly normal. Like we've done this before, like things have been normal between us. I'm tempted to do what I do best and pretend. It would be so easy to slip into the thought that this is my house and Beau is my husband. That we're happy and normal.

I don't do it though.

I stay where I am and soak up all the little details from being with Beau. I watch how he brushes his teeth and takes extreme care not to leave any toothpaste anywhere. When he washes his face he's meticulous. When he turns on the shower and pulls me close. He doesn't rush when he takes my clothes off. Beau and I shower and make love, that's what it is. It's slow and soft. The hot water from the shower head set into the ceiling falls around us like rain and it makes me think of storms, but this storm isn't wild or demanding. It's gentle and restorative, it relaxes me. When I come with Beau's name on my lips, he has to hold me up so that I keep my feet.

After, we dry each other off with slow touches and kisses that feel different from the ones we've had before. These are gentle and I feel shy when Beau looks at my naked body. I shouldn't be flushing and fighting the urge to hide from him with the things I've done with him, the brutality he's marked my body with. The filthy things I've said to him.

How am I shy?

If Beau notices, he doesn't let on. He just dries my hair and hands me a sleeping gown to get into. It's silky and black.

"This is your mom's, isn't it?" I ask when I'm dressed and he's toweling off his hair.

Beau makes a face and nods. "Yeah, it is. But I don't want to think about her when I'm going to get in bed with you."

I laugh and walk into the bedroom to turn down the bed for the night. "Fair point." I pause at the foot of the bed and dig my toes into the plush carpet. The bed is huge, a four poster affair with thick blankets and fluffy pillows that look like they belong in a boutique hotel, not someone's house. It's a beautiful bed in a beautiful bedroom in an even more beautiful house. It's easy to forget that there's evil waiting for us outside of its walls when everything is so peaceful here. The clock reads just after nine but I'm exhausted and I know Beau is too. When he comes into the bedroom I'm already nodding off in bed. He doesn't get in right away, but he does click off the light. I hear him go into the hallway and there's the sound of a door opening before his footsteps fade away. When he doesn't come back into hearing range, I sit up and glance towards the door. My heart starts to pound and I count the seconds until I hear him again. I get up to 600 seconds before I hear Beau at the end of the hallway.

"Beau?" I call out into the dark and he responds immediately.

"I could be anyone Nevaeh. Don't give away your position, calling for me like that."

"I know it's you," I say. "He walks too heavy. I'd hear him straight away."

Beau enters the room a second later and closes the door and locks it. "What does he walk like?" He asks and I feel the bed dip under his weight. The room is pitch black because we have the curtains pulled, even up here on the second floor. I didn't want to risk it.

"Heavy," I say and then try again, "he sounds like he's big. And he is, because I've seen him. He walks like he doesn't care who hears him. When he was running behind me, his boots on the pavement were the only thing I could hear." Even now I can hear the steady *thump-thump-thump* of him running behind me.

"He has to be in shape. There's no way he can be so big and fast. He ran like he could do it forever. Strong, too. When he tackled me...I should have died then, but I didn't. Somehow, I didn't."

I didn't die because I was too angry. The rage, that red hot, blinding rage, had fueled me. It was like when you hear about mothers that lift cars off their children when it's life or death. They gain superhuman strength they didn't know they had. My rage was like that. Superhuman. Utterly transforming and incandescent in its power. Would I be able to do it again? What if it failed me? What if this time, when I try to fight him off, it fails me and I end up just another name in the long list of victims? The name people wince and look the other way when you hear it. The name people feel obliged to say, "she was such a nice girl" and "she had her whole life ahead of her."

That's what The Reaper wants to turn me into. Just another hard to say name and an uncomfortable moment.

"How big is he?" Beau asks and scoots closer to me. I feel his legs rub up against mine and a second later he's hooking his arm around my waist to bring me against him. Our legs intertwine, and when Beau lays down, I go with him, my head on his chest. My stomach aches. I know I'll be sick soon if I don't try to calm down.

"Maybe 6'4 or bigger. He's as big as you," I say and start to trace the shape of Beau's hand beside mine where they rest on his stomach. "He's strong too and so, so fast. B-but the way he moves? He moves like he's the scariest thing out there. He knows nothing can touch him. Not the cops, not me, not anyone." My words end on a whisper, because my throat feels tight. It's hard to talk with how hard my heart is pounding. Even though I'm with

Beau and I know I'm safe in his arms, my body doesn't. I can feel my heart racing, it pounds against my rib cage so hard that my chest hurts. The pain is stress, I know that, but I can't stop it. Even from just talking about The Reaper, my body still thinks he's right behind me. I want to get up and run, even if there's nothing to run from.

Where would I even go without Beau? There's nowhere I would want to run to if he wasn't there with me.

I take in a deep breath and then another while Beau rubs my back. He turns us so my back is to his front and curls his body around me. We lay like that for a while with neither of us speaking. I stare into the darkness, willing myself to calm down. Beau at my back works like a charm and bit by bit, limb by limb, I relax into his arms.

"You'll be free." Beau kisses the back of my head and brings my hand up to his mouth. "I'm going to kill him, Nevaeh."

Beau means what he's saying. I know he does.

"I know you will," I lie into the darkness. As much as I want to believe the man I love, the boy I put away for a murder that marked us both, I know the truth.

No one can stop The Reaper.

CHAPTER THIRTY TWO
BEAU

NEVAEH LEANS CLOSE and looks into the pan that I've got pancake batter in. There's another pan going with bacon. I have just beat the shit out of a half a dozen eggs in a bowl that I'll cook once the bacon is done. The lake house is stocked just the way I thought it would be. There's fresh fruit and meat in the fridge along with a case of beer. When I went into the walk-in pantry, I didn't miss the two handles of Jack Daniels sitting right next to the bottled water.

Looks like my dad has been making more use out of the lake house than I realized. I bet if I went downstairs to the wine cellar that would be fully stocked too.

"I never pegged you for a cook," she says.

"I wasn't. Not before prison," I tell her and flip the pancake.

"What?" she asks and blinks at me in surprise, but I get it. Prison isn't exactly where someone thinks you'll learn to cook.

"They have culinary courses in prison," I tell her and her mouth drops open.

"They let you take cooking classes?!"

"Like I said, it was a culinary course," I stress those two words and then nod, "and yes, they did. I was the best fucking student in that class." I slide the last pancake onto the stack I've already made and start taking out the bacon.

"Sorry, sorry," Nevaeh says and holds her hands out at her sides in a mock curtsey with a grin on her face, "*culinary classes.*"

"That's better."

"Do I need to call you 'Chef' or something?" she asks.

I roll my eyes as I pour the eggs into the pan and point at the cabinet to the right of the sink. "Get the plates out and set the table."

Nevaeh gives me a mock salute and bounds off towards the cabinet. "Yes, Chef!"

I laugh and work on the eggs. "Shut it."

Nevaeh laughs on her way into the dining room with her hands full of plates, but I hear her say, "Yes, Chef!" once she's in the next room.

Breakfast is good. It's not the food that makes it good though, it's Nevaeh. I could be eating glass and a morning with Nevaeh would make me say it was the best breakfast of my life. I'm surprised by how normal she makes me feel. I haven't felt this way in a long time. Years. Whatever light Nevaeh carries around inside of her has pushed the darkness back enough that the noise in my head is quiet.

I feel like the kid that went to prison thinking he would be out in a month. The one that was sure the cops would find who really killed his girlfriend. The one that didn't know what it felt like to stab someone to death, using a piece of a chain link fence I spent every day for a week working on sharpening when I was outside in the yard.

I can be the dumb kid that doesn't have blood on his hands. I can be the one that didn't hurt Nevaeh or take from her what she would have given me if I'd just asked. I can be the man that might have noticed her with enough time and fallen in love with her like a normal fucking person.

I'm not normal though. Neither is Nevaeh. I fell in love with her with anger and revenge turning the thought of her into a weapon. But all of that calmed the second she said she loved me. All the anger, all the spite, every last bit of my drive for revenge crumbled to fucking dust. As twisted as my obsession and love for her is, as much as I know that I can't rely on myself to give her the happily-ever-after she deserves, it doesn't matter.

She's mine and she'll take what I give her. Right now, that's the side of me that's decent and kind, the one that lives to hear her laugh and notices how she takes her coffee. That's the side she gets right now. Nevaeh welcomes it as easily as she has the darkness rooted deep in me.

"Can we go for a walk?" Nevaeh asks.

We've been out by the pool. I've been walking the perimeter and checking my phone for time since that's all it's good for out here with the shitty reception that keeps going in and out. I spread a towel down for Nevaeh so she could read by the pool. We've been out here for an hour or so and I bitched at her to put sunscreen on, but the storm clouds that started rolling in half an hour ago blocked out the sun enough that I let it slide when she pushed back. There's a rumble and I look up.

"Looks like rain," I say. "I dunno. Maybe we'll stick around here."

Nevaeh sighs and throws herself back onto the towel she's laying on. "I need to move. Please? I'm so bored and I can't even text Sunny because of the reception."

I hesitate. The cops that are assigned to us should be coming by in forty or so minutes. They've been making sure to make their route every hour to hour and a half. I just saw Marcus, he's the younger of the two and more easy going than his partner. If I time Nevaeh's walk right, we can get back before it rains and meet Marcus at the front of the house.

"All right, but just for a while. They'll be by to check in and they'll lose their shit if they don't know where we are."

Earlier I thought Simon, the older of the two and someone I know from the parties my parents have thrown, was going to have a heart attack when he didn't find us after breakfast. We were in the wine cellar, investigating just how much time my father spent here by the amount of wine he had stored. When we came back upstairs, Simon had his gun out and was radioing Marcus for back up.

"Right, I thought Simon was going to shoot us when we came back upstairs," Nevaeh whispers and looks around like she thinks Marcus or Simon might be listening. Maybe they are, but I don't care. Nevaeh gets her shoes on and I get an eyeful of her ass. She's wearing a sundress, something that doesn't much look like an outfit my mother would wear. It's far too short, sheer and floral. There's a ruffle around the hem of it that only hits Nevaeh's mid thigh. It's definitely my father's mistress' dress Nevaeh is wearing. It makes sense, with the way this place looks kept up. It explains the fresh food and the linens that felt freshly laundered when we got into bed last night. I wonder if my mother knows my father is cheating. Probably not, if he's bringing her out here. I'm not surprised he's cheating, but I am surprised that he would play house with another woman.

My mother is vindictive and cruel when she needs to be. If she found out he was cheating on her, she'd bury him. Whoever it is must be worth it.

"I'm ready!" Nevaeh yells once she has her shoes on and I pause to look at her. Not just see her, but really and truly look at her. We opened the curtains up this morning to let the sun in and the late afternoon sun slants in and frames her. She looks so innocent and fresh faced. Her dark hair has a slight curl to it from my fingers and the smile she sends my way is bright and open. If I didn't know better, I'd say she was having a vacation, not hiding out from a serial killer. Since last night, there has been a shift in her and I can't put my finger on it. When we went to bed, she felt like stone in my arms. I could feel her heart racing. She managed to get to sleep, but it wasn't easy. Every creak of the house had Nevaeh stiffening and scooting closer to me until we were pressed so close that it was hard to breathe.

But this morning?

This morning she's been like a different girl. She's laughed and walked around barefoot and carefree. She's laid out by the pool and texted Sunny while she snacked and went through fashion magazines she found in the den. There's something not right about her. Even as happy as I am when I'm with Nevaeh, this feels off. This isn't happiness, it's a manic energy that has Nevaeh bouncing on her toes while I lock the door and watch the sky.

"The storm is almost here. We're going to need to come back sooner than I thought." I point to the sky and lead her towards the trail that runs from the house to the lake. It makes a big loop, so if we stay on it we'll be right back at the house. The loop isn't long, maybe a mile and a half, but I don't think we'll be able to do it before the rain hits.

Nevaeh pouts and drags her feet as she falls behind me. "Stop being such a downer. I'm sure we'll be fine."

Yup, there's definitely something up with Nevaeh. She's cautious and smart, so why is she acting like a careless pre-teen?

"Uh-huh."

She sighs behind me. "You're being so grumpy."

"And you're acting out of character."

"How do you even know that? It's not like you've spent time with me," Nevaeh tosses at me and then starts walking faster. The trail we're on is dirt and has a lot of uneven parts to it. The people that used to own the property had horses and would ride them down to the lake and back. Nevaeh shoves past me and almost eats shit when her toe catches on a rock, but I catch her arm and hold her up.

"Like hell," I tell her and drag her back against me. "I fucking know you and we both know it. There's not a thought in that pretty head of yours that I can't read. You're mine, angel."

She slaps at my hand and turns to glare at me. "You don't-I'm not yours. I'm just me. I don't belong to anyone, okay?"

"Keep talking like that and I'll take you to get my name tatted on your ass when this is over." I'm half serious when I say that. There were plenty of guys in lock up that had their women tattoo their names on them as a promise of waiting till they made parole. I never thought I'd be one of those men, but Nevaeh makes me want it. There's an appeal to thinking about my name sitting on the curve of her ass where I can see it. Nevaeh turns her back on me and marches off. The fast pace that she's walking sets an extra sway to her hips and makes her dress ride up slightly.

Oh yeah, I can see my name marking her perfect ass.

"Whatever," Nevaeh tosses over her shoulder as she stomps forward. When she stumbles I sigh and call out to her.

"Slow the fuck down or you're going to eat shit."

"You don't tell me what to do!" she explodes and turns back to face me with a glare on her beautiful face. "No one tells me what the fuck to do!"

I stop walking and cross my arms over my chest. "That so, angel?"

"Yeah! And stop fucking calling me angel! I'm not an angel!"

"You are to me," I tell her and Nevaeh jerks back like I slapped her.

"You're a liar!" She screams and points a finger at me. "I'm not an angel, you're saying that to make fun of me. You hate me for what I did." Her voice cracks and I see tears in her eyes. The wind kicks up and blows her hair across her face. Nevaeh pushes at her hair and tries to keep the skirt of her dress down when the wind flips it up.

"Nevaeh…" I take a slow step towards her and then another. She's wearing stupid sandals. Shoes that my dad's mistress probably only wears to walk around the pool and not on this shit trail. When Nevaeh tries to back up from me, her foot catches and she falls to her knees.

"Angel," I start when I see her shoulders shake. She's crying when she looks up at me.

"Stop calling me that! I'm not an angel. I fucking ruined your life!"

"Nevaeh-"

"I ruined your fucking life! You can't love me, that's insane!"

"And you shouldn't love me either after what I did to you!" I explode and get in her face when she gets up off of her knees. "It's insane that you want me after the way I fucked you."

Nevaeh's cheeks go pink at my words. "You don't tell me what's insane. No one tells me anything! No one! Not you, not the cops, not my fucking shitty mom or the goddamned fucking Reaper! *No one!*" she screams at me before she turns on her heel and starts running towards the lake.

I watch her for a second. It only takes one almost fall in her stupid fucking sandals for me to sigh and take off after her. "Nevaeh, get your fucking ass back here!"

"No!" Nevaeh's one word fucking answer floats back to me on the wind that's kicked up harder now that we're closer to the lake. I can see the white tops of the waves when they break and crash against each other. Thunder sounds above us and I push myself to run faster. We have to get inside. The way storms move in the prairie is unpredictable. We won't be able to make it back to the house before the storm breaks on us, but if I get her now we might be able to avoid the worst of it.

There's a curve in the trail with a boulder that marks it as the halfway point on the loop a few yards away and that's where I catch Nevaeh. There's a copse of trees here and some flowering bushes that I bet the previous owners planted. Stuff like this doesn't grow this way in the prairie. Not unless it was brought in by people. Most of Bloom looks the way it does because of the seeds and saplings settlers brought with them from the East Coast. This little copse of trees is the same. When I get to Nevaeh, I grab her around the waist and lift her up. She's going to fight me, I know that, so I keep her back to my chest and start to carry her up the path. The first raindrop hits me on the shoulder and then the arm. A second later, Nevaeh scratches the same place and throws herself back in my arms. She's trying to break my hold by bucking against me, but the shoes she's in don't give her the traction she needs so she just ends up having her dress ride up to her waist.

Nevaeh screams and I go still, because I know that sound. It's rage. Deep, dark, the kind of anger that feels old. "Get off of me!" Nevaeh screams from her chest. The sound of her words vibrates through my arms in time with the crack of thunder that splits the sky.

"Stop fighting me!" I give her a shake, but that only works to enrage the woman in my arms. She's not Nevaeh, or the girl that I've loved and despised. She's a force. She's the rumble of the storm rushing over the prairie. Sharp and bitter, destructive until the last wind gale. Nevaeh claws at me and screams.

"Let me go!" She throws herself forward and tries to stomp on my foot, but her sandal is too flimsy and the strap snaps off so that it's just her bare foot she's trying to bring down on me.

"He's going to kill me," she screams. My grip loosens when I hear those five words. "He's going to fucking kill me." I let her go and Nevaeh turns to face me. Her eyes are wild and she's not worried about how high her dress is riding. She stands there, legs spread and feet planted and throws her arms wide.

"I'm going to die!"

"No," I tell her, but she's not listening.

"H-he's going to cut me up into fucking little pieces like he did those girls. He's going to cut me open, Beau!" Her chest rises and falls fast and hard and it's then that I see her crying. "And no one is going to fucking miss me."

"I would," I tell her and try to make a grab for her. "And that isn't going to happen. I'm going to keep you safe."

"All that's going to do is get you killed!" Nevaeh shakes her head and throws a hand up in the air, "No!" She screams. "I'm not going to let him hurt you." Nevaeh turns and takes off at a run. She's running for the lake and even with one stupid sandal on her foot, she's making good time. I'm honestly too stunned to do much but watch her for a half second before I realize what's happening and take off after her.

"*Nevaeh!*" I yell. I'm gaining on her, but it's not enough. She's not following the trail anymore. She's cutting through the tall grass and she's almost to the water. Almost to the cliff that drops off and into the water. Fuck. The cliff. That's where Nevaeh is heading, not the water. I know what she's going to do. She's going to throw herself from the cliff. If she were to follow the trail we'd been on, we'd follow it alongside the steep cliffside before it emerged on the other side and headed back to the lake house.

Nevaeh isn't doing that, though. She's going to try to jump straight over the edge of it. The water isn't immediately there. If she doesn't jump far enough, she's going to land on the rocks below.

"Nevaeh, no!"

I put on a burst of speed and throw myself forward. My fingers slide over the flimsy material of her dress just as Nevaeh launches herself forward. Somehow I manage to get my arms around her. I can't stop though, so we end up slamming into the ground just an inch or so away from the cliff's edge. Nevaeh howls with rage when she realizes that I've stopped her.

"You motherfucker!" She swings on me and I take it, because I know it isn't me that she's seeing. Not right now. She sees The Reaper. So I let her make me her villain.

CHAPTER THIRTY THREE

Nevaeh

I'M LOSING MY shit. I know this, but I can't stop. "No!" I swing and claw at Beau. I try to bite his hand when it comes close to my face and kick at him when he pulls me into his arms. I'm sure he's trying to get me back to the lake house considering I just tried to throw myself off a cliff.

"Let me go!" I twist and try to wiggle out of Beau's arms, but he's too strong. I hate that he's so strong. I push at his arms and when they don't give I'm reminded that if he were The Reaper, I'd be dead. I fight harder. I have to get free. I can't let anyone hold me down. If I do, how am I going to fight The Reaper and win? I won't stand a chance if I can't get free from Beau. He has me half in his arms and my ass hangs out from where my dress has ridden up to my waist, but I don't stop fighting. I manage to get a leg free and drop my weight so that I'm able to throw myself backwards from Beau. I land on the hard ground with a grunt and swing at Beau when he comes close to me, but he's too fast for anything to land.

"Get away from me! You're going to die if you don't."

Beau grabs me and jerks me to my feet before he swings me up into his arms and starts marching back to the house. "Then I fucking die."

"No! No, no, no!" I push at him, but there's no moving him or breaking his hold on me. I try to lift myself up by pushing on his shoulder but it doesn't do anything to get me free. Beau just hitches me higher up and takes off at a jog.

He runs until we make it back to the little copse of trees that I took off running from. They're birch trees. They don't belong here, not on the prairie. I wonder who planted them but the thought is gone when Beau slows and shoves me up against the massive rock that's there. It's limestone and from the cut of it I know it was brought here, same as the birch trees. It doesn't belong and neither do I.

Why did my mom bring us both here to start over if she was just going to abandon me when I needed her the most? It doesn't make sense. None of this fucking makes sense. The birch trees and the limestone boulder or the fact that I'm with Beau Du Pont and he thinks he loves me.

Beau pushes the skirt of my dress up and shoves me down on the limestone until I'm bent over it with my ass in the air. "Beau!" I scream, but my voice is lost in the storm that's well and truly breaking over us right now. Rain falls hard and fast, pelts us like tiny knives. Icy water that cuts through my flimsy dress and makes my skin go numb.

"You want to act like a fucking brat?" Beau yells and holds me down with a hand at my back. "Then I'm going to treat you like a goddamn brat!" I barely have time to react before Beau's hand cracks across my ass. The water makes his blow sting far more than it should and I shriek as I try to get away from him, but there's nowhere to go. There's never anywhere to go when it comes to Beau. As much as I've told him it's not true, he owns me. He knows me. There will never be another person to know me like he does.

Beau spanks me again and my skin sings from the strike. He shifts and hits my other ass cheek. The burn evens out and it's not a scream that leaves my mouth, but a moan. I turn my face, my lips and cheek scraping against the rough surface of the limestone that still feels warm from that afternoon's sunshine.

"Beau."

He doesn't answer me. I don't know if it's because he can't hear me or because he doesn't care, but he hits my ass. The crack of his hand on my flesh morphs until it's pain and pleasure all rolled into one. That's the way it is with us. The way it'll probably always be. Pleasure tinged and chased with darkness that leaves me raw and weak from how much it shows me about myself. Looking at Beau is like looking at a mirror of myself. Our souls are both twisted and marked. With anyone else it wouldn't work, but our jagged and frayed edges fit together perfectly until we're whole.

"Beau!" I cry out when he stops spanking me. My body needs the pain. It quiets my mind, drowns it out until it's bearable and I arch my back, trying to chase after the kind of punishment that only Beau knows how to give me.

Beau kicks my legs apart and when he presses up against my bare ass, he's unzipped his pants and I whimper when I feel his warm thighs against my sensitized ass. "Beau, please, I-"

"Quiet!" He brings his hand down on my side and I jump. "Did I fucking say you could talk, slut?"

"N-no."

"I can't fucking hear you." Beau has to shout to be heard over the raging storm so I do the same.

"No!"

He leans forward and brings his mouth to my ear so that I can hear him when he says, "Then shut the fuck up and take my dick like my good fucking girl. Do you understand me?"

I nod and bite down on my lip when he starts to ease into me. Beau groans and grabs onto my hips to jerk me back against him. "That's it, take every fucking inch." Beau feeds me another inch and then jerks me back against him. His hips slam against me and I scream and claw at the limestone beneath me. My nail snags on the rock and pain shoots through me when it rips off.

"Scream for me, Nevaeh!"

Beau fucks into me and sets a pace that has my back arching and my injured hand scrabbling at the rock. Blood smears from my hand onto the rock but I don't care. The pain that Beau gives me amplifies the pleasure singing through my body. He changes the angle and when he slides home, I see stars. I squeeze down on his dick. I want to be closer to him, so much fucking closer than we are. I need him to keep fucking me.

"Don't stop. Oh, Beau! Beau! Please don't stop!"

Beau's hand covers my mouth and I scream against his palm. Even if his hand wasn't there, the storm would devour the sound. Beau's hand over my mouth is so much better, though. It sets a heat off inside of me that makes me feel primal and wild. Unfettered. The kind of woman that no one tells what to do, so much so that Beau has to force my submission. It's all a lie though. All he has to do is ask and I would give him the world, but that isn't what matters right now.

What matters is that Beau is forcing my submission. He's taking control of my body and showing me that no matter how much I rage, my body, my soul, my passion belongs to him. All of it. Every part of me. He is my god at this moment and for that reason I'm going to be safe because he said so.

My life, my fate, is his to will and when I cum, I scream myself hoarse with Beau's hand still wrapped around my face. I sag forward and Beau lets me go. He shifts his hold back to my hips and fucks me slow and hard.

I hear his voice but I can't make out the words. They rumble as sure and strong as the thunder that booms over the prairie and rolls over us, but his words are lost. Beau's strokes pick up speed and his fingers leave half moon bruises in my hips. My hips are already black and blue from Beau's brutal touch but I smile thinking of how I'll wear these new bruises with pride. How I'll press down on them for the first bite of pain that comes with that touch to remember exactly who rules over my body.

It's not me. It's not The Reaper and his bloody knife. It's Beau.

The storm doesn't let up and it's hard to see our way back to the lake house. Beau holds my hand tight and keeps me close to his side to shield me from most of the rain. I shouldn't have run out here like I did, but I needed to. There was something in me that needed breaking to remain sane. I squint and look at Beau. I'm grateful he recognized what was happening. I didn't.

I didn't and I almost threw myself off a cliff to stop The Reaper from killing me. Beau squeezes my hand and points ahead as he yells over the rain.

"It's just a little further!"

We went another way, opting to travel the full length of the loop that leads back up to the house. It was hard to get traction with how steep the trail was that we just came down and Beau said it was a lot flatter on the other side. I went with him because I only had one shoe after I broke the other and this side was far flatter, but it was also a longer distance to walk. Flash floods in Kansas are a regular occurrence and I'm glad the ground we're on is flat and open. At least we don't have to worry about being swept away by the water.

I wrap my arms around myself and shiver. I'm soaked to the bone and the rain is freezing, but that's standard in Kansas when it's almost October. I force myself to keep walking and keep my head down and so I miss it when Beau stops so suddenly that I crash right into him.

"What is it?" I yell, leaning close so he can hear me.

"There's something up ahead!" He yells back and points. I follow the direction he's pointing and freeze, because he's right. There's a shape up ahead, but the rain is coming down too fast and hard for us to see what it is. Beau moves forward but I dig my heels in when he tries to bring me with him.

"Let's go the other way, Beau."

He makes a face and shakes his head. "What? No."

"Please, Beau!" I pull on his hand and try to go back the way we came. I have a bad feeling about this. Whatever is up ahead shouldn't be out here. We're behind a gate on a secluded road in a place no one but the cops should know we're at. There shouldn't be anything out here.

"Come on, Nevaeh," Beau's grip on me is like iron. There's no fighting him so I let him drag me along. Every step we take fills my body with dread, even more so when I finally see what it is that's sitting on the trail ahead of us.

It's my mother's car.

I shake my head and grab Beau's arm. "Something's wrong. We have to go back the other way."

He looks at me then. The fear in my voice is enough to make him finally stop. "What is it?"

"That's my mom's car. She doesn't know I'm here."

Even if my mom did know I was here, her car shouldn't be on this lonely trail in the middle of nowhere. A thousand questions run through my mind. How long has it been here? Where is she? Who drove the car here? And lastly, did they know I would be the one to find it? They had to have known. Why else would my mother's car be here? It's too neat. God, why don't I have my phone on me? When we left the house my headspace was all wrong. I was feeling reckless. It's the only excuse for why I don't have my phone on me.

"Where's your phone?" I ask him. I want to call the cops. I programmed their numbers into our phones this morning. If we can tell Marcus and Simon, then maybe they can help us figure out why my mom's car is here.

Beau pulls out his phone and holds it out to me. I grab it and swipe up but there's no reception. "No bars," I tell Beau and he takes it back with a nod.

"Shitty reception out by the lake," he turns and glares at my mom's car. "Someone knows we're here."

I look with him at the familiar car that my mom has had since I can remember. It's only a few feet away now and I watch him make a decision. He raises himself to his full height and squares his shoulders. He's going to go investigate. Fuck.

I don't even try to stop him. It's no use.

We approach the car slowly and my eyes are on the driver's seat. I'm convinced I'll see my mom in the driver's seat but there's no one there. I scan the whole car and everything looks normal. It's still the same tan sedan that she's always driven. It's an old car, but it's sound. Even when we moved into our brand new house she didn't see the point of getting a newer car.

"We are not prideful. There's no use in getting a new car to keep up with the Joneses."

My mom really believed that by not getting a car, but moving into the nice house in the better part of town, she was avoiding any of the prideful behavior she loathed, even as she bought new designer clothes and bags. Her logic was screwy, but it let her keep her head up and judge everyone around her with impunity. That's why she liked church so much. It was free range to judge under the guise of concern. Beau drops down onto his knees beside the car and checks underneath it, but a few minutes later he comes up empty handed.

"There's nothing!" he shouts to me over the roar of the rain and tries the door. It opens. I hang back while Beau opens and shuts every door in his inspection of the car. I don't know what he's looking for but he comes back to me after a minute and grabs my hand.

"Come on. There's no one here."

We start back on our way to the lake house but I can't help and feel like we're being watched. I look back at the car. Its shape stands out but not for long. Not in this storm. It vanishes from sight after a minute or so of walking. It's another fifteen minutes until I see the lake house rise up out of the storm. The path that we took started on the side of it and now that we're on our way back I look for a way that my mom could have driven her car down past the lake house while we were here. The curtains we closed last night could have hidden her car from us but there's no road. If she drove her car here she did it without knowing about the trail. Why would she have done that? *When would she have done that?* I haven't spoken to her for the past two weeks and we came here straight from Beau's apartment. The timing feels off. Everything feels off.

I grab Beau's arm with both hands and pull him back. We're so close to the house, even in the torrential downpour there's no missing it. As eager as I was to get out of the rain, I'm nervous to do it now. Seeing my mother's car on the trail feels like an omen.

Something bad is about to happen.

"Beau, this isn't right. My mom's car shouldn't be out here. Why would it be out here?"

He wipes at his face and plants his hands on his hips. "I don't know, Nevaeh."

"We can't go back up there," I tell him and gesture towards the house.

"We have to go back inside. The storm is picking up. There's nowhere else to go."

"Beau, listen to me! That fucking car being out here is a message, or whatever! I know it is!"

"From who, Nevaeh?"

"I don't know! My mom? The Reaper? I don't know. But if we go back inside then we're playing this little game through and I have a bad feeling."

Beau watches me and at first I think he's going to tell me that we're going inside, end of story, but then he nods and grabs my hand. "Okay, let's go down the hill to Simon and Marcus. We'll tell them about the car and get a lift into town."

That sounds good. If we have other people involved, then we're doing the right thing. Going into town would be better than staying out here after we found my mom's car abandoned on a trail it shouldn't be on.

"Yes, thank you!" I have to yell to be heard over the rain. The storm hasn't let up since it broke on us, and as we walk around the front of the house I try to tell myself that's why I'm jumpy and nervous. That maybe there is a perfectly reasonable explanation for my mom's car to be where it is and that nothing bad is about to happen to us. I even start to believe that everything is going to be okay when Beau takes my hand and holds it. That lasts all of twenty more seconds because the front of the lake house comes into view. I watch as the lights inside of the house start to come on one by one.

Someone is turning them all on as they move through the house.

They're moving fast, it only takes a couple of minutes for the bottom floor to be lit up like the Fourth of July, and then the lights on the second floor start to come on too. The house is like a lighthouse that's suddenly sprung up in the middle of nowhere. The warm lights shining through the windows push back at the night and the storm, but it isn't calling us to safety. It's daring us to keep moving towards death. But even with a murderer inside, that's not the thing I'm looking at when it comes to the house.

It's the body I see.

Simon's body is strung up in front of the house. The light from inside shines out onto the front porch and shows us everything when the wind turns Simon's body to the side. I scream when I see the gash in their chest that goes down to their belly. They've been torn open, their insides trailing out of them and onto the ground below. Their blood doesn't stain the ground because the rain is coming too fast and washes it all away.

CHAPTER THIRTY FOUR
BEAU

THIS IS A fucking trap. I knew it was the second I saw Nevaeh's mom's car sitting out there on the trail. Getting a car out on the trail that looped to the lake isn't impossible, but it wouldn't have been easy for anyone that doesn't know the trail exists. It's a narrow path meant for horses and I see why the car got stuck the way it did with its front wheel wedged between a rock and the groove of the trail. I looked for keys when I searched the car but there was nothing, so I couldn't see if it would start. But with the storm there was zero chance of me getting the car to drive out of where it was. From the look of it, the car hadn't been there for very long. Nevaeh didn't think to check, but I pressed a hand to the hood and felt the still warm steel.

The car had been driven and dumped while we were on the trail. Whoever had brought it was still here and now a fucking cop was hanging with their guts out in front of the house. Beside me, Nevaeh screams, but she muffles the sound with her hands a second later. I grab her and turn her away from the body swaying in the rain. Fuck. Where the hell is Marcus?

I scan the area for anyone else but there's no one. Even if there was, I wouldn't be able to see much. Aside from the house that's got every light turned on now, it's dark from the storm and the rain is too fast to see more than a few feet in front of us. If Marcus isn't here there's a chance he's still alive, but seeing the way The Reaper split Simon open, I'm willing to bet Marcus is dead too. I'm sure the killer has the same in mind for us, with the way they're inviting us inside.

"Don't look at him," I tell Nevaeh and she hides her face in my chest. Whoever killed the cop drove the car on the trail. They're still here, and they're probably watching us right now. "Get in the car, we're driving to town now."

"Where's the keys?"

"Here," I tell her and hold up the keys that I locked the house with. Not that it mattered, because I can see the door open behind Simon's body. That open door is an invitation for me from The Reaper. That's the only one fucked up enough to do this, but who the fuck is it? I guide Nevaeh towards my car, but my thoughts are on the house. I want to go inside. I need to fucking know who has been doing this. It's not just Nevaeh they're after right now, it's the both of us that have been tormented by this sick fuck for years.

It wasn't Nevaeh's fault that I was in prison for so long. She was just a kid, but The Reaper? He took his sweet time sending that knife in to the cops. He stole those years from me, he took Carrie. Nevaeh squeezes my hand when she almost slips in the rain and I hold her up. Now he wants Nevaeh too. He's going to have to kill me first before he gets to her. I'm not some scared college girl. I'm as much of a killer as The Reaper is and it's his turn to fucking bleed.

I open the driver's door and scan the back seat, I'm not getting taken out like an extra in a B-List Horror movie. When I see there's no one there, I go to start the car, but nothing happens when I crank the engine.

I try one more time for good measure before I get out. "It's dead," I tell Nevaeh. Her face drops and she looks like she's about to start crying. "Hey, hey," I cup her face and stroke the side of it, "it's okay. We are going to be okay. I'm not going to let anything happen to you, remember? I promised."

"I know, I know. I know you won't." Nevaeh nods and grabs my hands in hers and forces a smile on her face. She's being brave and once again, I'm proud of her. I've seen Nevaeh hot with rage and felt her anger when she fights back. She's been beautiful in every fucking instance that she's refused to let herself be crushed, but seeing her fearful and willing to go on is even more beautiful.

I'm so fucking proud of Nevaeh.

"What do we do now?" she asks me and glances back at the house. She's thinking what I'm thinking. We have to go inside and whoever is in there is waiting for us.

"We go down the hill to the gate where their car was. Take that and get to town." My plan sounds reasonable but I know it's a pipe dream. Whoever disabled my car probably did the same to their car.

"Is your reception still out?" she asks and I pull my phone out. Just like before, the reception bars are nonexistent. She hands me back my phone. "Where's Marcus? H-he's not there, do you think he's okay?"

"I'm sure he's fine. Maybe he got away," I lie to her.

"He could have called for help," Nevaeh says and I hear the hope in her voice. She's not giving up yet, even if it's just to hope for the impossible. Good. I don't want her to lose that. Not when death has taken so much from us.

"Maybe he did," I say. "If we get to the car then we can use their radio too. Make sure help is on the way," I add to try and reassure Nevaeh. If I was the killer, I would have taken out the radio at the same time I ended Marcus and Simon, but I can't think like that right now. I have to get inside. That's where the Reaper is waiting for us. If I'm the one to take his head off then he can't get to Nevaeh. I have to find him and I have to fucking kill him. "There's a phone inside and keys to the car my dad keeps here. If we're lucky, they didn't fuck with that one yet." The garage is on the left side of the house, the door is by the stairs to the second floor. I'll have to walk past the living room and the kitchen, plus the door to the basement where the wine cellar is. It's a lot of ground to cover for a car I'm not even sure works, with a killer breathing down my neck, but it's quicker than going down the hill to the gate where I'm sure the only thing waiting for us will be Marcus' body.

Nevaeh nods and squeezes her eyes shut before she grabs my hand and looks towards the house. "Let's go." I go to tell her no fucking way. That it's too dangerous and I'll go on my own, but Nevaeh reads me like a fucking book the second I open my mouth. "I can't stay here. They could be out here and if they are, I'm fucked. We have to stick together like in the movies."

This isn't a fucking movie, but she has a point.

"All right, but stay the fuck behind me. I'm going to check Simon for his keys or a weapon. If I find anything, we are going straight for the gate." It's the smartest play I can make to keep Nevaeh out of the house. That's where The Reaper wants her. Why else would he have put Simon here like a neon sign and left the door open for us?

Whatever he's going to do to Nevaeh will happen in the four walls of this house.

Nevaeh nods in agreement. "That makes sense, okay."

"Don't fucking look at the body."

"I won't."

When we get close enough to the body, I drop Nevaeh's hand and go forward on my own. I take in The Reaper's handiwork. He's used ropes around his neck to hold Simon up and he's stripped his gun belt from him. I keep an eye on the door while I go through his pockets, but there's nothing. Of course there's nothing. Leaving a weapon for us would be too sloppy.

The Reaper has been one step ahead of us the entire time, why would shit change now when they have us exactly where they want us.

I go back to Nevaeh and think about saying fuck it. That we should just head to the gate and take our chances that maybe the car is open and the radio isn't fucked, but I can't because I know it's not true. The only way out is through this, The Reaper made sure of it. I look at Nevaeh. Thunder cracks and lightning lights up the sky and her beautiful face is there for me to see clear as day. She's afraid. Her eyes are scared but she still walks forward towards the house. I don't care what I have to do. I might not walk out of the house tonight, but neither will The Reaper. Nevaeh will be free when I'm done.

"You ready?" she asks and looks at me. But when she does, I don't see fear, I see resolve.

"I'm ready," I tell her and take her hand. We walk into the house together.

CHAPTER THIRTY FIVE

Nevaeh

SIMON IS DEAD. He's hanging by his neck in front of Beau's door and I have to walk past him. It takes everything in me not to throw up, but I do it. Beau told me not to look but I couldn't stop myself. The second he said it, it was like I couldn't look anywhere but at Simon's body. The Reaper gutted him like a fish from his belly to his neck. Simon's lifeless eyes stare off into nothing while he swings by his neck that is bent at an angle far too sharp to be natural. His neck is broken. I don't know if he did it before or after Simon was dead. I hope whatever was quicker happened first, but I've heard The Reaper kill.

There's nothing quick about the way The Reaper kills. He took his time with Carrie, made sure there wasn't an inch of her his knife didn't know. And she was alive for all of it. I hold on to Beau's hand tighter and we step over the threshold and into the lake house. The second we're inside, the pounding of the rain dies away. Outside it was so loud that if we weren't speaking into the other's ear, we had to yell to hear over the storm's roar. It's so quiet inside that I can hear myself breathing, no, not breathing, I'm gasping. I press my hands to my chest because I can hear that too. It's beating so hard that it makes my ears throb.

Beau looks at me and raises a finger to his lips before he leans in close to me. "We're going into the kitchen, that's where the keys are. We'll go to the garage next."

I nod and try to force myself to take normal breaths. I watch the stairs while we walk to the kitchen. The water dripping off of us leaves a trail behind us. When we left for our walk, all the lights were off, but someone turned every last one of them on. And, unlike last night, they've thrown open all the curtains. No, it isn't someone. I know who did it. The Reaper turned the lights on and opened the curtains. It wasn't just them daring us to come inside. They did it to make sure we saw them coming.

My hand shakes in Beau's and I fight to be brave. Why is this happening to me? I lead a quiet life and all I ever wanted to be was normal. This isn't normal. We get to the kitchen and Beau opens a drawer as quietly as he can and starts looking for the keys. They aren't in the first drawer. My heart drops, but Beau holds up a hand signaling that everything is okay and moves onto the drawer beside the first.

There's nothing in that drawer either, but Beau doesn't stop looking. He's on the fifth drawer when I think of something. There are no keys to find. The Reaper took the keys. I bite my lip and look around the kitchen. It looks just the way it did when we had breakfast, our dishes are even still in the sink. But everything is different now. This morning feels like it was years ago. How can The Reaper have come in here and made this place evil? He was here, I know it. He took the keys and he's waiting for us. I go to the butcher block that holds the kitchen knives and pull the biggest one out before I go to Beau's side.

"There's no keys," I whisper. "He took them."

Beau's hands clench on the drawer he's just opened and he nods. "Yeah, thought that too, but I didn't want to scare you."

Tears prick my eyes at his words. Beau was the boy that I never stopped loving, but that was the version of him I knew before prison changed him. When he came out he was a man with nothing but anger and darkness in his heart towards me. How we've managed to end up in this place where he wants to protect me leaves me feeling cracked open and vulnerable. So very few people have ever tried to truly take up for me. Sunny, Pastor Mike and now Beau. Few as they are, I'm grateful to have people that have cared for me and asked for nothing in return.

"We'll find another way," I tell him.

"If he took the keys the car is out and I'm willing to bet the phone line is cut too." He nods at the cordless phone on the counter and puts it to his ear with a frown. "It's dead."

I grip the knife tighter and point back to the front door. "Okay, so let's go to the gate. We can just start walking, okay? Even if the car is dead, we can just go."

"You need shoes."

Fuck. Right. I'm only wearing one busted sandal. I carried my shoes upstairs and there's nothing down here for me to wear, but it doesn't matter. I'd rather walk until my feet are bloody and raw then die.

"I'm fine, I swear."

Beau looks at my feet and shakes his head. I'm not surprised when he says. "I'll carry you," Beau decides. I don't fight him, I just let him pick me up and head for the door while I hold tight to the knife in my hands. Everything is still so quiet in the house. I can hear the storm through the still open front door, but that's it. We're almost to the door when we hear a thump above us. Beau freezes and we both look up at the ceiling. A second later there's another thump, this time louder.

"It's him," I whisper. Fear shoots through my entire body and I almost drop the knife. The anger that I felt when I almost chased after The Reaper is gone. I can't conjure it up. The only thing in my bones is fear at ending up like Simon. Gutted and lifeless, my eyes staring into nothing while the world goes on around me and The Reaper keeps killing.

Beau puts me down and nods at the door. "Go."

"What? No! I'm not leaving you," I argue but Beau shakes his head.

"I have to fucking end this. He's not going to stop coming after you. Never. He's going to keep coming for you over and over and I'm not letting him take you from me."

I'm set on arguing with him. Telling him that I'm going to face this evil with him, but he catches my face in one of his hands and grabs my jaw, cutting off the words I was saying, "Beau, I-"

He squeezes my face so hard that it hurts and my eyes water. "I'm the one that says when you die. *Me.* I'm the one that's going to fucking kill you if it's anyone, not that freak upstairs. I own you, *I earned you,* not him. Never him." Beau jerks my head back so that I'm forced to look up at him. I recognize the cruel look on his face. His eyes are cold, the man who held me last night, made me pancakes and let me sit by the pool is gone. The version of Beau I know the best and love the most is here now. The one that's all mine. His soul and heart are dirty, but they're mine all the same. He's killed for me before. He's going to do it again. Tonight.

"You're not fucking dying here tonight. Do you understand me?"

I nod because I can't speak, not with the way Beau holds my face. He brings me close to him and presses his mouth to mine in a brutal kiss. I almost drop the knife, but Beau takes it from me before I do and doesn't break our kiss. He doesn't let go of me either, but slides his hand down from my jaw to my neck and holds me there. The feel of his rough palm against my throat, that pressure right over where my pulse flutters, calms me. I reach up to hold on to his shoulders, run my hands through his hair and touch every part of him that I can. I pour all my love and longing, the obsession and devotion that I have carried for him for years, I give it all to him. I will him to feel just how much I love him, the depth of my love and adoration. I know he feels it. I feel the emotion coming back from him with how desperate and greedy he is with his kiss. He licks into my mouth and I part my lips for him. Our tongues move together, the breath I take in feels shared with Beau and I've never felt more connected to him than I do right now.

Maybe it's the murderer waiting upstairs for us that has me feeling this way, but maybe it's something else like fate and love and soulmates. That kind of magic. I'd rather believe in magic and destiny than in a psychopath, so I go with that. When we part, we're breathless and I almost burst into tears when Beau nudges me towards the door. There's the sound of a door slamming and the heavy tread of boots overhead. It's almost time. Beau tries to give me the knife back but I don't let him. He needs it more than me.

"Go, Nevaeh. Don't stop until you get to Bloom. I'll be right behind you."

Beau doesn't promise he'll be there, like he has to keep me safe. Last night I knew Beau meant what he was saying, but this time I don't know.

He's willing to make sure The Reaper doesn't find me again, that they won't be able to follow me and hurt me anymore, but where I hear the falter is when Beau says he'll be right behind me. I know what that means. Oh god, I know.

I want to cry. I shake my head and come forward a step but stop myself when he backs away. "Beau." His name gets choked up in my throat but the smile he gives me knocks it free. "Beau, no, please."

"I love you, angel. *Now go.*"

"I love you," I say back. It's the only thing I can say. Those are the only three words that will come out of me when Beau gives me one last lingering look and heads upstairs with the kitchen knife he took from me in one hand. He's willing to die. God, what if he dies? I stay where I am, watching Beau until he vanishes from sight up the stairs. I almost run up the stairs after him and beg for him to come with me. The only thing that would do, though, is tell the murdering psychopath exactly where we are. And Beau would never come with me.

"You're not fucking dying here tonight. Do you understand me?"

He's going to see it through and I say a silent prayer to whatever is out there that Beau lives. I need him to live. I deserve for him to live. Living means running, though. I turn to look at the door. It's still wide open and I can see Simon's body swinging in the wind and rain. I wonder if Simon tried to run. Did Marcus and that's why he isn't here? I take a hesitant step forward but stop.

I can't go empty handed. I gave Beau the knife. If I end up walking to Bloom, I'll need something to protect myself with. The Reaper isn't the only predator out there. I go back into the kitchen and grab another knife, it's small and easier to hold, which is good if I have to use it. I see a jacket hanging on a hook beside the basement door and reach for it, but when I do I see someone through the windows facing the pool. They're sitting with their back to the house. Even with all the lights on in the house, the lights by the pool are off and I can't see much of anything other than their silhouette. I forget the jacket and take a step forward and then another until I recognize them.

It's my mom. What is she doing here? Why is she sitting outside in the rain? A door slams upstairs and I hear the sound of feet running. I have to press a hand over my mouth to stop from screaming. I'm not supposed to hear this. I have to get outside. I rush forward, right to my mom and not out the front door like I know I'm supposed to. I go out the back door and shut it behind me. My mother has never protected me, not a day in her life, but somewhere in me I wish she would. I wish she had when I was fifteen and traumatized by Carrie's death, but she didn't.

She left me alone and told me to pray on it. We never spoke about that night. Not ever. So what is she doing here now?

"Mom?" I call out to her, but I'm not loud enough to be heard that far away with the rain. She's twenty feet away, so close to the edge of the pool. I edge forward and then stop. My mom's car was driven out here when no one knows I'm here. The only people that knew that were the cops and Beau's parents. I squint at the familiar figure and see my mom's dark hair plastered to her head. Her arms are on the armrests and she's leaning back slightly. It's a pose I've seen her do countless times when she's listening to a good story or relaxing at Church. My mother sits that way when she doesn't have a care in the world.

How did she know to find me? What was she doing with her car that far out? I haven't heard from her in weeks and now she's here. Something doesn't make sense. Why is she here?

I take a step forward but I freeze, because realization dawns over me. My mom knows where I am and so does The Reaper. She's been gone since the day of the first attack. The girl they found was killed that first day that my things arrived at the dorm. Where has she been with all of this going on?

I thought she'd just washed her hands of me and that's why she'd been missing this entire time, but what if she wasn't? What if she was there for every attack that happened? What if she's been involved?

I start moving again. My eyes are on her relaxed pose. She hasn't moved a fucking muscle. There's a killer in the house and she's sitting like she's enjoying the night air, not a storm that's surely bringing flash floods down around the county.

The only reason someone would sit like that is if they were safe. And the only way to be safe with The Reaper is if you know he won't kill you. The only way that would be possible is if my mom was helping him. I grip the knife tighter and keep walking forward. I half expect her to turn and yell at me, but she doesn't. I wait until I'm right behind her to speak.

"Mom, what are you doing here?" I ask. She can hear me, I know she can. I'm close enough but she doesn't give any sign that she did. This has to be part of her sick little game. Why am I even asking and hoping that she's not helping the murderer inside come after me? She would do anything to be free of me.

I glare at the back of her head. How did it never occur to her that I wanted to be any place but with her? How did she not know that I counted down the days spent in her home and kept time to when I would finally be free? It wouldn't make sense to her that I wanted out as much as she did, because she always thought I should be grateful. Forever indebted to her for the roof over my head and the clothes on my back.

The bare fucking minimum.

If she isn't going to give me her attention, I'll take it then. I reach out and grab her shoulder. "Mom!" I yell and give her a shake, but still she doesn't turn her head. I round her chair to get in her face. "What are you-" I stop talking and start to scream. I see why my mom didn't move or turn her head to look at me. Why she's been sitting without moving an inch in the storm.

My mom is dead.

CHAPTER THIRTY SIX
BEAU

I'M GOING TO kill this motherfucker. He's close. I can feel it, even if I can't see him. I walk down the hallway and past the bedroom I was in with Nevaeh last night. The door to it is open. I can see the bed still unmade, but there's no one in there. I think about going to the gun safe but it would take time, too much time and too much fucking beeping of that gun safe to do it without ending up with a knife in my back.

"He's as big as you. He's strong too and so, so fast. B–but the way he moves. He moves like he's the scariest thing out there. He knows nothing can touch him. Not the cops, not me, not anyone."

The lights on the second floor are on just the same as the first. I know I'm going to hear him coming, I just have to be patient. I just have to not do anything stupid. Prison taught me how to be still. I know how to wait, to look for an opening before I force my will to be done and take a life. All those times before, it was to stay alive or to follow orders from men I hated. I had no problem killing then. This is easy. I would do anything to keep Nevaeh safe. I go through the next bedroom and there's no one there.

He walks too heavy. I'd hear him straight away.

He's trying to be quiet this time, not at all like when he went after Nevaeh. Good. I want him trying harder now that he knows he's going up against someone his own size.

I continue down the hallway and enter the library. It faces the lake side of the house and overlooks the pool. I don't see anyone when I enter the room, but there is another room—my dad's study, that's connected to it. I head that way, but I only make it a few steps in when I hear the creak. It's slight. Something that you could mistake for the wind if you didn't know what to listen for or what someone sounds like when they're trying to move softly.

It's not the wind. It's that murdering cunt.

I barely have time to get my knife up when the door to my dad's study flies open and The Reaper charges out at me. He's big like Nevaeh said he was. Quieter, though. He slams into me and we both go down, but I bring the knife up and down twice and cut into him. My first stab goes into his shoulder and the second in his back. He grunts and turns, hits my arm and tries to knock the knife away, but I keep hold of it.

This isn't the first time someone has tried to get a weapon off me in close quarters. Probably won't be the last either, if I make it out of this alive.

I roll away from them and slash at the air to force them back a step as I get to my feet. The Reaper is already up and even though I felt the knife sink into him and there's blood on the floor between us, he shows no sign of being wounded. He's dressed in all black robes that make me think of the photos of liturgical vestments Pastor Mike showed us when he went over the history of the Church, but there's something wrong about them. It's not just the color, it's the cut and fit of the robes.

The Reaper wears black leather gloves and there's a hood pulled low over his face so the only thing looking back at me are shadows. I adjust my grip on the knife as we circle each other for a minute and I hear the tip tap of his blood hitting the hardwood floor. Outside, the storm rages and it's when a crack of thunder rumbles that The Reaper makes his move. He reaches into his robes and pulls out a knife of his own. It's military spec, the kind that's meant to do damage to bodies and I know if I let him get a clear shot at me with that fucking thing it's going to be hard to get back up.

His knife shines in the light and then he points it at me. "You've sinned. This is your penance." He growls and I almost drop my fucking knife.

I know that voice. I've heard that voice for years the same as anyone else that ever walked inside the walls of Crown of Thorns. I know who this motherfucker is and I hate that I never saw it coming.

No one in Bloom did.

"Vengeance is Mine, I will repay," says the Lord," The Reaper quotes and then he's on me.

CHAPTER THIRTY SEVEN
Nevaeh

MY MOM IS dead. I stare at her for what feels like an eternity but is probably only seconds. It's hard to focus on anything but my mother's face. Her eyes are closed and I'm glad for it. I couldn't handle seeing her like Simon. Lifeless and blank. Her body is tied to the chair, zip ties keep her posed in the chair. Without the extra support, I don't know if her body would be able to stay where it is.

She's been dead for a while. Even in the dark with the weak light of the house shining against her, I can tell. There's a flash of lighting and I stagger back a step when it makes everything daylight bright for a few seconds.

The Reaper cut her throat, but not just that. He cut a smile into her face, the corners of her mouth extend into a distorted grin. Her skin has been cut away, exposing her teeth and muscle.

"Oh my god," I whisper and clutch my knife tighter. I want to cut her free, but it wouldn't do any good, would it? She's dead. How long has she been this way? Why did he bring her body here? I squeeze my eyes shut, try and take in a deep breath. He killed my mother.

Did he kill her to get to me? Am I the reason why this happened to her?

"Mama," I choke out and fall to my knees in front of her. I have to get her out of here. I have to get her out of the chair. I grab the zip tie at her arm and start cutting through it. "Mama, I'm so sorry. I'm sorry. Oh my god, please wake up," I sob. I keep cutting through the zip ties but she doesn't wake up.

"Mommy, oh god. Mommy!" I yank at the zip tie. The rain falls hard and it's when I start working on the zip tie at her ankle that my grip on my knife falters and I cut my hand. The blade slices into my palm and the pain cuts through the panic flooding my brain.

"What am I doing?" I stare at my hand. The blood wells up for a second before it's washed away. I look up at my mom, but I can't look at her face. Oh god. What he did to her face. I look away, over her head and breathe.

"You can't help her," I tell myself. "You have to go. You can't help her."

I force myself to stand and take a step and then another. I have to leave her here. "I'm sorry," I tell her when I'm a step past her chair. I lift my eyes to the raging sky but freeze when I see movement on the second floor. There's a library there. I know it because I went poking around the house earlier for something to do and found a room full of nothing but the classics.

"My dad's office is through here," Beau told me when he found me reading. We'd left to make pancakes after but I'd wanted to go back to that library. The Reaper is there now. I see the flash of his blade, but he misses Beau. I watch as Beau lands a punch and slams the knife into The Reaper's shoulder. He drops the robed figure to his knees and hope fills me.

Oh my god. Beau's going to win.

I walk forward, transfixed by the scene playing out in front of me. The Reaper is on his knees and puts a hand against the window to push himself up but Beau is waiting for him and kicks him back. He stands over The Reaper and I see the knife he took from me in his hand. He's going to end it all. But before he can, someone else steps into the room.

It's another robed figure.

"No! Beau, look out!" I scream when I see them head for Beau. They're moving slowly, trying to be quiet and I don't know why Beau hasn't killed the man at his feet. What is he waiting for? If he waits any longer it'll be too late, the person at his back is going to kill him. My mother is dead but I won't lose Beau.

"Beau!" I scream again, but he can't hear me. I'm too far away and the storm is too loud. I have to get to him.

"No! God, please!" I scream and take off running for the door. I can't let this happen. It's not fair. He beat The Reaper. There were never supposed to be two of them. I slam into the door and rip it open. I fall to my knees when I manage to get in but don't stop moving and keep running. I sprint up the stairs, my bare feet slap on the hardwood stairs and I almost fall, but I don't stop running. I can't stop. If I do, Beau will be dead and then I'll have no one.

I turn down the hall and see the library door open. Beau swears. "I'm going to kill you both, motherfuckers!" My heart leaps in my throat. If he's cussing at them, he's alive. I'm not too late. Not yet. I slow down, walking with care. I don't think they've heard me yet. When I'm close to the door, I press close to the wall and crouch down. I edge closer to get a look inside the room. I see Beau, his back to the door that leads into his father's office and by the windows there's The Reaper. But there's another black robed figure standing with their back to the door. They're smaller than The Reaper, so I know they aren't who I faced down two nights ago.

They're someone new.

I wonder who they are, but the second they take a step in Beau's direction, I don't care. All I know is they're fucking dead. I push off from the floor and launch myself at them. Their scream pierces the air when I slam my knife into their back and we go rolling on the floor. I taste blood in my mouth when my chin hits their shoulder, but I don't let go of them. When we come to a stop, it's with them on top of me. I see the flash of their knife a second before they slash at me, but I raise my arm to block them and it's only my forearm they catch.

"Nevaeh, no!" Beau yells, but I can't look at him. My eyes are on the knife being raised above me with two hands. They bring it down with a grunt but I catch their arms and keep the knife above my head. There's a crash and a slam, the sound of the two men fighting fills the air and I want so desperately to look. I need to know Beau is safe but I can't with the killer on top of me.

"Fuck you!" I scream when they lean forward and put their entire weight behind the blade as they try to bring the knife down. "Fuck you, I'm going to kill you!" I bring my knee up and slam it into their back and throw my weight to the side. The sudden movement sends them over me and to the side with just enough room between us for me to get away. I roll away and get to my feet at the same time they do. That's when I see they still have their knife in hand but mine is long gone. Fuck it. There's an end table beside me and I grab the lamp next to me and hold it up.

"I don't need a knife to fucking kill you," I tell them and throw the lamp at them with all my strength. The ceramic shatters when it hits them and I grab the next thing on the table beside me. It's a heavy iron horse statue and I'm going to use it to bash their brains in. There's a crash and I look to the side. Beau and The Reaper are in his father's office. I start towards the door but the robed person in front of me moves with me and blocks me from getting in the office.

"What is wrong with you? Why are you doing this?" The questions come out before I can stop them. I don't expect an answer but I get one anyhow.

"You've been judged and this is your penance," a woman answers me and my heart breaks. I know that voice. "Thus I will punish the world for its evil and the wicked for their iniquity," she says. She reaches back to push her hood back but I already know the face I'm going to see.

"*Minnie*," I whisper.

Minnie gives me a mean smile and points her knife at me. "You're a real fucking pain in my ass, Nevaeh."

"What are you doing? Is someone making you do this?" I ask her.

She laughs. The sound is dark and bitter. "The only one making me do anything is you! You're making me do this."

I shake my head. "What? No!" I scream at her. "We were friends. I loved you and then you abandoned me!"

"Because you're a liar, Nevaeh. A filthy fucking liar that needs to be punished. But I gotta tell you, I never thought you were a whore. Guess that good girl act was all a lie too, wasn't it?" Minnie brings her hands up and raises her voice in a mimic of mine. "I'm a virgin and I want to wait till I'm married. Oh, I can't smoke or drink, it's wrong." She drops her hands and spits in my direction.

"You're a fucking liar, Nevaeh and now I'm going to cut that lying tongue of yours out of your head and make sure you never fucking lie again."

"You were my best friend." I say the words but even as I do, I know the truth. I was never Minnie's best friend. I was always held just a little further away than I wanted. I thought it was because I was needy.

Now I know the truth.

"And I hated every second of it. I was only your friend because how could I not be? You were the Mineral Belt survivor and my neighbor. Do you know the shit I would get if I wasn't your friend? I never liked you and your holier than thou fucking attitude. Always little miss perfect, always the center of attention because you wanted it that way. I hated every second with you, but I couldn't tell anyone. Only Pastor Mike. He understood me when no one else did. He knows what kind of parasite you really are."

Oh my god. Pastor Mike. What has she done to Pastor Mike?

"What did you do to him? Did you hurt him?!" Pastor Mike was always there for me when no one else was. What if something happened to him? What if he's somewhere cut up like my mother?

"Shut your mouth about him!" Minnie screams and points her knife at me. "You don't know anything about him! He saw you for what you were. The perpetually helpless victim."

I shake my head. That's not true. Pastor Mike knew what I'd been through. He'd never say that. "You're a liar," I tell her. The anger in me is fading. It's hard to stand in the face of Minnie. I loved her, thought of her as a sister and not a day went by that I didn't look for her. It was only in the past month that she'd abandoned me over the news about Beau. I wondered how she could have done it so quickly, cut me off from one day to the next like I never existed, but now I know.

She never loved me like I did her. She hated me.

"It's the truth, Nevaeh! You loved being a victim." Minnie slashes at me and I dance away from her blade. There's a thud and a sound of shattering glass in the next room, but I can't get around her to help Beau. "The one that got away from The Reaper. Well, you know what? Now you're just going to be another dumb slut who gets her throat cut. Just like that whore whose heart I cut out."

She killed Ali. Not The Reaper. *Minnie.*

She screams at me when she lunges at me and I dodge her. Minnie is moving too fast and slams into the end table I was just beside. She's still screaming, even when she's bent over the table and trying to turn when I bring the horse statue down on her. I hit her on the back of her head and her screaming stops. I don't, though. I bring the statue down again and again. I hear her knife hit the floor and I slam the statue into her once more before I step away from her. My heart is racing and I can hardly catch my breath when I turn to the office door. Minnie slides off the table and hits the floor with a thud beside me, but I don't look. I barrel towards the office and kick the door open. Beau's knife is gone and he's on the table with The Reaper above him. He's holding him back, but just barely. The tip of the knife is in Beau's chest and I can see blood blooming around the knife. It stains the white shirt he's wearing and I don't think, I act. I cross the room in two steps and swing the horse statue at The Reaper.

My swing goes wide, but I hit their back hard enough to give Beau the opening he needs to get away. He shoves The Reaper back and swings at him. The punch lands true and The Reaper's head snaps back. Their hood falls back from the force of Beau's punch.

I drop the horse statue and feel like the world tilts on its side when The Reaper turns to me and we lock eyes. "Pastor Mike?"

"Hello, Nevaeh." Pastor Mike sounds normal. He even smiles at me. I half expect him to say this was all a misunderstanding, but how can it be when he just had his knife in Beau's chest and he killed my mother.

"It was you? You're T-the Reaper?"

I can't believe it. How many vigils and sermons did Pastor Mike lead? *So* many of them. He stood at the front of the church and asked us to pray for the souls of those taken too early. How many parents did he comfort when they poured their grief out to him? Pastor Mike talked about the evil in the world and how we needed community more than ever, but all along it was his knife that cut and ripped Bloom apart.

Pastor Mike sighs and clasps his hands in front of him. The knife in his hand is so casually held that I feel like I'm the one that's wrong. The one that's losing their mind.

"The field is the world and the good seed is the sons of the kingdom. The weeds are the sons of the evil one," he says. Beau flips him off, but still Pastor Mike keeps speaking, "What kind of shepherd would I be if I let you descend into depravity on your own? It's my job to pull the weeds. To keep the world pure. What kind of pastor would I be if I didn't?"

"A sane one that doesn't fucking kill people," Beau snaps and rounds the desk to stand beside me. He takes my hand the second he's near me. "You okay?" he asks me but his eyes don't leave Pastor Mike.

"I'm fine," I tell him and swallow hard. "The other one was Minnie," I say quietly.

"*Fuck*," Beau breathes, but Pastor Mike's eyes go to the other room.

"What did you do to my disciple?" he growls. He's finally realized it's too quiet. That Minnie isn't coming to save him.

"I fucking killed her. You're on your own now."

Rage fills Pastor Mike's eyes and he stops holding his knife like a Bible. Instead, he points it at us and takes a step forward. "You are vermin! She was a pure soul and you defiled her!"

"No she wasn't! She was supposed to be my friend and you killed my mother," I scream back. "She was your most devout parishioner. Why did you kill her?" My mother would have given the Church anything. She might not have loved me, but she loved Pastor Mike. She loved Crown of Thorns. Nothing about her death makes sense.

"I killed your mother because she was a whore!" Pastor Mike explodes and he starts to pace the length of the office as he rants. "Your mother hid behind lies and deceit, but her deeds came to light soon enough. When they did, I purified her. Her adultery made her in need of redemption. For the Lord is vengeful and strong in wrath. The Lord is vengeful against his foes; he rages against his enemies."

Beau winces and sags against the wall. "Fuck his Bible quoting ass. I'm going to kill him," he says but I see how Beau is hurt. I have to keep The Reaper talking. I have to find a way to end this.

"Adultery?" I ask. "Who? Who did she sin with?"

Pastor Mike laughs and wipes at his face with the hand holding his knife. The casual juxtaposition of the bloody blade near the face I know so well makes me sick. He was never Pastor Mike. He's always been The Reaper.

"With none other than John Du Pont."

Beau makes a strangled sound at hearing his father's name and I understand. Outside of cleaning their house, I never once saw my mother speak to Mr. Du Pont. When did she find the time to be with him? How did I never know?

"I'll be paying your wicked father a visit when I'm done here. He has a debt to pay if he wants to save his soul like your mother did," he says and gestures around the room. "This house of sin made a perfect resting place for your mother."

My eyes water. I never felt close or loved by my mom, but what happened to her was more than horrific. More than anyone ever deserved to have done to them. The terror she must have felt at it being Pastor Mike, the man she trusted more than anyone, that tortured and killed her.

"You're sick. She trusted you."

"And she defiled her body with another woman's husband. She lost her right to salvation when she sinned, Nevaeh."

"When did you kill her?" I ask, ignoring his words. I don't care about the reason he had for killing her. "When?"

"The day I brought your things, of course," he tells me and I feel sick. "Made a rather neat go of it to deal with that slut's soul and collect your things," he pauses and looks at me with a sigh. "That was, of course, before you dirtied your soul."

"What are you talking about? You were always going to kill me because I lied," I say. Minnie wanted to punish me for my lie about Beau, but she also hated me. She was never my friend, but Pastor Mike? I trusted him like anyone else in town.

"No, you didn't mean that," he said and gave me a pitying look, like he was still the one that was right. The one meant to offer counsel. "You tried to tell them, but no one listened. I know this, you told me." It's true. I did tell him about Beau and my doubts because no one else would listen. Pastor Mike was safe. He promised to keep my secret. He promised Minnie the same. My hands shake. How close was I to being where Minnie is? Would I have fallen under Pastor Mike's hand if he'd pushed me to?

How close to the edge was Minnie that he was able to turn her into a killer? If it happened to her, it could easily have been me. Or anyone for that matter. Good, bad, evil. It's all relative at the end of the day.

"Then why? Why are you after me?! I trusted you!"

"Because you laid with him," The Reaper says and points his knife at Beau. I glance at Beau and see he looks pale. He's lost too much blood. He has one hand against the wall and glares at The Reaper.

"She fucked my brains out. No laying involved," Beau says. I know he's going to do something stupid. The Reaper's eyes go to him and when he takes a step towards him, my heart turns to ice.

I watch The Reaper sneer at Beau. "You were always so prideful. *Always*. That's the Du Pont family's greatest sin," he snarls.

"You couldn't stand me getting credit for your kill so you gift wrapped the murder weapon to the cops," Beau shoots back and even though he looks weak he laughs. "What's the matter? Your ego couldn't take people thinking I was The Reaper? You could have kept killing if you'd left Nevaeh and I out of this."

"There was never any leaving either of you out of this!" The Reaper explodes. "You survived me. Survived God's hand! No one is allowed to look upon the Lord! 'He said, you cannot see my face, for man shall not see me and live.'"

His knife flashes in the light when he slashes it at us along with his words. "You had to be judged. Retribution paid. The both of you forced my hand with your sinful behavior." He looks at me. "That was when your soul was done. You were going down the same path as your mother. I could not let evil like that grow in the world. You needed to be dealt with. Do you think I didn't see what you did at that party?" The Reaper asks, but he's walking towards Beau.

"The both of you, sinful, depraved souls. You watched him touch her, Nevaeh. You loved it. Minnie destroyed that temptation from ever happening again, but that still leaves you."

He means Ali. That's why they killed her. Remorse washes over me sharp and quick. She's dead for what happened at the party, but he's not wrong. I did love it. I watched Beau then, now I need The Reaper to watch me. I have to get The Reaper out of the room before he goes after Beau again. If he does, Beau won't survive it. He's not strong enough anymore.

But I am.

I take a step away from him and towards the door. I already know what I have to do.

"So why haven't you?" I ask him and start to walk backwards to the door. "Why haven't you dealt with me?"

The Reaper narrows his eyes and I watch the last piece of the man I knew fall away. "Oh, but I have," he growls.

"Really? Because I'm still fucking alive, you sack of shit! How is that dealing with me?"

Beau groans and holds a hand out to me. "Nevaeh, stop!"

"I love you," I tell him before I turn back to The Reaper. "You think you're big and bad? That you're the hand of God wiping sin away from this world? I don't fucking think so. You're a pathetic man. A fuck up that likes hurting people."

The Reaper stops, he looks at me. I have his attention now. "Stop your lies," he commands.

"How am I lying?" I ask. I'm just a foot away from the door now. "The hand of God wouldn't fail when it comes to killing a sinner like me, now would they?" Rage builds on The Reaper's face and he starts to come my way. My plan is working. "You are not divinely protected or appointed. Not until you kill me." I take one final step back as I say that, but my next move is a sprint. I turn and run out of the room with The Reaper a few steps behind me. We pass Minnie's body and I hear their strangled cry when they see her on the floor with blood coming from her ears.

Somewhere in the distance, Beau screams for me, but I keep going. I slam the door behind me and run straight across the hall to the master where Beau and I slept. I lock the door and almost trip as I go for the gun safe in the closet.

"4289," I chant as I rip the door open and fall to my knees in front of the gun safe there. "4289, 4289, 4289." I punch the numbers in with shaky fingers and the door behind me almost gives when The Reaper kicks it. The gun safe unlocks with a click and I rip the door open. Inside, there's a tray with the gun and a box of bullets. I pull it out and the bullets fall out of the box when it hits the floor.

I take a deep breath and try not to panic. The Reaper kicks the door again and I load the gun. I've only ever seen guns in movies, but I still manage to snap the magazine in place. The door flies open and I scream. I squeeze the trigger but nothing happens and The Reaper does not slow. He runs right at me, the knife in his hand raised high.

"Vengeance is Mine, I will repay," says the Lord," He howls and I know he's right. My hands are too shaky and I almost drop it when I pull the trigger, again to nothing. "I'm going to rip your soul out! It's mine!"

The safety, I realize. I never turned the safety off. I look down and hit the mechanism. The Reaper is only a step away. He's so close I can feel the warmth from his body. My hands shake while I disengage the safety and I almost drop the gun. I'm not fast enough. I know I'm not. The certainty of it sinks into me and a second later The Reaper slams into me. I go flying and the gun flies out of my hand and slides across the floor. I half expect a knife to sink into me, but it doesn't come. Instead, The Reaper grabs me by my hair and forces me to my feet.

I swing at him and miss, but The Reaper doesn't. He punches me and I almost black out from the pain of it. My legs give out and I hit the floor when he lets me go.

"You dirty fucking slut. You're just like your mother!" He screams at me as he starts to pace the room. "There was hope for you, Nevaeh. I thought you might be different, but in the end you proved me right. Just like all the rest."

I moan and roll to my side. My jaw feels like it's shattered, but I don't have time to process it before I'm kicked hard in the side. I scream and hit the wall from the force of the blow. I think he cracked a rib. I grab at my side and scramble away from him. Adrenaline and pain mingle in equal parts and force me to move. I have to get away. I have to find that fucking gun and blow The Reaper's head off. I force myself up from the floor and grab the perfume bottle off the dressing table beside me. The bottle shatters against the wall behind the killer in front of me and I grab another.

"Fuck you, you psycho!"

"You have been judged, Nevaeh. Your soul is found to be black and sinful." The Reaper points his knife at me and smiles. "You have sinned. Now repent."

I shake my head and hurl another bottle and then another. They hit him and explode into fragments. Glass flies back at me, but I don't stop throwing everything I can at him. "You're a murderer! How can you judge anyone when you're *killing people!*"

He shakes his head, "Not people. Sinners."

I think of my mother. She's dead and mutilated. Strapped to a chair in the rain and murdered by the man she devoted herself to. She didn't deserve that.

"They trusted you!" I scream. "*I* trusted you!"

"And now you'll reap what you've sown." He comes closer to me. Only a few feet are between us. If I don't move now, I'll be trapped in the corner with nowhere to go. There'll be nothing to stop the man that killed my mom from taking me apart. I won't let that happen. I refuse to let that happen. I scan the room for a way out and I see the gun. It fell beside the bed. The Reaper comes forward again. The bed is to his left and the next step he takes will bring him past the bed. Once he does, he'll see the gun that's laying just out of sight.

Time slows and I force my eyes from the gun to the monster in front of me. He's smiling at me. That smile makes my blood run cold. He's evil, psychotic, and everything I've ever feared in my life, but I'm going to stop him. The terror he's brought down on my home ends now.

"I'm not afraid of you," I say and his smile morphs into a snarl. He steps forward and I throw myself at him. My charge surprises him and he hesitates, taking a half step back before he recovers. The split second is enough time for me to make my move. I lower my head and slam my shoulder right into his stomach and knock him to the ground. I hear the wind get knocked out of him when he hits the floor. He coughs, but still has a hold of his knife. I don't care though, because I see the gun.

"I trusted you!" I bring my foot down and stomp onto his throat. I feel his windpipe crush beneath my foot and I do it again. The muscle and tendon there give and there's a strangled gasp from him as he raises his knife and tries to swing at me, but I'm too fast. It's not just adrenaline and pain that have me in motion. It's rage.

I'm so fucking angry. All my life I've done what I've been told, with Pastor Mike leading the way. And all this time I was nothing but a lamb being led to slaughter. I'm going to end this monster. He gasps and claws at his throat while he slashes at me, but I dart out of reach and scoop the gun up off the floor.

I can hear him behind me. He's moving again, but I keep my eyes on the gun. I can't fuck up again. The safety is off and I turn to fire at The Reaper, but before I can squeeze the trigger he stabs me in the thigh. I feel the muscle tear when he jerks the knife out and I howl in pain and fall to my knees. I fall against the bed with The Reaper on top of me. When he breathes, I feel it and the weight of him has me pinned to the bed.

"Sinful dirty woman," he spits at me. The words rumble and vibrate against my chest. He raises his knife and it shines bright in the moonlight, but I still have hold of the gun. I don't know if he doesn't realize I have the gun with the way he's taking his time. Maybe he knows I have it but doesn't care. For so long, The Reaper has been the thing we all fear. The demon in the dark that claims whoever they choose with no repercussions.

He never thought it was going to be me that ended him, but pride always comes before a fall and The Reaper is not the only one capable of vengeance tonight. I bring the gun up and fire. His eyes go wide when the bullet hits home, but he doesn't stop bringing the knife down. He's going to kill me and there's nothing I can do about it. I fire again and close my eyes and think of Beau. I love him so much.

I want him to live a long, happy life so I keep firing with my eyes closed, but the knife never reaches me. I open my eyes and look at the Reaper. His eyes are on me and blood drips from his mouth. The black robes he's wearing stain darker with his blood, but he's still holding his knife high. It's suspended in the air, a hand is there supporting it, holding it above me.

I fall back onto my hands and look up to see who it is that stopped The Reaper.

It's Marcus. The cop with the kind eyes stands there with one hand around The Reaper's arm and the other pressed to his side. Blood flows down his side and he looks weak, but he's still strong enough to hold the knife where it is.

"Shoot him again," he grits out between clenched teeth.

I shoot The Reaper again.

CHAPTER THIRTY EIGHT
BEAU

I **DON'T KNOW WHERE** Nevaeh is. She ran off with The Reaper on her ass.

"I love you."

Those were the last words she told me. I push away from the wall and go as fast as I can. I've lost a lot of blood, but I'm good. I can do this. I have to get to Nevaeh. I get to the door of the office when I hear the gunshots. Once, twice, a pause and then three more in rapid succession.

"Nevaeh!" I have to get to her. What the fuck is going on? Whose gun is that? The library is a mess. Minnie's lifeless body is sprawled out on the floor and her head is a bloody mess. Nevaeh made sure she's not getting up again.

I get to the hallway and that's when I hear the solitary pop of the gun go off and then silence. Fear settles into me. Whatever was happening is done. I can feel it in the air. When I stagger into the master bedroom, it's The Reaper that I see on his knees. Marcus stands above him and Nevaeh is on her ass, my father's gun in her hands.

"Angel," I say and she looks at me.

"Beau!" She's on her feet and hobbling towards me as soon as I speak. There's blood running down her leg and I know she's been stabbed.

"Are you okay?" I ask her, trying to reach for her leg. But Nevaeh throws herself at me so hard that I grunt and almost fall on my ass, but she holds me up. "Oh my god, I'm so sorry. I'm sorry."

"It's okay. I'm all right."

Nevaeh shakes her head and starts looking around the room. "No, you're not. You're bleeding out. We have to get you to the hospital."

"They'll be here soon," Marcus says and rips the knife from The Reaper's hand. "I called it in because this motherfucker," he yells and kicks The Reaper's motionless body, "tried to kill me." He stomps hard, brings his foot down on The Reaper, "You killed my partner!" He keeps stomping and it's Nevaeh that goes to him and stops him with a hand on his arm.

"I'm sorry. I'm sorry," she says. "I'm so sorry."

Marcus goes still and then the man bursts into tears. "Thank you."

Flashing red and blue lights greet us when we make our way downstairs. I feel faint but keep going while Nevaeh helps me to the door. There's a dozen cop cars, plus a firetruck and an ambulance, in front of the house. They're already working on getting Simon's body down when we get outside. It's still storming out but I hardly notice it.

Nevaeh and I walk out into the rain together. There's no other place in the world that I would rather be than beside her. We hold each other up while the storm beats down on us and washes us clean.

SIX WEEKS LATER

"I don't care if you don't want to do a couple's costume. We're doing it," Nevaeh tosses over her shoulder as she walks down the row of costumes. We're in the local costume shop and Nevaeh is dead set on us getting matching Halloween costumes. I talked shit because she expects me to talk shit, but we both know I'll give her whatever she wants.

"Fine, but no fucking tights," I tell her.

She laughs and looks over my shoulder. "That's it, you're going to be Peter Pan"

"Fuck."

Sunny pops out of the next row and holds up a pair of green tights. "I think you'd be a pretty hot, Peter," she says and gives the tights a wiggle, but I ignore her. Sunny's all right but if you give her an inch she'll take a mile. At least, that's what I've learned since we all moved in together a few weeks ago.

After the lake house and the news about The Reaper hit, my father was ready to give me whatever I wanted. He knew I knew about Nevaeh's mom and even though there's no real love between my parents, my father isn't of a mind to inconvenience himself with something like divorce. I asked for a house big enough for Nevaeh and me. Somehow Sunny found her way there too which is fine since it's a four bedroom.

I like her and she can cook Mexican food, so I let her stay. But even if I didn't, all Nevaeh would have to do is ask me and I'd shut my mouth and let Sunny do as she pleased. Plus, it was good to have Sunny around to help Nevaeh when she had to use crutches until her leg healed enough for her to walk. I eye her now as she moves ahead of me. There's hardly any limp to her walk now, but I still don't like it when she pushes herself.

"How about this?" Nevaeh asks and holds up a frilly gown with a big ass skirt.

"You want me to wear that?" I ask.

Nevaeh rolls her eyes. "Not for you! For me. It's Cinderella," she explains to me like that's obvious. "I'll be Cinderella and you'll be my Prince Charming!" She reaches over to a rack and pulls out a crown that she sets on my head with a smile. "You look so good! I love it! Come on, there's the matching costume over here somewhere."

I almost tell her I'm the farthest thing from Prince Charming but when she smiles at me I don't. For her, I'll do it. Nevaeh grabs my hand and I go with her willingly through the aisles.

"I'll be whatever you want me to be, angel. You call the shots."

I'll always be what Nevaeh needs me to be from now until my last fucking day. She's it for me. That's why I'm going to ask her to marry me tonight.

CHAPTER THIRTY NINE
Nevaeh

"**Y**OU REALLY GOT him in a pair of tights. I'm impressed," Sunny tells me. She's sitting in Beau's and my room, and applying stitches to her face with an eyeliner we got at the dollar store.

"Was there ever any doubt?" I ask her and she giggles.

"When it comes to you two? No way. He lives to make you happy."

I smile because it's true. Beau is the perfect boyfriend. I look around the room at the house, a house that he had his father buy for me to keep us quiet about what we knew. I thought about telling the truth, but this way no one knows what my mother did. Instead of the woman The Reaper painted her to be, she can be someone else. She can be the version of herself she wanted Bloom to see. In life we weren't close, but this way I can feel connected to her in some way with the secret I'm willing to keep for her

"How many parties are we going to?" Sunny asks.

"I don't know. I'm letting Beau decide," I tell her and keep doing up the corset of my dress. Everyone knows Pastor Mike was The Reaper. I thought Crown of Thorns was going to collapse. Everything he'd built was on a knife's edge when the news broke about the serial killer pastor from Bloom. They managed to pull it together with a new name, Tabernacle of Truth, and with a pastor fresh from a Kansas City Bible college. I don't know what their plans are, I don't go to church anymore. School is different, which I like. People don't hate me and when they stare it's because I'm with Beau. The staring was really bad when I had to use crutches to get around while my leg was healing enough to walk. I feel good now and it's healing up, even though I'll have a massive scar there. Beau doesn't care about the scar, but he does care about people staring. All it takes is one look from him for them to drop their eyes and pretend they weren't watching us. I've made more friends at Bloom State now and I'm even leading a group for the Death and Dying class. Professor Mrose is convinced I'd make a great Anthropologist so I'm signing up for a new course load for next year to test out the theory.

Things feel good. They feel stable and settled. It's a fairytale come to life, this stability and peace I have with Beau. I go to the bedside table where my earrings are and open the drawer to pull them out. The earrings are pretty, aquamarine with a little star dangling off the ends. They'll match my dress perfectly. Laying beside the earrings is a knife. It's the same style as the one The Reaper used. I touch it lightly, drag my fingers up the blade and down to the handle. I got it the week after the lake house.

There's a knock at the door. It's Beau. He looks so handsome in his Prince Charming costume. "You ready, angel?" he asks and holds his hand out to me. I know there's a velvet box tucked in the pocket his other hand is in. He's been playing with it all day. I didn't look at the ring inside though, I want that to be a surprise.

I take the knife out and tuck it beneath my corset before I shut the drawer with a snap of my hand. "Always," I tell him and take his hand with a smile on my face when I think about the night to come. It will be magical, beautiful and my perfect happily-ever-after, but if anyone tries to take it from me I won't hesitate to put them six feet under.

My name is Nevaeh Santiago and I will kill to keep my perfect ending.

THANK YOU

False Idols is the first book that I wrote and published as part of a community. And when I say that, I mean community in the most genuine sense of the word. From the very first word to The End, I have been supported by readers, authors, and dear friends and loved ones the entire way.

If you know me, you know that I'm a solitary and private person. It's in my nature to be an introvert but this book. This beautifully twisted and dark book was created with so much love and support that it humbles me to even think of how it came to be.

I want to thank my friends both virtual and IRL that kept me sane and supported. Thank you Brittany for never giving up on me. You are soul sister and my heart is full when I think about everything we've been through. Jeniya, you are the little sister I never had but am eternally grateful for you. I think we both know that without you this book wouldn't have gotten into readers hands. Thank you, Kenya! You have been such a good friend and I truly look up to you as not just an author but a woman that I would like to be more like for your constant encouragement, steadfastness and eternal optimism when it comes to the future of publishing. The sky is the limit! Aria, you've become such a dear friend to me and the way you came in like an angel baby to help me get these boxes done made everything HAPPEN. You are so loved and appreciated! Izzy, you've listened to me ramble about this book and have been an encouragement to write when I didn't feel like it. Watching you start your publishing journey has given me so much of my spark back. Kimberly, you're an OG and we've been through it since we were two readers in a podcast group that thought maybe we could become authors too one day. I am so proud of you and am thankful for your constant ear when I get excited about a story or need to work a plot line out! To my Arc Readers, y'all are seriously the light of my life. Every message and word of encouragement that you've sent my way has meant all the difference. I really don't think you know how much it means to me.

Special note of thanks to: Stephanie, S., Desi, Bunny Moon, Tanesha, Cass, Shannon Marie, Naj, Zahlia, Kenya, Alexis and Ashley for graciously being a part of the physical ARC team. It was really a learning experience for me and I am so grateful for how patient you were with me during the process! I hope this is the first of many times that I get to celebrate a release with y'all!

And last but not least, because he would throw a fit if I put him first on this list—the love of my life. Dustin. You are the partner my soul and heart has longed for and your support and love for not only me but this book has meant the world to me. I'm looking forward to forever with you.

ABOUT DARCY DAHLIA

Darcy Dahlia is an emerging author of humorous biographies. This is Darcy's third book. Darcy Dahlia is the darker alter ego of romance author Rebel Carter. You'll find a delightfully dark and spicy journey in each and every one of Darcy's works! You can expect monsters here, obsessive heroes, and heroines who give right into the dark side and love every second of it ;) When I'm not writing, I'm probably thinking about writing (which is why I had to make two pen names!) or on my merry little way to over caffeinated. I hope you enjoy and love the books I write, because writing my books is my dream come true!

Love y'all <3

Also by Darcy Dahlia

Gods and Sinners Duet:

God Complex: A Why Choose Dark Romance
Holy Sinner: A Why Choose Dark Romance—Coming Soon!

Monster Novellas

The Hunted Mate: Enemies to Lovers Monster Romance

www.ingramcontent.com/pod-product-compliance
Lightning Source LLC
Chambersburg PA
CBHW050917030726
47503CB00007BB/2332